Redemption

The Black Chronicle

Thank you for
your support

Capt Smithes

Chapter 1 - Fields of Fire

He could feel the pulse in his temple throbbing, "boom-boom, boom-boom, boom-boom." He could feel the sweat run down his back, each drop trickling and turning cold the further it fell, and as he overcame his fear, he opened his eyes and looked down the line of men he commanded tonight. They had just rescued him from Morg and had found themselves cut off with their path blocked, they had been under his command before but they weren't just his friends, they were his liability, he had to get these marines safely home.

"Captain Black, what are your orders? What are we going to do?"

That was the voice of Sergeant Rex, now he was a friend, a comrade from many a campaign.

"Captain, are you ok? What are your orders?"

He looked over the grassy hillock carefully and saw the building in front of them, motioning to the five marines to keep low. Suddenly he saw through the window of the building the distinct red armour of the Red Skull Sonder squad, the fear gripped him, they were elite troopers, he knew their chances of surviving was lessened now. The Sonder were a zealot group who believed it was their divine right to send all heathen into the next world, and they were most definitely heathen in their eyes, those they 'sent' would have to fight their way into glory or be cast eternally into the night. Their zeal knew no bounds as their own glory would be enhanced by the kills they amassed or by the glory of their own death. His heart grew heavy and his stomach ached with dread as the overwhelming feeling of accountability for these young marines lives sank in deeper, but now was not the time for doubt or fear, now was the time for action and decisions.

He motioned to the Sergeant, "Five marching round the east side," but as yet they were unobserved.

This would give them some advantage as these were their streets; they knew the best and quickest ways in and out of buildings, whereas the Red Skull kept to the main streets in case of ambush.

In signals again he motioned. "In five they will move with speed in two's into the building."

He knew they had one chance and one chance only, get behind them where their armour is weaker hopefully get a lucky shot with the photon bazooka. Sergeant Rex signalled and the first two, Bo and Red, moved across the seventy yards and through the door without being noticed, or so they thought, next went Sergeant Rex and Kollin but before they got half the distance, the Sergeant fell after a shot rang out, it was not the elite squad as they were still behind the building. He jumped up with the last marine, Kerk, it was a sniper, probably from the high tower to the west, they grabbed the Sergeant, another shot rang past his head narrowly missing causing a dust splatter close to his feet, and they dragged the Sergeant through the door. The Captain was furious at not taking into account the possibility of a sniper.

Captain Black barked out orders, his frustration clear, "Kerk, tend to the Sarge, Kollin and Bo block that door we don't want any further surprises."

The element of surprise was gone and their misfortune had not finished as Kollin and Bo closed the door and barred it shut suddenly the west wall collapsed completely and they were faced with an Infuriator, this was a one manned walker with a heavy bolt gun and photon cannon, it was just as surprised as the marines, whose faces drained and turned white. The Infuriator shot, winging Bo, the Captain, with his wits about him, shot the photon bazooka and for once fortune smiled as it ripped though the Infuriator's armour, stunning the crew man inside. Kerk moved quickly to Bo but too late the bolt had ricocheted piercing his side armour and entering his heart, he was dead instantly.

"Bo's dead, sir."

He could feel the pulse in his temple throbbing again. There was no time for doubt, Bo was beyond his help, and he was with the Almighty now, decision time again. Captain Black saw the Red Skull were now aware of them but were still moving down the east side of the building and with the new opening it gave the marines easy access to their rear. So trapped between an Infuriator and the Red Skull elite, Captain Black knew there was little option.

He knelt down to Sergeant Rex, "How are you, old friend?"

"I'm good, Gus, as long as you don't ask me to run but I can still fight."

Gus handed his friend the photon bazooka and pointed to the Infuriator, "If that moves give it another blast."

The Captain rallied the remaining three marines with blasters in one hand and melee in the other,

he cried,"To the Red Skull, all for the Almighty!"

They charged, faces flushed and hearts pounding knowing they had moments to live, shooting their bolt guns which bounced off the Sonder armour with no effect. Because of the ferocity of the attack only the trooper at the rear responded bringing his photon pistol to bear, Gus knew his life was almost over as he lead and was in direct fire of the pistol, again the pulse in his temple throbbed, "boom-boom, boom-boom, boom-boom." In his haste he misfired and the pistol exploded, killing him instantly, Kerk gave out a triumphant shout,

"Furious in unity, we will be strong for the Almighty"

The Almighty has truly given strength to their arm as all four marines crashed into the remaining troopers. Another fell as Kerk, on Gus's right, brought her mauler square across the chin of the Trooper smashing helmet and skull. But their superior strength of the troopers, who now had their wits about them, was clear as one by one Red, Kerk and Kollin fell to the rapid fire of the bolt guns. As each blast and each marine fell to the floor, Gus could feel his heart getting heavier. The Captain remained alone with three troopers facing him. He gathered his courage and with venomous rage swung his axe and shot his blaster. One fell as the closeness of the blast ripped open his chest armour taking half his arm with it and the axe fell with full force splitting the helmet of the second. But the Sonder Captain rose above Gus with his sword and pinned him down cleaving through armour, slicing nicely between his scapula and clavicle. Gus gave one quick prayer of thanks to the Almighty as he waited on his death, but then an explosion came from the building. Rex had followed orders and shot the photon bazooka into the Infuriator, which exploded shaking the whole ground and knocking the victorious captain down onto one knee allowing Gus time to take out the sword from his shoulder and slice the head clear off his shoulders.

"Let me assist you into the next world, dark brother."

Gus collapsed hiding behind rubble, still aware of the sniper, he was joined by Rex.

"Praise the Almighty, how did we survive that!"

He could feel the pulse in his temple throbbing, "boom-boom, boom-boom, boom-boom'" as the wave of pain, shock and unconsciousness rushed over him and his heavy heart remained at the knowledge he had failed Bo, Red, Kollin and Kerk.

The last thing he heard was the Sergeant's voice.

"They've found us; we have a pickup, Gus stay with me."

The darkness fell across his eyes and he became unconscious with the whooshing sound of the copter reassuring him that he and Rex were at least safe.

***

The beep of the heart monitor was the first thing he heard as the mist of his mind cleared, he tried to sit up but the poker hot pain in his shoulder stopped him, he collapsed flat on the bed, grunting in pain. A doctor appeared at his shoulder, he, like so many of this war, was a young man but more experienced than a man twice his age would have been before the war. He was sallow skinned with a goatee and over grown stubble in the places that should be shaven; he had a scar across his face. That scar will have its own story; his face was sullen and weary with obviously no time for this as so many more needed his skills. Gus was certain he was still alive thanks to this man's commitment and diligence. A war isn't won by how many you kill but by how many survive and thanks to these skilled men many do.

"Lie still, Captain Black, your wound is far from healed! I'm Lieutenant Patrick, you'll find some degree of discomfort as we had to perform surgery to save your shoulder and arm, it severed some nerves but we were able to repair them to almost full functionality thanks to the quick extraction. Please be assured we will do our utmost to ensure you have as little discomfort as possible."

There was a quiet pause as he wrote on the clipboard. "I have to discuss the method of pain control with your nurse; initially you've had an ISB to block the nerve pain prior to the surgery, so you will feel numbness around the wound and down your arm for a long period. But as the pain starts to kick in, as it obviously is, we will give you viscose injections of painkillers and anti-inflammatories medications, regularly until discharge. This should last for about 12-24 hours, after this the shoulder will be sore and you will be given painkillers. It is essential you take the painkillers before the nerve block has worn off and you take regular pain killers at the prescribed times as soon as you get discharged. This is to avoid unpleasant pain when the nerve block wears off. You will be given anti-inflammatory patches to be applied direct to the shoulder, cold compresses will also help. Ice packs will reduce swelling and control pain, crushed ice in a damp, cold cloth and placed on the shoulder for up to fifteen minutes. If you have any questions then ask your nurse, I will not see you again unless there are any more complications, I hope to never see you again. May the grace of the Almighty be with you!"

And as quickly as he arrived, he left.

A slender raven haired nurse entered the room, her smile was exactly the medication he needed and a sense of familiarity came over him but he felt different after she produced the syringe, face a Red Skull Captain, no fear, but he hated needles. She checked the bottle of medication, placed it on the tray and went over to the sink to wash her hands whilst scrubbing her fingers, the smell of the alcohol-based hand sanitiser wafted into his nostrils.

"So I hear you wiped out a whole squad of Red Skull, Captain Black, that's pretty awesome, Sir!"

"Call me Gus, and not on my own, there were five comrades in arms who fell with me."

Suddenly, he remembered Sarge.

"What about Sergeant Rex Yu, is he alright, did he make it?"

The nurse without turning her head said, "Yes, I remember him, he was discharged. The bolt in his leg lodged there but once extracted and stitched, he hopped out next day with crutches."

Gus was startled.

"How long have I been here?"

The nurse turned round.

"Well you had your surgery three days ago, so this is day four."

She checked the needle, checked the syringe before filling it with medication. She rolled the bottle between her hands and after removing the cap she pulled the plunger back on the syringe to the mark equal to the amount of medication she needed and inserted the needle into the rubber seal.

Again, Gus's skin crawled.

"Can't I get a pill?"

"No!!", said the nurse.

"You'll thank me later; it will hit the spot quicker."

She pushed the plunger of the syringe down, and forced the air from the syringe into the bottle. Pulling the plunger back she inspected the medication in the syringe for air bubbles, gently tapped the barrel of the syringe removing the last air bubbles trapped.

"Before you give me that, what's your name?"

She looked at him coyly and like a high school girl suddenly asked out on a date by the football captain said, "It's Melody."

She plunged in the needle with a lot less coyness causing Gus to squirm in pain,

"I'll be back in thirty minutes to apply your compress. You won't need another injection for eight hours, so you can brace yourself you big girl's blouse."

She smiled with a smile so large and bright that made Gus feel at ease and he watched her shapely figure leave as he lay back to rest. His mind couldn't stop thinking of Melody, how would you describe the most beautiful woman he had ever seen, she was someone who is just beyond beauty itself. Yes, the girl was 'pretty' or 'gorgeous' better described it, but that was not completely it. There was something else, a good personality in general. She was someone who respected, was open to what others had to say and think. This girl would be happy and lighten everyone else's mood. No begging for attention, but she doesn't hide in the shadows either. Yes, that was it; she was confident, intellectual, had priorities and had a loving and caring personality. His perfect woman would be conservative with her body no apparent tattoos or piercings, natural and acted herself, no heirs and graces. Yeah, there are plenty of guys who get the 'hottest' girl but they end up being miserable later in life because these girls are either very selective or just spoiled. He began to think of her chiselled cheeks, dimple chin, rosy lips, curly black hair and brown eyes.

He then physically shook himself.

"Get a grip Gus, it's the first you've met her. Must be the drugs addling your brain."

***

As he lay there he stared straight up at the ceiling. The dark brown patch on the ceiling reminded him of his old room in Grandfather's house. It had a similar stain, he reminisced about his childhood. Suddenly, the smell of the antiseptic, like a well-used and disinfected house covering sour smells of the sick and the dying, the smell of ammonia disappeared as his olfactory senses were overwhelmed by the memory of the smell of baking bread and his Grandfather's pipe smoke. It was a small house that he shared with three brothers and a sister along with his mother and Grandfather. His father had fallen at the battle of Jobo Creek where the Caledon Volunteers, faithful to the Almighty, clashed with the Red Skull. His memories of whining to his mother to let him stay up and listen to the stories of his Grandfather were strong. She almost always conceded and the four children gathered at his feet with their warm milk and cookie. Faces excited and tired, excited at the prospect of a story but more excited at being able to stay out of bed for a little longer.

"How do you begin a story like this?" said the old man, who sat in the centre of the room surrounded by his family.

"This country we live in used to be populated by strong, helpful and hard-working people where no one went in need as everyone helped out, when I was young in Caledon, it was a close knit community and the term, *minding your own business*', was somewhat blurred in definition, everyone's *business*' would be of common concern. Some would call it gossip but, on the most part it was friendly concern and motivated by compassion. If someone died or next door's husband had had too much to drink, again, or if they had not worked for a while and short on cash everyone would help out with some milk or giving them a job or a natter to get out the emotions and frustrations of life. If someone was hurt, ill or in any trouble not their own, there was never a need to call for help; it was given warmly, willingly without question by the kindly folks, who the expression 'mind your own business' was never expressed. They lived their lives unaware of how much they influenced each other and how much their actions would impact on the lives of each other, young and old, I am who I am because of these people and their acts of kindness and inclusion. They would be surprised at how long they have lived. Long after they have died, they live on in my memories and stories, people like Eru the baker who gave me my first job and Mrs Hockage our neighbour who would slip me a sugar candy when my mum wasn't looking and Jasper my best friend who helped me build our treehouse in the woods, but that was a long time ago, before the Red Skull had made their mark."

The children's faces screwed up at the mention of the Red Skull and Bobby, his younger brother hissed and booed. Grandfather continued almost unaware of their reaction.

"We used to be under no man's oppression, just under the willing service of a benevolent King, a King led by the Almighty's will. Now we live in fear of a cruel dictator. A dictator who illegally gained power over the Kingdom and his subordinates reign their still without any opposition."

Bobby booed again and they all joined in which brought a wry smile to Grandfathers face.

"Some say he isn't a man, a god, some say, yes but we know there is only one true God, and so does he. Maybe isn't an ordinary man but a god, by no means, he is something in-between. His legend goes before him, he is an Immortal who once lived with the Ancients but fell because of his treachery, the Ancients had been created to serve the creation by the Almighty, He who had created the spark of life and gave the Ancients one charge, serve the creation."

Sissy, his sister's face was now wide with wonder.

"But men and Ancients can show great evil as well as great love, this Immortal, Nefarious, chose an iron fist rather than the velvet glove of grace. He tasted power and liked it, as we know power corrupts and absolute power corrupts absolutely. From his corruption there rose a great and unruly race of men."

The children recoiled in fear, even they, so young, still hurt from the deeds of these evil men who had taken their father.

"He recruited this race of men as well as other Immortals, they are known as the Red Skull to us common people, and many fear them as they fear death or absolute annihilation as both often follow these evil men. Our only hope would be that they would never visit or have no need to visit us or our city as all who come in their path pray for death if it had not visited them already."

Sissy began to whimper but young Gus put his arm round her shoulder.

"Don't worry Sis; you've got four big brothers to look after you."

Grandfather called her over and sat her on his knee.

"Don't worry child. We here in Caledon remain one of the few strongholds of resistance against them and pray it remains so as they have never visited our city, let's hope the grace of the Almighty keeps it that way, but if they do they will feel a sting that day as our strong warriors show them how free people fight. Not everyone amongst us is friends, not like in the old days where talk was cheap and gossip did no more harm to you than a prick of a needle but we must be careful of our words today as a loose word can cause a life or even the fall of this great city."

Billy jumped up and wielding his toy gun and wooden sword.

Almost decapitating Jo he shouted, "Furious in unity, we will be strong, Caledon will never fall by the grace of the Almighty!"

Grandfather gave out a hearty laugh.

"With warriors like you Billy we will last a thousand years. But only if we remain vigilant until the day the Servant of the Almighty returns to restore the proper order, but we must remain vigilant and not be overconfident. There are those amongst us who would help the Immortals and the Red Skull,"

Billy spat into the fire.

"Vile dogs!"

Mother looked over and called out, "BILLY, that's enough of that language, calm down."

Grandfather tried to not show a smile at Billy's actions but his eyes gave it away.

"So," he continued, "as the great teacher Jonas has told us, *'My dear friends' don't believe everything you hear. Carefully weigh and examine what people tell you. Not everyone who talks about the Almighty comes from the Almighty. There are a lot of lying teachers loose in the world. Here's how you test for the genuine Spirit of the Almighty. Everyone who confesses openly his faith in the Almighty and his servant, who will come to return us back to the righteous way, he comes from the Almighty and belongs to his servant. And everyone who refuses to confess faith in the Almighty has nothing in common with his servant. This is the spirit of the evil one coming like darkness after the day; it will start without warning and gradually reduce the light until suddenly you will be in the pitch black. Well, here it is, sooner than we thought! My dear friends, you come from the Almighty and belong to his servant. You have already won a big victory over those false teachers, for the Spirit in you is far stronger than anything in the world. These people belong to the world that denies the Almighty. They talk the language of the evil one and the false ones eats it up. But we come from the Almighty and belong to his servant. Anyone who knows the Almighty understands us and listens. The person who has nothing to do with the Almighty's will, of course, will not listen to us. This is another test for telling the Spirit of Truth from the spirit of deception. ...'*

Mother looked over at Grandfather, motioned it was late and he needed to finish the story, he acknowledged.

"One day we shall see his true servant return and he will overthrow the false Immortal lords, but when will that be, no one knows the day or hour he will return but it will be as a thief in the night, he may even be amongst us now, but his presence will not remain silent for long, just as the great teacher Jonas has also said,

'...you will see another Sign, huge and breathtaking: seven Immortals shall come with seven disasters. These are the final disasters, you will see something like a field but it will be made of glass, the glass will be all shot through with fire and the faithful one along with the saved ones shall stand on the glass, the field of fire. They will sing the Song of the Almighty and his servant;

Mighty are your acts and marvellous, Almighty one, the Sovereign-Strong! Righteous are your ways and true, King of the nations! Who can fail to fear and to love you, Almighty, and give glory to your Name? Because you and you only are holy, all nations will come and worship you, because they see your judgments are right. ...'

On that day the Immortals will become mortal and the fear and dread of the tens of thousands of soul they have misled will be heaped upon them and they shall feel their misery for eternity."

"But what about us Grandfather, what will happen to us?" Sissy interrupted.

Grandfather brought her closer and whispered in her ears.

"Trust in the Almighty, dear one and you shall stand with the saved ones."

Then mother called, "Enough is enough, everyone to bed now!"

And as they trooped off one by one, giving hugs and kisses, Grandfather would say to everyone,

"Keep the faith and may the grace of the Almighty aid your sleep tonight."

After they were off to bed, mother would say, "I know they love your stories Grandfather but do you have to stir them up so with stories of glory and despair can't you ever tell them a nice story maybe one from your childhood, one without the doom and glory in it."

"Maybe tomorrow." was Grandfather's reply.

The children went to bed and to sleep without knowing that would be the last good night sleep they would get together.

Chapter 2 - Men of Steel

Mother finished her dishes and made herself a hot drink.
Exhausted from the day, she sat next to Grandfather.
They reminisced.
"I miss working in the mill; it was the best paying job."
Edina remarked.
Grandfather nodded.
"Especially if you were young, you were guaranteed to get
work in those days. It was hard and honest work."
Edina gestured with her hand.
"We all thought we had a job for life, a guaranteed future,
money in your pocket and food on the table."
Edina sat back after sipping her cup and sighed.
"I remember the day, I met Jimmi. I remember sitting in
my room brushing my hair, putting on my make-up and
slipping on my favourite red flowery summer dress. I was
getting ready to go to the factory dance."
Edina started to hum a song to her self.
"That was the song blaring from the radio, it's still my
favourite."
Despite her weariness she stood up and danced around the
room still singing to her self.
Grandfather laughed.
"I am thankful of that day; you have brought the sunlight
streaming into our lives everyday since."
Edina kissed Grandfather on the head and collapsed in her
chair; she picked her cup and took another drink.

Grandfather continued, "You were not a typical teenage girl!"

He gently held her forearm, "I suppose with you having no mother, you had to grow up quicker."

Edina's eyes grew deep in thought, "I could never understand why my friends always had clothes strewn all around or make up sprawled over their side table, dirty dishes not taken to the kitchen. I suppose it was because these were always my duties, I liked my room spotless, perfect."

Grandfather agreed, "You make a good mother and wife."

Grandfather looked across and took in the detail of her face in the firelight.

She looked back. She smiled, a cheeky smile, her high and wide apple cheeks also gave her a lingering smile. Her pretty blue wide set eyes revealed innocence but as you looked further you could see the deep pain that she had lived with all her life. She leant forward to feel the heat of the fire against her hands and then sat back brushing her long blonde hair with her fingers.

"I remember running down the stairs calling good-bye knowing no one was listening. Dad was laying in a drunken slumber, unaware and uncaring of where I was going or what I was doing. I slammed the door, I ran down the street to meet Rose."

Grandfather interrupted, "How is Rose, haven't saw her in ages."

"Me neither, think she's fine."

Edina continued, "We didn't have a care in the world. We always looked forward to the dancing and the fun. We ran into a group of boys, in the midst was Hugo."

She turned to Grandfather, "You remember Hugo, right."

Grandfather confirmed.

"I do. He was a brute."

"Yep," she confirmed, "he liked me but I had no interest in him.'*Well*,' he said."

Edina deepened her voice to impersonate Hugo.

"'*If it isn't Edina and her little sidekick Rose.*' He leaned forward, the smell of alcohol was so strong it almost made me gag, it disgusted me."

She recoiled as the memory of the smell came back to her.

"He grabbed my wrist."

She changed her voice again.

"*Where are you off to my love, if you're going to the dance can't I come too?*"

She rubbed her wrist as if it still hurt.

"I struggled but I was unable to loosen his grip. I could feel the twist of the skin and the bruising that would appear. Hugo had no idea how much he was hurting me, if he had, I'm sure he would have let me go. I asked him to let me go, '*I'm going with Rose not a drunken idiot like you!*' I said"

Edina smiled as she remembered her friends' loyalty.

"Rose jumped into the middle, in an attempt to make him let go but it only made his grip tighter, she defended me, '*Yeah ya stupid clown, she's going with me so let her go!*'

Hugo swept his huge hand across and hit Rose knocking her clear across the road."

Grandfather leant forward; these were details he had never heard before.

She continued, "He didn't know his own strength.'*You keep your ugly face out of it, this is between me and Edina, come on my love, take me to the dance and make all my dreams come true.*' He gestured to me to give him a kiss and pushed forward expecting to meet my lips but all he met was a slap."

Edina let out a laugh.

"That made him let go, I fell flat on the cobbled street with a thud. He was now in such a rage and grabbed Rose by the hair, '*That was your fault, why must you interfere, I just wanted a kiss and to go to the dance with Edina and you had to stick your big nose in.*' Everyone had disappeared by now not wanting to have anything to do with it. He made a fist and drew his hand back hitting Rose in the stomach; it was here your Jimmi arrived."

Grandfather smiled, "Always the hero."

Edina paused; a peaceful sadness covered her face.

"He saw what was happening from down the street and unlike the rest who ran in the opposite direction, he ran straight for the trouble. It was just like him he would never run away from a fight."

The crackle of the fire became apparent as she noticed a spark flying onto the hearth and dissipating into dust.

"Knowing Hugo for what he was, he gave no warning and ran full force, tackling Hugo and bowling him to the ground. They both rolled over a couple of times, Hugo was completely winded and Jimmi got to his feet first and before Hugo knew what was happening had him by the hair in the same way he had held Rose's. *'Feeling like a big man now are you? Tell me why I shouldn't punch your lights out?'* He let go and Hugo rose to his full height, he squared up to Jimmi and although he was over a foot taller, broader and probably muscle for muscle stronger, when Jimmi stood squarely with him and looked him straight in the eyes, he backed down. Hugo could clearly see he would have a fight on his hands, a fight he may lose and his ego couldn't take that."

"You are probably right." confirmed Grandfather.

Edina stared into the flames; she was almost telling herself the story.

"He looked over at Rose and then me, he realised himself what he had done, and he backed off slowly and ran as fast as his feet could carry him. Jimmi, the perpetual gentleman, went over to Rose to see if she was OK she held her stomach and was still a little breathless."

Edina came out of the trance.

"She was OK but she didn't want to go dancing anymore. She was concerned about me but I had only hurt my pride and bruised my buttocks from falling so hard. My dress was crumpled and dirty, my wrist a little sore but I was fine."

Realisation came over her face.

"It was that same night Rose and Bert got together, he took her home and Jimmi took me to the dance."

She mumbled as sleepiness began to overcome her.

"Jimmi was angry at Bert for taking so long to back him up but Jimmi was always quick to jump in, not like Bert, he thought things through."

***

Grandfather filled his glass again, he settled.

Although Edina called him Grandfather he was in fact Jimmi's father.

He had known Edina's father but he was never spoken about.

Edina startled from her nodding sleep.

"You knew my father didn't, you James?"

"Yes, I knew him well." replied Grandfather.

"We had been steelworkers in the mill like so many men in Caledon before us, a town built on steel. We struggled, worked hard, we had a friendship your father and I but only at work. Then there was the day of your birth, the sadness and anger at your mother's death. It changed him." Grandfather took a sip, "Enough of him!"

"Caledon was a good town then. Nothing was ever sugarcoated; the Caledon Steel Works was a hard environment. It helped you, prepared you for the realities of life whilst giving you the opportunities that work affords."

Edina stretched out and touched his hand.

"It was a tough place to work but it did give us all a good living and close bonds formed with everyone. We all looked out for each other; I spent more time with my steel worker friends than my father. I left him at home, walked into the steel mill and adopted another type of family; they were my brothers and sisters. The job was more than just a job, it was who we were, a part of our identity."

Grandfather smiled.

"I remember the day Jimmi and you got married."

Edina's face lit up.

"It was 2nd June in the New Forest, a Thursday: you had to work in the morning, but left work and went straight to the elder's house that transported you to the wedding venue. It was very traditional; we had a hundred guests for a sit down meal, three tier cake with decorations to match the two bridesmaids' dresses. Speeches from you and Uncle Eric."

Grandfather laughed.

"After the wedding ceremony and meal came the obligatory dance. Didn't Bert and Rose get engaged that night as well?"

Yes, yes they did." exclaimed Edina in realisation.

Grandfather sighed in a moment of pleasure.

"The wedding day passed by in a blur, it was possibly the happiest day in my long life."

Grandfather grinned, "It was an honour to walk you down the aisle."

Edina's face grew sadder, "Father had disappeared by that time."

Grandfather cursed him under his breath.

"Quince was a hard man."

"I know, he used the rule of fist."

Grandfather could see Edina becoming small as the memory of her father's abandonment and years of abuse permeated her mind.

"I don't think I've ever told you what happened that day, the day father left?" mused Edina.

Grandfather shook his head.

"Not in detail."

"That day Jimmi walked in on him raising his hand to me. He reacted in the same way he had with Hugo, he grabbed his hand before it struck, twisted it behind his back and pushed his face against the wall. *'You will never raise your hand against her again!'* he said. He turned to me and told me to go pack my bag. *'You're not staying here any longer.'* He bundled father to the floor, as I went to go upstairs. I could see he was embarrassed and dishonoured in his own house. It was too much. He grabbed a butcher's knife from the table and lunged at Jimmi."

Edina stopped as the next thoughts overpowered her.

"It's ok, you don't have to say anymore, Quince was a bitter man, I don't need to know and none of it was your fault.", reassured Grandfather.

"No, I want you to know how Jimmi saved my life from that nightmare, his memory deserves that."

She took a deep breath.

"He didn't see it quickly enough; I saw the knife slice across his hand as he put it up to protect himself. As the line of blood trickled down his palm and dropped onto the kitchen floor, time seemed to turn into slow motion which splintered into reality as I screamed in fear."

Edina took another deep breath.

"Jimmi had been in plenty of fights."

She turned to Grandfather.

"You know how impulsive he was. He acted first and thought later. He told me later he had never felt so scared. He could deal with a toe-to-toe street fight where you had the option to run away or friends might join in to support making the other think twice and back down but this was different. This was a matter of honour, a red mist fight where reason and tactics meant zero. Father didn't want to teach Jimmi a lesson, he wanted him dead and everything was in Father's favour. He wasn't using the weapon to frighten Jimmi, he was using it to win and winning meant Jimmi bleeding on the floor."

A tear rolled down her face, Grandfather squeezed her hand in comfort.

Grandfather spoke a little croaky as a lump formed in his throat in sympathy.

"He told me what scared him was that he had attacked Quince, he was afraid the law might take it as self-defence. For one of the few times in his life he regretted not thinking first."

Edina was still tearful.

"Jimmi said father was like a cornered animal, he felt like a dog circling a bear's den where the smarter part knows he should not have woken that sleeping bear. I couldn't believe my eyes, was my father really willing to kill a man in cold blood? My instinct was to get out of there but where would that leave Jimmi. I screamed, '*Dad, no!*'

Father lashed out, Jimmi disarmed him, knocking the knife to the floor. Jimmi tried to reason with him again, *'OK, sir, I've dishonoured you and I understand you can't let that go but this isn't going to end well if you continue this.'* I felt so helpless."

Grandfather interrupted and stood up to show what he'd taught Jimmi.

"I taught Jimmi well; in this town it was important he knew how to defend himself. Stand with your left foot firmly planted forward and the right foot resting on its ball. Standing slightly to the side, hands up, elbows tucked in, and fingers curled."

He threw a punch or two but then felt a twinge in his back which he held.

Edina gave a light laugh through her tears at Grandfather's foolishness.

"You look so like Jimmi right now and yes, that's what he did. My father was single minded, he lunged forward again throwing a punch at Jimmi's stomach. He was filled with alcohol, pride and ego; he was blinded to what Jimmi would do until it was too late. Jimmi deflected his arm, knocking him off balance exposing his back. He reached over pulling his arm back while reaching around his neck. Dad tried to throw him but Jimmi stepped backwards. He kicked the back of his knees, and kicked his heels bringing him down and placed him in a choke hold. *'Please Sir,'* he pleaded, *'I want to let you go but I can't till I know it's over. Stop struggling!'* Dad slipped into unconsciousness, Jimmi let go.

He had blacked out, I rushed over, kneeling beside him, I screamed, *'What have you done? Is he dead?'* He wasn't. Jimmi was just as distraught as me, *'He came at me with a knife, and I had to do something. He's just unconscious, he'll be OK. Let's get out of here before he wakes up.'*

I resisted, I couldn't leave him like that! I knew Jimmi was right, if I stayed I would suffer. He had only shown me anger or disinterest being the only child reared by a father, whose wife had died in childbirth and it was my fault, I took away the one thing he had ever loved."

The tears streamed now.

Grandfather stood behind her comforting her.

"It was never your fault."

"Jimmi had always protected me," she continued.

"My heart was torn but there was only one choice now, the road was set out before me. I leant over and kissed his cheek as he lay unconscious, I took what money I had and placed it in his hand. I took off the necklace which had been mothers and placed that in his other hand. I remember clearly what I said. *'This was always yours, I'm sorry mother was taken from you, I know you'd have been a great dad if it had been different.'* Jimmi repeatedly told me we needed to go before he woke up."

Edina broke a little smile.

"I remembered he was bleeding so I grabbed the biscuit tin we used as a first aid box, I took a swab and rolled it up insisting he grabbed it in a fist. *'We've got to go!'* I grabbed a bandage from the tin and my bag. We went to the door; I took one last look back before I never looked back again."

Grandfather could feel the burden of guilt on her shoulders.

"You have nothing to feel guilty about, you know that some say your father moved to Yar City and remarried but that's just rumours."

No one really knew.

Grandfather had become a father to Edina from that day.

"Jimmi always was impulsive," commented Grandfather, "hotheaded but always honourable."

His memories faded into those fateful memories he longed to forget but could not.

He took another sip from his glass.

"It was a bright sunny day, the day he left." turning to Edina.

"Do you remember?"

"I will never forget!" whispered Edina.

Haughtily, he pronounced with sarcasm.

"The proud 8th Caledon Volunteers marched to serve the Almighty against the evil of the Immortals and the Red Skull hordes who had seized the city of the Kingdom, Yar."

He sipped again.

"Forgive me, Almighty. The hurt has made me cynical." Edina touched his hand.

"None of us could have stopped Jimmi he wanted to go to war, no-one knew till he turned up announcing he had enlisted. I protested, you were furious but he wouldn't listen."

"His mind was like Caledon steel." concurred Grandfather.

"His mind would not be changed. He had heard of Red Skull's brutality from Bert and Rose when they spent six months in Yar."

Edina nodded.

"I remember! Bert had got a dream job. Easier work, better pay and a tied house. Rose told me how much she had hated it; she longed to be back home. They may be poorer but they were happier here, a far better place to raise a family."

"After we argued, I have to admit, I was proud of him. He was very proud to be an '*Eighth*'.

He made a good soldier; he would have been promoted if circumstances had been different."

Jimmy reached into a box beside him and pulled out a pile of letters tied with cord.

"Are those Jimmi's letters? I didn't know you kept them." exclaimed Edina.

"You can read them if you want. His description of his army life in the letters paints a detailed picture of the soldier's life. He loved the training, the drills, and the camaraderie."

He pulled out the top one.

"His final letter, dated 25 September, talks about the gentle slopes of Jobo Creek, he writes about their eagerness to get into battle the next day, to put their training into practise. Most of the letter tells about how much he loved us, his family."

He handed Edina the letter.

"He was proud of his boys, encouraged them to be a proud
Caledon man of steel in this difficult time, he looked
forward to the birth of his daughter, he asked you to call
her Cecilia, do you remember."
She nodded and opened the letter.
"He thanked you to, Grandfather for taking us in. Thank
you."
Another letter fell out from between the folds.
She picked it up and opened it, her breath caught.
"Oh, my! It's his letter to me, I can't! But I want too. Can
you read it to me Grandfather?"
He took it from her hand; she sank back in the chair, he
head against the head rest.
He began, solemnly.
"My dear Edina, fair and beautiful lover, right now is like
winter too me because I long for your nearness, but when I
return it shall be as if spring flowers are in blossom all
over. The whole world will be a choir, singing! The birds
will fill the forest with sweet song. Oh, how I wish I could
return to you right now but that day will be all the sweeter
when I see your face, hear your voice, your soothing
voice, your beautiful face. But duty calls and everyday
we're apart and you hear the birds sing, and then listen
carefully as they sing about our love. My life started on
that day we met, be strong my love, be courageous, keep
the faith."
Both sat in silence.
Edina broke the silence.

"It was a Captain Strong who knocked the door. They expected to win, the Red Skull force was small and reinforcements were days away. It was on the 26th of September that Jimmi, Bert and over two thousand strong steel men of Caledon were wiped out."

She leant forward, feeling the burn of the fire against her cheek.

She sighed, "Bert was killed outright but Jimmi was missing, presumed dead. The Captain apologised, the intelligence had got it wrong and the Red Skull were fully reinforced and led by the Immortal known as Morg."

The tears were flowing freely now between the both.

Grandfather concluded.

"Bert was brought home to be buried but poor Jimmi has no known grave and remains missing in action."

Grandfather reached for a small box, it contained photographs of happier days and Jimmi's diary , brought back by Captain Strong.

Grandfather tried to rationalise his grief.

"Jimmi was but one of the thousands of heroes now listed on the Jobo memorial in Caledon City square, we were not the only ones to lose."

But it was still his Jimmi.

He leafed through his diary, which he had read a hundred times before, trying to gain peace from the knowledge that Jimmi served the Almighty with courage, grace and pride.

But he crumpled over the arm of the chair, a broken man. These feelings he had hidden every day from Edina and those who slept in the rooms above. Those who he was now accountable for in the absence of his precious son, those who knew him only as strong and never weak, he must be the father, the man of steel that Jimmi would have been if he was here. If truth be told, Grandfather felt like he was no one. He was only an ordinary steel worker, not meant for the burdens this war had placed on him; he had raised his family and should now be enjoying retirement.

He gathered his tears, strengthening he said, "I will never understand why good men were led to the slaughter; it was a pointless, ill-planned affair. It achieved nothing but the deaths of good men and the maiming of many others."

Truly war is a leveller and as Grandfather comforted Edina as she wept over the letters, a final single tear fell like a raindrop that onto the fire place, it exploded and evaporated like the memory of his fallen son, the hurt is realised and then forgotten only to be remembered again with every fresh tear. But then he remembers the words of the Almighty. He stood strong and spoke with conviction.

"No test or temptation that comes your way is beyond the course of what others have had to face. All you need to remember is that the Almighty will never let you down; he'll never let you be pushed past your limit; he'll always be there to help you come through it."

Edina finished her drink and said goodnight, to Grandfather.

"Goodnight Edina." he replied.

He curled up in his chair and fell asleep in his misery but still remaining hopeful that he who promises never fails.

Edina climbed the stairs to her room, they only had two bedrooms, she shared one with Sissy and the boys had the other. Grandfather slept in his chair by the fire every night. Edina went through her thoughts, she would not sleep until she was sure she had done all her chores and everything was ready for the next day so that she wouldn't be scrambling in the morning for forgotten items. She looked into the boy's room to make sure they were sleeping, they all were except Gus who was almost there,

"Night, Mum," he said in a sleepy voice.

Although Bobby was the oldest, it was always Gus who had the broad shoulders, when news of his father's death reached them three years ago, it was Gus who stepped up to the mark, it was he who comforted her on that cold rainy day, her skirts hung heavy around her that day, heavily pregnant with Sissy and the other children clinging to her like vices, seemingly inconsolable. It was that day she stopped feeling young, it was then she realised that her gamble with Jimmi for a life time romance was lost and as she felt the tears rise again, cried to the Almighty,

"Oh, Lord, why do you ask me for so high a price?"

She went into her own room and moved Sissy who was, as usual hogging the whole bed, ensuring she was tucked in and sleeping. Edina then went over to the dresser and poured some water into the bowl, giving her face a splash and scrubbed her hands.

"O Jimmi, why did you have to take off on a foolish crusade? I need you more than this blasted country does!"

Edina had a strong faith and believed with all her heart but sometimes, just sometimes, wondered if maybe the Almighty had asked a little too much of her and her little family, more importantly, she hoped that she would not have to pay more in this approaching war. She had paid her price for peace, she sat at her mirror taking her brush and combing her hair.

She crumpled over the dresser, in a silent sob.

"Jimmi, I miss you so much. Lord, help me tonight, I've never felt so low."

Sissy began to rumble in her sleep, whatever dreams she was having. Edina leant by the bed stroking her hair, its ok baby, mum's here, everything's alright. She soon settled, so Edina went back to the dresser, removing her clothes and slipping into her night clothes. She took the brush once more and removed any remaining tangles and knots from her hair. She then slipped into bed making sure she did not disturb Sissy too much and reached down for her book, the Almighty's book, as she did every night. She opened up at the bookmark and read,

'This is the Almighty's word on the subject 'As soon as the evil days are up and not a day before, I'll show up and take care of you as I promised and bring you back home. I know what I'm doing. I have it all planned out, plans to take care of you, not abandon you, plans to give you the future you hope for. When you call on me, when you come and pray to me, I'll listen. When you come looking for me, you'll find me. Yes, when you get serious about finding me and want it more than anything else, I'll make sure you

won't be disappointed. This is the Almighty's Decree. I'll turn things around for you. I'll bring back all those who have been taken away, all those who have been driven out. This is the Almighty's Decree. I'll bring those who seem to have been lost, home from the place from which I sent them. You can count on it. ...'

She could feel her eyes becoming drowsy, as the Almighty's words of comfort soothed her weary soul, so she laid the book back under her bed, switched off her bed lamp and cradled her youngest, her precious Sissy, in her arms as they both took their last sound sleep together.

Chapter 3 - The Oncoming Storm

Grandfather woke the next morning at around six knowing that the children would be awake very soon, he always allowed Edina to sleep long at the weekend and he started making breakfast for the children. He could hear the first steps of the children rising, followed by various clatters, a low noise which slowly rose to a loud racquet as they collectively ran down the stairs expecting breakfast, all except Sissy who would always be last to appear making a slow sleepy appearance dragging her rag doll behind her. By this time Grandfather had made breakfast and laid it on the table.

Bobby called out, "I love Grandfather's breakfast."

There was a loaf of mother's homemade bread, with free-range eggs, a bowl of apples, Grandfather's freshly made biscuits, creamy butter and smoke-cured bacon with butcher fresh sausages. There was orange juice and lashings of cold milk and, of course, strong black coffee for Grandfather. After the food was devoured by the children, Grandfather chased them upstairs to get dressed, Edina, now awake slowly walked downstairs and sitting at the table was passed a plate of eggy toast dusted with powdered sugar and a tall glass of Volentia orange juice,

"It's important you get a right start to the day, and a good breakfast is the secret." said Grandfather as he bit into an apple and felt the tart, crispy, firm skin give way to his teeth.

***

Meanwhile, the 6th Caledon volunteer defence force watched the perimeters of the city they had guards on gates and patrolling the city walls, Caledon was an old city built when walls were necessary to keep out aggressors and in its history it had never been conquered by an enemy army. The defence force had always been a voluntary brigade since Gaelia had agreed unification under mutual consent. Many centuries ago, the King of Gaelia had been the rightful heir to both realms, so a political union was agreed, grudgingly but willingly. To this day, the people of Caledon and Gaelia still considered themselves a separate nation with their motto; "*Furious in unity, we will be strong for the Almighty*". The guard on the southern wall, considered his long day ahead as a sudden gust of wind swept along the top of the wall and the sound of doors and windows slamming shut echoed throughout the city, the wind came from the northeast as if out of nowhere.

"It's going to be a long one." he thought.

He momentarily looked into the city and saw a young girl, in a yard only two hundred yards from the wall, running to and fro, picking up fallen items and collecting the clothing from the clothesline. A heavy downpour was imminent and he shivered as another gust of wind blew across the wall.

Just as she took down the last piece of clothing from the clothesline, the rain began to fall. It started as a slow moving melody with a light drizzle tapping out the rhythms but it grew heavier. The sky darkened and heavy gloom spread over the city, he pulled over his hood. It felt a little eerie as it was nine in the morning but felt more like evening with the winds starting to howl adding the melody to the tune and the clouds making it so dark. Now the rain was drumming heavily on window panes, barrels, drainpipes, roof tiles, all adding to the percussion. Its force was strong, he saw people closing their front and back doors to prevent it from getting into the house. He couldn't put a finger on it but today he had a dread in his spirit, perhaps it was the dreary weather and the gloomy surroundings, he didn't understand why but he was feeling rather frightened. He wished this day was over and he was at home with his parents and family. He needed the comfort of their company, but it would be another seven hours before he could go home. He couldn't explain it, it felt like someone was looking over his shoulder, the feeling you get when someone's watching you, his neck hairs were standing on end but he just passed it as a moment of unreasoned dread and dolefulness.

"Give yourself a shake; it's only bad weather, sheesh man, what a wimp you are!"

Just then, an officer passed, he stood to attention and saluted. It was Captain Mark Strong but his friends called him 'Sparky', he was a wireless-operator in the RADAR rooms as well as a photon air gunner and had an insignia of an eagle sitting on a radio mast with the initials WOp/PhAG underneath. Most officers understudied other job in case of emergency, flight-engineers also trained as pilots. Sparky saluted back but swiftly moved on into what looked like a shack from the outside but led down stone steps and into a stone building a few hundred feet away. It had two floors with a security group occupying the first level, and the second, much smaller level housing the RADAR and wireless equipment. As he approached the door, two armed marines stood either side, they saluted, he punched in the key code and the door swung open. The room had a few benches, which were occupied by four further marines who stood to attention.

Sparky half saluted back, "At ease, marines, at ease."

He climbed the metal staircase and entered a second key code which allowed him into the second room. This room was a lot more high tech with touch operated, split screen oscilloscopes and multi-meters. The only piece of 'old' tech was a diesel driven generator kept in case of power cuts, which happened more often than you would think since the coup and Nefarious had forced himself as regent. Sparky stood before what was obviously the commanding officers desk.

"Reporting for duty on transfer from the west wall placement, Sir!"

"Stand at ease, do you have your transfer papers?"

Sparky took out the folded papers from his breast pocket and handed them to Major Paul.

"OK, Captain Strong, these seem in order. That's your station over there, you can start straight away."

"Thank you, Sir." said Sparky and he went to his position as ordered.

He was an experienced officer but he did feel slightly intimidated at this moment, the operator at the position said,

"Thank goodness, I've been on this post for sixteen hours, my name is Marty. Have a good one."

He quickly left after being discharged by Major Paul. Sparky had only been on the RADAR less than an hour when the appearance of Red Skull bombers on the screen startled him.

"Sir, Red Skull bombers sighted, two hundred miles out and closing."

This was a new tactic, bombers had targeted smaller towns, airfields and power plants but they had never attacked Caledon before, it was too far north and well defended. They had hoped those true to the Almighty in the south would be able to subdue this rebellion before they saw any war but this heralded a tactical shift in the Red Skull's attempt to subdue Gaelia and the city of Caledon. Caledon would not give up without a fight; this arial attack was an attempt to demoralise the population and force them to come to terms.

"Three hundred and forty eight Z31 type bombers escorted by six hundred and seventeen FK 2 fighters, Sir. One hundred and eighty miles and closing." exclaimed Sparky.

Major Paul turned white with shock.

"In the name of the Almighty, how can we defend ourselves against that?"

He grabbed the phone receiver and screamed.

"Full deployment of all arial defence, deploy all Eagles and man all photon-air gunneries!"

The Anti-Air defence of the city was divided into active and passive parts. The former was composed mostly of units of the Eagle Fighter Brigade under General Stef Pawlii, and anti-aircraft photon artillery and anti-aircraft photon-gun detachments under Colonel Kim Bear, admiringly nicknamed the Bear Brigade. The Eagle Brigade was equipped with fifty four fighter aircraft, vastly outnumbered but the experienced pilot knows, the best trained might find himself out manoeuvred by a passionate volunteer, especially one fighting for his survival and his home land. The Eagle fighter was a far superior aircraft to the Falcon but surely the sheer numbers would be their undoing. The Bear Brigade had eighty six pieces of anti-aircraft photon cannons, as well as a large amount of anti-aircraft photon-guns. The latter was composed mostly of volunteers and was supervised by Colonel Tad Boggins, known as 'The Boggers.'

***

At that moment Julia Caulks, the mayor of Caledon, had called an emergency meeting with General Pawlii. Mayor Caulks had had a rough few months succeeding to the position after the elected mayor, Bob Gillad, had died from a sudden heart attack and with the threat of the Red Skull, no time for elections. At the centre of her travails was the debate about capitulation to the Immortals. She considered it a real option but many, including the General, opposed her.

She had been called a witch, a traitor to the Almighty for even considering it but she was just echoing feeling already aired by the ruling government in the capital.

"Madam Mayor, there can be no capitulation, the Red Skull do not negotiate power. They simply take it, many consider your mayorship a joke, you are in a position of power you were never meant to hold, and we need to call for a council vote turning Caledon over to Marshal Law."

The Mayor stood up behind her desk slamming it with both palms as she did. Both hands stung with the force she had used but it did not sting like the sting of rejection in her heart right now at the suggestion of Marshal Law.

"Never, unless there is no other option!" she exclaimed.

But all her outrage could not wash away the attitudes she faced, there was no doubt her gender played a large part in people's confidence in her but there was another rather larger elephant sitting in her office, she had developed an alcohol addiction and everyone knew but no one broached the subject, until now.

"Madam Mayor," said General Pawlii. "It has become apparent that you are no longer fit for office, your service is appreciated especially in this hard time. Your commitment and long hours have been noted, which is why I would prefer if you declared Marshal Law instead of it being imposed upon you."

The realisation of what was being said struck the Mayor as the words of the General scraped over her soul like a rusty nail on a blackboard.

"You mean to replace me, without due process?"

"If that's what it takes, the Red Skull is all but knocking on our door and, frankly, Madam Mayor, you are no longer fit to lead!"

She began to realise, she saw the writing on the wall, and unless she changed her position anything she said would only be political posturing. In different days her alcohol problem would have been a relatively minor issue, swept under the carpet whilst it was '*dealt with*' privately, but in the larger drama which was unfolding it could not be overlooked. Caledon needed leaders with a clear mind and people needed to have confidence, it would be central to any evaluation of Mayor Julia Caulk's leadership.

The General leant closer and spoke softer.

"You know, Julia that I have always supported you in most of your decisions, at least publicly, but that's not what matters at the moment, now is not time to show any wavering or weakness of any kind. It's a matter of trust about speaking directly to the questions and concerns. It's about what we value and not who will be cast aside. It shows us that even those in high office are expendable for the greater good, being in office means holding up to your convictions but also means taking the proverbial bullet when needs must. Madam Mayor needs must!"

She straightened her suit jacket, maintained her position of authority, in her mind she had the words to justify her position about the democratic cultural institution of long standing in Caledon and how important values from our past need to continue to be part of our present and part of our future. Then the phone rang, she grabbed it angrily.

"I said we were not to be disturbed!"

The caller on the other end apologised,

"Sorry, Madam Mayor, but we are under arial attack from the Red Skull."

The Mayor's stomach sank like a stone, she switched the phone to speaker, the caller continued,

"The General is required immediately at HQ there are reports of over three hundred bombers."

"By the Almighty!" said the General.

"Our conference is over and I expect your resignation within the day."

He marched out of the office leaving the door ajar. Mayor Caulks slumped in the chair, now finally realising that the only thing that mattered now was survival and all her posturing was meaningless, her spirit sapped away from her as did her grasp on power that morning, politicians were no longer useful, Caledon now needed soldiers.

***

General Pawllii marched into the HQ, with determination, marines standing to attention and saluting as he went. Colonel Bear joined him in his march to the war room coming from her offices,

"How true are the reports?" he barked at the Colonel.

"The call came from Major Paul of the south wall RADAR position, its three hundred and forty eight Z-type bombers in ten formations escorted by six hundred and seventeen Falcon fighters, sir, less than ten minutes out. Full arial defence has been activated but the numbers are against us sir.", she replied.

Initially the air defence was successful. The Eagle Brigade shot down forty three enemy aircraft, while anti-aircraft artillery, the Bear brigade, had shot down a similar number of enemy bombers. However, the brigades also suffered losses; it had lost thirty eight Eagles, or approximately seventy per cent of its initial strength. The Bear defence started to crumble as eleven AA batteries lost there commanding officers due to the incessant bombing. They blasted Caledon every hour, guided by the fires set by the assaults. The raiders continued attacks that lasted until 4:30 the following morning. For the next consecutive five days, Caledon was bombed day and night. Fires consumed many portions of the city. Residents sought shelter wherever they could find it. In the worst single incident, four hundred and fifty were killed when a bomb destroyed a school being used as an air raid shelter.

"They came every night like wolves in the dark." described the local newspaper,

"Every night Caledon is ringed with fire and stabbed with fear. They come mostly just after dark, now, you can sense from the quick, bitter firing of the guns that there will be no rest this night."

***

On that first night, the Black family could hear the sirens wail, the grinding of the aircraft's engines overhead. In their room, Edina, Grandfather and the children huddled for safety, with the curtains drawn across the windows, they felt the shake from the guns. They could hear the

47

boom and the buildings crumpling like paper under the heavy boot of the bombers, tearing buildings apart. Like a bully standing on their sand castles at the beach unaware and uncaring about the time and care taken to perfect it, only wishing to crush spirits in the same way he had crushed your creation. Half an hour after dark in the first day Grandfather went to a high, darkened balcony that gave him a view of Caledon. Gus and Billy followed, the rest stayed with Edina. As they stepped out onto the balcony a vast inner excitement came over Gus, an excitement that had neither fear nor horror in it, because it was too full of awe. He had seen big fires, but he had never seen the whole horizon of the city lined with great fires. Scores of them, perhaps hundreds.

There was something inspiring and dreadful in the awful savagery of it. The closest fires were near enough for them to hear the crackling flames and the yells of those trapped inside and the brave firemen trying to rescue them, their efforts to control the fires were courageous but mostly futile. Little fires grew into big ones, big ones died down under the firemen's valour, only to break out again later. They saw a new wave of planes flying over. The motors had an angry pulsation, like a bee buzzing in blind fury, as the days went on the guns did not make the same constant overwhelming din as in previous days, was it because the attack lessened or was the brigade getting fewer in number. Their sound was sharp, nearby; and soft and muffled, far away. They were everywhere you could not escape the noise night and day. On day two, Gus continued to watch the bombing, it had stopped in early morning but had restarted again just after night fall, into the dark shadowed spaces below, and whole batches of incendiary bombs fell. He saw two dozen go off in two seconds. They flashed terrifically, then quickly simmered down to pin points of dazzling white, burning ferociously. These white pin points would go out one by one, as the unseen heroes of the brigade smothered them. But, while he watched, other pin points would burn on, and soon a yellow flame would leap up from the white centre. They had done their work, another building was on fire.

On the morning of day three, the greatest of all the fires was directly in front of him. Flames seemed to whip hundreds of feet into the air. Pinkish-white smoke ballooned upward in a great cloud, and out of this cloud there gradually took shape, so faintly at first that he wasn't sure he saw correctly, the City Hall was on fire. It was surrounded by fire. It stood there in its enormous proportions, growing slowly clearer and clearer, the way objects take shape at dawn. It was like a picture of some miraculous figure that appeared before weary volunteers and soldiers on this battlefield calling them to duty and inspiring them to make one last effort to withstand the oncoming storm. The streets below were illuminated from the glow. Immediately above the fires the sky was red and angry, and overhead, making a ceiling in the vast heavens, there was a cloud of smoke all in pink. Up in that pink shrouding there were tiny, brilliant specks of flashing anti-aircraft photon bursts. After the flash you could hear the sound. Later that evening, Gus could see the City Hall emerged from the flames of one of the most devastating raids ever; the clouds were pink instead of silver. And now and then through a hole in that pink shroud there twinkled incongruously a permanent, genuine star. The old fashioned kind that has always been there, a symbol that although much was changing below, the heavens remained the same as the Almighty was not affected by the acts of evil men and the faithful must remain, ever shining. Below, the city grew darker and all around below was the shadows, the dark shadows of buildings and bridges that formed the base of this dreadful masterpiece. After the raid was over, when all were resting or asleep, Gus and Billy went out among the fires, this was the first they had left the house, the first they could see the devastation up close. The sense of excitement and dread of what they may find ran through them; Gus was struck by the monstrous loveliness of Caledon, once proud and peaceful, now lying with her belly slashed open with great fires, shaken by explosions, its dark regions along the River Pannch sparkling with the brightness of the flames as if fireflies had been trapped in the water, all of it with a ceiling of pink that had, not less than an hour ago, held bursting photon shells and the grind of the vicious engines. Within him he felt the numbness of disbelief, the excitement and anticipation knowing they could return in another hour or so, the wonder in their souls that this could be happening at all.

Billy turned to Gus with a tear in his eyes.

"It's like the end of all things has closed in."

The crows filled the sky, the houses were burning in flames gold and red. People were running everywhere and every direction with eyes full of tears or dread. Children sat among the rubble, some as if unaware of the devastation played games, others searched rubble whether for food or family was unknown. Grandfather had been absent the last few days, he volunteered to help search for survivors, Billy and Gus both now knew they must do the same. These things all went together to make the most hateful, most beautiful single scene they had ever known.

Billy spoke again, now with tears streaming.

"Why did they do this, why did they do this, so much fury and fire, they didn't have to do this?"

Gus took his brother in his arms, who was now sobbing like a baby, he comforted him.

"This is not the end, the day of the Almighty has still to come, and we still have hope. As the Grandfather taught us. The Almighty has said, '*Let the strength of peace run through My hand when we walk away from the storm.*' And Billy we will walk away from this storm, fear may grip us now but then we will not be afraid. Right now, I am sure of where I stand, in the strength of the Almighty and not in the fear of evil men. Once more, the strength of peace will run through this land."

As they separated and slowly walked back to their reasonably untouched home.

Billy did not smile, instead his tears turned into anger.

"Gus, we will take back our own. Whatever else comes upon us, we will take back our own."

They continued to walk as the rain beat on them, thunder moaned from the heavy clouds, a reminder of the further onslaught to come. They arrived back in their house to find everyone eating including Grandfather, taking the opportunity during the respite. Edina was furious.

"Where have you been, it's not safe out there."

Nobody smiled as Billy recounted what they saw, they all knew, including Sissy, what was lost.

Grandfather said, "Trust the Almighty, in time all pay the cost of their actions and the Red Skull will be no different. For the innocent then peace of mind is their reward, for the treacherous their reward is set."

After food, Grandfather motioned to Edina that he was returning to help with the rescue efforts.

Billy caught this, "Grandfather, Gus and I are going with you, we can't just sit here like frightened children, we're young men, we can help!",

"No way!" exclaimed Edina.

"It's dangerous and you're too young."

Billy never disrespected his mother but he was adamant.

"Mum, we want to, NO, need to help. We can't just sit here and do nothing, if you stop me I'll just go anyway!"

Grandfather stepped in.

"Billy, that's enough, apologise to your mother!"

Billy's eyes dropped but he apologised.

Grandfather continued, "I'm just going to search for survivors, they won't be near the fires and let's face it

Edina, if a bomb were to hit here they'd be just as much in danger. They are strong and four more willing hands will be welcome to the rescue crew."

He took her hands in his, "I will look after them."

Edina consented; she took both boys in her arms, kissed them on the head.

"Be careful, my strong young men."

The boys followed Grandfather who reported to his allocated rescue squad, he approached a man who was obviously in charge, they both looked over, and the man nodded and then approached them with Grandfather.

"Hello boys, I'm Renee, these buildings have recently collapsed and may have people trapped in them. They will also have supplies we can take and distribute amongst those in need. The stronger men will move larger pieces, you will move the smaller ones or if we find supplies you will take them to the store master over there, he is Mr Montagne."

Just at that a cry came from one of the searchers.

"We've got a live one here!"

Everyone rushed to help and a frantic search for the survivor began. It had been an eight-story building and had collapsed a day ago. The building was a garment factory that made low cost clothing for workers. So far they had found thirty people dead but had saved fifty three trapped souls, some with serious injuries, others with minor, a few with none so they also had joined the rescue efforts. Only the ground floor remained intact, the remaining floors had come crashing down. Cranes and diggers were used but when '*a live one*' was found people used their bare hands to remove the concrete blocks and angle grinders to cut the iron rods to save further collapse on those people who were still trapped. Gus couldn't believe his eyes as he looked at the building collapsed before him, it could only be described as a chaotic scene and frantic search for the person trapped under the rubble, everyone was dusty and dirty, but all thankful that it wasn't them, they were the lucky ones. When it was realised there was someone still alive people seemed to come out of nowhere there were firemen, police, and construction guys digging out, because someone was down there. It was crazy right now but a good kind of crazy. Two construction workers in hard hats ran past him climbing onto the rubble. He could also see a few pedestrians heading into the rubble as well. Very quickly people were placed in a line of twos passing rubble from person to person forming a human chain, meticulously moving buckets of debris out of the building in a search for the survivors and before long they had uncovered a twelve year old girl.

One police officer kept saying, "Be careful, in case there are any unexploded missiles or bombs, we don't need a second explosion."

They got the girl out. They slowly passed her from person to person laying her carefully on flat ground as the paramedics treated her. The one thing that struck him was how, just as quickly as they arrived, they all dispersed back to their tasks, the paramedics placed her on a stretcher and then their ambulance, it whisked her away with sirens blazing and then he was again amazed at how quiet the scene was. No one seemed shaken or rattled. The site itself was quiet. No shouting, no sirens, no noise except from those quietly removing rubble once more, as if nothing had happened.

They continued working for another hour or so and then the sirens once more sounded.

The same police officer called.

"Take shelter, stop work, fire fighters report to stations!"

Grandfather led Gus and Billy to a stairway; it led down into a basement.

"We'll be safe here till it's over, then we will go home for some food and then we can come back again."

The bombers attacked the munitions factories and shipyards, wave after wave of high explosive photon bombs and missiles and incendiary bombs were dropped over a nine hour period, the boys tried to sleep as the streets outside were devastated with fires once more raging, and more people trapped in collapsed buildings. By now, people were used to the bombing and as the siren wailed to let them know it was over, their expressions could have been misunderstood as complacency but that was not the Caledon way. No, it was just their unwavering courage and heroism in the face of a relentless enemy. They returned slowly back home, looking forward to mum's food and the warm reception of her arms at how thankful they had returned safely.

"But Grandfather, why do we go home now, surely it's just after the bombings people need most help?" exclaimed Gus.

Grandfather smiled at his logic and enthusiasm,

"Firstly Gus, were no use if we aren't strong, we need to go eat. Secondly, the professionals, the firefighters and police officers need to control the fires and make it safe for us to return to help."

"Oh, alright."

Gus's unwavering faith in his Grandfather's word brought pleasure to the old man.

The boys, of course, ran on ahead of Grandfather, they heard people talking saying it was the worst yet, two ladies were talking.

"The father next door, of nine year old Janae, was killed outright when the Moore Plaza collapsed on top of him and John Horn was driving to pick up his daughter just before the last attack and a missile hit him direct, nothing left but a hole."

They turned the corner expecting to see their two storey house only to find it was in rubble. There was no way to explain the anger or sadness they felt at that time. Billy fell to his knees, Gus remained strong but speechless and Grandfather, a good few minutes behind collapsed completely, it was as if all strength sapped from his legs and arms and torso and finally his head.

He fell into a heap on the ground and lost complete consciousness.

Chapter 4 - Just Stay Alive

As quickly as it started, the bombing ended on day five, the onslaught which had become part of the expected day just didn't happen. The people of Caledon would be granted two days respite before the land fighting started, when the first Red Skull armoured units would reach the southwestern suburbs of the city. Despite Red Skull radio broadcasts claiming to have captured Caledon, the Volunteers of Caledon would not capitulate that easily. General Pawlii and Colonel Bear stood in the HQ war room with many officers surrounding them and Mayor Caulks in the background, now as a political and civilian advisor having succumbed to the very strong suggestions of General Pawlli five days earlier to step down.

"What is our current position Colonel?" said the General wearily.

He had slept little over the last few days and survived on black coffee and whatever half sandwich he had placed in front of him. Colonel Bear was little better but both being professional soldiers, apart from the bleary eyes and the occasional half drooled speech, still looked sharp.

"As you know." she replied. "From the very first hours military facilities such as infantry barracks and the airport and aircraft factory were targeted, they also targeted civilian facilities such as water works, hospitals, market places and schools. In addition, civilians were strafed from the air with bolt gun fire, in an attempt to produce terror amongst the civilian population."

"Red Skull scum!" said the Mayor, rather louder than she intended.

The Colonel continued, "As you know, we have three Destructors in port including the AS Priority which was undergoing repairs, as well as the AS Solidarity and AS Joshua, both had just been refitted with photon cannons. They joined the defence of Caledon, firing a tremendous barrage at the Z31 bombers; it gave them a kick in the teeth they did not expect."

The Mayor interrupted again, "We have to take this opportunity to evacuate the remaining civilians whilst they muster their forces for a land attack."

"What are the civilian's stats Madam Mayor." asked General Pawlii.

She quickly responded, "Five hundred and twenty eight civilians are hospitalised beyond being able to be moved, six hundred and seventeen people are seriously injured but with proper support can be transported, we have a hospital ship in the port who could cater for them and transport them to the Burgh, which I believe, is still untouched by the Red Skull."

She stood up and looked straight at the General and gave a huge sigh.

"Stef!"

He quickly turned round at the mention of his first name.

"Our biggest problem is that almost all the housing estates were completely wiped out; we have one hundred and forty eight thousand civilians who have lost their homes, how on earth do we keep them safe whilst keeping enough soldiers behind to halt the oncoming storm?"

The General remained unmoved.

"Thank you for your input, Julia, Colonel Bear what troops do we have left?"

She replied, "We have over one hundred thousand soldiers who have been garrisoned from outlying areas, some are retired from service and have come back to serve the Almighty. We have around thirty thousand militia from the general population and twenty thousand police and fire fighters."

The General looked perplexed.

"What about armaments?"

Colonel Bear spoke confidently.

"We have enough armaments to defend the city till the Almighty returns, it's the man power we lack, sir."

He thought again, this time for a long time.

After five minutes the Mayor spoke.

"Stef, what about ....."

"Be quiet, Julia, let me think."

She stepped back feeling snubbed.

The General continued staring at the wall for a further ten minutes then he spoke.

"Madam Mayor, you will supervise the transfer of the injured to the hospital ship, I will send instructions for it to set sail to the Burgh once the transfer is complete under the protection of AS Joshua."

"What of the rest?" said Julia.

"Patience you infernal woman! Major Hardrheind will oversee the evacuation of the civilian population with the exception of any who can be drafted into the Militia. Colonel Bear please arm all police and fire officers with bolt guns and select a contingency, they shall be the armed escort for the civilian evacuees who shall head to the fort town at the Vale of Lamont. Please also place general drafts order for all able bodied to join the Militia, start plans to strengthen our defences, they are coming and we had better be ready for them."

There was silence.

Then General Pawlii, called out.

"Step to it, on the double!"

Both Kim and Julia looked at each other, Colonel Bear saluted and both left.

The General then turned to another officer.

"Captain Smig, I need to address the city arrange for a press conference."

***

Grandfather came round, lying flat on the ground with a police officer beside him.

He sat bolt upright.

"Gus, Billy, where are you?"

"It's alright, sir." said the officer.

"They are safe and helping in the rescue operation, they're clearing rubble like the two strong young men they are, you should be proud."

"I've got to help, Edina and the children were in there!" exclaimed Grandfather.

"Now, sir, you just lie there, a medic is on his way to check you over, you'll be no good to anyone if you collapse again. Lie there and rest." insisted the police officer.

Juat then, a familiar face appeared, it was Rose.

"Hey, James, you do as the officer says, there are plenty helping, I'll stay with him officer, I'll make sure he doesn't get up to any trouble."

Grandfather crumpled emotionally, his face became small and childlike as the tears streamed down his face falling in between the wrinkles and following their contours, a proud man, broken.

"Why, Rose? Why us? Why did this happen? First Jimmi and now Edina and the children.

Oh, Lord, the children!"

He was now uncontrollable as Rose took him in her arms and joined him in their requiem of tears as memories of their fallen heroes and lost families overwhelmed them.

After a full ten minutes, Rose spoke.

"I remember what you said to me James, when the news of Jimmi and Bert came through; asking why just gives us more questions and not answers. Today we will do what we have to do, we will take today but tomorrow we will begin again, we will recover and rebuild. The Almighty has a plan and until it becomes clear we will find meaning and purpose every day, we will live on because to die has no purpose. The Almighty's word reminds us,

'Even when we walk through the shadow of Death Valley,
I'm not afraid when you walk at my side. You nudge me
gently in the right direction and make me feel secure.'
And what I like about that verse, death is only a shadow,
fleeting and flees when the light appears."

With that a lightness came over the old man's face as the
pieces of his shattered life lay before him, he rediscovered
the internal core of strength that his long years of faith
afforded him.

The rescue team continued to search amongst the rubble
and as they were about to break through a large concrete
slab, a worker was cutting iron rods when suddenly he saw
what looked like a grey, silvery stick just moving from a
hole.

After looking closer he realised it was a leg and then heard
a child's voice calling,

"Please save me!"

He immediately called over police officers and
firefighters. The officers ordered workers operating heavy
machinery to stop and using infrared video detection
equipment, located the exact positions of all who lay
beneath. Gus heard the news and climbed the rubble, a
firefighter caught him or else he would have been down
the hole.

"Let me in, I've got to get them out."

The firefighter dumped him down on the broken concrete
and brick.

"Sit there and let us do our job!"

A small voice cried out again, "I'm still here!"

Gus jumped up again and made to go for the hole.

"It's Sissy, my little sister, I've got to get her out!"

The firefighter grabbed him again and held him down this time.

"We are, son, but you are now stopping us. Sit still or I will get the police officer to remove you from the scene."

Gus realised he was being over reactive.

"I won't move, not till I'm told, I promise."

At that a female police officer came up beside him with Billy, the same officer who had been attending Grandfather.

"I'll stay with him." she said.

"You go and help, it's alright, and she'll be out soon." ..

Sissy's voice could be heard again.

"I'm not hurt but my mum and brothers are, please hurry!"

Handsaws and drilling equipment were brought in to cut through the iron rods and debris, the rescuers worked for forty minutes before finally pulling Sissy from the rubble, amid cheers from the crowd. She was relatively unhurt, a few bruises and scrapes to her legs and arms, she spotted Gus and Billy and ran through the rubble.

Her first reaction was to slap Gus on the arm.

"You said you would protect me!"

She then grabbed him and the emotions inside realised into a flood of joy as Billy and Gus hugged and kissed her and cried.

"I think you should all go to your Grandfather, I think he needs to know the news." said the police officer.

"I will keep you updated, let the workers do their job."

"There are still two boys Bobby and Jo and my mother Edina!" said Gus.

"Thank you, we will let you know." replied the officer.

The three children ran to Grandfather, his face nearly exploded with joy on seeing Sissy.

"By the Almighty, how is this possible? Praise the Almighty, you are alive."

"Yes, Grandfather."

She threw her arms around his neck; he felt it heavy as she squeezed so hard it took away his breath.

"I was really afraid, Grandfather."

"I know my sweet Sissy and so were we all. Tell us what happened, dear one."

Sissy sat down on the rubble like she was sitting on a chair in the kitchen, crossing her legs.

"We'd been in the house as usual when we heard the sirens; Bobby went up to the balcony to watch. I told him not to, it was too dangerous but he just laughed. Mum was getting us ready for bed when a big bang came from the top of the street, Bobby came running, and he was screaming that we should hide. Another big bang from the bottom of the street and then one landed right on top. Mum had already put me and Jo in the cupboard under the stair to protect us but Mum and Bobby were still outside, the cupboard door was still opened, I saw the cooker fly by. I could see Mum she was sleeping and had bricks on her. I could hear Bobby at first saying, *'Are you alright mum?'* I told him she was sleeping. He said he was trapped and couldn't move. Jo was beside me but he was sleeping

64

too and his leg was bleeding. We were there for ages and Bobby stopped talking, I think he fell asleep to. I began to feel sleepy when I saw sunlight and shouted out. And here I am, Mum will be OK, won't she Grandfather."

"Let's wait and see, my love."

About another forty minutes later, the police officer returned.

"Hi, Gus?"

"Yes, that's me!" he replied sharply.

"You're a responsible lad, I need to talk with your Grandfather, can you take Billy and Sissy over there, and where that lady you know is."

"Rose, do you mean Rose?" he asked.

"Yes, she's helping by giving out tea and sandwiches; maybe you can get some for your brother and sister whilst I talk with your Grandfather."

"James." said Gus.

"Pardon?" said the officer.

"His name is James, and yes, of course I will."

He said it with a great deal of pathos as he gathered his siblings and herded them towards Rose, his arms and legs were heavy with tiredness, his back ached but the biggest and sharpest pain was the dread in his heart as he knew why they were being sent away, the news could only be bad news.

He got tea and sandwiches passing them to Bobby and Sissy who wolfed them down as if they had not been fed for a week. He did not want one as he felt a stone in his stomach and tried not to think of what she was saying to

Grandfather, it was too frightening to contemplate. He sipped the tea; it made his teeth hurt as there was too much sugar in it but he welcomed the warm, sweet drizzle as it slowly ran down his throat hitting the stone in his stomach.

The officer approached James.

"How are you, sir?"

"I'm ok, young lady, please call me James. Have you any news about my family?" he asked with urgency.

"That's why I'm here." she replied.

Grandfathers' face turned grey.

"Are you alright, James?"

"Yes, yes just tell me."

***

The General sat at his desk waiting for the half dozen news people to settle, the television stations and masts had been obliterated and only short wave radio remained after the carnage of the Red Skull raids. That was sufficient for their need as the General cleared his throat in anticipation.

The press had already been notified that he would be making a statement and no questions would be answered.

"In just the past few years, we have witnessed major political changes in the Kingdom and now a massive onslaught on our proud city of Caledon which can only be the precursor to full fledged invasion of our beloved Gaelia. Thousands of people have been killed; others have been left homeless without possessions. We were given little warning of the arial attack we have just endured, showing the cowardly nature of our enemy, cowardly perhaps but powerful and relentless. We have been swept along in the unavoidable path of these evil men. Some of us have been left intact, but few of us, most have been left in shambles, rubble and debris. As survivors we have been left dazed, tired, angry, confused and devastated. Our lives have been shattered, like the tree struck by lightning, and we may never be the same again. But these days are strong reminders of how vulnerable we are to the unexpected, the loss of a home, or the loss of a loved one shatters a person's world, destroys what was once familiar and upsets the normal sense of safety and stability. Viewing images of destruction, waiting and worrying about safety of family and friends have left many of us feeling shaken and unsure. We are left splintered, shaken and denuded. The impact of this traumatic event will be felt for years, and for many of us whom have lost everything, a lifetime. But now there is no unexpected surprise, no reason to be unprepared. We will pick up the pieces of our shattered lives and find ways to keep on living, everyday taking up the challenge. We must discover our internal core of strength, our faith must remain firm. Today we are reborn, the labour has been long and costly but this is the turning point we will send them a wake-up call that the people of Gaelia do not succumb to bullies and the actions of evil men. If they want this land it shall be at the cost of our extinction, every last man, woman and child must play their part in the fight against the banality of evil. Every able bodied adult aged between twenty one and fifty five will join the Militia to strengthen our arm and hold back these devils, exception being single mothers and fathers who are the sole guardian of their children, as well as the ill, infirm and injured. All who are injured and in need of hospital care shall be transported to the Burgh by the hospital ship in the port. All else shall be escorted to the Vale of Lamont via land by armed escort. Please report to the proper stations to get your instructions. We have seen and believed every good thing that the Almighty has done and that what He has done before He will do again. He will fulfil his promises and as we remained faithful to Him in the good times, we must remain true in the bad. He will do it because He is the Almighty. He will fight for you, alongside you, whether you take arms, or take care of those in need or help rebuild our great city and nation, stay strong and steady. Obediently do everything asked of you. Together even one of you, single-handedly, shall put a thousand on the run! Because the Almighty fights for you, just as He promised you, vigilantly guard your souls against the seed of doubt. The darkness must come before the dawn. As we stand in the rubble left us by the Red Skull, let these stones be a witness against us, they have heard every word that we have said to the Almighty in the darkness and the flame, they shall be a standing witness against them that they cannot cheat on the Almighty or those who remain faithful to Him.

Furious in unity, we will be strong for the Almighty and may His grace be upon you"

The General stood and left, waving away the press with their questions.

***

Grandfather sat on a bench in the hospital ward with Gus on one side sitting straight as a poker but eyes fixed and dazed, Sissy on the other grabbing hold of his waist and sobbing as if she would die if she let go. Billy paced up and down the corridor. The police officer had told Grandfather they had found three people Bobby and Jo was dead. Half of Bobby's face and body were crushed with the falling debris, he would have died quickly, firstly going unconscious with shock and then bleeding out. The gas and water mains had burst; Jo had died of asphyxiation from the gas.

It was a miracle that Sissy was still alive. She had already been treated, she had felt dizzy and nauseated, and she had told Grandfather she had been sick whilst waiting in the rubble. When they dug out Edina she was still alive with serious crush injuries to her chest. She, and the bodies of the boys, was taken to an ambulance and then Edina was rushed to the nearby Military Hospital for treatment.

On arrival they had found evidence of internal bleeding caused by the crushing.

The doctor appeared at the door.

"She is still asleep but you can go in now."

The doctor had already explained to Grandfather that her injuries were too severe and, if the Almighty afforded her grace, she had only a matter of hours left. As they entered the room the boys stood on the left side both holding her hand, Grandfather lifted Sissy onto the bed.

"Remember what the doctor said, you can cuddle her but gently or you will hurt her."

She sat quietly on the bed whilst Grandfather held Edina's right hand. Grandfather's thoughts wandered, today he was hurt, he felt mortally wounded and responsible, as if he could have made the difference if he had been there. It was an odd sensation, he was numb but yet it was hard to not focus on the pain. It seemed to be the only thing that was real, it tore a hole in his stomach and when he thought about his dead grandsons, it stung. He would remember everything about today, he would not let one memory escape ever. He knew, as he had believed and taught, that everyone goes away in the end but he had it in his mind he was the next one, at seventy, he was the next to go, not Edina and certainly not his grandsons.

Billy spoke up, "What will become of us Grandfather?"

Grandfather's throat was dry and he could feel a lump, he knew he would begin to cry if he spoke. Gus could see his Grandfather was struggling so he spoke.

"My sweet brother, everyone goes away, everything changes in the end. All we have here is fleeting and you can have it all, it's just dirt and dust. But we will start again; we will move with the rest, we keep going we must find a way. Life goes on. We can live again, we must concentrate our energies on our lives, and we have survived. We will have to cope with this every day, the loss, but if we do not rebuild a new life as a memorial to those we have lost then we may have just as well died with them. Yes our lives will be changed forever. Our old dreams are gone; we need to dream new ones and not mourning what might have been. That's what mother, Bobby and Jo would have wanted."

Sissy, who had been lying, gently, on her mother's legs, suddenly sat up.

"She moved!"

Everyone looked at Mother; she opened her eyes very narrowly, slightly squeezed Gus and Billy's hands and mumbled almost incoherently.

"You're a good boy, Gus, just like your father. I love you all. *Just stay alive*."

She closed her eyes again, her arms and body went limp and exhaled her last breath.

Billy immediately let go of her hand, ran out of the room confused, delirious, calling for the doctor. Sissy was screaming.

"She's ok; she's moving. She's moving!"

Gus stood there still holding her hand placid and peaceful. Grandfather kissed her head.

"It's OK Sissy, you can hug her all you like now, and you won't hurt her. She's gone to be with father and the boys."

Sissy wailed uncontrollably, the doctor barged into the room, quickly examined her and pronounced her dead.

Edina and the boys were all cremated in the hospital furnace, they all then went to register for evacuation as they had been instructed and were heading for the fort at the Vale of Lamont within the day.

***

General Pawlii marched defiantly into the war room,

"Let's show these dirtbags how Caledon soldiers fight,"
He barked out orders.
"Colonel Bear, shouldn't you be at the Forward
Command?"
She stood to attention.
"Just leaving, sir, finalising tactics with Colonel Tomas,
your chief of staff."
He was not impressed,
"Is there something wrong with our communications that
you had to do it in person?"
"No, sir."
"Well, let's get a shift on Colonel."
She left immediately to attend her command post.
Pawlii continued to bark.
"Status, Colonel Tomas."
He replied, "Most of the city authorities have been
withdrawn with the civilian population or are on the AS
Joshua, together with a small contingency of the police
forces and fire fighters. They are about to set sail and the
city should be completely evacuated of all citizens by
tomorrow."
"What about the enemy?" Pawlii growled.
Tomas bent over the maps in front and pointed,
"We expect our first attack from the 4th Scorpion Division
under the command of the Immortal Morg. If our Intel is
correct they will be the first to reach the outskirts of the
city."
Pawlii interrupted.

"I want barricades and anti-tank barriers constructed starting at the outskirts gradually drawing inward every two hundred yards making passage with vehicles almost impossible, leave a route open for our traffic but make it a maze with routes impossible to pass smoothly without u-turns unless you know them. Use the militia for this. There will be skilled labourers in there who can work quickly and effectively. What is our troop strength?"

"We have eighty five battalions of infantry with photon cannon gunneries and forty five Militia batteries; this has been strengthened by the communique issued by your self."

"Who is in charge of the conscription?" asked Pawlii

"The Militia is under the command of Major Paul." Tomas confirmed.

"He's a good man, evokes confidence hopefully enough to counter any panic that may start once the battle starts, after all, the Militia are essentially still civilians."

Pawlii looked a little more satisfied.

"Good work, Tomas. Let's crack on we have lots to do."

Intel had indeed been correct and the first to attack were the 4th Scorpion regiment.

Pawlii had not left the War room once.

"Can someone please give me Intel?"

Tomas rushed to the table.

"They have managed to break through the initial positions and started their march towards the river Pannch."

He was interrupted by Colonel Bear in forward command.

"The suburbs of *Radjow, Zyn, Ras and Piasno* have all been captured; they are reforming to attempt another assault on our western borough of Grec, where they were advancing. We have halted them at Opaska thanks to 13th infantry."

Pawlii slammed the table.

"We must hold Grec; we cannot let them have the junction at Opaska."

"I have every confidence that even if they do break our defence of Grec, they will not take Opaska." boasted Bear.

"And why are you so sure Bear." demanded Pawlii.

"That crossing is defended by the 40th infantry and commanded by Captain Mark Strong." Bear replied confidently.

Pawlii's expression changed.

"I too am now confident; Captain Strong is a good man."

***

Captain Mark Strong had been assigned to the 40th Infantry Regiment reinforced with Militia, who had named themselves *'Children of the Lion'*. He was an experienced officer whom had served overseas in several campaigns. He stood watch over the 40th Company and the *'Children of the Lion'* on a barricade which was erected at the crossing of *Opaska and Grec* square. He was a tall man, 6' 6", very broad shoulders. His head was shaven bald, and had a very impressive goatee and twirl moustache. He appeared at first to be an imposing man but actually loved by those who knew him as he was fair and was able to tell amazing stories, which he often did at night in order to allay any fears the troops might have. His laughter and humour brought spirit and bravery into the heart of anyone who would listen, his mere presence increased hope that the 40th had lost before he was assigned as Captain. He stood on the barricade with one foot forward and his binoculars out. He had heard fighting the first day in the suburb of Grec and although many had urged him to deploy and assist those placed there in its defence, he was a disciplined soldier; his orders were to defend this crossing and retreat once it became no longer defendable to reinforce those behind, not those in front. He was looking for signs of the 13th Company who had been assigned to the defence of Grec, they would have been given the same orders and, as Grec had obviously fallen, they could expect reinforcements. There was an explosion to his left about eight hundred meters away, he didn't flinch or dive for cover, he just turned his head and looked with his binoculars.

There was a huge dust cloud and slowly he could see remnants of the 13th marching through the cloud, bolt gun fire came from their right, he now lowered his binoculars and went down on to one knee.

"Suppressing fire, 222 degrees, southwest," he barked down his communicator.

The remnants of the 13th quickly joined them, he spoke with a Lieutenant who was obviously wounded but stood tall.

"Report!" said Captain Strong.

"Sir!", said the Lieutenant.

"We were outgunned and out flanked; they attacked head on at first but then came from our right flank, where a unit of Militia was deployed, worse than useless, untrained rabble."

"Secure that talk, Lieutenant! Just the facts," snapped the Captain.

The Lieutenant continued, "Our Captain was captured about midday, it was then we started to retreat with about a third of us left who are still able to fight the rest are dead, captured or wounded."

"Thank you, Lieutenant have all your troops report to medics for fitness, all wounded will report back to 3rd Company behind us and those severely wounded to the military hospital in HQ, you will supervise this and escort them."

The Lieutenant saluted and left to carry out his orders. Mark returned to his position but now crouched and cautious, the cloud had dispersed and for the moment the bolt guns had ceased, the suppressing fire had done its job and as the open square before them was just a killing field for anyone trying to cross, the Red Skull had stopped to assess their next move.

Mark sat down with his back to the barricade and called over his Lieutenant.

"I want you to send out two reconnaissance squads from each flank and where's the radio operator? I need to know what the lookout tower can see."

Lieutenant Smith disappeared quickly to carry out his orders, replaced by the radio operator,

"Contact the lookout position, I need info!"

Within minutes, the radio operator handed Captain Strong the communicator.

"Whom am I speaking with?" he asked the radio operator.

"Corporal MacDonald." he replied.

"MacDonald, report."

Corporal MacDonald replied, "We are being advanced upon by the 4th Scorpion Division supported by artillery and Pincer V tanks, they also have motorised units but they have been useless because of the barricades. Initial reports said they had over two hundred and twenty tanks but most of these must have been redeployed, Ochoa and Wolf Districts are taking a battering, but I can still see around eighty. When they attacked Grec our 75 mm photon antitank guns were well placed, firing at point-blank range immediately stopping a good half dozen causing road blockage to those behind, you won't need to worry about the Pincers for a while. They are regrouping; you are in no immediate threat. MacDonald out."

Captain Strong bellowed.

"Lieutenant Smith, where are you?"

Smith appeared dutifully.

"Yes, sir?"

"Update on our defensive position." he demanded.

"As ordered, the Militia have been placed in outlying buildings to the left and right flank of the main defence. They have covered the streets and empty building with gallons of turpentine and sugar from a nearby factory."

He paused, "They await your orders."

Captain Strong stood silently, still observing.

"Continue your duties." he eventually said.

Within the hour, the fighting recommenced, Pincer tanks approached the flanks but the Militia ignited the turps as instructed and the tanks were destroyed without a single shot from the Militia. Seeing their flanks now blocked by their own burning tanks the 4th Scorpion tried a frontal assault. Taking their position behind the barricades erected, reinforced by the able bodied from the 13th, the 40th held their ground repelling the infantry assault. The 4th Scorpion suffered heavy casualties and had to retreat. Their force was further weakened forces by redeployment eastward to help thwart the Pannch River counteroffensive. The 4th Scorpion Division alone lost over half their tanks in that one assault. There was no more fighting that day.

Chapter 5 - Beware the falling donkey

That evening the 40th company of Caledon volunteers was further reinforced by artillery and thirty three Victor tanks. They, along with the 16th company of Naval Marines, started an offensive on the left flank of the Red Skull forces advancing towards Opaska in an attempt to further relieve the 40th and regain Grec. This bought Captain Strong's troops some time and that early evening they took advantage of the rest.

"Captain.", called out one of the Sergeant.

"Tell us about your tattoos."

The Captain had tattoos all over his body; each one told its own the story.

"Well!", said Mark.

"I have a bulldog here." pointing to his left arm.

"For those noobs and grunts who don't know, only veterans of the battle of Jobo Creek have these, so if someone with a bulldog tattoo gives you an order, then you'd better listen and pay him respect."

He then pointed to his chest.

"I have a gargoyle on my chest which reminds me of my wife and kids!"

He gave out a huge belly laugh.

"Give them grace, Almighty, and may I join them soon."

He bowed his head for a moment.

He continued, "I also have a dragon for every Red Skull officer I have guided into Glory."

He had three.

"I look to add another, this campaign."

He sat down and was passed a tin mug of black coffee.

"My favourite is this one on my right elbow; we were travelling in Malai on a motorised transport, just routine reconnaissance. When suddenly, BOOM!"

He jumped up and lunched forward causing two or three of the Militia to startle and scalded one with some of his coffee.

"The transport in front blew up, it was a land mine. We were then ricocheted with bolt guns but none of the weapons could penetrate the vehicles armour. We couldn't leave those in the front vehicle, so we trooped out in formation laying down suppressing bolt gun fire. The fire ceased and the rebels scattered, the medic, two grunts and me. I was a Sergeant then."

The Sergeant gave out a cheer.

"And you were no good at it, so they promoted you!"

"And your promotion is due!" replied Mark.

"We got to the vehicle, pulling out the survivors and dead. A grunt and the medic helped the survivors to the other vehicles. Carrack and I started to strip the vehicle of valuables and weapons before we took off the brake and pushed it to the side. Just at that, from nowhere a wild dog jumped out of the bush and in seconds Carrack was dead, I raised my gun to shoot but from my left another knocked me flat. It was on top of me, snarling, drooling. These weren't ordinary dogs, big as a man, jaws that'd snap your bones in a single bite and teeth two inch long. I was lying on my back, thirteen stone, snarling dog on top of me who wanted my head for an appetiser. I called out, *'Almighty, give me strength.'* Then, a donkey walked past, like, where did that come from?

This distracted the dog for a moment, I pulled out my garrotting knife and plunged it into his neck, that just made him angry but he reeled back letting me get to my feet, I jumped on his back, it was like riding a pony, I grabbed his neck with my left arm holding on to the garrotting knife like a handle, and his head with my right and twisted with all my might. I heard it crack like rotten wood under me and he fell dead with a thump, shaking the ground and trapping my left leg. The rest had been shot or scared off by the rest of the squad."

"So why the tattoo of an old man with a beard Captain? Surely a wild dog would have fitted more?" asked a grunt.

Sparky stood to his full height and looked square at the grunt.

"You will also see a tattoo of a donkey falling which reminds me of what the prophet Achan said, the Almighty used a donkey to warn him of a foolish mistake he was about to make.

He said, *'Beware the deadly donkey, falling slowly from the sky, you can choose the way you live my friends but not the way you die.'*"

He sat back down.

"I have the face of the Almighty tattooed on my right elbow, because that day when I called on him He gave me power to overcome a more powerful enemy, to deliver me from a certain death and tomorrow He will do the same, call on Him and He will give you power to your right arm."

He spoke with authority and all those within earshot suddenly felt their courage rise,

"You see, men of Caledon, when law becomes unjust, rebellion become duty. Fear is obligatory when faced with possible death but courage is a choice, tomorrow we choose courage!"

***

Mark was at his command position most of the night; he had a few hours sleep and was now having some tea, strong tea. He was poring over the map, considering his placements. Most of his Militia was on his right flank, supported by the 16th naval marines. On his left were a veteran squad of Caledon volunteers, they had faced Red Skull before, with the main force and regular troops defending any main thrust through the centre. It was barely 3am and Captain Strong received information over his intercom from MacDonald in the tower.

"Updated intelligence, Sir!" scrambled MacDonald's voice over the earpiece.

"Report!" he barked.

"The Red Skull have moved units in the night, snipers have been spotted in the Smith building with reports of the new Infuriators being deployed as well."

The Captain had never engaged an Infuriator, he had never seen one, and they sounded amazing machines.

The report continued.

"On the right flank elements of their infantry are advancing trying to outflank us; they may think we have been weakened here because of the bombardment we have already received."

"Thank you, await orders."

It would have been true that the right flank would have had been weak after that last push but thanks to the retreating 13th and advancing 16th they were more than reinforced.

He spoke out loud but only to himself.

"It'll take something more special than that to catch out Sparky."

He ordered a squad from the 16th with two units of Militia to advance on the right and engage.

On the left, he had decided to lead the veterans, the snipers could not be left unattended, they would decimate them piece by piece throughout the day and, if the Almighty was gracious, he may see an Infuriator. Most would be glad if they never saw one, but not Sparky. The 16th started their infiltration movement; they walked at double time and set up beside a large tenement in Campbell Street. Lieutenant Allan looked back and saw the Militia taking supportive position in the rear, Corporal Jodie, after scouting ahead, reported back. Two mechanised units were advancing, these units had TX17 weapons targeted by drones, take out the drones and the weapons became a lot less effective but with the drones deadly accurate.

Lieutenant Allan instructed Groza and Jon,

"'*Sky*' sharpshooters, take positions on the second floor. On my call, target the drones."

He turned to the rest.

"All you other grunts lay down a volley of bolt gun fire and then charge the support troops of the mechanised unit."

Five minutes later, they were deployed and in position.

The Lieutenant ordered.

"Sky, execute."

Groza and Jon spotted three drones, before the Red Skull had a chance two drones were down.

The Lieutenant ordered.

"Grunts volley."

Shooting their bolt guns into the advancing units, a TX17 blasted into the second floor, Groza dived into cover in time but Jon took the full blast, blood and bone splattered and shattered covering Groza, he quickly regained his position and, as ordered took out the last drone and joined in the bolt gun volley, he would mourn his comrade later. With no drones the mechanised units were reduced in firing capacity, the front section was all mowed down but they returned fire quickly.

The Lieutenant motioned to five marines on either side to outflank and engage in close combat, leaving the rest to continue firing. Marines were all specialist with melee weapons and hand to hand combat, few would survive an attack from veteran marines.

Once in place, Corporal Jodie Pond signalled.

"Grunts in place!"

The Lieutenant replied.

"Grunts, execute!"

***

Meanwhile, on the left flank, Sparky was advancing with his veteran volunteers they took up position about two hundred yards from the building where the snipers were, the report wasn't completely accurate, there was a tactical squad supporting them. Marines liked to get close and dirty, volunteers preferred to shoot from a distance due to their lighter armour. They took position behind a wall and after the spotter had identified the positions of the snipers, Sparky ordered open fire on the building.

With photon bazookas and volley of bolt guns they soon had the sniper company decimated and the tactical squad pinned down. One last blast from the bazooka and half the four storey building collapsed.

Sparky ordered a squad into the building to finish off the remnant and secure the building.

Suddenly, three Infuriators came from the left. Sparky's wish had come true, they were inspiring. Fifteen feet tall walkers with reinforced armour, bolt guns would just be as effective as spit balls, two arms, one had twin heavy bolt gun and the other had a photon cannon. These were operated by one man inside an armoured hood. He stood there with his mouth open in admiration and a childlike expression on his face, like he had just found a toy he'd always wanted under the Christmas tree.

The fact that bolts were whizzing past his head seemed to make no difference to him at that moment.

"I would love a go in one of those!"

He allocated command to the Sarge and took a squad of volunteers equipped with antitank weapons, more than enough for these walkers, but his intention was not to blow them up, he wanted to capture one. The Infuriators split, two concentrated their fire on the main force who could do little but hide behind the barricade with the violence of the attack from them and the other pinned down the squad securing the building.

***

On the right flank, Lieutenant Allan and the marines discharged a volley, then a second and a third before engaging the infantry. You could feel the fear rush over them. He charged an infantryman but he avoided his shot by jumping on the wall ledge using it to project him higher and dropping onto the infantryman, who was knocked him sideways, still winded the infantryman rose and lunged forward with a knife he had pulled from his boot only to be rebuffed by the sword of the Lieutenant. The infantryman stepped back and took a few seconds as he realised this was no ordinary man and his death would be no easy thing to obtain. One last thrust and Lieutenant Allan side stepped allowing him then to roll forward and stand directly behind his enemy, thrusting his sword deep into his back and with a final twist he withdrew the sword and the man fell in a heap on the floor. From the balcony, a shot rang out, it missed him barely and ricocheted off the wall another soldier lunched at him with his fists but he dodged giving him a kidney punch in the side, a second slashed at him with his knife, it stuck in his armour but did not pierce through to the skin, the first punched again and this time caught him full on his face. It bloodied his nose and he felt the warm blood trickling down. He drew the bolt pistol from the fallen soldiers holster and aimed it squarely at the soldier with the knife, discharging the weapon, launching a bolt which clearly exploded into his chest and dropping him dead immediately. He then spun round and sliced the other soldiers head clean off. The Red Skull infantry began to withdraw, so Lieutenant Allan ordered retreat and joined the Militia who were firing randomly into the much weakened Red Skull forces, the Militia held and the Red Skull retreated. Lieutenant Allan stood with his heart pounding and fuelled with adrenaline he stood before his men, raised his blood soaked sword and cried, "Furious in unity, all for the Almighty!"

***

Meanwhile, Sparky and his six men came in from the left until they were behind the machines of destruction.

Sparky spoke, "Zed and Sunny take the Python antitank and keep an eye on those two only fire if they make a move towards us or when we attack the other. Do not fire at that one that one is going to be mine!"

"Yes sir" they replied and they set up the Python.

"Hacker and Pak, you're the decoy, move a hundred yards back and in ten minutes start firing your bolt guns at the single walker, then duck. That'll give me time to get close and figure out how to get into it."

They both looked at each other realising they had the tail end of the job.

"Yes sir!" they said as they deployed.

"Marthus and Prothus, You're with me."

They carefully came in behind the Infuriator who was trying to find and pick off the squad in the building, then as planned Hacker and Pak fired their bolt guns which bounced off the armour barely denting it, the Infuriator turned in their direction letting off its bolt guns in an arch as it turned, Sparky could hear the high pitched whine of the cannon charging ready to take a blast.

"Marthus and Prothus cover me, shoot at anyone you see."

He ran the twenty yards, under its legs and jumped to attach a 'sticky' grenade to its underneath, the Captain spotted what looked like a hatch and a lock into the hatch. He dove to the side and landed in a pile of rubble about ten yards away as the grenade exploded, just as he expected, it was enough to knock the walker sideways and the hatch door open. The operator crawled out to be met with a hail of bolt gun fire from Marthus and Prothus. Sparky returned to the walker and with the three together, they got it on its feet. He couldn't resist, he climbed in and apart from there being no hatch, it was operational. He looked and saw his squad, still pinned down behind the barricade. Over his telecom he gave the order.

"Zed, Sunny. Fire!"

The left Infuriator exploded as the antitank weapon hit it from behind as did the right one after Sparky hit it with the newly charged cannon of his new toy. The squad behind the barricade stood up and cheered loudly at the realisation of what the Captain had done, this was muted by the rumble of Pincer V tanks as everyone dived for cover again. Sparky looked across and coming through the side street of the half blown up building were three Pincer tanks in single file hoping to position themselves and blast the barricades in front.

Captain Strong called in his intercom.

"Full retreat, back to fall back positions!"

Enemy support troops came beside them the tanks and began strafing the barricades.

Sparky, hearing the whir of photonics recharge, got inspiration, the four storey building beside him was ready to fall after the bombings and explosions of the last few days it was a miracle it still stood.

"A miracle!" he said out loud.

"Almighty, I call on you again to bring strength to my right arm."

It was less than ten yards away, he spoke quietly to himself.

"Beware the deadly donkey, falling slowly from the sky, you can choose the way you live my friends but not the way you die. Today my sweet Elizabeth, I will finally be with you and the kids in Glory."

He fired his cannon straight at the wall, Sparky and the Infuriator was completely crushed as the structure of the wall crumpled, weakening the base and the full four storey wall collapsed crushing the Red Skull troops and burying the tanks, allowing the volunteers to escape.

***

General Pawlii's whole plan was pinioned on his attempt to buy time for organisation of defence of Caledon, any military historian would concur he was successful. It was clear to Morg, Red Skull Commander that Caledon would not go quietly and would be defended at all costs. General Pawlii managed to gather enough forces and war material to successfully defend the city for several weeks.

As a result of this, Morg withdrew his Scorpion Divisions in fear the losses he was enduring would thin out his ranks too much. He wanted to conquer the city not trap his troops in pockets of fighting, they withdrew back to Canto. Caledon positions were now being held by the weakened Infantry Division. However, the lack of food and medical supplies were taking their toll on both sides. The water works had been destroyed and all boroughs of Caledon experienced a lack of water, including Red Skull forces.

Pawlii was not thwarted by the overwhelming force of Red Skull but by the political situation which had become very difficult. The President of Gaelia had instructed General Pawlii to consider negotiation with Morg, not capitulation, negotiation. This lack of support from the Burgh made further defence of the city seem pointless. When Colonel Tomas handed him the communique from the President, he picked up his empty mug and smashed it against the wall.

"Bloody politicians!"

Everyone stood to attention; in all the heat of battle he had never lost his cool once, until now.

"Tomas contact Bear and get her back here."

He now spoke in a disparaging way.

"His high and mighty President has ordered we take a negotiations team to meet with Morg and agree terms."

The two met near Canto, a cease fire agreement was signed and all fighting halted. The real terms were no longer in their hands but in the hands of the politicians meeting in the Burgh.

Despite the ceasefire, several units declined to put down their weapons and Colonel Bear herself had to visit personally. The Red Skull withdrew to outlying areas of the countryside, outside the walls of proud Caledon city.

***

That evening, Pawllii, Bear and Tomas sat in the small office beside what had been the war room with a well deserved tipple.

Pawlli raised his glass.

"I salute you; let us pray the sacrifices of those we commanded will not be in vain."

Bear and Tomas stood in respect.

"To those we lost."

Both sat down.

"It was a close thing, sir, but we prevailed." Bear commented.

"No ranks tonight, first names Kim. Call me Stef. Your first name is John, isn't it Tomas?"

"Yes, sir. I mean Stef." answered Tomas.

Bear nodded in agreement.

"When the 3rd Scorpion Division broke through lines along the Pannch River nearly cutting us of from you, I thought it might be the end."

Tomas replied," No way were you letting them off with that, you hit them hard and pushed them to the south keeping the east road clear. The fighting was heavy and our first counter offensive failed. We were reduced to infantry and armoured units. The fighting was so fierce and was so intense that at one point we only held a narrow strip of land along the Pannch River, leading towards the Kaman's Forest. My men were almost cut of from my command post in the Morin Fortress."

Pawllii had sunk into his armchair, enjoying the dissection of tactics.

"You did well Kim losing there would have meant losing Morin and that would have been defeat."

"Your praise is welcomed, Stef. It really did though, it provided important relief to the defenders south and west of the city." stated Bear in confirmation.

Tomas stood and raised his glass.

"To the service of Caledon Volunteers, who in conflict have been distinguished, earning proud reputations and causing the formidable Red Skull troops to be afraid. Whether they were supply men, ammunition handlers, engineers, artilleryman, infantryman, tank men or marines we always give them a fight. In our proud history, Caledon volunteers have always been sent to add firepower at the toughest point in fights. Yet again we took the sharp end and stuck it back up their own backsides."

With that he sat down.

Bear laughed.

"You're a good soldier John but a lousy speech maker."

She sipped her glass.

"Truth is that with the winter drawing in and the ground wet, it made it difficult for them to move as easily. The first seventeen hours were the worst; they destroyed one infantry division, badly crippled two others, cut one armoured combat command to pieces, and caused over four thousand casualties. The personnel situation in the Pannch was grim."

Both Pawlii and Tomas listened with interest.

"The counter attack began with the 16th and 28th Infantry bolstered with militia who had bore the brunt of the initial attack."

Tomas concurred, "They may have been untrained and undisciplined but they did their fair share."

Bear continued, "During the daylight hours, the direction and size of the attack was only vaguely perceived as the 3rd Scorpion was deployed over such an extended front that it was impossible to provide a defence in depth. The plan, as you both know, was to deny the enemy use of the road network. The 33rd Artillery Group, with support of the 15th Infantry and newly arrived 101st Marines dispatched from Morin fortress, they pushed so far forward in support of the 16th, that the 33rd Artillery had only five guns left. You had moved the 28th Marines,

John, in defence of Ochoa and Wolf. So to plug the gap they moved forward, discovering twelve more guns that had been abandoned. When the enemy broke into the open, they came under heavy fire from the 33rd with its newly bolstered armoury. The Artillery men who had no role because of the lack of artillery, armed themselves with small arms fighting as infantrymen with the Militia. This rallied these men and successfully captured a half dozen Dervish howitzers. With these they fired over four hundred rounds in a few hours. This bombardment and the 15th forming a roadblock in Siber street delayed a company of Pincers."

Bear jumped to her feet.

"Wait a minute. Major Cotter!" she bellowed.

Major Cotter's head popped out of an adjacent room.

"Yes, sir!"

"You were in command at Siber Street, weren't you?"

Looking perplexed, he replied, "Yes, sir."

"Come over here and report."

The Major marched over to be surprised by a glass thrust in his hand.

"Sit down and tell us all about it." demanded Bear.

The Major took a minute and then began.

"During the fight for Siber Street, the 5th Pincer Division occupied the area from the police station down. I realised the building could not be taken by the unsupported infantrymen and militia, so manoeuvred a battery of Dervish howitzers we had claimed into position to fire on the building."

Pawlii interrupted, "I remember that, we got reports that Siber Street had been taken and then within the hour we had it back. Sorry Major, continue your story."

"More Pincers moved in on us, we set up my division command post in the police station. I again repositioned the Dervish howitzers sited as single pieces around the outpost position. I equipped the 101st with some '*sticky*' grenades and deployed them in bomb craters as tank destroyers. When they passed they stuck them to the rear, weaker armour and boom. Our narrow streets did not suit these beasts."

Bear raised her hand to halt Cotter.

"See that speech you made earlier Tomas, well I heard from a Captain under his command," she motioned her head toward Cotter, "that he gave a truly inspiring speech, can you remember it."

Cotter hesitated.

"I think so but I'm sure the General doesn't want to hear it."

"Damn right I do, speak man.", confirmed the General.

"Stand up and speak up. Get everyone in here. Listen up men, this will inspire you."

The Major felt under pressure but he tried to remember.

"I think it went like this."

He took a breath.

"Your combat has been outstanding. You have without exception proven yourselves to be good soldiers. In this next assault, we will come out fighting, not just for the Almighty or for this fair country of Gaelia, for you and your families. Let this be your motivation pure and simple, Come Out Fighting! This may be one of our roughest fights but we will punch a hole through their lines, Come Out Fighting!"

The Major finished, all three senior officers stood and applauded, Bear pointed to Cotter and addressed Tomas.

"Now that's a speech, John, that's a speech."

Pawlii moved over to Cotter and shook his hand vigorously.

"I'll do the paper work, son, but you are are no longer a Major. You are now a Colonel, a hero of Gaelia."

Turning to all those listening he said, "Do you want to know why, because under this mans command of the 33rd he provided the means for the defence of Morin fortress. His military spunk and ingenuity gave us all the time we needed, time for me to send reinforcements."

He took the newly appointed colonel by the elbow guiding him to his own chair and sat him down, topping up his glass.

"Thanks to this man and all of you in this room we continue to be a city that has never been conquered by an enemy force. The Caledon defenders at Modin, towards the end were reduced to fewer than twelve thousand soldiers and Almighty knows how many militias. We got reports that the enemy forces were preparing for an all-out assault. The report numbered them at over seventeen thousand. It looked bad."

He perched himself on the arm of his chair, almost mournfully he continued.

"We had, for a long time no communication between us and Modin, the fortress was shelled day and night with artillery bombardment. The forces on the eastern bank of the Pannch were attacked on a daily basis."

He stood back up, with gusto.

"All were successfully counter-attacked. I could almost empathise with Morg. If it had been me, I would have had enough. He sent a final all out assault on all fronts which was yet again repelled but with heavy casualties."

His head lowered in exhaustion, the Cotter stood.

"Sir, I am honoured but please retake your seat."

Pawlii sat down again.

Bear continued, "It is true we were in dire straits, we had been at the spear point of the attack and the entire Corps was reeling. Confusion reigned, by dusk, the Red Skull advance at our expense was formidable but we never lost hope. Everyone took arms, the rear echelon soldier, headquarters officers, supply and technical service troops, and those men who show up during every battle, the lost, the separated, the stragglers, every man was an infantryman, a Caledon man of steel. We were poorly armed and hastily organised but we made the difference between effective reserves and none, between a line holding and being broken through. Colonel Langly reinforced us."

She raised her glass towards a tall blond officer at the back, he returned the gesture.

"After heavy fights for several days the Red Skull 23rd and 31st Infantry Regiment was almost annihilated by our defence and the tactics of Major," she paused to correct herself, "sorry, Colonel Cotter. Remnants of the 16th and the 28th broke through the Red Skull encirclement ending the battle of Morin Fortress and essentially the siege of the city."

Bear placed her glass down and stood to attention before Pawlii, saluting.

"It was an honour serving you, sir, and we agree that it is you who is the true hero of Caledon."

Everyone in the room stood to attention and saluted.

Tomas rallied a cheer.

"To General Pawlii, Hurra, Hurra, Hurra!"

They all replied in unison.

"Hurra, Hurra, Hurra!"

Chapter 6 - The Quiet Years

The Immortal Cutler, Red Skull Ambassador, met with Fedrix, President of Gaelia; there had not been a Prince in Gaelia since its first union with the Kingdom. It was agreed that all Gaelian troops would cease resisting the Red Skull; domestic political power would remain with the rightfully elected Gaelian Houses of Assembly and Delegates. The Gaelian Army would also remain under their command but would be required to fight in defence of the Kingdom, in return. Red Skull would have garrisons in Gaelia's three major cities Caledon, Askdean and the Burgh. Red Skull would also have ten unelected, co-opted representatives in both houses.

The 31st amendment was added to the constitution, one which had previously been unwritten.

"There shall be liberty of the Press. No person must be punished for any writing, whatever its contents may be, which he has caused to be printed or published, unless he wilfully and manifestly has either himself shown or incited others to disobedience of the laws, contempt of religion or morality or the constitutional powers, or resistance to their orders, or has advanced false and defamatory accusations against any other person. Everyone shall be free to speak his mind frankly on the administration of the State or on any subject whatsoever."

Gaelia was linked with the Kingdom, as it had been for over four hundred years before the Red Skull removal of its elected government. For now, Gaelia remained a self-governing and independent realm, domestically at least if not internationally. This was not a popular decision and caused discontent, many felt that the country's and Almighty's interests were being disregarded to the Red Skull's advantage. Other concessions were made such as their remaining a university in the Burgh and having its own national bank. In the next few years, there were clear signs of a growing separatist movement and increasing disenchantment with the union.

***

Grandfather had taken the children as instructed to the registration office. They were bunked up in the local community hall before being transported to the Vale of Lamont. These were uncertain and anxious days in their sojourn in the Fortress of the Vale of Lamont, but in three days they had been allocated a prefabricated house on the outskirts of Lamont, they arrived safely and were able to settle down to a normal life. Those first few months, they lived next door to Rose, amazingly.

James was well able to support his family as he secured work shortly after their arrival. He was employed as a gardener in the local estate for several months and then got promotion to the position of foreman of a large group of workmen. This was a new experience for him as he had always worked in heavy industry but he took to it like a duck takes to water, both boys worked in the gardens like James in later years, starting with weekend work and then Billy, as an apprentice, he made it a career and a business.

All through these years, James, with the help of Rose, maintained one long and constant vigil lest anything befall the children, he would never forget Edina's last words, "Just stay alive!" He would not do anything that might jeopardise their welfare; no parent was ever more devoted to their children. They received a good education, Gus, went to the Burgh University and when Gus returned home to Lamont, it was his custom for Grandfather and he to take walks on Saturday mornings after breakfast. One of their favourite walks meant climbing the high hill near their home, they had a panoramic view. To the northwest, on clear days, they could see the sea; they would talk about many things but on those days, they would talk about the days in Caledon. To the north was Mount Herron with its snowy peak monopolising the skyline, almost a thousand feet of the upper slopes glistening white with perpetual snow. Far to the east they could see the valley which would eventually lead to the Burgh built on the rocky hills of Ravenhead. A little south and the east, through the Ravenhead valley, was the town of Dopolis, which was famous for its theatres and arts. When they did not climb the heights to view the distant landscape, they strolled through the countryside and studied nature. This was one of those summer Saturday mornings, they sat on a rock looking northwest towards the sea.

"How is Sissy, Grandfather?"

"She seems distracted, more than usual that is."

Grandfather gave a wry smile.

"She has a new boyfriend."

101

"Oh! That'll explain it. She always was the popular one, always loads of friends." stated Gus.

"We were fortunate, when we moved to Lamont. We were given a house next to families with children close to her age. The Almighty was generous, we were next to Rose. She was a good help."

Gus smiled, "Rose is the only person I've ever saw challenge you, telling you off. I remember she was always telling you not to be so protective, especially with Sissy."

Grandfather nodded.

"I was in constant fear something might happen to her if she were allowed to play in the garden with the other children." he chuckled.

"Rose convinced me I was being too protective, she was becoming self-conscious and self-centred."

Gus splurged, "Yeah, she's none of those."

Grandfather gave him a disdainful look.

He continued, "It was understandable how you felt, we have lost so much. I appreciate the burden you have carried in your heart for us."

Gus leant back on the grass he sat on.

"I have some memory of the 'tin hut' but my happiest memories are in the cottage, it was comfortable and helped heal the scars of Caledon."

"It came with the job, always seemed cramp to me but you boys became strong in mind, body and soul whilst we live there. Lamont has been good to us, a good school, the temple had a good youth programme and you both got weekend work in the gardens of the estate."

Gus mused, "It was hard work but I did enjoy having money in my pocket."

"It made you strong, in muscle and personality." confirmed Grandfather.

"Do you ever miss Caledon, Grandfather?"

Grandfather smiled again, widely.

"I did contemplate moving back to Caledon, At that point, I had never fully given up the idea that you ought to grow up in Caledon, but with the reasoning of a female, Rose convinced me that Lamont was a better place to rear and educate children."

Gus agreed, "Rose is a very persuasive women but she was right."

"When I thought about it logically," confirmed Grandfather," it made sense. Billy was now 16 and was just about to start his apprenticeship in the estate, you were 14, doing well at school and Sissy 5 just starting school. You were all in excellent health, it was just me romanticising."

Grandfather sighed, "It was around that time my health had deteriorated, I could only work part time but with Billy having started work, more than made up for the loss of income."

Gus nodded, "I always felt sorry that Billy had to stop school to start work."

Grandfather shook his head.

"You were always the smart one; Billy was desperate to start work."

"Well it has worked out. Billy is an excellent landscaper and has built his garden centre at the village spring from nothing and got us the new house."

"You've all stepped up, Sissy is a good help with home duties." confirmed Grandfather.

"She never talks about Caledon, do you think she has any memories?" enquired Gus.

Grandfather shook his head.

"If she does they are buried deep, she does talk of some memories of her mother before the tragedy and her death. I think she talks with Rose more about that."

Gus could see contemplation on his Grandfathers face.

Grandfather continued, "Sissy was an inquisitive child and we often have long talks of an evening.

I thought I'd miss those when you went to the Burgh but Sissy has replaced you."

Gus smiled in confirmation.

"You are good to talk to; you always have an answer, no matter how searching our questions are. You never fail to give us the right answer and make sure we fully understand it."

"You make it sound easy." Grandfather said with some perplexity.

"You had some crackers but Sissy even more so. The ones I can't get, Rose picks up the slack."

Gus changed the subject.

"It's good that Billy manages to keep our roof garden in tact."

"Nope," replied Grandfather.

"That'll be Sissy, with a little help from me."

"I spent a lot of time on the roof garden," he mused, "working on my geometry, geography, physics and philosophy. You've done us proud, Grandfather."

"How is your ear? Does it still bother you?" Grandfather enquired.

Gus held his right ear, "I can feel the blood pulse through the vein when I'm a little stressed. That's the payment I get for too many winter nights on the roof garden. It was that year the great snowstorm happened, heaviest snowfall in twenty years, snow fell ten feet deep. Sissy wondered where I was and found me sleeping in the snow. She woke me and in her hurry to get out of the snow her hand slipped on the stair bannister and she fell down the stone stairs, she broke her left ankle that day."

"I forgot about Sissy breaking her ankle. I was worried for a while about you, thought you were going to lose all your hearing because of that infection." replied Grandfather.

"Hearing is fine, just the thumping."

Gus changed the subject again.

"Billy's business seems to be booming."

Grandfather agreed.

"It has trebled in the last year, the house is almost paid off and he's saving to send Sissy to University as well. He's a grafter."

Gus's chest stuck out.

"I'm proud to be his brother, mum would be proud as well."

He paused.

"Is that a telescope on the roof, that's new?"

Grandfather nodded.

"Billy bought it to look at the stars, think he's going to pick your brains about it."

"It'll be a pleasure. I've got some books in my dorm, I'll bring them next time." he confirmed.

Grandfather looked with pride at Gus.

"You do know how proud we all are of you getting into University and being appointed a Master of the Burgh Temple."

"It was Christiana, the elder, who recommended me; I often read the words of the Almighty before he speaks. I like it there, it's a bit more liberal in its interpretation of the words of the Almighty, but you can mingle more freely with people from all over the Kingdom. The debate is invigorating and free thinking, vibrant, I have learned a lot and been inspired by Christiana."

They both sat silent for a few moments.

It is true he secured much of his intellectual and theological education from the tutors of the university but his real education, that equipment of mind and heart for the actual test of grappling with the difficult problems of life, he obtained by mingling with his fellow students. It was this close association with his friends young and old that made him the officer he became later. It was here he got to know the human race; Gus was highly educated in that he thoroughly understood men and women and devotedly loved them.

Grandfather broke the silence.

"I got a letter from your senior tutor."

Gus sat up startled.

Grandfather laughed.

"Don't worry; he just wanted me to know you were an excellent student. He remarked that he had at times learned something himself from your searching questions."

They both sat silent for a while.

***

Gus looked out towards the sea. He again broke the silence.

"I remember that day we left Caledon, Grandfather." said Gus.

"Police squads urging us to evacuate the city if we were able."

"I remember it like it was yesterday."

Grandfather's hands moved slowly to and fro to help him tell the story.

"They put us onto trucks after that awful night sleeping on the floor of the community hall."

"I slept fine but I think I would have slept on glass I was so tired." replied Gus.

Grandfather continued, "They loaded us on trucks along with bags of rice, mats, blankets and tools. I don't remember how long we travelled but they were in no hurry and constantly stopping.

The streets were busy, seemed like everyone was leaving."

Grandfather paused, he suffered from shortness of breath, and he took out his inhaler and puffed.

"When we reached the outskirts of the city, the world changed for us. We were city people, the countryside was alien to us, we saw an abundance of slopes, needled trees, browns and greens, higher rising land, and stout oaks, but nothing to our eyes of obvious value just outstanding beauty."

Gus smiled widely.

"We soon adapted Grandfather; we soon became country bumpkins, eh"

"I remember your face Gus." remarked Grandfather.

"When we moved into the small prefab we had, you couldn't believe they were asking us to live in a tin hut."

Gus laughed loudly, "But you did us proud getting that promotion and the tied house that came with it. And Billy, I'm so proud and thankful to him for all his hard work. I mean to repay him Grandfather!"

His voice had conviction in it.

"I know Gus, I know."

Grandfather continued reminiscing,

"The first night we could not even make a fire, the wood was damp and we didn't know how to, we huddled together in the blankets we had been given. There were still too many things to think about, the first days were new and different in a way that was not much fun for you and the other children. You had nightmares for months haunted by the fires, falling houses, and your mother's death."

"I still sometimes get them, Grandfather." announced Gus.

"The next day we started meeting others, that's when we found Rose was right next to us, remember Grandfather."

Grandfather replied, "By the grace of the Almighty, I do not know how we would have survived without Rose, a genuine gift from the Almighty."

Gus sat back as the heat of summer's day began to rise, it was a warm summer.

"She gave us extra blankets and showed us how to light a fire. We were able to boil some rice and opened up tins of meat."

Gus's face distorted.

"I've never been able to eat tinned meat since those days; we ate so much of it early on. I think all we ate for a week was rice and tinned meat."

Grandfather grimaced but then smiled.

"It was a mixed blessing, the nights would have been unbearable without those extra covers, and don't forget the berries Billy found, days to be thankful for, days we will never see again, thank the Almighty."

"They were days of fatigue and hunger, every day I went to try and find some food. There was a small stream nearby, so there was plenty water if we ran out of our ration of bottled water. And Billy found a fishing pole, he went every morning to catch fish, remember the first one he caught, he was so excited till he brought it home and then realised he had to gut it."

Grandfather guffawed.

"His expression was priceless, it went from victorious to confused to dejected, I had never did it either but I worked it out. I soon got to the guts of the problem."

Grandfather laughed loudly at his own joke, Gus chuckled having heard it so many times before. Grandfather's eyes lit up as he remembered another story.

"Do you remember you came home with daffodil bulbs? You had found them in the ground and thought they were onions, we had them boiled up and everything, when Rose came by to see how we were."

"Yeah!" said Gus.

"She started screaming at us, *'What are you doing, you can't eat them, there poisonous.'* "

With a sigh Grandfather spoke.

"We survived the might of the Red Skull but nearly killed ourselves with daffodils."

Gus contemplated the irony in Grandfathers statement for a moment and then lightened the mood. "Remember the toilets, first month we had to use the communal toilets, it was just a big hole in the ground, the stench was overpowering. On a warm day and the wrong wind you could smell them all over the town, the local residents of Lamont would complain bitterly."

"Sissy wouldn't use them, she would urinate out the back, as did you and Billy, don't think I didn't notice. As for the other, she pooed in an old pot and I had to carry it down."

"You got me to do it once." interrupted Gus.

"I came back infuriated and embarrassed saying 'Never *again, I would never do that again.* "

"What was the problem, Gus, apart from the obvious one?" enquired Grandfather.

"I slipped and tipped some out, it went over the trousers of Jenny Smith who was passing, she looked at me as if I had three heads."

Another laugh from Grandfather.

"I always wondered why the Smith family didn't speak to us much after that, I didn't know that till now, Gus."

"Well it was embarrassing.", he replied.

"You children were resilient, I am so proud of you, your mother would be so proud of you."

"We had better start back Gus, they'll be expecting lunch as usual."

***

They headed down the hills past the farmers fields and into the suburb they now lived. In the kitchen were Sissy and her *'friend'* Nathan. When Grandfather entered they both looked suspicious. As if they'd been doing something they shouldn't have been doing, they hadn't but their faces made them look suspicious. Cecilia Jamesina Black had little memories of Caledon, she only knew three strong men in her life, her Grandfather, Billy and Gus, they were among the fortunate and found. She had learnt early the importance of prayer and chatted daily to the Almighty in a natural way, not like the elder at the temple, who used big words she could not understand. She was sure the Almighty would understand them but was not convinced He enjoyed these conversations, she was sure He enjoyed the conversations she had with him. She remembered the early days in Lamont only as days when she couldn't sleep for the cold and weeks of day after day wondering what she was getting to eat, pangs of hunger but all outweighed by the love and attention she got from her three strong men. Now that Gus was away, Sissy had to taken over more chores, such as setting the table before meals, she had done so. Others included milking the family cow and caring for the other animals. She had learnt to make cheese and Rose had taught her to weave, she soon became an expert weaver. Nathan sat opposite; his father was the local greengrocer and had deft fingers on the guitar. It was an innocent friendship to begin with but as adolescence came it turned more romantic, she had found a fourth strong man. When asked by her friend to describe him she said, "He's tall, dark haired, and a gorgeous smile. He has a way of making me feel safer than I ever have before, he's seen me at my absolute worst and still wants to be my friend. His laugh is like velvet and the wicked sense of humour inside of him is pure excellent. He doesn't judge me, just tries to help. I can't express how blessed I am to have him right now. Oh, and he has gorgeous blue eyes, he's funny, smart, the nicest guy you'll ever meet, down to earth, has a smile that's to die for, have I said that already? He can be shy, awkward, the sweetest person I've ever met, a little stupid sometimes and doesn't realise how perfect he is. He's got the most beautiful smile and I just get lost in his eyes. I melt whenever he giggles in this really cute way. It makes my day whenever I can make him laugh because he makes me laugh all the time.

He can sing as well and plays guitar, and is friendly to everyone. He's pretty great. The kind of guy I could just sit and spend time with for hours without running out of things to talk about. He's kind of immature, but so am I, so that's that. Overall, he's just a super nice guy, and that's what really counts and did I tell you about his smile."

Grandfather spoke, "What have you two been up too?"

"Nothing.", replied Sissy.

"We went for a walk."

Gus sneered, "You went for a walk, in the countryside what about all the insects you hate so much."

Sissy cocked her head, "I'm not eight anymore! OK, I still don't like all the fleas, ticks, jiggers, centipedes, and the midges in summer, I mean, what was the Almighty thinking off creating midges but I don't mind some of the bigger, furry ones like rabbits and deer."

Nathan decided to join in on the sneering.

"What about snakes, rats, and spiders. Rats and spiders are bigger and furry."

Sissy shivered and the gently slapped his shoulder.

"Don't talk about spiders, why are there so many, it's all very unnerving at times."

Both Gus and Nathan chuckled, as Grandfather started lunch.

Sissy drew daggers.

"I don't know what you see as funny. Why does there have to be so many spiders? By the hundreds they are, it's my living horror. Remember, Nathan, on our walk today into the woods and as I passed under a low limb and a big one landed on my neck, down it came crawling all over me."

Nathan teased her.

"You were screaming for ages, I swiped it off you but you kept screaming, '*Get it off, get it off.*'"

He laughed again.

Gus could see Nathan was good fun, good to have chatter with, a laugh or just be frivolous with, both liked to play pranks.

Gus retorted, "I hope you're keeping up the Black boys' tradition of 'winding up Sissy'?"

Sissy's daggers drew longer.

"Don't you encourage him?"

Nathan threw up his hands innocently.

"What do you mean? I'm sweetness and light."

Sissy voice was getting higher and faster.

"What about the time you hid in the bin and jumped out on me or when you put talcum powder in a balloon and burst it over my head, I jumped a mile as well as being covered in powder."

Gus splurged in laughter at the thought of Sissy covered in talcum powder.

Sissy did not appreciate it.

"Not to mention the countless fake bugs in bed or bag."

Nathan got defensive.

"It's not as if you haven't got your own back."

Sissy lowered her chin, placing her hand over her mouth.

"I don't know what you mean." she said coyly.

Nathan threw his hands up in protest.

"Like the time I had fallen asleep on the couch, you put shaving foam in my hand, tickled my nose with a feather and watched me smear it all over my face."

Sissy giggled.

Gus patted Nathan on the back and then kissed Sissy on the head.

"She's learnt from the best. So where did you walk."

Sissy responded, "Just the pond, I love paddling in the shallows, Nathan found a small boat in the reeds, it was still watertight, kind of, so we often spend Saturday's investigating."

Nathan interrupted.

"When we were younger we would pretend to be pirates in search of treasure or explorers finding new lands or just float and see where we would end up."

He got excited.

"One day we found a large partially submerged log that was floating in the pond; I pulled out the white birch branch. It was about two inches in diameter and eight feet long, the branch showed beaver damage at its base."

Sissy joined in, "I thought it might be beavers, we had never saw one, we spent the rest of the day looking for beavers."

Gus shook his head.

"You don't get beavers in Gaelia."

Sissy cocked her head again.

"We know that now!"

Sissy continued, "Mostly, we just watched the small waterfall, unless the water levels fall. Then you can see reeds and dead weeds floating on the surface, the water would become murky around the mud flats where the lily pads grow. One day I found a lily pad the size of my arm. I couldn't wait to tell Billy!"

The room fell silent for a moment, Sissy reflected. In all the years of her life, these years were the most enjoyable, the best days of her life.

They all sat and ate lunch, not knowing it would be the last Grandfather would prepare.

***

That night, they all went to bed. Grandfather was tired, he fell asleep quickly. Then, he woke but not fully, that half way where if you just fall over again you'll be fine but yet you're still aware of your surroundings. He noticed a light, it came from the bottom of his bed, was he dreaming, he could not tell. It became brighter and out of the brightness there sat a man. He was tall with very bright blue eyes that looked like the pure ocean and black flowing hair. His presence lit up the entire room, so big and so beautiful to describe him would not be possible.

"I am dreaming ", said Grandfather.

"No," said Andreas, "but it is time, you are tired and you have finished your service. The Almighty requires no more of you, Edina and your other children wait for you in Glory."

"But I cannot leave, I am still needed." he argued.

"What about Jimmi, you said nothing of Jimmi."

"No longer are the concern of the living yours, it is time to live as the Almighty intended, no more sorrow or pain, just sweet fellowship." replied Andreas.

"But how do I get there, friend?" asked James.

"Simply rest and take my hand, when you take your last breathes here on earth then you will take your first breath in Glory." answered Andreas.

James' mortal body lay back down and breathed his last as his eternal one took Andreas' hand, the light dimmed and nothing but darkness and death was left in that room. The next morning, Billy came into the room as Grandfather had not wakened and he realised he would not, he was in Glory. Gus came into the room behind Billy followed by Sissy. Gus grabbed Sissy and took her straight out but not before she realised what had happened.

"Grandfather!" she screamed.

"Take her out Gus, I'll deal with Grandfather."

Billy made the phone call to the doctor and the funeral home and the elder.

It left them feeling empty but Sissy was the worst affected, she felt like she was suffocating, like when you dry swallow a pill. All her glands around her neck ached with the pain of trying to stop crying, she wondered if she would always feel a sinking feeling that she could never run away from. They all gathered in the kitchen, around the table they had ate lunch the previous day but with no Grandfather. Rose was making tea and the elder also joined them.

"Why was he taken?" said Sissy.

"I will never understand? My heart feels broken."

No one responded, no answer could be given. Sorrow that you cannot hold back had swept over that house. Numbness ran throughout their bodies with soulful cries that cannot be expressed.

Finally the elder spoke, "Let us pray to the Almighty."

They bowed their heads, "We enjoy warmth because we have been cold, we appreciate light because we have been in darkness, the same token, and we can experience joy because we have known sadness. Almighty and Father to us all let this family feel warmth in equal measure to the coldness they feel now, let light fill their lives as the darkness has encompassed them and let joy be as deep as the sorrow they have had to bear."

The funeral was three days later, Gus looked at his Grandfather's face, it was worn and lifeless as he stood beside the coffin to say his goodbye. A tear rolled down his cheek as he touched his hand, leant over and kissed his cheek.

He spoke, "Tell them your stories Grandfather as you take your rest, and tell mother how we stayed alive."

James was cremated as was the tradition, and the next morning all three walked up the hill Gus and Grandfather had so often walked, they faced the ocean, looking towards Caledon. Gus opened the urn of ashes and in silence watched as the wind carried Grandfather away towards his beloved Caledon.

Chapter 7 - The Prophet and the Martyr

Gus returned to the Burgh after a while to complete his studies. As he travelled, sitting alone on the train, his thoughts about his Grandfather still engulfed him. His Grandfather was an old man and his death a peaceful one but with someone who had lost so much any loss of a loved one would sting. His attention was distracted. She sat in the opposite aisle but across from him in the train, as the whir of the engine and the clack of the wheels of the train made its continuous noise suddenly all he saw and heard was her. Her chatter and flirty voice, he caught a waft of her perfume and a glimpse of her cleavage. As he heard a rumble underneath the carriage which broke his concentration, he suddenly realised he was staring. The houses and vegetation flew past but he found it hard to pay attention to anything else but this girl. She was slender, small, her face had slightly less than sharp features, round playful eyes which Gus kept catching as she kept looking over at him but then quickly looking away as she caught Gus's eyes. She had a stray strand of hair which kept falling down over her face, she would, endearingly, try to flick it into place every few minutes. Finally she gave up pretending to not notice Gus and when their eyes caught again she smiled at him. It no longer felt awkward as they acknowledged one another, she was dressed in a black suit with a red low cut top, chewing gum but there was something electric about her he could not describe. She spent the rest of her time chatting with a young man across from her, he had sallow skin and swarthy beard, as the train pulled into the station they went their separate ways, this was the first time he saw Melody, unknowingly.

***

Ten years passed under the rule of President Fedrix, who had been voted in under a promise of *'Democratic Change'* but how does such an obviously mistrusted President stay in power. The rumours were always about rigged national election in his favour. Tactics like slowing down the voting process in the opposition strongholds, allowing the Red Skull to supervise the electoral count, paying collaborators to subversively pressure people into voting for him, having armed guards outside the polling booths, losing or spoiling certain voting boxes all help a corrupt man keep power, little did he realise how fleeting and fickle power can be. How it all comes to one pinpoint that changes everything. The factor of time meant things can be forgotten and atrocities of war overlooked by new generations. Apart from throwing himself into his studies, he increased his activities in the Burgh Temple. His favourite was the summer conference which attracted youth from all over Gaelia. At the conference the atmosphere was always thick with excitement, the music was youthful, deep bass drums and intermittent chorus from a diva like singer. They danced on chairs, they talked and chatted and laughed, these were days of laughter and excitement. The excitement of youth with one mind and one purpose in the one room all waiting excitedly to hear from the elder as he proclaimed the goodness of the Almighty and the virtue of following him with all their heart. It was being part of the team for this conference that he came to the attention of Christiana, becoming one of his inner circles. Gus stood on the steps as Christians gave that speech just before the massacre in the Burgh square, it was he who bundled Christiana to the floor, shielded him down the steps and escorted him down King's Place.

***

Lillibet was an eighteen year old girl from the Burgh; she was only eight when the battle of Caledon was fought, so knew little of its awfulness except for stories told by old men. Her best friend was Annie, she was only a few months younger having become friends at the temple youth group. Lillibet was skinny, wiry some would say, a shock of long straight red hair, and piercing eyes. Her smile was an interesting smile, naughty, playful and sweet, like she had a secret and wants you to pry it out, like she knew something you didn't, a smile that makes you smile. She had an uncanny ability of knowing who was genuine and who was not to be trusted, she was also not afraid to say what she really thought but never in a mean way, although her comments could be cutting, they were never meant to hurt. Annie was different, a gentle soul but a wise soul, an old head on young shoulders. She was pretty faced with curly blond hair and unlike Lillibet, very shapely, there was more than one boy's head turning when she walked down the street. She was passionate, positive and confident, she knew who she was, got up when she fell and never gave up. She defined fashion, beauty and attitude in her peer group. Truth be told they both could hold court at the social events they attended and usually had a group around them; they were indeed leaders and not followers setting the tone with their friends on a regular occasion but were completely oblivious to their power over others. They did not revel in it or use it to their advantage; it was just the way it was. Their friendship was an intense relationship like teen girls have but maybe more so. You know how some girls get so attached to each other they can barely stand to be apart; well that was Lillibet and Annie. When they were at school they would dare each other to wear outrageous clothes or hair styles, they would never be seen together with exactly the same outfits and hair styles but they were literally joined at the hip. When you were talking to one of them you could tell they were thinking about what the other was doing. One day, Annie was sitting with a big group in the school lunchroom when she accidentally knocked her drink onto her lap. Some laughed, the more cruel said she had wet herself, the laughter began to mount, Lillibet did what some would call strange, she poured water on herself, the cruel ones stopped laughing and left in a storm while everyone else poured water on themselves too and laughed.

Annie gave Lillibet a huge hug and said, "You are a true friend."

These moments were not unique, there were many, like when Lillibet was sick with flu and Annie camped out in her room. They talked for hours and Annie helped Lillibet catch up on her homework even though she hadn't done her own; she even fended off annoying little brothers. Lillibet had fallen asleep and a knock came to the bedroom door, it was Dan, her six year old brother.

"What do you want, Dan?"

"I want to see Libus."

That was what Dan called Lillibet,

"You can't!" said Annie.

"She's sleeping."

"What's wrong with Libus?" asked Dan.

"She just sick." replied Annie.

"Is Libus going to die?" asked Dan,

"No.", she said with a giggle, amused by Dan's childlike innocence and worried expression.

"She's just got the flu."

She closed the door.

In friendships, its actions that count big or small, actions that show loyalty, honesty, trustworthiness, or willingness to make a sacrifice when needed. Lillibet, on another day told Kaitlin, a snobby girl, exactly what she thought of her. Kaitlin grabbed Lillibet by the hair and pulled out a chunk. Lillibet made a fist and hit Kaitlin square in the eye. Annie pulled them apart and held Kaitlin down.

Just then a teacher appeared and Annie took the blame for Lillibet because she knew her father would punish her severely for getting into another fight. Countless times they would hold hair whilst the other was sick, going together clothes shopping, those moments when they would just sit together not talking, or when they finished each other's sentences. Often what you look for in your best friend is good judgment, they had found that in each other, friends who would confide in each other and trust them to keep it all a secret, someone who would really tell you how bad you look in that outfit, even though you really like it. Romance complicated the relationship a little, when Annie got 'serious' with Arty but in true friend style Lillibet stood back, no longer a friendly critic but now an unbiased cheerleader. It didn't last. Arty was too in love with himself to love anyone else.

"I'm sorry I ignored you for that prat Arty." said Annie.

"Hey.", said Lillibet,

"Life rolls on, we're still friends and now we have one prat less to worry about."

Annie laughed and hugged Lillibet, she did that a lot.

"I love you for that, I've learned my lesson, and next time I'll listen to you when you tell me he's a prat."

The girls heard about the special assembly at the square and their curiosity rose, they were advised to stay away.

"What do you think Lillibet? Should we go?" said Annie.

"Try and stop me.", exclaimed Lillibet.

"It's going to be momentous, the buzz in the air will be unimaginable, it's about time someone told these Red Skull where to go and elder Christiana is the one to do it, it'll be historical, as well as hysterical."

Annie's face grew worried.

"I don't know it'll be busy, I think it would be best to leave things alone instead of stirring things up."

Lillibet jeered.

"You big woose, you don't have to go but I am. If you do I'll meet you in the square at ten beside King's Place."

"Ok.", said Annie with a stammer of uncertainty.

"I'll meet you there tomorrow then."

***

Christiana incited the Gaelians to call for their independence; he was in no doubt that he enjoyed the support of large sectors of the population, by the fact that he had united so many in the struggle which culminated in an organised protest outside of the House of Assembly.

Ambassador Cutler stood at a window overlooking the gathering, there had never been so many assembled before in an age.

He called over his Lieutenant and said, "Prepare the Guard and await my orders."

Christiana stood on the steps and addressed the large crowd.

"Here in Gaelia we are descended in blood and in spirit from men of vision, men and women who dare to dissent from accepted doctrine if we know it too be wrong. As their heirs, we must not confuse honest dissent with disloyal subversion. We do not yet advocate outright rebellion but we must stand strong against any deviation of our faith. President Fredrix has brought such deviance into our midst. The words of the Almighty are clear; it is our duty as citizens within this democracy to know when to obey, and when to disobey the government. You are all reasonable; you can clearly see what needs to be done.

Maybe it's time to act. We need to send our political leaders a message. We will not lie down. Our freedom and liberty has been hard won, paid in full by the blood of heroes. If we let it slip away, then we will surely slip into the darkness of tyranny. Can we allow bourgeois politicians to make decisions which contradict our traditions? We do not have a democracy!! We have a republic! Which will soon become a dictatorship, this can only lead to the detriment of the common worker, and will you sit by and do nothing, while your rights are stripped away from you? All in the name of Nefarious, whose existence daily defames the name of the Almighty? The Red Skull grossly underestimates the threat before them. They would call me a terrorist, an antagonist, but when did this occur? Many of you know me and knew me before the Red Skull arrived, not in peace but with arms, so who is the terrorist? Who is the antagonist? Who created me by crushing political resistance and empowering fundamentalist like me? There accusations are rich coming from them. I am a citizen of Gaelia, they are the invaders."
He paused for a second, allowing the effect of the last statement to sink in and the cheer of agreement to desist.
"I truly wonder if they think we don't know what freedom actually is. Freedom will not be taken away from us through the use of arms. Freedom has nothing to do with laziness, sloth, gluttony, greed, and the likes! A free man will not take pride on having smitten a sleeping enemy but the Red Skull do. Here our cry today, we are no longer asleep! We are no longer going to bear the shame, simply

like one who has been smitten. The weak and politically correct believe they have accomplished something. Go ahead and believe it. I am laughing at you, we are laughing at you! Today my aim is to remind you of where we came from and to remind you of where we are, disenfranchised by a politician who cares more about his position of power over the people whom elected him. You have read, learned, studied, and applied the words of the Almighty. We have always believed that ignorance is tyranny in itself, so have always allowed freedom of education and speech. Red Skull means to take that away and replace it with false doctrine. Tyranny can only be defeated by never compromising. You all truly understand your own value and potential and have achieved so much more than any corrupt nations and people. My words will be criticised, demonised, and mocked but ask your self, what do we do for the good of our humanity? I tell you now, we rise, we stand in the name of the Almighty and we take back our freedom!"

That day the crowd chanted.

"Freedom!"

That day was not a day of honour and as the crowd's momentum grew, the local police began to struggle as the crowd swelled, moving as one, as a wave about to crash on the shore. The emotion was tangible; it left a tingle on your tongue.

Cutler motioned again to his Lieutenant.

"Deploy the Guard!"

The Red Skull moved on the crowd that day and what was witnessed was horrific.

As they marched on the House of Assembly they were warned by the police to disperse but the crowd continued to chant.

"Freedom!", and marched on, this was enough reason for the Red Skull to act. They lined up and on command fired their first volley above the crowds' heads.

"Disperse quietly and calmly!"

The police officer said again but they were not going to be convinced or dissuaded from their right to protest as the 31st amendment stated.

So the Red Skull let off their second volley, this time directly into the crowd. Lilibet was near the front of the crowd, she had come to see history but this was not the history she suspected she would see. Her plans to meet Annie there had not come to fruition; she could not see her in the mass of the crowd. As the first volley rang, she screamed and crouched in fear, then the second bang of bolts and she saw a young man being killed as he attempted to crawl to safety, and was outraged at the cowardly act of the troopers. She saw the dead young man being dragged into one of the buildings by his friends. She then watched as five men crawled towards an alleyway, King's Place, where she should have met Annie. Shots continued to be fired into the crowd, Gus pulled Christiana into that alleyway. She turned round and felt a bolt whizz past her and explode into the body of the man behind her, he fell before her as she crawled on the ground, the true terror gripped her like a claw had grabbed her soul and was ripping at it. She began to scream as she lay on the ground beside the dead man, trying to get to safety. She looked round and saw another man as his body jerked with bolt shots and it continued to writhe on the ground. He landed on his front with his head towards her. She could not believe the inhumanity of the murderous troopers before her. The cowardliness of shooting into an unarmed crowd, shooting people in the back as they ran away, shooting people on the ground as they lay dying or trying to crawl away, trying to save themselves. She now began to fear for her friend as well. She remembered Annie's concern and now wished she had listened to her wisdom. Another volley was shot, she caught Annie's eye, and she also lay prostrate on the ground but was still alive. They crawled to each other and took each other's hand, still crawling, attempted to take cover behind a wall. The Red Skull soldiers continued to fire at the marchers, Lillibet and Annie huddled behind the wall; bolts were hitting the wall behind them. They didn't see the bolts; they just heard them, each devastating blow exploding on impact, the precise, streamlined, hard object focusing its kinetic energy onto a small area, the high pressure causing massive stress to a tiny spot, causing it to penetrate rather than simply impact. High powered bolt guns making the bolt go through the target rather than be stopped by it. Lillibet felt a bolt graze the sleeve of her jacket as she cowered, she looked at Annie as a bolt blasted through the wall and pierced her left shoulder exiting with an explosion of red.

"Oh, Annie, your shot!" said Lillibet.

She automatically placed her hand over the wound.

"We need to get out of here!"

She helped Annie up and ran taking shelter in a nearby building.

Lillibet ripped strips from her sleeves for a make do bandage, dressing the wound.

She watched through the front window and saw more, a young man and what looked like his father being shot in the back and head. She saw others, a small group being pulled through windows to safety. She saw two people move a small distance out from the rest of the group; one of them was only a child, as they did so they were shot and fell onto some shallow steps.

"We can't stay here either, Annie, are you able?" said Lillibet.

Annie nodded, Lillibet gave her a shoulder and both walked through the building and out the rear door into the alleyway, they turned and noticed two troopers in the alleyway she froze on the spot but their backs were towards them. At that a young woman appeared wearing a white uniform, she silently motioned to them and helping to support Annie under her other shoulder, quietly helped them around the corner and into an ambulance. A third trooper came up between the other two troopers, knelt down and fired a shot which hit the pavement about two feet in front of the nurse, she felt the bolt hit her trouser leg and temporarily fell to the ground but just as quickly got up and climbed into the ambulance which sped away, the sound of bolt fire becoming quieter till there was no more shooting, the contrast of the silence was almost unbearable.

Lillibet broke down in tears as the nurse tended to Annie's wounds.

"It's all right, dear, she's going to be fine. Wish I could say the same about the future of Gaelia.

By the way my name is Melody."

***

Once they had reached a safe place, Christiana spoke to his small but close group.

"Today the Red Skull have revealed their true agenda, so today, we begin to reveal ours. Some of you must now retreat to our strong hold at Fort Lamont. General Pawlii, although remaining under the watchful eye of the Red Skull has remained faithful to the Almighty, you shall gather the faithful and call to all in secret. Fort Lamont is our stronghold where the faithful will gather and be strengthened. I shall travel encouraging those around us to rally, we shall go underground but only till the day we rise."

Over the next few days the inner circle dispersed, Christiana travelled with two who were faithful, David and Deborah. Gus, as instructed enlisted with the Loyal Burgh Navy, enlisting as an officer in the Marines.

***

After hearing news of this atrocity, groups began to form. People began to awaken and becoming conscious of the power that was being given away, a similar protest was organised in Askdean.

It was the beginning of the war of resistance.

In Askdean the citizens were generally wealthier; it was a magnificent city built from marble and granite. After the massacre in the Burgh, tumults and bloodshed disturbed the streets but not openly, the underground terror against the Red Skull started here. Red Skull collaborators disappeared. The mayor, not wishing to disappear made the resistance aware that he was cooperating under extreme duress and would assist them in any way to return the city under the authority of the Almighty, his name was Gess Flora. Riot and flame engulfed the city, Cutler declared Marshal Law over the city sending Morg to oversee. Askdean was famous for its temples and cathedrals, it's most famous was known simply as *'The Kings'*. The owner of the land around it, a collaborator, had already agreed the shops and stalls on his land could trade on the Holy Days, forbidden in the Almighty's Edicts. Anyone going to worship would have to walk past a long line of shopkeepers pushing their goods, this, at best, annoyed most but enraged some. The more impetuous youth would harass the shopkeepers and try to incite a reaction. A crowd gathered in the narrow streets leading to *'The Kings'* Temple, the days anger began when stalls and merchandise were spilled over, angry words between youth and shop owners began to spark like little flames that start a forest fire, all over the streets leading to the Kings Square. The violence started when some men, collaborators, already in arms, started to attack worshippers trying to reach the temple. One man was struck in the face after asking one of them to move aside, another was stabbed and another kicked in the side, back and head by a group of men. Then the men of greater influence decided to meet with Mayor Flora, to convince him to speak with this land owner, that he may revoke the shopkeeper's new rights.

***

John, the elder, and twelve men from the King's went to Mayor Flora, to implore him and remind him of his promise. As they arrived, they were not greeted by Mayor Flora alone but also by Morg.

They complained bitterly.

"We have worshipped in this temple for centuries without incident, this man Sebastian must be made to desist from issuing licences to sell on our Holy Days."

Morg stood silently, creating an ominous atmosphere of fear and dread amongst those in the room. All were aware of his kinetic abilities as an Immortal.

"What do you say, Mayor Flora?" asked Morg.

The Mayor who had been sitting at his desk now stood.

"These men represent the vast majority of the citizens of Askdean; we have a duty to them, the shopkeepers and Sebastian."

At that Morg turned his head to look at Gess Flora, he lifted his hand towards him, gave a little twist and the Mayor's neck snapped, he fell to the ground dead.

Morg now turned fully to face the delegates of the people.

"Never trust a politician; they have the ability to say yes and no at the same time."

Two of the group ran out of the door in sheer terror, the rest, also gripped with fear remained.

Only John showed no fear he set his eyes like steel on those of Morg.

"I can see my attempt to persuade you to join the Red Skull cause would be futile and although your friends are like schoolchildren gripped with dread, not you, my friend.", stated Morg to John.

"My name is John, it is only the Almighty I fear and I am not your friend. I have spoken with the Almighty about many like you. He assured me then and I know it now, that when this day arrived He would give peace this world could not fathom and he has. In times of tribulation, I take courage that it is fleeting because He has overcome the world, overcome you."

John turned his back on Morg, this caused a reaction of anger in, he raised his hand but wisdom and experience spoke into his anger.

He thought, "To kill this man would only create a martyr, he must be broken."

John addressed the other men.

"Brethren, rejoice, be made complete, be comforted, be like-minded, live in peace; and the God of love and peace will be with you. Today is the start of a long day of night but be strong, be a voice clear and loud proclaiming His glory and grace."

At that Red Skull guard entered the room as previously instructed by Morg.

"Arrest the elder John, the rest escort out. Tell the crowd what you have seen today. Let them know I crave chaos, it feeds me. Rebellion is my '*entrée*', it is war that is my '*plat du jour*', have no doubt war is coming, and it must."

John was taken to jail and the rest released to tell the tale, the official line was that John had killed the Mayor, hence his arrest but few believed it. This injustice and oppression caused more violent incursions, the people assembled around the temple with the loudest outcries; but it was the purpose of Morg to drive the people to insurrection, and he gave his troopers orders to plunder homes.

The fight moved underground with small guerrilla groups being marshalled from the King's, one assault was on the military garrison where John was held. Phineas, an ex-Caledon volunteer, became leader of the sedition; he led the assault to release John. Many were slain; Morg had been spending many a night talking with John. Phineas became over confident and on the assault of the garrison was himself killed, as were the Captains under him. The conflict erupted into a bitter and uncompromising struggle. The underground movement had one aim, the impeachment of parliamentary government and the establishment of new political parties which would fight the Red Skull and uphold the edicts of the Almighty.

Despite small victories, the guerrilla groups had to retreat into the poorer suburbs such as Nestoria.

***

The Burgh Massacre and Askdean uprising was passed off as an act of sedition against the government, all meetings in temples across Gaelia where restricted and an edict of how these meetings were to be performed passed. This did not go down well amongst the more orthodox temples and many elders refused to follow the '*guidelines*'. Those who refused were thrown out of temples by government officials and many held illegal meetings, they were held in barns, lofts, cellars and even in fields on the hillside far from the watchful eyes of the Red Skull. Christiana became a wanted man and as, one by one, his fellow elders were killed or captured, he alone bore an anointing only a few others had. He was named the '*Ghost Prophet*' by his enemies because no matter how hard they tried, who they tricked or convinced to deceive him, they could never capture him. They also indulged in a more insidious weapon of propaganda spreading lies and slanders about Christiana in which they were aided by the media. The only time they did capture him came when he was overheard in a Burgh public house and recognised, he had lodged with a friend who were also under observation. The next day access was made to the house on the pretence of searching for illegal goods. Christiana was seized and handed over to the Red Skull who dispatched him to the city of Yar for the personal attention of the Nefarious.

The Captain of the Red Skull looked at his scrawny, lanky frame and said, "This cannot be the scourge of the whole nation whom the Red Skull have had so trouble much with? I can now see why you are called the *'Ghost Prophet';* you are only one meal away from death."

The next day, they set sail on a ship to Yar; the Captain of the vessel came, out of curiosity to see this Ghost Prophet.

"You have a reputation, preacher, but as I stand here it does seem to be untrue, the one who cannot be caught has been caught."

Christiana stood as best he could with his chains restricting him.

"Truth be told, the Almighty warned me of the troopers as he always does but this time I was instructed to allow myself to be captured. I was told I would meet a leader of men and I would change the course of his life as the wind changes the course of a sail."

The Captain was taken aback by the prophet's confidence.

"Your words suggest that you were captured for the sole purpose of speaking to me?"

"Well.", said Christiana.

"Let's test it, I was also told strange things, he was a lover of the light but worked in darkness, he was a lover of Lily but this was lost and he used to have a heart of steel.

Do these words mean anything too you?"

The Captain's face drained of blood, he staggered and sat down on a crate beside the makeshift cell in his hold.

"I was reared in the city of Caledon and fought as Militia in the initial struggle against the Red Skull but as the politicians made their deals, I lost heart as that struggle took from me my darling wife Lilly, I believed in the Almighty once but He has taken so much from me, I lost all hope."

The prophet came as far forward as he could.

"Well, it would seem the word is for you,
'The Almighty is with you, O mighty man of steel, He has placed you here in the darkness so when the time is right you can shine and the darkness before you will flee.'"

The Captain smirked.

"With me? If the Almighty is with me, why has all this happened to me? Where are all the miracles and wonders our parents and grandparents told us would happen, the fact is, the Almighty has done nothing and wants nothing to do with us, he has turned us over to the Red Skull. Maybe their interpretation is correct, he is a malicious god who only craves our destruction with rebellion and fealty to the Immortal lords being the only way."

Christiana looked him straight in the eye, at first the Captain dropped his eyes because the strength of conviction from Christiana was overpowering, and he knew he had taken the easy road. He gathered his courage, lifted his head and looked straight back.

"The Almighty has a job for you, you can either go in His strength that is yours or remain hidden in this ship's hold till Glory or death takes you."

With all disdain removed and in complete earnestness the Captain asked, "How and with what could I ever serve the Almighty again? Look at me; I am a weak man, reduced to transporting prisoners for the same enemy who took everything from me."

The prophet now, somehow, stood full height as though the chains that bound him were not even there.

"If you are a man of Caledon then you know what secrets you have been told, you know what strengths, what tools, what abilities you have. You are also aware that all of these are fuelled not by might or by strength but by the spirit of grace. Redemption and justification is what fuels you and assures you that as we serve, the grace of the Almighty will be with you. You know that one man who is justified and redeemed can stand against a thousand and remain victorious."

Suddenly the Captain stood taller; his face gained a stature it had not shown for an age.

"Guide me elder, what should I do."

Christiana spoke, "My fate is not to meet Nefarious that belongs to another. Loose my chains and those of my friends give me a boat and we will make our escape."

Without hesitation the Captain followed instruction.

"Now.", said Christiana.

"Give us ten minutes to make our escape and then raise the alarm with the Red Skull guard, you will assist them fully. It is clear the Almighty wishes you to remain in the darkness until the day of your destiny is revealed, it will grate you, do nothing which is abominable but do cooperate till it is your time."

"As you say elder." replied the Captain.

Then Christina stopped dead and said, "Wait, what is your name, I know it not?"

"It is Gideon!" he stated proudly.

"Your name suits you, powerful warrior and bearer of light, may the Almighty's grace be upon you."

The elder and his companions left the hold led by the Captain; they climbed into the life boat which had oars and a sail with the Captain lowering them into the sea and further speeches of farewell imploring the Almighty's grace on all. The Captain did as requested, waited ten minutes then alerted the Red Skull guard; they did not take chase but instead informed the Scorpion copter base on land that quickly dispatched a copter in an attempt to recapture them. They had managed to get quite far from the ship and could clearly see land, only a few miles away. Without notice the sea becalmed and increased the danger of capture, they could not yet see but could clearly hear the whirring of a copter.

Waving his hand to the east, from where the desired wind for the sail should have came.

"Almighty, give us shelter in this barren open place, give us a sudden wind and let us have a swift and safe passage unless our work is done."

Before he ended his prayer, with the distant hum of the copter still in their ears, a sea mist came from what seemed nowhere covering them in a thick blanket. They sat silently as the engines of the copter came closer till it passed overhead unseen, as they must have been to the copter crew. As the engine noise faded into the distance once more, the wind rose and the flapping sails filled like blown bladders, and he and his comrades were saved being blown along with the mist till they beached. The news of their escape was quickly released and every Red Skull squad was put on alert. By now the stories of his escapes were legendary. He gave hope to the faithful and brought frustration to those opposed to him, he very much became a heroically romantic figure. Over the next few years, dogged by spies, and hunted by Red Skull, it was spoken by both as being a man of great personal strength and his hairbreadth escapes became bedtime stories told to the young and old by both camps. Amongst these many tales was the night he stayed in lodgings in Dopolis, a commanding officer of the Red Skull, who was separated from his squad, sought shelter for the night. He spent that evening with Christiana, enjoyably talking of many things including the Red Skull doctrine but remained unrecognised by the Commander. The following morning the Officer inquired after his companion of the previous evening and was told that he had left earlier to seek a hiding place; it was then obvious who his companion was. It is said that the Officer was so surprised to learn that Christiana was a harmless and discreet person that he resolved not to pursue him further and returned to barracks, his name was Arix. On another occasion, whilst leading a field meeting after a heavy fall of rain they were found by Red Skull as they began to pray. Christiana along with the others fled in all directions, he fled towards the river intending to cross and go to friends on the other side. On reaching the river he found it flooded and decided to stop and pray, which he did in the shelter of some bushes. On rising from his knees and about to enter the surging river he was astonished to see pursuing Red Skull landing on the other side of the river. It seems that they had ridden past him in the gloom and hurried across the river before it became impassable, if he had not stopped for prayer he would have been caught in midstream. Or, the time he hid in a cave. They used the latest infrared technology but remained unfound, the trooper stood next to him whilst he crouched, his boot even touched his but he was not discovered. Or when riding on a borrowed Cobra motorcycles, travelling to the next town, he came across a squad of Red Skull, he drove his Cobra full pelt towards the crown of the hill where, just before the crest, he threw himself into a hollow with some bushes. He fully expected his pursuers to find him and as the squad rode past, he flinched causing the bush to move. One trooper, taking no risks, let a hail of bolts loose into the bush but not one hit him, they scattered either side, he felt one skiff his left ear which bled. The scar left behind he called his reminder of grace. Amazingly, they rode on and did not examine the bushes; there he lay until sunset when he was able to make his way to a friendly farm. He was chased through bogs, he escaped but his pursuers were drowned or the time he slept in a sheep pen and woke with the sheep all sleeping on top of him, whilst a squad walked past and he was unnoticed as the sheep, obviously following the request of the Almighty, had settled on top of him to conceal him.

Whilst he held a meeting on the moor, once again mist was involved.

He preached that day on these words.

"Fire and hail, snow and ice, hurricanes and mountains all obey the orders of the Almighty"

When Christiana preached he did so with deep melancholy, yet his sympathy, tenderness, and racy humour kept it light. His keen insight into human nature and his intense realisation of the Almighty's fatherly care bred in him a familiarity. He was a man whose nature was moulded by the circumstances of this time but also fashioned by the grace he lived by daily. He was always received with awe by his hearers, who trembled respectfully at the strange intuition he had in every situation.

On this occasion he referred to the treacheries of the Red Skull;

'The plowers plough the fields and draw their long their furrows. These are the tracks that they must sow their seed and the fruit they grow is the fruit they must eat. So is it for those who betray the Almighty and do not seek his redemption, the seasons will come summer and winter, frost and fresh-weather, till the world's end; and at the sound of the last trumpet, when all are in a flame, their fruits will bum. Then the plowers will lose their grips of the plough, there will be yelling and screeching that will be among all his cursed seed, clapping their hands, and

crying to the hills and mountains to cover them from the face of the Almighty and his servant. I cry now and implore you as faithful to cry also. Let the Almighty arise, and let his enemies be scattered; let them also that hate Him flee before Him. As smoke is driven, so drive them, as chaff is separated from the wheat.'

He then bent down, lifted some dirt and scattered it to the wind, suddenly stopping, as if someone had whispered something in his ear.

"Red Skull and they are close."

A young boy who had been placed on guard came running into the midst,

"They have found us and they are so close that escape seems hopeless."

The crowd began to panic but the elder calmed them.

"If the Almighty does not save us today it simply means our earthly task is done and we serve him in Glory instead."

He bowed his head in prayer, "Almighty if today is the enemies' day then let them have it but I ask that you cast your cloak over us, save us this one more time and we'll keep it in remembrance, telling it to the commendation of your goodness and grace."

As he prayed, the mist covered the hills and the fugitives.

The Red Skull squad once again passed by only yards away and all remained unnoticed. He became such an agent of change and rebellion that Cutler issued an edict which required all persons to aid in his arrest, and none were to offer him help or support of any kind. If any person were to willingly cooperate with him they would be as guilty of his crimes and punishable along with him to the full extent of the law. It is a measure of the respect that the people had for him that he eluded capture for over three years after the edict was given. Throughout the next few years, the severity of the Red Skull, especially towards the disciples of Christiana increased, their bold repudiation of their authority was a political danger which could not be ignored. The Red Skull troops called this the Hunting Fields. Revolution was in the air.

***

In Askdean, elder John remained the prisoner of Morg. Morg would visit him daily and they would spend hours in debate. John, although young, just twenty seven, was a stalwart for the Almighty, he was born in a village not far from Askdean. Both his parents died whilst he was fairly young and was reared by his uncle who, was not the kindest man but held to the ways of the Almighty. From the early age of ten he was completely convinced that he would be an elder. Some found him precocious, cocky was one description, but the young John was just confident and assured in the grace of the Almighty. He had learned to read the scriptures by the time he was seven years old and would preach about the Almighty's love and grace to whoever would listen, in his early teens, his uncle introduced him to the sons' of local 'worthies' where he learnt how the world worked. He graduated from the Burgh University at aged seventeen, youngest graduate ever. After leaving university he returned to Askdean and continued his biblical studies, becoming a master of the temple and then finally an elder. It was here whilst watching some of the atrocities of the Red Skull that he determined for himself, with a new found zeal, that he would be a witness for the Almighty standing against all that Red Skull stood for.

After his arrest Morg spent many days with him.

Morg tried constantly to break him.

"One of your brave men declared his faith before he was executed for sedition, as an example his head and hands were hacked off and positioned on the Upper Millergate."

John was unmoved.

"I also heard that some of his adventurous friends stole the corpse, removed the head and hands from the spikes on the bridge, burying them secretly so as this martyr could not be defiled any more."

John, unlike other elders, who proclaimed a peaceful solution, was an eager advocate to do battle against tyranny and was not shy of being antagonistic. He was recognised as a fervent believer but a fluent and gracious preacher well able to get his point across to the crowds who came to listen to him. Morg found him a curiosity, he had met many who had faith and fervour, many willing to die for the cause but in the end fear was evident, even without his kinetic ability you could see it in their eyes. They were aware that they were about to enter glory but did not seem prepared, not ready yet of the unknown. He assumed it was because their faith was not as secure as they stated, that they, as the deluded Red Skull troopers, had simply accepted a faith they had not even fully understood. As an Immortal, he knew the truth, he had spoken with the truth but had chosen to follow and make his own truth. John acted as an Immortal should, as someone who had been beside the Almighty when the world was created and stood in awe and wonder at the creation. As someone who had felt the first wind and smelt the first rose and saw the first wave and knew the plans of the Almighty to be true. But he was a mere man, where did this confidence, self-assurance and unbending faith come from. The surety of the man was impossible for a mortal but yet, it was real. Whenever Morg entered into the prison cell that John occupied, it hit him like a familiar smell, a citric smell which spoke of cleanliness but knocked you backwards with the pungent smell of eternity he had only ever sensed before in the presence of the Almighty and other Ancients and Immortals.

"Have you again returned, Morg, is my conversation that addictive that you cannot live more than a day without it?" enquired John.

Morg could not believe that this man after weeks of isolation and very little food could still be so straight and discerning in his statements.

"I do not speak with you because of a desire to know you personally better, only to dissect your reason to better understand your kind."

John laughed with quiet confidence,

"And, of course, if you can break my spirit and employ me to talk about the benefits that the Red Skull offers in preference to the orthodox ways that will serve you well."

"I have never hidden my agenda in our conversations." replied Morg.

"No," said John.

"Only your purposes behind that agenda."

Now Morg gave a laugh but not one that brought cheer, one that brought malice causing anyone who had any goodness in them to cringe and recoil.

"I only seek to impart and learn wisdom from someone who so clearly has obtained wisdom far above anyone else of your race." he stated.

John answered, "I'm sure you speak as a far greater expert than all the experts combined and if we mortals were to seek that wisdom we would need no one else to tell us anything about living, nothing that would be of value. But don't forget that I and the good men and women of Gaelia have a brain and know that the Almighty plays second fiddle to no one. It doesn't take an expert to know these things which is why so many believe and why the Almighty made his message so simple and clear cut that it would take an academic simpleton to confuse it."

Feigning hurt as if his comments had offended him, Morg retaliated.

"Am I being ridiculed by you calling me an academic simpleton, surely that is not the way of the Almighty, it is the way of kindness, grace and mercy, my friend, your words are intended to cut."

John was immediate with his answer.

"The surgeon only cuts the harmful growth from the body to prevent the rest of the body from becoming ill, if truth be a surgeon to you then let it cut."

Morg stood tall and sneered at John.

"So this is the man who has conversations with the Almighty! Reduced to ridicule without mercy speaking as if he was a man who never did wrong and is himself not in need of a surgeon! It's easy for the pious and in bred to point their fingers in blame at the outsider who come with different ideas and notions from their own interpretation and culture, for those who are secure to pour scorn on those who struggle daily with doubt and fear."

John looked from left to right as if searching for something.

"I see no Red Skull struggling with doubt and fear only those you persecute and dominate with the very fears and doubts you speak of. It is you who invests in fear and doubt for your own gain. You are like bandits who reside safely in high security houses, insolent blasphemers who live in luxury while speaking of the atrocities of the poor and down trodden, atrocities you have caused, you think you have bought and paid for a god who'll protect you but that is the biggest deception, because it is one you play on yourself."

He paused, as if someone was whispering in his ear, Morg caught the sense of citrus again as John continued, "But why don't you ask the animals what they think, they seem to have more wisdom than you, let them teach you. The birds sing every morning and make it clear what is right, if you listen, they can tell you what's going on. Put your ear to the earth, even the growing roots cry out to the Almighty, they know the basics, let them teach you the basics. Listen, as the fish tell you their stories of what has been agreed before time began, before even your creation Immortal one. It is clear to all with eyes that the Almighty is sovereign, that He holds all things in his hand."

With a look of admiration seeing he has understood more than most, Morg replied, "You are right and more wise than I give you credit. I have heard all you speak of, I have heard the cries of every living soul, breathing, and it would seem common sense, as common as the sense of taste? But do you think, elder, that you have a corner on wisdom that I have not heard. I now see where your strength comes from, the presence of the Ancient is with you, be clear, I not only have heard this truth, I have smelt, tasted, touched and saw this truth you describe, but yet it did not ring true. It excludes rebellion, the one thing you humans excel in. With clear choices you still choose the wrong, a fork lays before you, one with a clear road, the other leading to danger and you choose danger. You are more like us than you dare imagine or wish or have the audacity to believe, you crave freedom but choose oppression because you cannot cope with the responsibility true freedom brings."

John sighed weary, not of the conversation but off the circles Morg tried to make.

"You have now revealed your ignorance, we may act like you but you can never act like us. Yes we have the capacity for destruction but from that chaos, like in the beginning, the Almighty brings order. You can talk from now till the Almighty returns but your false tongue will reveal itself, it will trip itself up. Why? Because true wisdom and real power belong to the Almighty and you may have felt, tasted and touched the truth but you have never embraced it. You may have stood eye to eye, toe to toe with truth but its integrity was far from you because you abandoned integrity when you choose your own road of danger. From the Almighty I have learnt how to live but unlike you I have also learnt what to live for. If he tears something down, it stays down, but what you tear down keeps rising and gets stronger every time. He holds back the rain and there is a drought, the flood you are trying to hold back is too strong and he will one day let loose what you cannot contain, like a flood it will engulf you. Strength and success belong to the Almighty and you may feel you have these but they are fleeting, you have denied it in your heart for so long that it has become like a myth to you, a bed time story not to be believed. You know both deceived and deceiver must answer to him. Experts will be stripped of their expertise, those with wisdom will feel like witless fools, kings will lose their royal garments because they will seem like rags, sages will keep silent and he will disarm the strong and mighty. He shines a spotlight into the cave of your heart and hauls deepest darkness into the noonday sun. At his bidding nations rise and then fall as world leaders loose their reason, groping in the dark without a clue, lurching and staggering like drunks."

A sudden look of understanding crossed John's face and though he had been saying all this whilst looking at the ground suddenly looked straight at Morg, into those eternal eyes.

"And though we are the same, we are different. When I chose wrong, I may also chose redemption, for you Morg there is no choice, no redemption, your only hope is that the truth be a lie because you are forsaken. It is clear but not with your eyes, focus your heart Morg; you know that this is your fate."

Morg stood and could not respond immediately as he was once again staggered at his discernment, "I have saved you because we needed no more martyrs but tonight you have sealed your own fate, I have no more use for you."

He left, addressing the guard, "He is one of the stiffest maintainers of his principles that ever came before me, tomorrow execute him. Make it as public and bloody as you can, let his death bring fear, let there be no hope left."

By this time, elder John was not a sturdy man by any means being rather delicate and fragile, the excessive length in jail, long taxing debates with Morg, broken sleep and irregular diet showed itself in his physical stature. Despite poor health, his execution the next morning did exactly what Morg feared, created a martyr whose spiritual stature shone beyond the pale physical wreck of the man that stood on the execution dock. He was shot in each arm and both legs, they hung him upside down, to let the blood drip and so he would slowly die as the shock took control. In what to others would seem an act of mercy, and some say it was, Morg stepped up and placed a bolt into his head to end it quickly, for an Immortal this was mercy.

Chapter 8 - So you want my Job!

Gus joined the Loyal Burgh Marine Corps, as did many of the young men of Gaelia. It was all part of the master plan set out by General Pawlii and Christiana almost ten years previous. Christiana was a peaceful man but he was not a stupid man. He knew force would have to be used in order to remove the Red Skull threat from Gaelia. General Pawlii had stripped out all the military equipment from Caledon before he had handed control over to Morg. He had built a bastion of strength and old virtues in Fort Lamont where he had infiltrated the best corps of the Gaelian army with men he could trust as well as the remnants of the brave Caledon volunteer with the strict instructions to build the fiercest armed force, most loyal to the Almighty and each man trained with the motto of Fort Lamont engraved in their conscience, *'Spare no enemy, Sacrifice no friend.'* Only those who had went through the rigours and testing of a temple education, that and passing the intense physical nature of the corps were allowed to join the marines. Young men and women flocked to the temples to be considered for admission to the corps of the new Gaelian Army. For many they saw the opportunity of adventure and the possibility of travel. For others it was simply to earn money and have employment as their world was just starting and had been turned upside down by the Red Skull invasion. Yet others it was patriotism, a chance to fight against a totalitarian regime, for a lot it was just plain revenge. This whole initiative helped the country out of the turmoil of the conflict because jobs were created to support the effort. There were thousands of young people out of jobs and the promise of a regular pay was attractive, there was a tremendous feeling that the Red Skull aggression had to be stopped at all cost. There were many routes into the military life, many went down to the recruiter's office and simply enlisted but Gus entered one of the service branches as an officer. The military was always his option, growing up hearing the stories of glory by Grandfather could do nothing else but push him to follow his father's footsteps. The Caledon volunteers would have been the obvious choice, like his father, but the Marines had the reputation of being the best, and he wanted to be a leader of the best fighting force. The thought of going through the toughest training regime imaginable did not faze him as it was this training that made them the most admired branch of the military. Their logo, a marine standing victorious on the head of a dead dragon, had something to do with it as well. Gus had earned his bachelor's degree, easily meeting the educational standards; he still had to go through Officer Candidate School, a relentless ten week platoon leader course. The entire ordeal tested his mental endurance and leadership abilities.

Marines' basic training was in Courage Barracks, just south of Fort Lamont. He arrived late in the evening on the first night; he didn't know what was going on. He was told to put his bags down, then pick them back up, repeatedly, all while someone was marching around screaming at him and the rest. Then he had to run up and down stairs, pointing at his locker and repeating his military number. He then had to strip down naked, run through the cold showers, then get dressed again without drying and ordered to go to sleep but the whole night Drill Sergeants shouted at anyone who actually fell asleep, yelling, screaming, making them get back up, get out their clothes run through cold water get redressed, still wet and ordered to go to sleep.

The next day, was hot, the first thing he heard was shouting, lifting mattresses, emptying beds, screaming into faces.

"Good morning princesses, did I wake you from your beauty sleep and you all need your beauty sleep, I've saw prettier toads, I've saw more attractive fluff from my backside than you. Get your sorry butts up and to the barbers, NOW!!!"

He quickly dressed, with DS barking all the way.

"Quick step, Quick step, you slackers."

Gus sat on the chair with the clippers buzzing around his head, standard hair cut was zero.

DS shouting, "We cut your hair short to make it easier for me to get into your head."

DS stopped beside Gus.

"Am I in your head yet soldier?"

He bawled into his ear.

"Yes, sir, you are sir." replied Gus.

The DS was tough and gave no quarter, he would continually shout as he pushed you on in the task,

"So you want my job! You will have to do better than this, you want my job? Who would want to babysit a bunch of wet lettuce leafs like you?"

They were in ninety degree heat; hair shaved, in full uniform, boots, doing drill after drill after drill. Gus was doing another fifty press-ups, DS stopped at the soldier beside him, and he lifted his boot and pressed it down on his head.

"Is that sore soldier?"

He replied, "No, sir, not sore, sir!"

The DS barked back.

"By the Almighty it should be sore; I've got my boot pressed against your head."

They all stood to attention, DS turned to the soldier two down.

"Are you standing to attention, soldier, ARE YOU!!!"

The soldier replied, "Yes, sir, I am, sir."

"Then why, by the Almighty, are your arms bent, should your arms be bent when you stand to attention, should they?" barked the DS.

"No, sir, poker straight, sir." replied the soldier.

"Well," said the DS, "Why are you standing there with bent arms, soldier? You know what to do, quick step, and quick step!"

The punishment for not standing to attention with poker straight arms was to do one hundred laps of the parade ground, flapping your arms saying, "I am a bird, I am a bird."

Each evening, the DS chose one soldier, who hadn't put in enough effort that day, their task was to bring to his quarters one hour after mess a full cup of hot black coffee, the cup had to be exact full to the brim and if it was not, he would spend that night in the brig. Everyone ended up in the brig because after a full days drilling their arms and legs were weak and shaky and found it impossible to carry a full to the brim mug of coffee without spillage, but not for Gus, the only cadet to achieve it, that night as he returned to the bunkhouse, to the exasperation of the DS and utter disbelief of the other cadets.

"How did you do it, how did you manage to carry it without spillage, you must be made of steel?"

"Simple!" replied Gus.

"Once I poured the coffee in the mug, I took a big mouthful, it was burning hot but, I did not swallow it. I walked to the DS room and then spat the mouthful back in his cup, a perfectly filled mug."

The bunk erupted in laughter and cheers and back slapping, DS heard the raucous and sat sipping his coffee wondering,

"How did that boy do that, no one has ever done it before?"

The noise died down and Gus said, "Anyone got any blister cream, my mouth is in agony!"

***

They got up in the dark and collapsed in their bunks early at night, everything was done in a hurry, DS always yelling at you.

"So you want my job! You'll have to do better than that, precious."

Sleep was a luxury you rarely got the benefit from but you learned to work with people in a way you would never do in civilian life, you learned teamwork, problem-solving, trust, and most importantly, how to shut up and take orders without asking why. Marching in formation, somehow seemed very important, as did learning how to clean and use various bolt guns and pistols. All the meantime Gus was getting more fit and in better shape, they were well feed but were taught,

'Only take what you'll eat and then eat all that you take.'

Friendship became important and, as the competitiveness grew, Gus gained a few enemies but you learned to respect everyone. Whatever Gus was before he started, he was a stronger person and a valued team member when he finished. He did his best, and then tried to add ten per cent.

Whilst trying to sleep after a long day on week five, his bunkmate asked him,

"Gus, I'm struggling how do you keep it up?"

"I know, it's hard for me too." replied Gus.

"Every day I tell myself, hundreds of people have done it before me. Don't doubt yourself, Gus, and don't doubt your cadre."

He paused.

"DS is just teaching us to stay alive, and how to keep other people alive. He's teaching us how to do his job. If you can't do it, don't do it but if you can, keep going. Keep going, concern yourself with two things, where you are at that moment and where you're going to end up, how we get there is not our concern."

Gus sat up, leaning on one arm and looked over the side.

"DS has one goal and it's not to wash you out of the program, but to train you to be the best you can be, better than you can even imagine."

He lay back down.

"I have a dream every night, I dream of the day when I stand on the parade ground to attention as DS walks up to me and calls me a Loyal Navy Marine for the first time. That will be a feeling that will never be repeated."

The weeks continued, Gus was exhausted, demoralised, had tears of pain, joy and laughter. Years later, on reflection, he said that those ten weeks were the most fun he had ever had without a girl! Gus's ability, from a young age, to keep a cool head helped him make it through the mental toughness, working for years in the estate gardens and with his brother in the garden centre, carrying heavy loads, digging and working heavy machinery had helped him get into top physical shape, there was A LOT of physical training, and the course wore his body down but he came out stronger and fitter than ever before. Gus's quiet wisdom but direct manner proved to work well in leadership, his ability to empathise with those he commanded but yet remained aloof, to be friendly but not friends, to be commanding but not commandeering. He was first trained to be a provisional infantry officer, all had to have this training as any could be called to lead an infantry squad at any time. He was ranked as a special operations officer because of his education and skill in languages. For the next eight months he served aboard the AS Justified, they patrolled the northern coast and sea protecting trade convoys against pirates, General Pawlii had also negotiated a secret trade agreement with the northern countries, ensuring that the Red Skull were unaware of the arms and other items that had been embargoed in case of revolution.

***

One year on from the massacre, Elder Christiana and General Pawlii met in a secret war room at Fort Lamont. President Fredrix had lost control with both houses of government suspended and leaving power effectively in the hands of Cutler. The Burgh was subdued but Askdean was in turmoil as those loyal to the Almighty carried out guerrilla warfare against the Red Skull and Morg. The killing of Elder John had strengthened their resolve to resist Morg at all cost. Christiana and General Pawlii now had a hard decision to make, were they ready for all out war against the Red Skull? They had a strained relationship as they often disagreed as to how things should be done, Christiana preferred a political solution but General Pawlii was growing impatient and blamed the bloodshed of the Burgh and Askdean massacres on Christiana's hesitance. Christiana resisted General Pawlii's suggestion of an invasion of the Burgh wishing to keep civilian casualties to a minimum. Their conversations were always a frank exchange of words, General Pawlii had managed to prevent the knowledge of the secret army falling into Red Skull hands for over ten years and knew, as loyalties were now splitting, that it would not be long before Cutler would hear of his treachery and order troops against Fort Lamont. The time to act was now. But Christiana felt that if they encouraged the guerrilla campaign, weakening the Red Skull, the day would come when they could simply march in with little or no opposition. General Pawlii's advisors, especially General Bear who now lead the guerrilla warfare in Askdean, had spoken of how they had felt gravely hampered by the restrictions and many were angered that they could not show their hand and fight with their brothers in open combat.

General Pawllii gave Christiana a report from General Bear which clearly said, "It will not be possible for us to keep our growing forces hidden, unless you are able to show some new facts or strategies, we should not prolong the start of open conflict any longer."

Christiana sat in his chair with his head in his hands, he was tired.

"It was I who first suggested this tactic and, to all intensive purposes, it has been successful so, if we reinforce the security measures will that not buy us more time."

General Pawlii remained standing, with his foot tapping, obviously restraining his temper, not wishing to disrespect the elder.

"The object was to prevent the Immortals from gaining full control and allow us to rebuild our forces without this information leaking out. Now I humbly request and suggest the time has come to show our hand. You have no idea of the enormous inconvenience and friction which this delay is causing."

Christiana stated, "Your proposal for me to speak with the people over the radio inciting them to revolution does not sit easy with me after all it was my speech on the steps of the Assembly Hall that led to so many innocents losing their lives. I feel it would be ineffective and look like we are begging for help at best or not telling the truth to these people about how strong we are, at worst. The proposals you are putting forward are very drastic and would seem like we are putting all our eggs into one basket."

The General nodded his head, "It is a death or glory approach but I do not trust the politicians to rally to our cause unless we show force, the only politician I trust is Julia Caulks, Mayor of Caledon, and even then she only knows a limited amount of information, I will tell her nothing more until that city is fully under our control."

The elder gestured in agreement.

"Although, I also have faith in Julia, perhaps our first action is to secure that city; the Almighty has shown us favour in that Morg has been moved to Askdean along with most of the Red Skull, there only remains one battalion. We should wait until the last minute to tell her our plans, though, to prevent any leaks. These are huge issues we two struggle with; if we err even a little then much will be lost."

The General turned slowly as he felt a change in the atmosphere, slowly and increasingly a citric aroma began to fill the room.

"It would appear that the solution is about to be given to us Stef, have you ever spoken to an Ancient?"

A growing light appeared in the corner and out stepped Andreas, standing eight feet tall, his piercing blue eyes transfixed Stef as he stood motionless and in disbelief.

"How are you, Christiana, my friend?"

"Very tired and wishing rest but ever faithful and wait for instruction."

Andreas placed his hand on the head of Christiana,

"Breath easy and know the grace of the Almighty."

You could physically see a change in Christiana; his face lightened and appeared as a man ten year younger. His posture changed as he straightened in his chair.

Andreas then looked at the General.

"Your anger and frustration is justified, Stef, there is no doubt that what the Red Skull do is heinous and cowardly but, given what I am about to say, we must endure the knowledge that they may target innocent civilians with their acts of terror, they will receive their reward."

Andreas stepped forward to administer grace to the General but he, instinctively stepped back.

"Do not fear, I only wish to assist you but will not if that is your wish."

Stef stepped forward again and Andreas lay both his hands on each shoulder.

"May the grace of the Almighty fill you."

Stef felt a surge of power, like electric but more like a refreshing and bringing an overwhelming sense of wellbeing, if he had been a less stubborn man, he may well have collapsed at the first touch but his pride prevented that and he stood strong but feeling a resurgence of faith and hope.

Andreas continued, "Red Skull has but one goal, to dissuade the loyal, so as they abandon hope and the Almighty. We wage a global war on the terror of the Red Skull, everywhere Nefarious seduces mankind into believing that war is the path to glory. They teach that the eagle cares not for the world it flies over, only looking for its next prey which it seeks to devour, but this is a misunderstanding as the eagle is not separate from creation but part. As is the smallest bacteria, which is, in fact, more powerful than the eagle in its devastation. Nefarious claims lordship over the smaller countries as a shallow excuse to protect the smaller powers against an invisible enemy but never submits his great power to the judgment of the small powers. Nefarious has only one desire, to rule or to destroy what he cannot rule. Nefarious resists the truth. The truth is that great nations like yours are destined to shed your blood for those who are lesser in stature but for now you must take the scoldings of these lesser powers and your people who see your apparent inaction. Do not expect all to declare war against the Red Skull, they have been instructed not to until they also are given the signal. To expect otherwise is foolish and proud, they are not dogs who you can expect to jump through the hoop whenever you snap your finger to suit the convenience of the overlords, which is the Red Skull way. You must continue to listen to the symphony of paternalistic overlordship spoken by Nefarious and the Red Skull, deal with internal politics, although its rank smell fills your nostrils till it nauseates your stomach. Consider this, you have strength at sea as well as on land, gain supremacy there, but to do so you must first regain control of your ports, your fleet is your ace in the hole. Cutler will soon give you opportunity, take it and then claim your actions as political. Direct your attacks at the weak points, gain access to the head and cut it off, the Red Skull is a seven headed monster and each must be taken individually, the beast is too strong to kill in one blow, the Almighty's will is a flawless gem, heed to it. There is still strength in the east and the north remains as strong as ever despite some deep wounds but Gaelia is the strongest opportunity to resist this evil but in your desire to show strength you may instead show weakness. Nefarious mistakenly assumes that Gaelia is subdued seeing this rebellion in Askdean as nothing more than a pin prick which brings him frustration as it deprives him of his greatest general, Morg, in his eastern campaign. A poisoned pin prick can cause just as much devastation as a blunt blow to the head. The Almighty has no heed of politics or politicians, boundaries and kingdoms all blur in his eternal view, so not for political reasons, but out of His preferred way He advocates an abundance of caution. The Almighty takes a long while before He moves swiftly but when He moves, it is swift. Be prepared to move on his command but He would have you walk, not run, we are not dealing with a single malevolent individual who will fall with one swift blow but a cancer which needs treatment and surgery to be removed. Gaelia is a tough and resilient nation, so are its people. I'm supremely confident that Gaelian's will pull together, take care of each other, and move forward as one proud nation. And as they do, the Almighty will be with them every single step of the way."

At that the bright light returned, the citrus smell faded and Andreas was gone.

"It looks like we have to wait further.", sighed the General.

Christiana gave a gentlemanly snigger.

The General sat down at a desk.

"In light of what I have just heard, I suggest plan B, Operation Aeetes, as all-out assault seems too great a risk. If the quest of our Golden Fleece, the complete defeat of the Red Skull is to be on a slower road, knocking out the dragon's teeth one at a time, then as Aeetes did, we should plant and water our dragon's teeth. We send covert units into Askdean and we may find others will spring up turning them against their aggressor, then rend them from our cities to the last man."

The elder agreed.

"Although it makes me extremely uncomfortable having the fate of the world in our hands, settled with a nod, it is clear to me that we can no longer stay our hand. We shall release our dragons slayers and regain control in part, in hope that the people of the Burgh shall rise with us."

"The threat that faced us a decade ago is not the same." answered the General.

"Believing us subdued and conquered, Nefarious has moved his might to the North where they are engaged, he cannot move them against us quickly and he dare not as the beast in the North would devour him if his strength did not stay there. He is overstretched, whatever we choose will act as an irritation against him, an itch he cannot reach or ease. Instead of grace and kindness his mind has turned into one of military-minded crudeness and totalitarianism."

"All will be rectified in time, tell me of the forces we have then?" asked Christiana with a reassuring voice.

They continued into the night making plans, the tension now removed.

Whether it was because they had come to an agreement or the after-effect of the visit of the Ancient Andreas but their plans became clear and set, they would reinforce Askdean with marines from the AS Justified sent as covert forces. This time though, they will begin to take and establish parts of the city starting with the port, slowly winning back the trust and loyalty of the people. As they agreed the last of the finer details, Colonel Smig knocked on the door and entered on the General's command.

"Sir.", he said.

"We have just heard from our contact in Yar, the Black Hawk, Cutler has ordered the vessel Shard to stop and search the convoy coming from the north countries."

Both Christiana and Stef looked at each other.

"As prophesied." they said at the same time.

The Colonel looked blankly as if out of the loop which he clearly was.

"Does it have escort?" asked the General.

"Yes, Sir, the AS Joshua, a good old girl but the Shard is faster and better equipped."

The General grabbed the orders he had just written and passed them to Smig.

"Put these orders into action, order AS Justified to engage the Shard with fatal consequences, instruct the AS Joshua the same if they detect it within firing range."

"Yes, Sir!" replied Smig.

The General turned to Smig.

"Colonel Smig? Do you understand my last orders?"

"Yes, sir!" he replied.

"Sink the Shard at all cost."

"Thank you." said the General.

"Make it happen."

AS Justified was a focus for national pride with her flared clipper bow and an extraordinary top speed, she had been described as one of the most beautiful warships ever built and would outrun any ship at sea. Earlier in the decade cutler decided having a Navy was utterly useless.

He concentrated his might on land and air forces. All the heavy ships of the Kingdom Navy were reduced to scrap, their guns removed and used for city defences. Morg persuaded him to keep the battle cruisers Shard and Scimitar, however, an attack by guerrilla unit midget submarines whilst in port at Askdean badly damaged the Scimitar, its wreckage remains in the bottom of that port with its bow still visible as a constant reminder that Askdean was still not subdued, leaving the Shard to operate alone.

Cutler signalled Shard.

"The enemy is attempting to aggravate the difficulties of our Northern land forces in their heroic struggle by sending an important convoy of provisions and arms to Askdean. We must prevent this!"

Cutler informed Morg, "The vessel Shard will attack the next convoy headed for Askdean."

The Shard set sail, unaware that she was being lured into a carefully constructed trap with the convoys providing the bait. Shadowing the westbound convoy, and forming the anvil for the attack, was AS Joshua who accompanied the convoy, the hammer was AS Justified approaching from the west. The Navy knew of the Shard's position, the Burgh Resistance had intercepted the communications between Cutler and Morg. This was confirmed by, Black Hawk, who notified it had indeed sailed. When Shard was only an hour from the convoy, it was clear she was unaware of the AS Justified and expected to engage the older, slower, less powerful destructor AS Joshua. She was unaware that AS Justified approached from the west. When they opened fire, Shard was taken totally by surprise, and a blast from AS Justified destroyed the Shard's radar leaving her sailing blind, facing both AS Justified and AS Joshua who had left the convoy to outflank the Shard. The Shard made an attempt to attack, the newly joined in battle, Joshua, but as she attacked head on, over shot, hitting next to the port side of the ship, Joshua's experienced crew brought her about and shot a full side on barrage inflicting damage on Shard's starboard side. The Admiral on board the Shard had orders from Cutler to withdraw *'If heavy forces were encountered'*. So he decided to withdraw and thought to use to the full her speed advantage. He could only hope they would be unable to follow her except as shadows in ever-increasing distances, rather than pursue her. He however had not expected to meet AS Justified who was not only equivalent in speed but faster. The Shard blindly, shot a ten blast broadside towards the Justified catching her on the bow, still believing she still had her greatest weapon, speed, sped off again. However, her escape bid was foiled when one of her engines took a direct hit from the Justified who replied in kind, slowing her dramatically. Admiral Fury, commander of the AS Justified realising the Shard would fight to the last withdrew slightly and ordered an attack with torpedoes. A total of fifty five torpedoes were fired at Shard, and eleven found their target, it was as good as over.

The Admiral of the Shard sent a communique to Admiral Fury.

"I shake your hand for your tactics; I only ask you rescue my crew, those that survive."

Admiral Fury replied, "Until the last of the Shard sinks, I will show the grace of the Almighty to any stranded sailor, shall I expect your presence on my vessel."

"No." was the reply.

"My fate rests with my ship, my glory in her last throws of resistance against both our enemy, the sea."

The Shard disappeared, the Justified picked up the survivors. Before the battle was over General Pawlii had sent dispatch to Cutler explaining his actions and how he had considered the Shard's actions as a breach of treaty and he had ordered his ships to defend themselves against boarders. He finished by stating that he hoped this would be settled amically with no loss of life but he would defend Gaelia's sovereign rights as agreed in the treaty. Both vessels sailed with the convoy to Askdean, dispatching marines into the city along with the arms and supplies from the northern countries. Lieutenant Black was amongst them.

Chapter 9 - The Pretend War Ends

The massacre at the Burgh square was a monumental turning point in the fight against the Red Skull, the long years of apparent peace made the stories of atrocities seem as exaggerations made up by troublemakers, anarchists and conspiracy theorists. Complacency was the order of the day, but the sacrifices made that day by unarmed men, women and children, almost certainly changed the apathy. This was the day that marked the downfall of Nefarious.

***

After the massacre, Lilibet and Annie were rushed to the Loyal Burgh hospital, Annie was now sleeping after being administered a sedative, so was completely oblivious to all that was going on, for Lillibet it was the worst time in her life, not knowing if her best friend was going to live or die, she spent most of it in the hospital waiting room. Everyone was busy and no one could tell her about Annie for such a long time.

Eventually, Melody returned, "How are you Lillibet? Do you need any medical treatment?"

"No.", answered Lillibet.

"I've scraped my left knee and elbows but there fine, what about Annie?"

"She's fine." replied Melody.

"Let's have a look at those elbows."

As Melody reached out to examine them, Lillibet pulled away.

"I'm fine, I tell you, tell me about Annie!" she shouted.

"I will take you to see her but not till you calm down and let me have a look at those wounds!"

The blood rose in Lillibet's face, she was about to scream but something broke in her and she sat in the chair in a slump and floods of tears ran from her. The frustration of being unable to help, the guilt of convincing her friend to come with her to the march, it all became too much to bear and broke like a dam into torrents of tears.

Melody came beside, put her arms around and comforted her.

"Your friend is going to be fine, it's only a flesh wound but what would she think if I let you go untreated. I've sorted her, she's fine, now let me sort you."

Lillibet gave into the logic and Melody treated her scrapes and scratches.

They stung and then the pain eased as Melody applied antiseptic and wound dressings.

Once done, in a calmer voice Lillibet asked, "Can I see Annie now?"

"Follow me.", replied Melody.

"She will be asleep but she will also have to stay over a few nights, do your parents know?"

The realisation suddenly hit Lillibet, they knew they were at the square, they must be frantic.

"No they won't."

"Well, I suggest you don't spend long with your friend and go home to tell them. Annie will need an overnight bag anyway."

"Yea!" said Lillibet as she walked into the room.

She sat down next to her, holding her hand and apologised to Annie, the tears came again. Annie was fully fit in a couple of months, apart from the odd twinge when she moved her shoulder the wrong way. She had developed a little arthritis in her wrists and elbows. As soon as she turned eighteen, they both marched down to the enlistment office and signed up for the Caledon Volunteers, they trained at Fort Lamont.

**

As instructed by Andreas, General Pawlii played a political game. On one hand pledging feigned compliance to Cutler in the Burgh whilst being completely non-complicit on the other, in fact he began to show a great deal of Chutzpah for a man who had always been conservative in his mannerisms.

He sent a communique to Cutler.

"I would like to inform you of my intentions and reasons for recent events, it is with great regret that the AS Justified fired upon and sank the Shard, it was an act of self-defence as the Shard was threatening the sovereignty of my vessels and I am led to believe the Shard was the first to fire on AS Joshua."

He continued, "The grace of the Almighty shown to your men who survived the sea will surely prove that this was in fact an act of defence and not of war. I would like you to consider this as you are clearly wise and are aware of our ancestors. You have studied what they learned from their ancestors and know our culture would not allow such

175

an act. If I had not acted as such the rebellion that you now have in Askdean would have spread as wildfire to other cities. I am a newcomer at this, with a lot to learn, and not too long to learn it, so I ask for your patience and indulgence as we forge a new unity between our people. Why not let me be taught by someone wise, such as you, instruct me in what you know from experience? Can mighty pine trees grow tall without rain? Can luscious, red tomatoes flourish without sun? Blossoming flowers look great before they're cut or picked, but without soil or water they wither more quickly than grass. Without your counsel and patience, we may do the same. So, as gesture of good will, allow me to send troops in support, I will send troops to Caledon allowing you to dispatch the remaining battalion there to support the efforts suppressing the riotous behaviour of the Askdean rebels, ungrateful brood. I will also keep troops in reserve for dispatch to Askdean; I cannot ask them to fight alongside the Red Skull as that would prove too contradictory in conscience to many of the soldiers as well as to the nation as a whole. They can however be used as a cordon, ensuring your troops receive supplies whilst embargoing supplies to the rebels, any rebels found being immediately handed over to your authority as the criminals they are, to be punished as they lawfully should. I would also inform you that some of my soldiers have deserted their posts and, because of mislead loyalties, joined the rebels of Askdean. This will not be tolerated and any further traitors will be dealt with severely. I again thank you for your wisdom and grace in these difficult and politically sensitive times."

Of course, this was all just subversion and smoke, he dispatched his troops to Caledon and the last battalion of Red Skull was sent to reinforce the troops in Askdean leaving Caledon, for the first time in a decade, fully in Gaelian hands.

***

As AS Justified approached the port of Askdean, the disembarkation of the battalion of covert Marines was hindered by heavy weather; some of the vessels to be used were flooded with the heavy rain and high waves. It would take time to make the affected assault boats seaworthy as required, it was considered that the whole operation be abandoned but in view of the latest meteorological reports, it was decided delay was the better option and the operation would begin in the next twenty four hours when the weather forecast was far more promising. That night was difficult; it was not the swell of the sea that kept him up, or the noise of his newly acquired corporal, Rex Yu, throwing up in the toilet because he was sea sick. Not even the other grunts playing cards because they couldn't sleep, no; it was the tense eagerness to get the job done. They were already meant to be in the midst of conflict and they would have been if it wasn't for this sudden gale. It just gave him and his men more time to think about what they were about to face, they had the training and were confident they would achieve their goals. As he jumped from his bunk and walked down the passageways, he looked at the faces of his platoon and wondered how many of them would survive tomorrow, how many of these faces would he be seeing for the last time? He then thanked the Almighty for tonight's bad weather; he had granted them one more night of life, one more night of camaraderie and friendship.

"Don't stay up too late, dog faces; we gotta squeeze some Red Skull plukes tomorrow."

He raised his voice, "So, hit your racks and get some shut eye."

He walked back a happier man, lie down and slowly fell asleep.

The Minerva groups, Gus's squad, were to land at dawn the next day on the South Pier, where it was expected to be best defended, as the time approached the weather also rapidly improved and conditions were perfect as they climbed aboard the assault boats. They were using boats to keep the landing quiet; copters would be heard miles out and alert the Red Skull to their plans. As Gus climbed into the assault boat, he looked around at the men, they all looked nervous, anxious and a streak of dread was evident in all their faces, they were impatient to get it over with, the impatience was not heroic just impatience. There was a relief as well; that at last the plans so often talked about was now turning into action. Their anxiety was on behalf of their friends, not of themselves, they were much too excited and interested in what was going on to think of danger. He caught the face of Corporal Yu, he wasn't particularly outstanding in features or stature, in fact very slight, you might even question how he managed the marine training, his nose was crooked, and his eyebrows were thin and ginger, like his hair, green eyes and no chin. In his report, it said he had lived in Caledon before the invasion, newly married and one child. Then the Red Skull attacked, like so many who had lost much, in fact, he had lost all. He had served seven year as a grunt but now promoted to Corporal.

Rex sat with his thoughts until Gus asked him, "How are you, Rex?"

He looked up startled; he almost always had that rabbit caught in the headlights look.

"Just having a private word with Father."

His eyes looked upwards indicating the Almighty,

"I was just telling him, we better not be looking for a second chance because we may not get it today. But it is our place to have hope, we are doing something noble after all."

"Good idea Rex!"

Gus got the attention of his troops.

"As we maybe on our last journey before glory, let's bow our heads."

Gus coughed to clear his throat and spoke a little louder.

"True to your word, you let us catch our breath before we jump off this precipice into the unknown. When we are at a crossroad, send us in the right direction. Even when the way goes through Death Valley, I'm not afraid when you walk at my side. You are a trustworthy Father who makes us feel secure, let us trust you this day and every day from now."

The whole boat looked up and called out as one.

"For the Almighty!"

As they moved closer to the shore, Gus looked across at the other boats and saw two parallel rows of assault craft, about one hundred and fifty feet apart, heading towards the horizon and the shore. The sea was so calm that not a man felt any sign of sickness, not even Rex. When they landed at South Pier they jumped in the swell knee deep and waded ashore. In the early light, as they landed a Red Skull Officer spotted them and fired his photon pistol and succeeded in piercing the second assault boat opposite, the flames and exploding ammunition looked more like a fireworks display than warfare, he was quickly mowed down by bolt gun fire, up till that point there had been no evidence that any enemy existed. The second boat had Captain Cochrane, commander of Minerva, who was instantly killed in the explosion leaving Gus in command. They were due to move along the dock towards the Red Skull positions before they knew it, thanks to the impromptu fireworks display; they were in the midst of the fray. They reached the first warehouse and found the position very unpleasant. The Red Skull was on three sides, and at no place more than fifty yards away; shooting was concentrated and incessant. Gus crouched behind a wall and took his bearings, he could feel the pulsing in his head and if honest a little nauseated. They had two main objectives, secure a warehouse where suspected resistance fighters were being held captive and secure a bridge which would ease passage of reinforcements from Neptune. The warehouse was immediately in front and the vital bridge a further three hundred yards along the road. To crown their sorrows there were Infuriators. These diabolical machines left them no quarter, for the first time ever; Gus heard the terrifying whistling whine of photon cannons charging before the enormous sound of discharge and explosion.

Rex whistled, "So that's what death sounds like."

The Infuriator fired again, there were explosions all around, bolts flew past like fire flies.

They entered the main warehouse, securing the exits and taking position at the flanks rear and front.

The smell in the warehouse was putrid.

"Corporal Yu, take a squad and search the upper floors, see what you can find." ordered Gus.

Rex took his squad and in details climbed the stairs they entered a room where all the windows were blacked out and the smell was over bearing. Rex felt uneasy, there was an air that inspired fear, men and women of lesser stature would have hesitated before entering. A marine lit a flare and walked in, the smell overpowered her and she vomited where she stood. The red glow created shadows and things were unclear as they progressed forward, the Marine could see now what the smell was, temporary cells and in each cell were people. They had obviously been mistreated, emaciated, in rags and had been left in their own excrement and urine. Most were dead, a few barely alive. Rex leant forward, he was devastated at the atrocity before him, he felt irritation then annoyance and finally rage at the blatant disregard for life. He turned to radio Lieutenant Black, the rage growing in him, suddenly, out of the darkness, a hand reach out and touched Rex on the shoulder; he jumped and pulled his bolt pistol.

It was a survivor.

"By the Almighty, I nearly blew you away. Help this man, and look for any more that's still alive."

He radioed down, "Lieutenant Black, you'd better get up here."

The man fell on Rex, grabbing him around the waist and nearly knocked him over.

"Get him out of here, I said, move any survivors down stairs and give them water."

They moved him out. Gus arrived and got a report from Rex, Gus ordered him to post sentries, lookouts and snipers. They had to hold position there until reinforcements came along the coastal road from Neptune in the south and Mercury in the northwest. They had lost forty men in the initial assault on the warehouse but were holding fast for now.

***

The forces were divided into five groups led by Major James, Commander of Vulcan, retaining a floating reserve and command base. He turned to his second.

Captain Msipha, "Update!"

Msipha snapped to attention.

"Neptune landed near a heavy gun battlement four miles along the coast from Minerva to secure it. They made landfall unobserved."

James looked puzzled.

"How come!"

Msipha replied, "The lookout post at the lighthouse was unmanned which allowed quick advancement."

***

The Lieutenant in charge of Neptune looked around at his men, they stood between the orchards nervously clutching their bolt guns, fearing that at any moment they might fall victim to snipers. As he reached the edges of the defences of the gun placement, he could see one guard, the Lieutenant motioned with hand gestures for the Marine next to her to move from behind and with a cutthroat gesture, made it clear what she expected. The marine made his way behind the guard and at the right moment, made his move. Many would say that slitting somebody's throat with a knife is a silent kill. It is anything but silent; the enemy will gurgle and thrash around until his brains run out of oxygen, creating a lot of noise in the process. No, if you want a silent kill, you put your blade at the indent of the base of your enemy's skull where the bone is thin and slam it upward at a forty five degree angle. You'll scramble his medulla oblongata and the motor senses are cut off immediately. The guard was dead, as he slumped down; the marine caught him and let him down easy, sliding him down the length of his body. Without warning, as he turned another Red Skull came around the corner, they were both surprised. The Red Skull pointed his bolt gun at him but before he could fire the marine grabbed the muzzle and barrel, gave it a twist and turned the gun so as he held it. He pulled the trigger, the point blank range exploded into his chest armour, some of it ricocheted off, and the rest found the cracks on the armour between the arms and neck and exploded into his chest.

One ricocheted and caught the marine in the soft flesh of the left leg. He felt it, searing pain, which made his knee buckle, as the shots rang, the bunker came to life; a small squad poured out of the doors but the Lieutenant had her marines positioned for the fight and the Red Skull were slaughtered without a single shot being fired by them. Everyone of them had the sensation of being at the centre of an explosion as bolt after bolt hit them, loud bangs and blinding flashes of light all around them. The ferocity was so great that they felt no pain, only a violent shock like an electric terminal and a sense of utter weakness, being stricken and shrivelled to nothing. All of this happened in less than ten seconds. Their knees crumpled beneath them, falling, heads hitting the ground with a violent bang. Having accomplished this task, the Lieutenant motioned to her communications.

She called Vulcan.

"Neptune has secured our first objective."

Msipha informed James.

James ordered, "Inform Neptune to move along the coastal road and form a reserve for Minerva."

The Lieutenant cleared the area securing the heavy gun and rapidly moved along the coastal road.

***

James enquired from Msipha.

"Has Mars group assaulted the Island of Marlon yet?"

Msipha replied, "Yes, sir. They have secured its oil and arms stores. The Red Skull troops where few in number and the Askdean workers who were many, aided the marines. The workers grabbed tools as weapons and although a dozen were shot in their charge the small Red Skull squad were overwhelmed."

Msipha detected a wry smile on James' face.

"Did you know that I was born and bred in Askdean?"

Msipha shook his head.

James continued, "Times have been hard in Askdean since the first day of resistance, Red Skull used repression to try curbing *'the threat of terrorism'* relying on the hope that most *'decent citizens'* wouldn't react but submit because *'decent people'* have morals. But we citizens of Askdean never considered the Red Skull as more than parasites, cockroaches needing to be crushed. They will not expect the conquered to react in a ruthless manner. They have received the wrath of justification felt by those who had been so roughly oppressed. The line had been crossed; the weak have risen triumphant against the oppressor."

Msipha interrupted Major James.

"The transport carrying Mercury has moved past Marlon Island, they are about to disembark on the north western shore."

James replied, "Inform me when they reach the refinery and Red Skull communications have been cut, before they hit the oil refineries."

Ten minutes later, Msipha reported again.

"The Mercury has thrust forward; they have split into four attack points. They have already come under heavy attack with a number dead before the boats were fully on shore. Captain Chafe has reported three squads of Red Skull and two tanks defending the refineries."

James grunted, "Tell them to use extreme force."

***

Captain Chafe received his orders as he sat with the first two attack points pinned down on the shore south of the refinery.

He spoke into his communicator.

"Groups three and four move forward in the flanks in two columns, try to take out some of this heat and use the blasted bazookas, we didn't bring them for decoration."

The third group caught the tanks from the back by surprise in a pincer movement in what can only be described as a hailstorm of fire. Both tanks exploded as they were hit from behind by the bazookas. The fourth moved further North to take over the telephone exchange, leaving it wrecked, then returned to assist first and second.

Captain Chafe reported back to James.

Msipha barked, "It's Captain Chafe, sir."

James grabbed the communicator.

"Report!"

With the noise of heavy gunfire above him.

Chafe reported, "The tanks are destroyed, the remaining Red Skull forces have rolled backwards into the refinery taking defensive positions to hold it despite our assaults. Both sides have had heavy casualties."

At that moment, there was a large explosion twenty feet from Chafe.

"Blast it!", shouted Chafe to those around him.

"I thought we had neutralised all the heavy arms, find whoever is shooting those rockets and make it stop."

Chafe gathered himself.

"Sorry, sir. As I said, the armour is neutralised," he paused, "well most of it. We hold the western shore, communications have been destroyed but the status of the full missions' success is still in question, we still have a lot of fight left in us. I don't think the battle is over by a long shot."

James responded, "Good job, Captain Chafe. Regroup and mount a second assault."

"Yes, sir!" replied Chafe.

He looked over his barricade; two marines were pinned down in the midst of a firefight hiding behind a truck, wheels still spinning and passenger door open, smashed into the side of a wall.

Chafe turned to his left side.

"Take another marine and assist those trapped."

He turned to his right.

"On my command lay down suppressing fire."

He took a deep breath.

"Fire!"

The two marines launched their daring mission in full sight of the embattled Red Skull to rescue two marines.

There was another rocket and explosion.

"By all the fiery hordes, will someone kill that Rocket launcher." screamed Chafe in exasperation. The suppressing fire had caused enough distraction to retrieve the stranded marines.

Fourth group, after setting up heavy bolt positions on a windswept stretch of road north, blocking any Red Skull effort moving South in support, began firing into the Red Skull positions.

"Thank the Almighty, reinforcements at last."

Chafe spoke into his communicator again.

"We have opened fire on the target and are engaging them in combat."

At his command, the second assault began under the glare of illumination flares fired by the Red Skull.

Mercury attacked, firing missiles and throwing in cluster bombs.

Twenty minutes later, Chafe gave his final report.

"The Red Skull forces had been overcome; we will crater the coast road between North and South to hindering any reinforcements."

Msipha replied, "Can you send a party by landing craft to destroy a small billet of Red Skull forces just south of your position."

"I'll send Sullivan with a detachment." he replied.

Captain Sullivan landed in the area of the billet and with her small raiding party immediately entered the building, they found the Red Skull had vanished and discovered the most prominent Quisling of the city hiding in the cellar, his name was Jonathan Oliver, former Deputy Mayor, and they also detected a slight smell of citrus.

***

Minerva continued to encounter very stiff opposition from Red Skull infantry who fought to the last man. In the buildings they were established with snipers, who took up positions on the high towers west of the port. The opposition was severe in degree and skilful in quality having been augmented by a detachment that had been moved into the barracks for recuperation but there is no doubt that the fighting spirit, marksmanship, and efficiency of the enemy was of a high order.

Major James was unclear of Minerva's position and communication had been cut.

Major James turned to Captain Msipha.

"Get over there and find out why they're not communicating, let them know that they need to communicate even if they're dead."

Minerva had lost two wireless sets early in the fighting and visual signalling was limited.

Minerva was in the midst of very bitter street fighting, pushing steadily on from house to house. Their casualties were particularly severe with many NCO's either killed or wounded.

One NCO very much alive was Corporal Yu.

"What's the extraction plan for the prisoners, Sir?"

Gus sighed, he was weary with the weight of losing so many men already, and half his platoon was dead. Very few spots on earth could lay claim to the shear loss of life in such a short time experienced on the cross over between Tyrol and Bridge Street, it became the focal point for the attack of the port. The cost was almost half of the men that had went in three hours previously. So fierce was the fighting that at the battles end, the area was so scorched that the grass hadn't even begun to grow almost a year later.

"The biggest concern for me, Rex," replied Gus, "It's how much longer we can hold out without reinforcements, our communication is nil. I need you to cross the *Styx*."

This was the name dubbed by the troops for the death row between Tyrol and Bridge Street,

"See if third group has managed to fix their communication device, if so tell Major James we are desperate for the support from Neptune and Vulcan, send immediately."

Rex accompanied by a marine came out of the building on the rear flank, flares were lighting up the sky, an Infuriator was in front but they were unnoticed until the marine made a noise not a big noise but the Infuriator heard the noise and let off a sweeping volley from its heavy bolt gun the grunt stood there and Rex jumped in to pull him down. He would have been shot if he hadn't. Rex rolled a grenade which exploded underneath the Infuriator crippling its legs but not its guns. It continued to fire a hail of bolts from all directions, they both jumped to their feet and took cover again, a bolt hit Rex in the shoulder it stung but his armour held. They ran for their objective, this time a bolt clipped the grunt on the ankle, he fell but again Rex stopped picked him up and helped him to a safe place.

"By the Almighty you are a troublesome one."

Finally, Rex arrived in the building across the street and located the communications operator,

"Have you got that to work yet, marine?"

"Yes Sir,", came the quick reply.

"It got hit by a misfiring smoke grenade when we disembarked but I've got it cleaned up and operational again."

"Well signal, Vulcan, immediate assistance needed from Neptune and Vulcan.

Resistance heavy. Position in doubt. Immediate advice requested."

The signal was received from Minerva; Captain Msipha was already on his way with Captain Chafe and Neptune progressing down the coastal road.

The Marine reported back to Rex.

Rex replied, "Send in at once, second group required if objectives are to be completed, strong opposition being encountered in centre and North of the port."

Major James ordered the rest of Vulcan to engage.

Captain Msipha and the first wave of Vulcan had almost reached the landing place at South Pier.

***

"What's your name marine?" asked Rex.

"It's Dance, Sir. Deborah Dance, born in the Burgh." she replied.

Rex scowled, "I don't need you full birth certificate, I'm not picking you up at a club."

The Marine stood straighter.

"No Sir, sorry Sir."

"We are crossing the Styx in five, inform your NCO."

As intimated, Corporal Rex and Marine Dance headed out into the *Styx* in five, Rex knew, from experience, not to travel back the way he came as a sniper would be waiting. They instead went into the building in front and then planned his journey behind walls and upturned vehicles,

"Dance, stay here whilst I scout ahead, if I'm not back in five, follow on if safe."

The Marine, huddled down with her communications pack, replied, "Yes Sir."

Rex moved off, Dance waited as ordered and in around three minutes, the door Rex left through opened but it wasn't Rex. It was three Red Skull. Before she could respond, the three surrounded her, the first stepped forward and raised his bolt pistol. Her training taught her that it was empty; he had discharged all his bolts.

"You might want to check you've got rounds in your gun before you point it at anyone."

She stepped forward grabbed the pistol and wrist and twisted it and him, kneeing him in the small of the back knocking him to the ground, she felt the second coming up behind her so round house kicked him in the stomach but the third elbowed her in the back and head knocking her down.

The other two grabbed an arm each pinning her down the third walked slowly towards her intending to kill her. Suddenly, he was struck in the back with the butt of a bolt gun, it was Rex. The Red Skull fell to the ground, one jumped up, he palmed him in the chest spun round grabbed the third by the neck and head butted him. He drew his katana, sliced off the head of the second thrust his sword threw the belly of the third and raised both arms high he brought it down onto the first, still lying on the floor, finishing him off. Rex liked his katana.

Red Skull armour couldn't resist its sharp steel.

Dance kicked one in the stomach as he lay there.

"Thank you, Sir, I owe you, they caught me unaware."

Rex did not show any reaction.

"It's war Dance, there are no favours in war, we look after each other, just be more aware next time. Now grab that communication device and follow me."

Within ten minutes they reported to Gus and re-established communication with Major James.

***

Neptune had arrived driving forward into the port as reinforcements. Mars had landed from Marlon Island. Captain Sullivan took her detachment forward into the port, where she assumed command of the remnant troops. Minerva had suffered heavy casualties and was operating in small parties, very determinedly and under the leadership of junior NCO's, but making slow progress against the Red Skull infantry posts and snipers. With the arrival of reinforcements, they went forward with Captain Sullivan and Lieutenant Smith and taking control. Sullivan despite being wounded, with great coolness and complete disregard for personal safety, reorganised her forces and directed the drive through the port until, when she judged the situation to be well in hand, she left Lieutenant Smith in charge and returned to her operations HQ. When Msipha arrived with the first wave of Vulcan, they came under a hail of fire from a nest of heavy bolt guns. Captain Msipha took a six man squad and approached the gun nest from the left flank, whilst under fire from the rest of the squad the heavy bolt crews were unaware of their approach. Marines threw smoke grenades to cover their advance. Captain Msipha was first to reach the nest, leapt the barrier and shot his bolt gun felling two Red Skull instantly, an officer grabbed him from behind by grabbing his shoulder and his waist picking him up over his head and slamming him down. He hit the floor like a dead weight with the wind taken out of him but instinctively he pulled his bolt pistol and shot the full clip they all bounced off his armour making only dents and scratches. The Red Skull officer laughed picked him up again but this time by the throat. Msipha punched with both left and then right, which hurt the Red Skulls officer's pride more than him. Again he threw him, slamming him against the wall as he fell his hand felt the butt of a photon pistol, which had fallen from the officer's holster in the initial struggle, just out of reach. The officer walked towards him, Captain

Msipha turned round onto his back the officer lifted his foot and planted it with force on his chest. He could feel the pressure on his rib cage as the ribs began to crack under the pressure. The butt of the gun was at his fingertips, he moved it closer to his grip millimetre by millimetre. The officer also saw the pistol and Captain Msipha's attempt to reach it. He reached down, releasing enough pressure for him to stretch that last inch to grab the gun.

"Time to punch out."

He shot the pistol, it took the officer's head and shoulders clear off.

After securing the position, Captain Msipha reported to Lieutenant. Minutes later the main task force from Neptune arrived supporting in the drive through the centre of the port and along the water front.

Major James ordered Mercury to move around the peninsula and then southwards from their position in the North, to close on the rear of the enemy.

The Major spoke to Lieutenant Black who reported.

"The firing has died down at the southern end, the opposition is nearly finished. The southerly demolition tasks have been started almost immediately. I will go forward to reconnoitre and will report again soon."

Gus climbed the tower to the west of the port and, from the top, searched the area to the southwest and to the north as far as the dam which supplies power to the electric light station. He could see the final fire fights between Mercury and the retreating Red Skull. He made to go back but he when reached the bottom floor, he turned the corner and ran into a Red Skull trooper. They both were taken by surprise, and entered into hand to hand combat. Gus gave a shout throwing the enemy off guard and charged faking a strike which made him flinch, losing his balance. Gus struck his shoulder quickly, grabbed his arm and pulled it behind his back jerking it upwards quickly dislocating the enemy's shoulder. He thought he was alone but out of nowhere six more Red Skull appeared. Gus threw a grenade, there was a lot of shouting as they ducked for cover, the explosion blew them backwards. As he recoiled from the blast, ringing in his ear and blurred vision, he heard the blast of bolt guns and saw shadows walking towards him. He went to draw his pistol but his holster was empty, he stood ready, expecting death but was surprised to hear.

"Are you OK, Lieutenant?"

His vision cleared and standing in front of him were four men in long coats with red epaulets. The Red Skull squad laid dead, apart from the one whose shoulder he dislocated, being held at gunpoint.

"I'm fine, who are you?" asked Gus.

"See that red we wear, it's as a sign of the resistance, and we wear the colour to remind us of blood these devils have shed. We need to get out of here, we're not safe."

The Red Skull was thrown to the ground, the one speaking put a bolt in his head, he slumped dead.

"Why did you do that!" shouted Gus.

"He's scum!" was the reply.

"Never again will you shoot an unarmed man, he may be scum but we are not. We show wrath in combat but mercy and grace in victory, never again. DO YOU HEAR ME?"

"Yes!" he replied.

"That's yes Sir!" screamed Gus who was now in his face nose to nose.

"Yes, Sir."

Gus turned to the rest.

"The most important thing we can do is stay alive.", he pointed to his heart.

"In our hearts and in our heads."

Now pointing to his head.

"We CANNOT become like them, we must remain better. Do you all hear me?"

They all replied, "Yes, Sir!"

Gus turned, looked back at them over his shoulder.

"Follow me!"

Lieutenant Black returned to the operations in the port and communicated to Major James.

"I have made contact with the resistance; the Red Skull defence is overcome. Minerva has now carried out its allotted tasks; the port will be unusable for the near future, restricting resupply for Red Skull troop. Raiding parties under command of Lieutenant Smith have attacked all remaining gun placements, destroying all that could not be moved and allocated to the resistance."

James responded, "Good work, Black. I will join you soon."

James ordered the small parties left at the refinery, the southern gun placement and Marlon to destroy all targets and then rally with the main force. All of the industrial targets were destroyed; landing craft dispersed ferrying the wounded and the captured prisoners back to AS Justified.

Major James, issued orders for the remaining troops to disperse and relocate in the city along with the resistance movement. That day Lieutenant Smith received promotion to Captain as did Gus, Rex Yu became a Sergeant and Marine Barr his corporal.

As he gave his field promotions, Major James addressed his officers.

"The Almighty gave free will to men in spite of His knowledge that it would lead to sin and thence to suffering. The infinite value of each human soul is not knowledge; He loves us not because we are loveable, but because He is love. Evil has its parasitic existence, it creeps up on you like ivy on a tree, beware of regret and bitterness serve him in grace and mercy. Furious in unity, we will be strong for the Almighty."

Chapter 10 - The Long War Begins

Morg raged as he paced in the Mayoral office in Askdean, having received a communique from Cutler about the sinking of the Shard.

"Must I do everything; can that fool not see Pawllii is pulling the wool over his eyes? Release Caledon back to that mongrel whom I scrapped with ten years ago."

He read further.

"A cordon, a cordon, a ring of death waiting to choke the breath from the last of the Red Skull in Askdean."

A knock came to the door.

"Enter.", he called out.

"Report. Sir." said the Red Skull Major.

"South Pier is under attack, it would appear a battalion of Loyal Navy Marines have landed and are currently attacking our troops in the South Pier and Marlon Island."

The Red Skull Major grabbed his head as excruciating pain shot through it, the rage in Morg grew to a crescendo with his kinetic power spilling over like a poisonous gas, unseen but deadly.

His anger knew no boundaries and the Major collapsed as the pain increased, it was like thorns pressing into his brain. He collapsed and blood flowed from his ears and nose, Morg screamed and the whole room exploded into splinters, glass, wood, everything disintegrated as the power of his wrath burst and shattered violently and noisily with the internal excessive pressure of his frustration. Two officers ran into the room to see what had happened, still angry he drew his broadsword and halved the first one in two from his left shoulder in a forty five degree angle to his opposite waist. The second officer quickly reacted drawing out his axe, parrying Morg's next strike. This stopped Morg in his tracks as he realised that someone had dared to stand against him.

Morg stood back and re-sheathed his sword.

"Your name soldier?" asked Morg.

"Captain Arix, Sir." was the reply.

"You are wrong! From now on you are Major Arix, second only to me, ensure you do not fail me."

Morg left the room, closely followed by Arix leaving the debris of the chaos behind.

Morg stood in the battle scarred landscape of South Pier, it had been estimated that the Pier would be unusable for six months, meaning supplies would have to be air dropped or sent by land, neither sufficient to supply his army occupying Askdean.

He turned to Major Arix.

"I have been the victor of many campaigns, and when fed with mistrust and chaos people become desperate. Desperate people give up on the false notions of the benevolent Almighty they have been force fed, their friends and brothers become fickle as a gulch in the desert. In good times they're gushing with water from the melting ice of good intentions but in the bad they're dry, gullies baked in the sun, looking for every opportunity to better their own circumstance before their brothers. Their friends expect the water of compassion, they hope for a cool drink of grace. They arrive so confident but what a disappointment, they get there, and their faces fall, one look at their dry words lacking intention and they shrink in fear. I have underestimated these Gaelians. Report, Arix."

Arix stood to attention.

"They attacked by sea catching most of the detachments by surprise, they rescued the prisoners, captured supplies on Marlon Island and destroyed the refinery beyond repair. The communication exchange has now been repaired and we found this dog, cowering in a corner in the cells."

Two Red Skull troopers frog marched Jonathan Oliver in between them, they threw him to the floor, and he lay there a moment before standing to his feet. The previous night, Captain Sullivan, had been presented with former Deputy Mayor Oliver in much the same way. Since the death of Mayor Flora, the political responsibility of the city had fallen on him, not that he had any responsibility as Morg used him as a puppet. Captain Sullivan questioned him, gaining valuable information that would assist the infiltration of the Marines into the resistance. The house they found him in had been a retreat for Jonathan, who was escorted by four Red Skull for protection, not that they cared for his safety and abandoned him, on first news of the invasion, to his own devices. Jonathan Oliver had spoken of how he'd feared for his life and regretted everything he had done over the past year as he had now seen the light. Captain Sullivan did not believe his words being anything more than an attempt to save his weakly life. He had been a tall man, whom had obviously lived the good life, before the uprising, he was thinner in face and girth than he had been but the evidence of sagging skin from his neck and trousers which fitted imperfectly, held up by braces rather than the bloated stomach which had previously held them up. On consultation with Major James, it was agreed that they had neither the stomach or resources to rescue such a quisling, Jonathan had expressed a desire to redeem him self, so he would be left for the Red Skull. If he survived, he would act as a double spy, pretending to work and spy for Red Skull but used by the resistance. It was agreed to only give him false information and to trust anything he said with suspicion. So they threw him in an empty cell where they had found the prisoners earlier that morning.

"Do you have anything to say? Weasel?" asked Arix.

Jonathan now had bravery in him, born of the need to earn trust as well as the complacency which he now had for his own safety. The realisation he should be dead but still alive, his lost faith in the Almighty was resurfacing, and maybe he had a purpose for him after all.

He responded, "Why do you treat me so harshly and talk to me in such derogatory terms? It's not as though I have ever asked you for anything. I have never asked you for one thing, have I ever begged you to go out on a limb for me. Confront me with the truth and I'll shut up. Show me where I've gone off the track, what's the point of all this pious bluster? You pretend to tell me what's wrong with my life, but treat my words of anguish as so much hot air. Are people mere things to you?"

Arix stepped across and hit him across the cheek with the back of his hand, on contact the armoured glove broke Jonathan's nose, the crack was clearly heard, the trailing fingers scraped across the near eye and, as Arix's hands were large the lower part of the glove caught his trachea as he completed the arc of the slap, he could feel the pressure on his carotid artery and choked a little as he struggled to breath for a moment with the impact and felt the warm blood trickle down his throat.

He regained his composure.

"Look me in the eyes! Do you think I'd lie to your face? Think it over, no double-talk! Think carefully, my integrity is on the line! Would I be standing in front of you if my loyalties were not true? If I had betrayed you would I have not run with the rebels as their denizen into their rabbit holes, because scared rabbits they are! They did not kill me because they threw me into a cell, to kill me later at their ease, but when they heard the mighty Morg was imminent they scurried away into their lair of cowards with their tails between their legs. Can you detect anything false in what I say, mighty lord Morg? You can discern good from evil?"

It was true that he could not find deceit in his words but he did detect a new found bravery which hindered Morg sensing any other emotion other than this because of its strength within his character.

"I detect no deceit." replied Morg.

"Tell us all you know."

Jonathan Oliver continued, "They spoke of mutiny, they spoke of Pawlii and how he had become weak and they could no longer stomach his bile. They spoke as if the attack was unauthorised. As of the AS Justified, it was unclear if the whole ship was mutinous or just the marines, they transported the prisoners and wounded back to the AS Justified but the remaining dispersed into the city to join the resistance. There were names, Captain's Sullivan, Smith and Black; they deserted taking four hundred Marines with them, the rest returned to the Justified, mostly wounded or dead."

Morg stood with his back to them for a time, no one dared speak or approach him.

"Thank you, Mayor Oliver, as that will remain your title, you may return to your office in the city centre as I will have use for you in the future."

Mayor Oliver left.

He turned to Arix.

"Clean this mess up, I shall return with the Mayor, report to me tomorrow, we will counter strike."

***

This attack on the South Pier was destined to bring disaster to the residents of Askdean. The huge numbers of people by far outweighed the amount of supplies that could feasibly be airdropped or transported by land. It became obvious just how dire the situation was to become. In reality, the numbers didn't begin to factor in other variables, including weather conditions and aircraft being shot down by the resistance. To compound this further, some of deliveries were hopelessly unsuitable for the situation on the ground, one delivery dropped twenty tons of red wine and summer uniforms in the middle of an approaching bitter winter. Beyond the obvious suffering of the troops on the ground level, it took a heavy toll on the citizens. General Bear, leader of the resistance developed stress induced eczema of such a severity that she was forced to completely bandage her hands and a tic in her right eye that would eventually take hold of the entire right side her face, she was so appalled by the conditions the citizens were facing since. She and her soldiers reduced their rations to the same level as the citizens; she lost twenty six pounds in weight in two weeks. Living conditions were unimaginably terrible. Rats became a staple of most people's protein intake. Resistance and citizens alike would go around picking dead animals clean of meat; they had to strip their dead comrades of their uniform to outfit the continual stream of new draftees. The Red Skull called the slum areas 'The Calidarium', meaning the cooking pot. The war lasted four years before things changed. During that time, Gus Black grew in stature and fame, he became known as the 'Bane of Morg.' His fame as a sniper and leader of daring insurgencies into Red Skull territory became legendary. He was much more than just a sharpshooter, his improvisation of the equipment at hand was ingenious, with a photon rifle and an attached scope he could kill anyone up to two mile away, and he could even take out enemies who were taking cover behind walls. He developed the 20mm bolt for the bolt gun, which was brutally effective. He established a sniper school, his students, forty in all, went on to kill over one thousand Red Skull during the course of the war. '*The Calidarium*' was in the northern sector of the town, it had been a slum area and was never a priority for Morg, and he considered all mankind as scum, so why would he want to associate with the scum of the scum. Its tight knitted streets with many layers and countless basements and subterranean tunnels made it ideal for the resistance and perfect for ambush should the Red Skull venture near. Its geographical name Nestoria was shortened to the '*Nest*' by the local. The houses were grouped hazardously often on slopes or below floodplains, pollution was huge from fires and poor sanitation. It was located beside the city garbage dumps. The only railroad that ran through it was an industrial one which had previously transported oil, these tracks were used little now and the carriages and trains lay empty. Many became temporary barracks for resistance fighters, energy transmission lines also spanned overhead. The houses generally were small sized and mostly single-storey but houses were built on houses towering three or four houses high. They were built from concrete, corrugated iron, plastic sheets, and wood, anything people could lay their hands on, the streets narrow and often unpaved; there were few open spaces, certainly no parks. On the edge of the slum was the last remaining functional temple in the city, Hope Temple, it remained untouched because of its location. It continued in the work it had done for centuries serving the community of Nestoria every minute of every day caring for people in need with community centres, soup kitchens and charity donations providing food, shelter and housing.

***

Morg sat at his table, eating the morsels placed before him, Arix stood behind.

"We must demoralise these insurgents, we must catch these heroes and show what cowards they are. They dare not face us in open battle; they know they would be annihilated."

He paused, "What do you suggest Arix?"

Arix stood motionless.

"There is only one that carries their hope; we must cut off the head of the beast, this renegade Black. If we get him surely they will crumble."

"What of Bear, she still breathes?" asked Morg.

"She is a wreck of a leader held together with bandage and tape, she presents as an imbecile. Reports have come in from our sources that Black operates around Hope Temple of Nestoria; he still clings to his false hopes instilled in him by the elders of the Temple."

Morg finished what was on his plate, sat back, and sighed.

"Send Sandl with a platoon of troops to find out what he can, at any cost."

Arix saluted, clicked his heels and left the room. Gus and Captain Sullivan would often attend Hope Temple. Outside of Christiana, elder Alieti was one of the greatest, best and most learned of elders. After service, they would help in the soup kitchen and then spend time in conversation in the lounge of the elder's house, just across from the temple. The conversation was at times heavy but on other occasions they came within an inch of killing themselves with laughter. On this occasion they were speaking of art, discussing the works they had studied in university, which seemed such an age ago, in a different world. Gus spoke fine words and dainty phrases about the painter Hainey but both Captain Sullivan and Alieti discharged some venomous sarcasm of his work being a mere pupil of McGill, and did not come anyway near the artistry of 'The Master'. Gus continued to wax lyrical in grandiose speeches, priding himself in his apparent inexhaustible knowledge on the subject. Sullivan leant back and made hand gestures behind her back, in jest, intimating she thought him a big mouth. In the heat of the talk, suddenly someone broke wind; it was exceedingly loud and distressful in odour.

"Wow!" said Alieti.

"I haven't smelt one like that since my days in the barracks."

Alieti got up and opened the window wide.

"Was that you who laid that egg, Sullivan?" asked Gus.

"Not me that is most definitely a boy's one. A mere dainty female such as I could not possibly have delivered one that was so stately and in such bulk."

Alieti still stood at the window getting air because the stench was truly awful.

"It was certainly not me; such an unholy stench would not have come from the belly of one as holy as me."

Alieti said in jest.

Gus remained silent except for the belly laughing which all three were in the midst off.

Sullivan said, "In the great name of the Almighty, I proclaim my innocence."

She stood up, one hand in the air and the other on her heart.

"Before the sinless hosts of heaven I swear that desolating aroma, nostril clogging rottenness, foul stink from the pit itself was not formulated by me or anything human."

They both turned to Gus who was in a full fit of giggles.

"OK, OK, I did it, but I don't understand your complaint, it was so poor and frail a fart, compared with what I normally do. I was ashamed to call the weakling mine in such august company. But bear with me till I can make amends."

Gus stood up, bent over and let out such a godless blast that both screamed protests and held their noses. The smell was so dense and foul a stink that the previous seemed like roses. Gus sat back down but almost fell off his chair with laughter.

"I apologise, I don't seem to be able to do justice to my usual powers of propulsion. I can try again if you like."

Alieti waved his hands vigorously.

"No brother, no, please, no more. If you have need, please avail yourself of the indoor plumbing."

Sullivan piped up.

"I think I will though before this mustard gas suffocates me or makes me blind."

Whilst waiting for Sulivan to come back, Alieti and Gus spoke.

"So why did you volunteer for this, surely there were less traumatic ways to serve Gaelia?" asked Alieti.

Gus combed his fingers through his hair, grabbed his coffee, which had grown cold.

He drank it anyway and grimaced.

"What can I say, the Almighty sent me on this mission, the fact that it's secret, that we pretend to be rebels appeals to me, I swore when I was younger, first to my mother, to stay alive no matter what. Second, to avenge her and my siblings, when I heard of this top secret mission, I grabbed it with both hands."

Alieti passed him some buttered bread and freshened his coffee.

"Did you notice that guy in the service today?" asked Gus.

"No, which one?" asked Alieti.

"The small, stocky guy, balding head, had a grey suit!" replied Gus.

"He's just started coming round, think he is a town hall official, his name is Doge, I think, Doge Eom, I think, why?"

"Don't know, just a hunch, he looked suspicious."

Sullivan came back in, "Who looked suspicious?" she said.

Gus explained.

"Yeah, I saw him too; I'm with you on that one spent too much time looking around himself."

Sullivan sniffed, "What's that smell?"

Gus looked at Rikki.

"Enough, Rikki, we've moved on, build a bridge."

"No, seriously, it's like lemons."

"Yes, friends, sit down." said Alieti.

"We are about to get a visitor."

The light grew and from it stepped Andreas.

"Peace, friends and servants of the Almighty, I come with news, a gift and a warning. You all have found that there is a difference between living and being alive. God is kind, you have not let the crowd sweep you along heading in the wrong direction, you have chosen to fight through and step out of the crowd. Your actions bring influence but it also brings destruction, this is the path you have chosen. Today is salvation day in this home but not for all, the Almighty restores the lost and guides them to glory. Today is a day of glory but not for all. It's easy to get disoriented, confused and lost, do not hesitate, if you do you will fall but be sure before you heard of the Almighty, He knew your name. He stands at the door, He will let you in. He'll put your enemy in your hands; you can do whatever you want with him but remember it's the sick that need a doctor. It's the sinner who needs a saviour. Its judgement that makes the sinner hide from the Almighty but it's His grace and mercy that makes us run to Him."

He turned to face Gus.

"He sees the potential inside of you even when you can't see it. Fear or faith can make you do crazy things, you have chosen faith, be confident in the Almighty, not surety in your own abilities alone. Honour isn't about pride it's about recognition of faithfulness. The Almighty recognises your faithfulness and entrusts you with this dagger of Promethium."

Gus took the dagger, it seemed elegant, dignified even, but brutal, the short length meant, to be effective, the combat would have to be incredibly close and intimate, the way a Marine liked it.

Andreas continued addressing them all.

"Just because you're in a storm doesn't mean the Almighty doesn't want you there. He did not say you would have a storm free life, just a storm proof one.

The Almighty is closer than you think, focus your heart and not your eyes and it'll become clearer. Red Skull approaches the temple, they look for Gus, he is the prize Morg seeks, and go now they approach."

Alieti jumped to his window, he saw Red Skull approaching about five hundred yards away.

"I will deter them!"

He left the room and ran downstairs.

"What will we do?" said Sullivan,

"Pick a window, ready your rifle Captain, hunting season has come early."

Sullivan went to stand up but Andreas grabbed her arm.

"The Almighty will catch you when you fall; your place in glory is fixed."

This statement caught Sullivan by surprise, almost took her breath away. The light decreased and Andreas was no longer there, Sullivan grabbed her rifle and took position at the next window.

Sandl marched up the steps with twenty Red Skull; Alieti met them at the top of the stairs.

"What are your intentions in approaching this holy place? This is a place of hope." demanded Alieti.

"My master Morg has a question for you, so, listen to me Alieti and make sure of your answers if you wish this to remain a place of hope. He asks why have you ganged up against him with the insurgents, especially the dog Black, we have heard you give him bread and respite, even praying with him for the Almighty's guidance, setting him up as a hero against your liberators."

Alieti lowered his eyes.

"We give bread, respite and guidance to many; it is our service as it has been for decades at Hope Temple. I have heard of this Captain Black and heard there is none as true of heart, none more honourable either. Who has told you that I aid him?"

Sandl now stood beside Alieti, they stood toe to toe, almost nose to nose, his intention to intimidate him had not worked, Alieti stood firm.

"Morg has eyes everywhere and today his eyes were on your temple, answer my question before my patience fades!"

Alieti responded, "I may have prayed with him for the Almighty's guidance? But don't accuse me as if I have been involved in any wrongdoing, me or my temple."

Sandl was as cool in his response as Alieti; he knew a shaded truth when he heard it.

"Be sure, Alieti, with that answer you are going to die, your next answer will determine whether we include your family and your precious Hope Temple."

Suddenly, there was a shot, it was Sullivan, she had aimed for Sandl but the Red Skull next to Sandl moved in front and instantly dropped dead.

Sandl ordered his henchmen.

"Destroy the Temple and kill the elder."

Within minutes the elder was dead, another shot, this time Gus and another Red Skull down.

Sandl signalled three troopers ordering "Follow me."

He had seen the gun flash.

The rest of the squad burst into the Temple, intending to massacre all inside. The doors swung open with great force, the troops went through in details, the building was empty, unknown to them elder Alieti, ex-Sapper Marine had set a sixty second delay timer attached to six satchel charges, a demolition device, with components of plastic explosive, a carrying device such as a satchel and a triggering mechanism, this had been in his hand and triggered the moment he was shot. The satchels also contained homemade grenades, iron shrapnel and glass bottles filled with petroleum, the troops stood no chance. The explosion was immense, those closest were torn apart by the shrapnel and glass they and the next line were engulfed in a petroleum fire ball the two at the rear were thrown clear down the stairs with the explosion fortunate to survive with mild shrapnel wounds and scorch marks. The windows had blown out and smaller incendiary explosions were heard as the fire raged into the eves, as the bell tower collapsed, the whole temple gave way to the fire. The two surviving troopers stood in the debris and shrapnel and heat, disbelieving the desperation and fanatical actions of these stubborn people. Meanwhile, Sandl had taken his small detachment in the direction of the flash, towards Gus and Sullivan in that upper floor. He directed his troops as there were only two ways out, through the front door or over the rooftops. He remained with two troops facing the door whilst he directed the sniper, to watch the gap in the roof. The explosion did not even make Sandl flinch, instead he simply ordered the two surviving troopers.

"Get your wits about you, both through that door, flush out the rats."

Red Skull being extremely disciplined followed his orders without question and once again burst through a door but this time no explosion. Sullivan and Gus both realised it was time to get out of there; they heard the door being burst open.

"So, what's the plan, Gus?" asked Sullivan.

"Shoot our way out the front door, that's suicide."

"No.", said Gus.

"We go to the roof, jump the gap and keep going till we're in the alleyways of the Nest."

"Sounds like a plan, let's do it."

They moved out into the hallway of the upper floor, they could clearly hear the troopers moving towards them and up the stairs, Sullivan threw down two grenades, one explosive, one smoke, the troopers dived for cover and were again covered in debris and shrapnel. Gus and Sullivan climbed the attic stairs; they sat either side of the attic window.

Sullivan said, "Good option Gus, where now? We're trapped and they've got a big surprise for us outside the front door, we can't go through this window they'll see us."

They could hear the troopers moving again, "We've got to go Gus."

Gus spotted a hatch which looked like it led to the roof.

"There!" shouted Gus and pointed.

Sullivan saw it, they both moved together, Gus punted Sullivan through and she lent back down pulling Gus up. His feet disappeared just as the troopers smashed through the door. Sullivan looked over the edge, her head spun.

"I don't like heights Gus, and that's a good ten feet jump." said Sullivan.

"Don't be foolish." he replied, "We'll do it together, ready, 1-2-3!"

Gus ran, jumped, rolled and stood up, feet apart on the opposite roof but Sullivan hesitated.

"I can't do this Gus, you go, and I'll keep them busy."

She threw another grenade down the hatch.

"Come on Sullivan!" shouted Gus.

She stood up, screamed at the top of her lungs and ran for the gap, screaming as she leapt. Suddenly, there was a bang, the sniper had saw Gus jump and waited for the next with his crosshairs fixed and as Sullivan jumped her fate was sealed, the bolt entered her chest, through her heart and exploded through her back. In the microseconds, time slowed as Gus called her name and their eyes met, despair gripping them as she was blown sideways with the impact and fell to the ground. He looked down at her broken body; legs bent backwards and blood oozing from her wound.

"For the Almighty, glory is now yours."

He caught a glimpse of what looked like Andreas but just for a moment. Gus saw the head of the first trooper at the hatch, he let off a couple of rounds causing the trooper to fall and giving him time to cross the other roofs and into the alleyways of the Nest, as planned, but the plan hadn't worked. He knew that his plans were not always the plans of the Almighty; this war had claimed two more friends.

Chapter 11 - Guilt and Redemption

Gideon followed the instructions Christiana gave him, he continued to serve the Red Skull transporting goods by sea between the Burgh and the Kingdom's capital, Yar. The people of Yar were blissfully unaware that Gaelia and Askdean were in the throes of revolution, they were also blissfully unaware of the Rock Island internment camp just thirteen miles off their coast which held prisoners from the first incursion of the Red Skull into Gaelia, mostly from the battles of Jobo Creek and Caledon. Men and women long thought dead waiting their fate from a master who had all but forgotten them, Nefarious had more important things to deal with. Gideon often detoured via Rock Island to drop off or collect supplies; he knew its purpose but could do nothing to change it. That was about to change as he sat in the pub, 'The Scarlet Promise'. He sat as he always did, alone, he had few friends and even they were more acquaintances, he trusted none. Before him was a plate with spiced pulled pork, some uninspiring cheese, tomatoes, bread and a flagon of cider, it had been over four year since his encounter with Christiana and he again began too doubt. Had the elder tricked him with his words, just too escape, or had he simply not obeyed the Almighty, had he misunderstood the instructions and had been abandoned by Him. Guilt was a feeling that he was familiar with, he called it his 'bothered conscience.' It was a feeling of culpability for his lack of activity. He felt guilty and responsible that his inaction was causing further suffering, he saw the deeds of these cruel men and did nothing, was he condoning them. He was filled with regret and guilt, he felt ashamed, unworthy, embarrassed about his inaction. He also knew he was feeling guilty about things he was not responsible for, events which were out of his control, he knew this was also unproductive and detrimental. He had not been punished by the Red Skull but rather rewarded, as it was he who had raised the alarm, as instructed by Christiana. The Red Skull increased his contracts and business had never been better, this increased his feelings of guilt. He bit into his cheese, feeling the softness squeeze between his teeth, it really was an unimpressive cheese, no real flavour, he followed it with some crispy bread and a swig of his cider which was fresh and sparkling, the bubbles tickling his pallet and flowing down his throat. He looked over and saw a group of well-dressed men, unusual considering the 'type' of pub it was, it being small also meant he overheard most of their conversation.

"No!", said a tall, blonde skinny youth with a pimple on his nose.

"She can't meet him or thank him, his identity must remain a secret, there are many escapees he has helped and all have taken on new identities or been transported back to fight 'them' in their own countries, his secrecy it what makes it possible."

The group lowered their voices again and he could not hear for a moment, then a larger gentleman leant back on his chair.

"The last time that happened we had to meet with that blasted fool Percy Falcon to try and dissuade him, all because his imbecilic son got caught by the Red Skull, and his dull wife boasted to everyone how he had helped her son escape. Once Percy, his loyalties clear, heard what had happened, he headed for Captain Chase, the Red Skull officer he knew, with the intent of disclosing his identity, fool of a man."

He leant back in and the voices became mumbled again.

Then the skinny youth spoke.

"We lost two good men that day in the skirmish but Falcon was silenced, beware the folly of mothers gratitude."

A third man then spoke, a bit louder than needed, he was older and had hearing aids, which meant he spoke louder because he could not judge the volume.

"So why are we here discussing this in one of the dens of Red Skull?"

The skinny youth hushed the elderly gentleman, "Not so loud!"

They grouped together again, nothing but mumbles could be heard, they then sat back and all three looked at Gideon, its blatant obviousness startled him.

The skinny youth stood up and walked towards him.

"Would I be having the pleasure of addressing Captain Gideon?"

"You would!" he responded.

"Captain Gideon, born of Gaelia and owner of the merchant ship '*The Fleece*'?"

Gideon was beginning to become impatient; he did not suffer fools and did not like answering the same question twice, even though it had been asked differently.

"As stated, yes, what is your business with me?"

"Please forgive me for being obtuse, but I have to be sure I am speaking to the right man," said the youth.

"I have one more question, if I can beg your indulgence?"

Gideon nodded, the youth asked, "Does this mean anything too you, '*The Almighty is with you, O mighty man of steel, He has placed you here in the darkness so when the time is right...*"

Gideon interrupted, "*...You can shine and the darkness before you will flee.*"

The youth sat down at the table, "I see I have indeed found the right man!"

He opened his jacket revealing a letter which he pulled out and handed to Gideon, he took it, opened it and read it.

It read:

Dear Gideon,

Christiana, whom I believe you aided, has brought you to my attention. Let me introduce myself, for secrecy sake, until we meet, I can only be known to you as Black Hawk. We are a secret society who assists captives of the Red Skull escape and either rejoins the resistance or gain new identities. Our lines have been disrupted and we need new methods of distribution, our mutual friend has recommended and commended you, meet with me this night at midnight in the upper room of the 'Lady's Balcony' on Market Road.

I look forward to your attendance.

Yours in the Almighty

Black Hawk

The youth asked, "Are you finished reading?"

Gideon again nodded, the youth took the letter, struck a match, set it alight and carefully watched it burn disappearing into ash and smoke.

"This cannot be spoken of again, will you be attending?" again Gideon nodded, it was all too surreal for words.

The youth continued, "It was a pleasure speaking with you, Gideon."

He and the two others left leaving Gideon behind. Gideon finished his meal, it was after nine, so he lit his pipe and sat back waiting till the time of his appointment.

Later, he stood outside the *'Lady's Balcony'*. It was ten minutes to midnight as he walked through the door, the bar was surprisingly busy.

He saw the skinny youth and approached him.

"Good evening, Gideon, I didn't introduce myself earlier, my name is George. Room fourteen is where you'll meet him."

He climbed the stairs, the smell of the tobacco and stale beer rose, his nerves also rose as he felt the butterflies in his stomach, every squeak of the stair became prominent as he realised, at last, almost four year later, the elder's prophesy was about to become true. The guilt he felt only hours ago was replaced with elation, if redemption was a feeling, this was it.

He approached room fourteen and knocked the door; from inside he heard a voice.

"Enter."

He opened the door and entered, he saw the elderly gentleman from earlier and then as he rose from the chair a grey haired thin man. He was easily fifty, he walked towards him with the aid of a stick in his left hand, and he reached out his right hand in welcome.

Gideon took his hand.

"I think time for subterfuge is over, many know me as Black Hawk but you will know me by my real name, my name is Black, Jimmi Black. You can call me Jimmi."

**

Jonathan Oliver was sitting in his office dealing with the daily administration his office deemed necessary when Morg barged in, he had been hunting Gus Black for almost four year now but never ever got as close as that day at Hope Temple.

"Mayor Oliver, the dog Black is now in the Calidarium of Nestoria, I have been informed he will be in Hope Cafe within the hour, I need your police force to cordon the area whilst I apprehend him."

The Mayor picked up the phone and arranged it as Morg requested, once Morg left Jonathan moved to the right side of his desk, opening the drawer revealing a communication device. He had kept his promise to the resistance providing them with Intel about every move the

Red Skull made. Morg took a squad and set out to catch his bane, to end the hope of the resistance. Morg arrived in the market place which led to Hope Cafe. It was past noon and, if reports were correct, Gus and his entourage should be inside. They entered the market place like hooligans which made everyone breathe heavily in panic as they arrived. All the stalls were open, flying insects buzzing around due to the heat and time of day. There were lots of pigeons who scattered in flight, up till that point, you could hear the constant cawing of the crows but when Morg entered the square they stopped.

He stood at the edge of the left hand side of the road as people rushed away. The noises were very loud; people chattering in fear and confusion, dazed with not knowing what they should do and Red Skull copters buzzing over-head. He walked past a woman in an old yellow dress who had laid out all her vegetables on her stall, his very presence and rage within him caused them to wither as he passed. Gus, Rex and Deborah were meeting Captain Francis Smith there; they were sitting with coffee and thick chunks of buttered bread, waiting for 'Smithy'.

Deborah spoke, "Don't you ever get disheartened Gus, when is this war going to be over."

Gus replied, "No one told us this would be quick, not like other missions, just a quick forty eight hours then back to cozy barracks, we knew it would be for the long haul.",

"Ha," retorted Deborah.

"Cozy barracks!" she said with contempt.

"Maybe for you officer types, you probably had Jacuzzi's and a masseuse but us grunts had to make do with hard bunks and shared showers. Though, a warm shower would be good right now, shared or not."

She sipped her coffee and took a large bite from her bread.

"That's good butter, didn't get that either in the grunt hut!"

Rex grew easily annoyed at Deborah; she talked too much when nervous.

"Stop your bellyaching, least you had somewhere to flop back then, now were like foxes without a hole, sure gets wearying hiding and running from the zit heads all the time, but were still alive unlike so many who got off that boat the same day as us."

Rex picked up his cup.

"To all who've fallen!"

The others picked up theirs as well, "To all who've fallen!"

Deborah continued, she'd learnt to ignore Rex when he was morbid.

"You've got family Gus, right?"

She knew not to ask Rex about family.

Gus replied, "A brother and a sister, the rest are dead, they live in the Vale of Lamont."

Gus could see Rex wasn't comfortable with the subject.

"That's what keeps me going, hoping to return to a normal life.

As the Almighty has said; 'We couldn't be surer of what we saw and heard, the Almighty's glory, His voice. The prophetic Word was confirmed to us. You'll do well to keep focusing on it.

It's the one light you have in a dark time as you wait for daybreak and the rising of the Morning Star in your hearts.' That's what keeps me going."

"Amen!" responded Rex.

Just at that a communication came over the radio, it was Smithy.

"White Dove to Hope's nest, come in, over."

Deborah picked up the communicator.

"Hope's nest to White Dove, where are you, coffees getting cold, over",

"Got a message from Slack-man, Grey Wolf at door, imminent, suggest the sparrows fly with extreme haste."

Rex jumped up and looked out the window.

"By the Almighty, he's outside and by the look of it he's well supported; I can see at least a dozen Red Skull."

The cafe owner came out of the kitchen.

"Your only hope is the sewers, there's a drain in the kitchen, it's tight but you can make it."

Rex responded, "We gotta go, it's Morg himself and he's heading for the door,"

The three went into the kitchen just before Morg entered the cafe. Gus and his men were huddled far back, ready to go down the drain; Gus held them back in fear that Morg would hear the scuffle.

The cafe owner approached Morg nervously.

"What an honour Sir, do you wish refreshment?"

Morg looked at the table they had sat at, still with coffee and bread on it, he sat down.

"Give me coffee and tell me about those who were just here, where and when they left."

The cafe owner began to sweat bullets, he knew Morg could tear the information from his mind if he chose too and he could tell if he lied, his only option was to stall.

He walked to the counter.

"Let me get your coffee first and then answer your questions, my Lord." Morg had sat at a table next to the kitchen door, within reach of a skilled assassin such as Gus.

Rex whispered to him.

"Can you believe it? This is the day the Almighty was talking about when he said, *'I'll put your enemy in your hands.'*"

Gus thought, "I could just creep up."

He felt the Promethium dagger, was this destiny, a sharp jab and Morg would be dead.

Then he remembered the whole promise the Anointed had spoken, *'He'll put your enemy in your hands, you can do whatever you want with him but remember it's the sick who need a doctor, it's the sinner who needs a saviour, its judgement that makes the sinner hide from the Almighty but it's His grace and mercy that makes us run to Him.'*

He turned to Rex, "Do as I say, you and Deborah go down the drain, stealthy. They will take me, they won't kill me, I'm too big a prize, my life is in your hands, rescue me at the right time."

Rex nodded, Deborah was dumbstruck in disbelief but both followed orders. Gus took out the dagger and crept up, in one swift move he leapt and he clipped some hair from Morg's head, rolled over and stood up.

Morg reacted but then remained standing.

"I believe I'm the one you are looking for Immortal."

Morg felt his head where it had been clipped.

"It would seem you missed Black, not that any mortal weapon you have can hurt me."

Gus stood firm.

"The Almighty has stayed my hand that I should so much as raise a finger against you or you would be lying dead before me."

Morg laughed, not a joyous one but one that came from the deepest grave, it caused Gus's heart rate to slow and he felt a slow shiver run down his back.

"And how have you spared my life, maggot, for that is what you are compared to me, and no more harm can you cause me than that of a maggot."

Gus held his tongue; he wished to say so much more but knew his next response would say it all.

"I am armed with faith and a weapon which will even bring fear to your cold heart."

At this he produced the dagger, for the first time ever, a mortal saw fear in an Immortal's eyes, Morg had not felt dread for millennia but today it gripped his heart and if it were possible his heart would have stopped there and then. The only way for his existence to cease was from a Promethean blade to simply scratch him, he would not die, Immortals can't die, and he would cease to exist.

Morg stepped back; he spoke to the cafe owner who crouched in fear under the table.

"Leave now dog, while you can, this moment is only for the ears of great men and Immortals and you are none."

He took his leave and ran out the door, shouting.

"Don't shoot, don't shoot."

They didn't.

"And what now mortal, you have the weapon but no longer the advantage." dared Morg.

Gus replied, "This very day with your own eyes you have seen, that just now, the Almighty put you in my hands. My men wanted me to kill you, but I wouldn't do it. I won't lift a finger against you till the Almighty ordains. Today is not your day. Look at this, look at the dagger, you dare not even touch it in case you nick yourself and you cease to exist, I have studied in the temple, I know what it will do. I could have cut you, ended your existence but I didn't. I'm no rebel I defend my cause and yet you hunt me down to kill me like a dog. Let's decide which of us is in the right. I may die and the Almighty may avenge me, but you are in His hands, not mine and that is what grates you, No matter how far you run, your destiny is still His to decide and that is your downfall. Not mere men like me. So be assured that my hand won't touch you. The Almighty asks you now, answer if you will, He hears all; *'What does the mighty Morg think he's doing? Who do you think you're chasing? In fact it is you who is being chased! The Almighty is your judge."*

Gus paused for a breath.

"Oh, that he would look down right now, decide right now and set us all free of you!"

Morg stood for a moment in contemplation, astounded by the immortal words being spoken by this mortal man, and then said, "You wish an answer?"

Morg looked skyward, arms spread, "It is true, you've shown me grace today even after all the evil I have committed you have treated me generously but what choice do I have now, I have chosen my route, I have chosen wrongly. There is no alternative."

Morg spoke again to Gus, "The Almighty put me in your hands and you didn't kill me. Why? I cannot fathom the depth of grace and faith in men like you, I am jealous, envious of this great gift the Almighty has given you but am unable to share it, this gift of redemption. How I long to be favoured and justified but my course is set. Today you have shown me grace, I will show mine by making your death quick."

Morg called in his captain, "He has a dagger, take it and guard it with your life."

Gus handed him the dagger without a struggle and proceeded outside with his hands on his head. The Captain kicked the back of his knees and Gus fell.

"Enough!" cried Morg as he came out the cafe.

"I don't want a hair on his head touched."

Gus smiled at that, even Morg hadn't realised his irony.

***

Whilst Gus distracted Morg, Rex and Deborah escaped down the sewer and came up on the street a few houses down, as they climbed out. A rattle of bins caused Deborah to swing round ready with her bolt gun. She stopped in time, it was Captain Smith. Deborah stood to attention.

"Sorry Sir thought you were a hostile."

Smithy laughed, "It's OK marine, are you going to assist your NCO?"

Rex remained in the sewer trying to get out but found it difficult as Deborah stood in the way, she assisted.

"I have planned our escape but where is Captain Black?"

Rex explained the situation,

"Not good." expressed Smithy but quick to think.

"OK, they have to pass the intersection of Hill Street and Queen's Lane, I have insurgents in that area, and they can cause a blockade with a vehicle or two forcing them into Queens Lane. Deborah and I will position ourselves to snipe with you, Rex, on the ground, objective to free Gus, agreed."

"Yes, Sir." they both replied.

Smithy continued, "Deborah, start with the driver and then officers and NCO's working your way down, do not fire till I fire first, Rex take your opportunity when you see it."

"Yes, Sir." came the response and they sprinted off Smithy leading, launching there daring rescue mission.

***

Gus was bundled into the back of a motorised patrol unit. There was a smile on his face when he asked the trooper next to him.

"Far too warm today, I hate heat, what about you?"

The trooper shook his head with conviction and unbelief, did this guy not know what just happened.

Gus teased, "You guys are pretty tough but loyal Marines kick your butts every time."

The trooper head butted him and he fell off his seat.

The Captain called out, "Stop that, Morg said he was to be unharmed!"

Gus gathered himself, sat down him, and wiped the blood from his nose.

"I think you may have some discipline issues Captain."

The Captain did not react as he climbed on board; Gus felt the rumble of the engine starting with its grinding noises and smell of burning oil. They moved along Hustler-Gate and turned into Hill Street, as predicted by Smithy. His friends had moved quickly and the patrol found an upturned truck blocking their way, wheels still spinning and people arguing, smashed into a house wall.

A Sergeant leaped out of the patrol vehicle and guided them into Queens Lane before he went to untangle the mess ahead.

"Blast these locals."

He looked up and gained reassurance as a pair of copters flew overhead, as he approached, the man nearest waited till the trooper was at point blank range, pulled out a bolt pistol and shot him in the head, he fell dead instantly.

A second trooper, seeing what happened, dashed off the rear yelling, "Ambush, Ambush."

Smithy, positioned in a balcony, fired killing that trooper dead, Deborah fired and instantly killed the driver causing it to veer and smash into a wall. Rex, hiding in an alleyway, gulped and prayed,

"Almighty make me fast and accurate."

He already had his pistol and katana in his hands; he gathered his courage and moved.

Troopers were now out of the vehicle and firing back but in the confusion of the three shots from three directions there response was uncoordinated. Deborah killed a second and then a third with Smithy killing a fourth. Rex rushed at the vehicle, a trooper fired but missed; Rex raised his pistol and shot him in the chest. Gus stood up and bundled over the guard next to him and then elbowed the next who was just about to shoot at Rex. The first guard thrust the butt of his gun into Gus's stomach who bundled over winded. Rex was now close enough and parried the next troopers bolt gun spinning him round and sliced him down his back with his katana, yet another lunged at Rex with a knife which he blocked with his arm and brought his katana across his chest, he then caught a third behind the knee slicing the leg clear off. Gus swung his bound hands round catching his guard clear across the jaw just as Deborah shoots him, splattering blood all over Gus. Rex rushed the next, barging him to the ground, pushing the gun nozzle with his hand, misdirecting the shot killing a second trooper, knocking him down to the ground. He then swung round catching the first in the midriff. The last trooper aimed his bolt pistol at Rex's head but fell as the blast of the photon pistol, fired by Gus, felled him, piercing his armour, exploding in his chest.

Rex, covered in blood, knelt down.

"Thank you, Almighty, for today's protection."

Just at that the marines who had caused the *'traffic jam'*, Bo, Red, Kerk and Kollin joined them.

Bo cut Gus's bonds, Gus found the Captain who took his dagger, redeeming it from his possession, and Deborah and Smithy took their leave as well escaping through the narrow alleyways as more Red Skull appeared at the entrance of the lane. Gus took his newly formed squad as they burst into the busy street. A young woman ran in front of Gus, he narrowly missed her. His mind wandered to that day on the train when he noticed that pretty girl, maybe his mind was just distracted or wishing he was anywhere else but here, he remembered the young, happy woman, her hair long, curly and black, and her pretty red top. The gravity of the situation returned, knowing they were being pursued, he looked at the building to the left it was large. Busy with people coming in and out of the front door, the windows were dirty but it was too noisy and crowded. If he went that way any troopers following would be indiscriminate, everyone would be in danger, they needed somewhere spacious away from the crowds, and he led the men down the street, pushing through the crowds. The day was hot and Gus could feel the sweat forming beads on his brow. His back pack suddenly felt heavy, it was old and dirty with holes and seemed burdensome, just like this task, and suddenly he began to grudge the mission. The daily hiding, the dirt and grime and just longed to be back home in Lamont or in the temple at the Burgh where so many good memories were made. The street led to a park with a wooded area, he led his men through, coming to rest on a grassy hillock overlooking some empty buildings. He could sense in his men a range of emotion, excitement, nerves, frightened, confused, worried, frustrated but also hopeful, he could sense them because he felt them also. He could feel the pulse in his temple throbbing.

"Boom-boom, boom-boom, boom-boom."

He could feel the sweat run down his back, each drop trickling and turning cold the further it fell, and as he overcame his fear, he opened his eyes and looked down the line of men he commanded tonight. Hope drained as he looked over the hillock to see a squad of Sonder Red Skull elite heading their way, that day was not over and was yet to end in tragedy.

Chapter 12 - A Prolonged Conversation

Morg marched through the South Pier, troopers opening up before him.

He saw the destruction, Captain Arix came beside him.

"One person with a belief is equal to a force of ninety-nine with only orders, I believe if you promote a rogue and he'll sue you for damage, if you knock him down and he'll do you homage. But Arix, my friend what if he is a prince and not a rogue?"

He turned round to walk away.

"Clean up this mess and meet me at the Mayor's office. We have a mole; I know where his den is?"

Morg returned to the town hall, Jonathan Oliver had now moved to the lounge area of his office having just finished lunch.

Morg spoke.

"We need to converse, Mr. Mayor, ask your staff to bring more coffee as we have stories to tell, both of us."

Jonathan did as he was instructed and cautiously approached Morg.

"Stories, my Lord, what stories do you speak off?" asked Jonathan.

A lady entered the room with a tray of coffee and hastily left.

"*True redemption is when guilt leads to good.'* Have you heard that expression before Jonathan?"

Jonathan was about to speak when Morg placed his finger to his lips indicating he did not require an answer. Jonathan knew this was not a good sign. Morg used his first name; it felt as if he was being summoned by a teacher who used his full name only when he was in trouble, trouble more terrible than any teacher could ever give.

Morg continued.

"We all know many sayings that can be quoted like this, and they all mean the same, they suggest you must not oppose the powers that be, that to fight against superior force or meddle in matters that are above your station are futile and wrong but yet the residents of Askdean continue to resist despite myself becoming the power. The superior force, reducing them to the infidels they are, they still resist. Can you explain this?"

Again Jonathan began to speak but again Morg motioned for silence.

"I begin to understand that their traditions are more than mere romanticism, so that any undertaking I try which have been proven successful in my vast experience would seem foredoomed to frustration. My experience has shown me that men are invariably inclined to do evil. They formulate rules to restrain their desires, otherwise they shall have anarchy and anarchy is too uncomfortable for them. The Red Skull is taught to embrace anarchy, that death and glory, fire and fury are their precepts, their Niyama. They join our forces because they become weary and disillusioned by heretics and hypocrites who forever mouth dismal proverbs and demean their human nature as a repulsive action to be cast aside for some false unreachable divine nature. It is these very people, always harping on, who drive souls into my arms to pervert into the Red Skull way. They complain with excessive protests that our way is evil and pessimistic but we see it's optimism, the truth that it will all become nothing. But again and again my cynicism is not met with hypocrisy but bravery, grace and, today, mercy. So here is my question, the one you may answer. Have you been against us since the first day at South Pier making your treachery honourable, your actions heroic or have they played on your corruption and bought you with false promises. Tell me your story and don't rush, I have nowhere to go, today I received divine mercy and I wish to bask in it."

***

Jonathan realised he had been found out. He slumped in the chair, took some deep breaths and prepared to tell his story. Jonathan, unusually, felt free, as if a great weight had been lifted. He had lived in a secret world for too long, watching his words, couching his answers, and living under a fog of deceit. Now he was free to speak as, he whom he hid from could now see him clearly.

His persecutor was now his counsellor, his enemy now his empath.

Jonathan spoke.

"You are correct, I have been working with the resistance since the invasion but whether it was bravery or heroics are debatable. I have served you well as Deputy Mayor and was loyal to you and the Red Skull cause. My traditions came from the temple, I knew their precepts but although they recognised that everyone has problems and encouraged them to trust, they could not conceive that not everyone had faith, I did not; my addictions and desires overwhelmed me. The way of the Red Skull appealed to my carnal nature, the wild abandonment and disregard for the consequences or the person seemed to be freedom without responsibility. As desires become demands and you begin to lose control, vague unease becomes fear, fear becomes terror and then terror becomes shrieking hysteria. Instead of freedom you find yourself bound, not by rules, which was your fear and reason for rebellion but by guilt and a never ending, ever consuming, never satisfied thirst for more."

He paused and looked at Morg; he remained motionless but intent in his listening.

"I was a wreck of man, huddled in the corner of the cottage in fear as the noise of battle in the distance raged on South Pier, it wasn't even close. My Red Skull escort had left me, they had never respected me, and they left me for dead in their pursuit of glory. I overhead their conversation before they left, they sat in the small smoke filled room crammed with their bunk beds, one stood in the doorway with his bolt gun slung over his shoulder, his armour had some pockmarks across his back and shoulders from bolts that had glanced him in previous fights, he spoke,

'I long for the look of fear on their faces as I shoot and kill them, their faith in the Almighty does them no good that day, I watch as the life empties from their eyes.'

Then the noises of explosions came, the distinct sound of bolt gun fire, they, all four, rushed out of the room likes dogs hearing the sound of a car and wishing to go chase it.

They heard cries of, *'For the Almighty,'* their training and discipline left them, their instinct kicked in and they were filled with rage and a desire to fight.

The NCO rallied them.

'Our duty is here, shall we abandon it?' he asked.

'There is no glory in protecting filth; our calling is higher.' replied a trooper.

The NCO nodded in agreement.

'Remember your training, do not let them flank us, we shall find a unit and join them in the fray. When we open fire, we move to another spot quickly before they can shoot back.'

They disappeared out the door and I heard no more except the occasional sounds of bolt fire and explosions, I was gripped with fear for what seemed like an eternity. Suddenly, I saw a bright light, I thought my protection detail had recanted their hasty decision and returned with a vehicle to evacuate me, when suddenly a mighty man dressed in ivory robes stood before me, I fell to the ground as one who was shot, motionless, and unable to move or speak. At first, my thoughts turned to death, surely this was my judgement but these thoughts faded like wisps of smoke from a fire as heaviness covered my whole being.

The whole room lightened and suddenly tones of melody filled my ears. Like siren song promising the joy of heaven, harmonies and voices wed as in marriage to produce divine sounds that would breathe life into the dead. Impenetrable sounds, undisturbed songs a millennia in age which induce pure consent of heart. Music that could only be sung before a king, I felt myself rising as if being assisted by the arm, before me stood a sapphire coloured throne and the Almighty was sat upon it. Ancients lifted trumpets and blew, a thousand voice host accompanied by immortal instrument of golden tones.

The mighty man spoke; *'Spread out! Think big! You're going to take over the nation; you're going to resettle desolate cities. Don't be afraid, you're not going to be embarrassed. Don't hold back, you're not going to come up short. You'll forget all about the humiliations of your youth, and the indignities will fade from memory. Your redeemer is the Almighty, known throughout the whole earth. You felt abandoned, devastated with grief, but the Almighty welcomes you back, now, with enormous compassion, He's bringing you back.'*

The light faded as in a dream, and a Marine Captain stood before me, I wondered if fear had made me delusional but longed to renew that song again, to keep in tune with Heaven, to live with him, and sing endlessly in mornings light. The Marines treated me harshly but no more than I deserved and with more grace than the Red Skull had ever. A few hours later I stood before their commander. It was then my doubt left, it was then I realised that one sees clearly only with the heart, anything essential is invisible to the eye. It was clear to me that the Almighty had chosen me. I saw clearly that grace was not dependant on action but now lay before me, a test that I must pass before I could receive the fullness of His promise, I had purpose, not bravery, not heroics, purpose and it is that you strive against, it is that you cannot comprehend."

Mayor Oliver went to the cabinet and poured two glasses of red wine, as if he was passing time with a close friend instead of the scourge of Gaelia, an Immortal who could extinguish his life with a single thought or extend his death with excruciating agony. His confidence lay not in his own strength, his confidence lay in the promise the Almighty had given and not yet fulfilled.

"So," he said, "You said **WE** had stories, do you have one to share?"

Jonathan stretched out handing the glass towards Morg. Morg slowly looked up, surprised at how calm Jonathan was.

"I too have heard that eternal song that gives you glad tidings of things far better than anything imagined," he took the glass from Jonathan.

"There are gardens, where the river of life flows beneath and above. Salvation is the words of that song, salvation of mankind, salvation that removes from their breasts any hatred or sense of injury. I remember walking in those gardens of perpetual bliss where fellow Ancients entered from every gate with the salutation, *'Peace be with you, Peace! Peace!'* My portion were these gardens, beneath which the river of life flowed and on the hillside, beautiful mansions each with their own throne of dignity reserved for those who were to yet be justified by the Servant of the Almighty. It was in these groves of cool shade when Nefarious first planted the seed of doubt in my heart, he was known as Serbius then and I was called Janus. Doubt is the easy road, if I knew what I know now, faith is the strong route, strength of heart but where you get that strength is what has eluded me till now. Nefarious whispered words of sedition, words of discontent, *'Why should these justified receive the reward of our hard labour, they are to receive our consolation through grace? Every fruit of enjoyment will be theirs, they shall have whatever they call for in this lofty Paradise they were unable to climb to on their own merit.'*

He spoke of the Almighty being addled in mind after all his eternity He had become senile, he spoke of other Ancients who were discontented. He failed to mention it was he who had placed that discontent in their hearts, we rebelled, we were cast out, and we were left with one option, corrupt mankind and overthrow His kingdom from below. I have spent a millennia and found mankind was already corrupt and easily convinced of the falseness of the Almighty, until the battle of Jobo Creek when I first encountered the men of Caledon, where I encountered one particular man of steel."

***

Back in Yar, Gideon had settled in a chair by the fire, having finished supper and taken out his pipe.

"Do you mind if I smoke? It's a nasty habit I know."

"Of course," said Jimmi, "Now I can tell you my story and why I have brought you here."

Jimmi sat down, very slowly, his leg still hurting from the bolt wound he received at the battle of Jobo Creek. His bones creaked from the years of imprisonment in Rock Island; he lifted his foot, which was missing several toes from the frostbite he received swimming the icy winter sea to escape Rock Island, onto a cushioned stool to rest.

He relaxed and asked, "So you were a Caledon Volunteer I hear, fighting in the battle of Caledon."

"Yes," said Gideon, "I served in the 4th infantry under Captain Mark Strong, an inspiring man taken from us too early like so many in those times."

"I understand." said Jimmi.

"I too lost everyone; I also served under a Sergeant Strong at Jobo Creek."

Gideon stopped puffing his pipe and his eyes opened wide. "You fought at Jobo Creek?" he exclaimed.

"Yes, and it does my heart good to hear Mark survived to fight another day, he must have gained promotion and well deserved. As you are aware, following the defeat of the main Loyalist army at Yar, President Charles withdrew to gain support from Gaelia in the form of the Caledon Volunteers. He hoped to raise further militia from the Kingdom as well trying to retake Yar. He was barricaded into Regent Castle where he had been resting for several weeks from the war.

Whilst there, the Loyalist western army was defeated at the battle of Langly Forrest, another blow to morale but news of the Caledon Volunteers advancing from the north towards them raised hope once more. The President's army was scarcely adequate for the task ahead, it marched to Jobo Creek, which had a small force of Red Skull, he had hoped a small victory there would bring confidence to his troops and bloody the nose of Morg who advanced from the South, intel said he was days away."

***

Morg continued his story with Jonathan.

"As the Loyalists approached, the Red Skull withdrew and marched away as instructed. They were to appear unwilling to fight, but I have led many a campaign and know the benefit of propaganda and false intel, the President's army occupied Jobo Creek, making plans to attack the next day expecting little resistance, they had marched into a natural ambush with bog on two side and the creek on the third, unknown to them we had copters flying in carrying three battalion of troopers from Yar expecting to arrive before dawn the next day. I ordered heavy artillery to be placed on Kilman Hill, five miles away; they would barrage the creek an hour before we arrived."

***

Jimmi took a breath and a sip of his glass.

"Jobo Town was a Loyalist stronghold from the beginning, its circuit of walls was substantially repaired and strengthened and an outer ring of earthwork defences constructed. Field Marshall Byron directed operations against Red Skull General Brier. Although Brier had gained control of much of Jobo Creek, he unexpectedly withdrew, Byron, a proud, foolish and inexperienced in war had thought they had lost the stomach to fight."

***

Morg sat forward rearranging objects on the table kinetically, arranging his battle field to demonstrate his brilliant strategy.

"Byron held the crossing into the Loyalist north preventing him from being surrounded or allowing Brier to gain a foothold. So, Brier's forces stormed the crossing around 2am the previous day and attempted to scale the walls nearby. The attack was thrown back, but Brier set up a close blockade of the area."

***

Gideon asked, "Why didn't Byron press his advantage?"

Jimmi sighed, "Because he was a blustering fool, that and he became over confident. We marched in that previous afternoon with a two thousand strong force. It was a wonderful sunny afternoon as we marched into Jobo Town. I suppose we were all blustering fools. We all had this beautiful idea that it would last a few weeks at most and then we would be back home with our families, we were leading a triumphal procession for the Almighty without ever having fired a shot, we marched with heads held high as the crowds cheered and celebrated the victory we hadn't yet won. The evening was a different story, cold, wet but expectant and hopeful, and then it started."

Morg became animated as he described the scene, he enjoyed war.

"The heavy artillery fired as instructed at 5am, they did not know what hit them, we must have decimated a quarter of their forces, once the firing stopped, Brier's subordinate Colonel Michael led a determined assault on Jobo Town's outer defences with his troopers. Major Jones' forces advanced under cover of darkness and stormed the eastern suburbs at dawn, gaining control of the district outside the East-gate. They moved lighter artillery into the newly captured area and began bombarding the inner walls from close range, opening a breach."

***

Jimmi now leant forward.

"As we stood in readiness to attack, the guns fired, we could do nothing as explosion after explosion came reigning down, we hid in our dug outs knowing that we were defenceless against a direct hit. Mud and blood sprayed everywhere; we were far from the glory and shine of the parade. I lost many friends, men who had come to fight for their country, for the Almighty and died cowering, not out of cowardice but out of inability to fight against such an overwhelming force. As quickly as it started, it stopped, after such an eardrum shattering noise, the silence was quite threatening. It promised worse to come and it kept its promise, silence covered us like an unwelcome quilt on a warm evening. Then, we heard, low at first, the whir of copters, like a small hum or the beginning of tinnitus, you're not even sure at first if you are hearing it or was it just ringing in your ears after that barrage of noise you just endured. But then, you see that others can hear it too and as you look up you realise how overwhelmed you are, there were forty '*Cockroach*' class copters, they can carry up to one hundred troopers each. We all expected the sunrise, instead the skies were blackened by the flying hordes of Morg, hope drained from us only to be replaced with despair, and we were told Morg was days away but here he was."

***

Morg was now standing and gesticulating.

"I arrived! Flying on a Cockroach, have you ever flown a Roach?"

He looked directly at Jonathan.

"No!" came the reply.

"Riveting, absorbing, it will grab you, the sheer insanity as I stood at the tailgate exit ramp, I saw the last of the artillery attack, it flashed with a beauty that only man in his insatiable desire for destruction could create. From that height the beauty of war is at its purest, it becomes more than blood and guts, it becomes passion and its earnestness helps define you. The artillery stopped as we approached and the only noise we could hear was the powerful engine of the Roach just about to deliver, so vividly, the devastation of a Red Skull air attack. We strapped into our harnesses.

We wouldn't land; we would jump release and be ready for battle in a matter of minutes, immediately in the midst of the grit, grimness, and chaos of war. Nothing nails that feeling, that mood that experience with such gripping authenticity. It is then, you realise, and this is the real thing, the intense, compelling, gut wrenching reality of warfare. Courage is only a myth; it's the adrenaline rush which stimulates the fight or flight during these intensely dangerous assaults. By this time, Colonel Lansdale, loyalist commander, had already pushed the main body of Loyalists across the bridge south of us, making the resistance stiffer than we had expected. More sauce for the dish."

He smirked at this comment.

"He planned to work around behind on the eastern side, trapping us between his Loyalists and the Jobo Town garrison."

***

With his hand caressing his cane, Jimmi said, "The whir grew louder, the troopers dropped from the rear of the copters, we fired our bolt guns skyward, many we shredded as they fell, they landed dead before us but there were too many and too quick and responded with their own bolt gun fire, that day we felt the rain of fire fall upon us. They fell like minuscule meteorites, tearing armour, skin and bone, I looked to my right as I took cover and there lying beside me was Bert, my schoolboy friend. Tore apart by the shards of death, his chest tore open, his left leg missing, blood dripping from his mouth. I had touched my first dead body and it was my friend, my emotions raged, once the hail had finished we charged, crossing the bridge and advanced northwards towards the newly won Red Skull position on Hooke Heath."

***

"The battle raged for several hours." explained Morg, "Colonel Michael detached five hundred troopers from the besieging force and marched down to support me. Langdale withdrew closer to Jobo and took up a new position on open ground at the creek. The Loyalists in the city observed Michael's movements and sent out a force of around one thousand volunteers under Lieutenant Gerard to attack the rear of our column. However, Gerard could not march directly out through the eastern suburbs because of the besieging army; he had to manoeuvre around from the north. At Hooke Heath, on the fringe of the eastern suburbs, the Loyalists were attacked by my units. We pinned them down in heavy fighting, Gerard was unable either to attack Michael or support Langdale."

***

Jimmi was very emotional now.

"I gripped my bolt gun tighter, Sergeant Strong gave orders and we charged, discharging our bolt guns into nothing. In a few minutes we engaged troopers, we knelt down and opened fire, mines and hand grenades blew up in every direction. Every few minutes we would jump up and fire again pressing on and on. Now we were in the midst of the battle, we had imagined the enemy's opposition to our attack would be very different and we were overwhelmed that we were suffering so many casualties. Their artillery had done well to soften us up. The sight was pretty grotesque, heavy shells had torn huge craters in the earth, in amongst the debris there were torn bodies and limbs of soldiers, death had taken a terrible harvest here. They lay, silent, stiff, ripped apart, the landscape left an incredible impression on us, and it was from a nightmare. The air tasted sour. Our nerves were on edge for whatever might happen next, sure enough, it came. Everywhere there was confusion and death, suddenly we began to rush forward through the gaps in the wire and swarmed towards the Red Skull. Swathes of smoke covered and then revealed us; flashes of bolt gun lit it up like lightning in the clouds. These gods of war, these Red Skull, shot their lightning bolts with no fear, sun streaks gleamed in the smoke which swirled upwards, dancing around one another. Then the wind slowly carried the smoke away, revealing us in the open with no defence. I followed on behind the volunteers in front, we moved forward at the double across the ground. My pace slowed down when I came across someone. He was lying at the side of a crater, covered over with a coat, badly wounded and in the last stages of his fight with death. I spoke to him but he couldn't hear me. I knelt beside him in an agonising silence trying to give him comfort; it wasn't long before he breathed his last breath. I squeezed his hand and asked the Almighty to speed him on his way to glory. Sergeant Strong ran past.

'Let the dead bury the dead, your duty is not finished,'

I followed. A heavy bolt gun exploded rounds in rapid succession at our feet, we ran behind a wall for cover, as the bolts continued, the soldier beside me looked across, we both saw a volunteer's legs with no torso, and it had been severed in the artillery barrage. The soldier beside me finally could take no more, he was gripped in panic as he realised his own mortality, he started to scream and ran, only to be mowed down by the heavy bolt gun, which took his head clean off. Sarge directed us up the right flank as he went down the left. The bolt gun followed us and caught the legs of my companion knocking him clear off his feet, I again dove for cover, the bolt gun continued firing, the sheer force of the bolts moved his body a clear three feet backwards. The Sarge threw a grenade, destroying the bolt gun nest and then we both grabbed the volunteer dragging him to cover.

'Dress that man's wounds.' he ordered.

At that, a trooper appeared, Sarge, caught his ankles turning him round and falling him to his face, he drew his knife, driving into the base of his skull instantly killing him, a second trooper shot and he dove and rolled to the right gaining his feet and drawing an axe from his back, he rushed the trooper and shoulder barged him to the ground, bringing the axe to bear full force on his chest as he swung round like a dancer to maximise the downward force of the axe. It was with graceful but brutal precision he fought. I looked and saw more troopers advancing. I shot blindly with my blundering fighting skill, a bull in a china shop in comparison to the grace of the marine. Suddenly, in the near distance, stood the figure of evil, Morg, he was a tall being; he looked like an ancient god, perfect stance and tone of body, very solid and very quick. He mowed down two volunteers with his photon pistol and severed the head of another with his broadsword, as he turned and advanced I caught sight of his face. It had an ageless expression on a youthful face; his eyes were deep and dark. They had witnessed beauty in its utmost but evil in its most dreadful, being in his presence caused despair to creep into your soul like dampness into your bones. He was dressed in black, his face pale but his long flowing hair was purest white. He held a photon pistol in his right hand, his broadsword in his left and a long blade hidden in his boot. In wild abandon, Mark and I lunged towards him; with some kind of energy force he pushed Mark and slammed him against a wall he slumped. He walked up to the Marine raising his broadsword; I shot randomly at him with my bolt gun. They penetrated but seemed to do no harm. He turned with a look of disdain. I shot again but this time he used an unseen power to turn the bolts back on me and they shredded my leg, I collapsed onto one knee and awaited my death but I suddenly felt strength, knelt beside me was a man dressed in off-white.

The Almighty has not abandoned you, today is not your day to gain glory, peace be with you."

***

"The new recruits from Caledon fought well; it was exhilarating." exclaimed Morg.

"I stood fighting, enjoying the blood lust, a marine charged at me with his axe but I pushed him aside, as I swung my sword to plunge it into his hateful heart, bolts penetrated my back. I turned round and saw a Caledon dog, hate filled his eyes, and he shot again. I returned his hail of fire upon him and he fell before me, and then I saw someone I had not seen in a millennia, it was Andreas, an Ancient like me. A onetime close comrade and he comforted the dog. He spoke to him, what, I could not hear, he then looked at me. His eyes pierced me and for the first time I felt a stab in my heart, a sour feeling in my stomach which I had never felt before, I now know it to be guilt. Andreas left; the volunteer stood and spoke words of power, divine words.

'I walk in the right direction, the direction that leads not only to peace but to knowledge. When a man walks in the right direction, he understands more and more clearly the evil that is still left in him. When a being walks in evil he understands evil less and less. You understand sleep when you are awake, not while you are sleeping. You can understand the nature of drunkenness when you are sober, not when you are drunk. The Almighty asks you Morg, What does the mighty Morg think he's doing? Who do you think you're chasing? In fact it is you who is being chased! The Almighty is your judge."

I had never been confronted like that before, it stopped me in my tracks and today, it happened again, the same words, the same question, and the same guilt."

***

Jimmi leant back, "I did not know where I gained the strength, the words were not mine but inspired by the touch of the Ancient. I collapsed and the sky above began to spin as blackness took over me. Next I knew I was in the hospital of Rock Island with my leg badly dressed, I had been told that I nearly lost it too infection but it was saved by the doctors, I spent five year in that hell before I escaped and took on the guise of Black Hawk."

***

Morg sat back down.

"The battle was almost won, we had eliminated three quarter of that pathetic Loyalist army, Michael joined forces with me after he had deployed troopers in the lanes around the creek; others were positioned to cover the flanks. I then advanced towards Langdale, who led his infantry forward to meet our attack. My troopers poured in volleys of shot from the flanks at Langdale's advancing troopers. Badly disrupted by the bolt gun fire, the Loyalists were soon broken, they scattered, some fleeing back northward, others following Langdale himself towards Jobo. The final stage of the battle was a confused mêlée in the early evening beneath the walls of Jobo as Langdale's retreating infantry blundered into the fighting between Gerard and my troopers. More infantry were sent out from the city to cover the withdrawal of Gerard and Langdale, but they too were driven back by our triumphant Red Skull, Byron rejected all calls to surrender Jobo.

The Red Skull encircled the town and maintained a constant bombardment of artillery, under the severity of

Byron's command. The defenders repulsed attempts to take Jobo Town by storm and mounted raids of their own to harass and disrupt us. Conditions worsened as the siege continued over the next few days, with many citizens dead or dying, the mayor finally persuaded Byron to surrender. Byron was a fool, I killed him"

***

"So, Gideon," said Jimmi finally.

"Now you know my story, I shall ask you about your chore. It is time to return to Gaelia, to the Burgh then on to Caledon, can you take me, but it must be in secret!"

Gideon replied, "I was promised long ago that the Almighty had a purpose for me, I have endured the menial tasks of the Red Skull but it all has had only one direction, one goal, tonight it is revealed, you will have your transport."

***

Morg stood, two Red Skull Guards appeared.

"We have both revealed some of our inner selves today, do not fear your life as I still have purpose for you, my path, once clear has now become mired."

He turned to the Guard.

"He is not to harmed, allow him to continue his business but do not let him out of your sight."

Morg left, Jonathan continued to sit by the fire sipping his wine, as if it were any other day.

Chapter - 13 A Day of Contrasts

Gus woke in hospital from his sleep woozy and fuzzy-headed because of the pain relief.

His first thought was, "Where am I?"

The confusion and bewilderment left as he noticed familiar things all around him. He looked out at saw his favourite nurse, Melody. On his right sat Rex, Rex was speaking but he couldn't focus on anything, everything being said went straight over his head. He went in and out of consciousness several times, on one occasion, he even thought he saw Grandfather, he wondered whether he was dreaming or hallucinating. He was so doped up on meds it felt like being under a lot of pressure, like he was stuck in the bottom of a swimming pool but able to breathe. His most prominent memories were of Melody, who seemed to be always there and the feeling of exhaustion. Time moved really fast but everything felt really slow, he watched the clock on the wall.

He could hear the radio, He knew what songs were playing, but it was as if only a few lines of each song played before it went to the next one. Finally, he woke enough to engage in conversation, it was a good feeling waking up from a good rest in a warm bed. He heard Melody working beside him, he felt himself extremely attracted to her. She was close enough that he could smell her body odour, it smelt like butter that was just starting to go off. He felt her hands as she placed a cuff on his arm to take his blood pressure.

"You brighten up my day every time I see you."

Melody smiled, what girl doesn't like being told they make someone's day clear and bright, especially from someone so handsome.

"That's cheesy." she replied, "but thanks."

She smirked again at the thought she was bright and sunny, her tired face refreshed. It was sweet and lifted her spirit. The closeness of Melody excited him, he watched her as she breathed in and out, the softness of her hands, the gentleness as she placed the stethoscope on his brachial artery. Her touch was sensual too him, it felt good to have her so close, he studied her face, the curl of her eyelashes and their blackness. The deep brown eyes with green specks, the oval shape, even the wrinkles and tiredness in her eyes seemed attractive to him. He admired the sharpness of her features, her high cheek bones, her dimples; he took time to study the fullness of her lips. She bit her bottom lip as she concentrated and then licked them, too moisten them. He longed to reach out and simply stroke her face but he didn't want to startle her.

She took off the cuff.

"You're blood pressure is a little higher than usual, are you feeling OK, Captain Black, you're looking a little flushed?"

"I'm feeling great." he replied.

"In fact, never better and call me Gus."

"That's good because you have visitors who have been waiting."

"Let them wait." he grabbed her hand.

"I'd rather you visited me.", he stroked her long slender fingers with intimacy.

She didn't resist, at least for the moment.

"I can't, I've got work to do.", she insisted but still did not resist.

"Promise me you'll be back." asked Gus.

She looked down at the floor coyly.

"No promises."

She withdrew her hand and left the room. Before she left completely, she stopped at the door and looked around. She admired Gus, he was tall, muscular, she loved his bright blue eyes, and she could look into them endlessly. She had heard that men with blue eyes were kind hearted, gentle and loving. The curve of his lips was sexy, he was extremely handsome. Obviously athletic and very strong, she enjoyed his touch, she also wished to remain. She cursed the fact she had to work, she took one last look at his muscular torso and left to get the visitors.

A few minutes later, Rex and Smithy entered the room; there was suddenly an effervescent atmosphere as the comrades and friends met. An onlooker would have assumed they hadn't saw each other in an eternity, the truth was, it had only been a few days but conflict had taught them each day might be their last, the assumption of meeting someone again was never made.

The assumption that they would meet in glory was more of a reality. Every time it was a feeling off elation, as if they had found a long lost childhood friend.

"Look at you all tucked up nice in bed, you big softy. We've travelled through the pouring rain and waited for hours just for you to wake up.", said Rex.

Smithy nearly broke his neck looking backwards at Melody, admiring the shapely ankles and calves of her legs.

"Well, well, who was that little beauty? Are they all like that?"

Finally turning to face the right way round and talking to Gus.

"You leave that one alone Smithy, I got a feeling about that one, she's special."

"You keep that kind of feeling to yourself, bud. I don't want to know and if you mean a stunner as being special, she's more than special, mate." concluded Smithy.

Lieutenant Patrick entered the room.

"Much to my disapproval, you have been ordered to accompany these men; General Pawlii wishes to speak with you."

He turned to Captain Smith.

"I am telling you Captain, in my opinion, he is not fit enough to be discharged yet and I will be recording my concerns."

"Don't worry, Lieutenant, I've watched his butt for the last four years, I'll make sure he doesn't over extend himself."

The Lieutenant walked away shaking his head.

"Marines, think they're invincible!"

Rex moved to the wardrobe and took out Gus's combats.

"So guys, I've been told nothing, I know I'm in hospital but where?"

Rex shook his head.

"Been told nothing, what are you talking about, I've hardly left your side and told you the whole story. You've been sleeping for two days."

Smithy laughed that infectious kind of laugh that sparkled.

"It's probably you telling him your stories that's made him sleep as long, I know they usually send me to sleep.", he chuckled again.

Rex just looked at him straight faced; he rarely smiled let alone laughed.

"Let me tell you what our auspicious friend tried to tell you, you're back in Caledon, Gus, whilst we were in the midst of our little incident with Morg, General Pawlii was informed about your little secret, the knife."

Panic spread over Gus's face.

"The knife! Where's the knife?"

"Stop your panic!" said Rex.

"I've got it somewhere safe."

Gus breathed a sigh of relief.

Smithy continued.

"When he heard you had a weapon that could kill Morg we were extracted.

So, we're here to take you to see the General, it's apparently time sensitive and of utmost importance, you've been here nearly a week and things are changing fast."

Gus finally finished dressing although his boots were too big.

"Nothing changes in this army, the quartermaster has only two sizes: too large and too small."

The three soldiers got to their feet and left the room, as they walked up the corridor Gus heard his name, it was Melody.

"Gus, Gus, wait a minute!"

He stopped and turned round; she caught up and pushed a piece of paper in his hand.

"Just in case, call me."

She stood on her toes and stole a soft kiss from his lips.

"Don't get the wrong idea now."

Gus stood speechless, it was completely unexpected but that kiss confirmed to him that she was someone he could not continue to even breathe without, breathing became of little consequence. Melody could see he was overwhelmed, perhaps embarrassed, she became embarrassed and began to gibber in her embarrassment,

"I'm sorry, I didn't mean...I...I...sorry, it was kind of a surprise attack, sneaky you might say."

She said, in a voice breathier than she intended.

Suddenly, he reached out and grabbed her, giving her a long lingering kiss. When they stopped she giggled, blushed and skipped away.

"Smooth, man, very smooth." said Smithy cynically.

Rex joined in, still slightly in awe about what he just witnessed.

"Isn't it rude to interrupt someone mid-sentence by kissing them?"

"Apparently not." confirmed Smithy.

"Especially if you're gibbering with embarrassment, very machismo, Gus?"

"OK, guys!"

"Enough with the friendly fire, I could see she was getting tongue-tied, so I helped her out."

Smithy slapped him on the back.

"You certainly did, my boy, you certainly did. No point in hesitating when a fair maiden is in obvious distress. A positively knight in shining armour."

They all laughed and as they walked along, leaving the building and climbing into their vehicle.

***

Rex drove with Gus in the passenger seat; Smithy had jumped in the back. The rain was torrential, as they moved along, the wipers were going at double time, barely enough to see the road, the squeak and rapid movement annoyed Gus just slightly, but it wasn't that that annoyed him. Here he was, injured after serving in a hell hole for over four year, just having possibly met the love of his life and, again, the Marines have a mission, again, the Almighty is demanding his service.

He couldn't help but think,

"Haven't I sacrificed enough, isn't there someone else who could do this?"

He longed to be back in the hospital to take the chance and find out more about Melody.

To simply go on a date, like any normal person. He watched the rain running down the car side window as the rain eased into a steady pour. He saw a park with trees, and children, sheltering underneath as they had been caught in the downpour. It brought him back to reality, it reminded him of his childhood days in Caledon, when the rain was the only thing that could spoil his day, it brought him satisfaction to know that once again children could play in Caledon with no apparent Red Skull threat and he had played a part in that. A stray tear caught him unaware and ran down his cheek as he remembered his family and longed for their company too, he straightened himself up in the chair.

Rex caught his tear, "You ok, sir?"

"Yes.", he replied.

"Memories catching up, that's all."

"I understand." replied Rex.

Within a few minutes they were at HQ and all marched together to General Pawlii's office.

Both Smithy and Rex stopped at the door of the office.

"Aren't you coming in?" asked Gus.

"No, we have been instructed to bring you here and then wait to escort you back to barracks."

Smithy smiled with his usual contagious smile.

"It's all yours buddy, enjoy."

They both sat on leather armchairs positioned opposite the office precisely for that reason, waiting until you were summoned. Gus suddenly realised the gravity of the situation, gulped, took a deep breath.

Smithy spoke.

"You sure you don't need the bathroom before you go in, in case you're a while?"

He smirked.

Gus shook his head, knocked the door and entered after he heard a muffled, "Enter!"

He quickly scanned the room, there was General Pawlii at his desk, and standing beside him was Colonel Bear. She had aged and still had an intermittent tick developed in the Askdean campaign. Sitting to the right in a lounge chair was Christiana; he stood and stretched out his hand.

"Gus, it's good to see you, seems like an eternity but the Almighty has been gracious to you I hear."

He continued shaking his hand and then said, "O blast convention."

He threw his arms around him and gave him the biggest hug you can give. He was genuinely fond of Gus and thankful for all the help he had given in years past at the Burgh Temple, he knew it was Gus who saved his life that day in the square. Gus was taken completely by surprise and half- heartedly patted him on the back, his military training would not allow any more emotion than that.

"Thank you, elder; it is a pleasure to see you also, certainly one I did not expect today."

Christiana sat down again and Gus stood to attention.

"Stand at ease, Captain." said Colonel Bear.

As he did he now noticed a fourth person who sat in the corner, he could not quite see his face.

He had not noticed him till now because of the emotional response of the elder, he was an older man with a walking stick.

"Reporting as ordered General."

"Yes, Yes." said the General.

"Perhaps you should sit down, we have a lot to do today and I need to bring you up to speed as well as confirm some rumours I have heard."

Gus sat down next to Christiana, as did Colonel Bear, the General stood up and started to pace.

"OK, business first, I think you know everyone in the room except for this gentleman, for the moment we shall call him Black Hawk. You will be aware he has been our agent in Yar for many years now but has returned with important information, but that is for later."

***

Black Hawk, now known to us as Jimmi Black, was beside himself, he had thought for years that his family had all been killed in the battle of Caledon but now, he had found out he had children in Lamont he had now been told that they had identified another son, who was a hero of the siege of Askdean. When he entered the room, it was confirmed to him as he saw his father walk into that room, he was the exact double of James, his heart was pounding, he so wanted to run to him, embrace him, kiss him and when the elder did, he felt twangs of jealousy but that was replaced with pride as he realised how highly respected his son was in such high places. He could never have hoped for such honour if his life had been different. He held his emotion and impulse, he knew his time would be soon enough, he quietly prayed.

"Thank you, Father for your grace and mercy."

***

General Pawlii continued.

"Tell me about this knife?"

Gus explained, telling about the occasion with the Ancient and the incident with Morg.

"You were able to kill Morg but you chose not too!" exclaimed Pawlii,

"I had every intention to kill him but then I felt a check in my Spirit." explained Gus.

"I remembered the words of the Ancient and knew in my heart that the Almighty had a further use for Morg. What that is, I do not know but my conscience would not allow me to take his life."

Christiana interjected, "If it was a matter of conscience, we cannot condemn the man. He has proven himself time and again to be faithful in his service and has proven himself to be a good judge of circumstance. We cannot doubt his intentions were honourable, even divinely prompted."

Pawlii snorted, whether in disagreement or frustration could not be told.

"Where is the knife now?"

Gus replied, "My NCO has it in a safe place."

Pawlii continued, "Will you hand it over for our safekeeping?"

Gus paused, the silence became a little unbearable and certainly surprised the General who expected and immediate, "Yes, Sir," as was the norm.

The answer he got was even more of a shock, Gus stood up and to attention to show the General he meant no disrespect.

"No, Sir!"

The General swung round; he was not used to his troops being insubordinate.

"Explain yourself."

Gus took a deep gulp as he knew he was risking his military career.

"It was a gift from the Almighty, Sir; it was given to me for my use. I am sure if the Almighty had intended it for anyone else He would have given it to you, I don't believe I am simply a middle man, a messenger; I believe I am meant to be its keeper."

The atmosphere grew thicker, the General's face grew redder and he was about to burst upon the Captain in a tirade of anger when Christiana stood up beside Gus, placing his hand upon his shoulder to show his support.

"The Captain has a point! General, does it really affect our plans if he keeps it safe instead of us."

Christiana paused and gave him a steely look.

"Not really."

The General's face colour decreased as he began to realise the common sense being spoken.

"Sit back down, Captain Black. I have some more news and some questions. Firstly, and despite your questionable decisions, you are being given the new rank of Major as recognition of your service and bravery in the recent conflicts, congratulations."

Gus was taken completely aback, today was a day of contrasts.

"Thank you, Sir."

"Let me update you as to our present situation." interrupted Colonel Bear.

"It has become obvious that Cutler regrets the incursion into Askdean. He has seen what an error it was, which has now tipped the blunder into a catastrophe for them. Besides being an unnecessary conflict, it has served as a distraction from our activities at both Fort Lamont and, latterly, Caledon. Without yours and others sacrificial service they would have gained the extra resources and attention needed to stop our build up in arms. In this sense, the last four year of bloodshed in Askdean has proven a necessary evil that had to be endured for the greater good. We who have survived need to count ourselves blessed. Their actions made thousands of young people feel disenfranchised and eager to rebel against the agents of their fate, an insurgency was beyond inevitable. Morg made three decisions that, in fact, proved crucial. He killed elder John which created a cause, he gave his officers too much authority which resulted in the *'hunting fields'* and ordered extra troopers in support of a new counterinsurgency instead of strengthening the civil police force, which would have been accepted more readily by the general population. It was a gamble which did not pay off, Cutler opposed the surge and was sceptical of the new strategy, he recognised that Morg, a superb strategist in battle, had no experience in civil matters. However, thanks to important information brought to us by Black Hawk, we are now aware that Cutler has also withdrew his forces, including Morg, from Askdean, leaving Jonathan Oliver with civic responsibility, his motives and loyalties are unclear."

"If I may interrupt, Sir." asked Gus.

"Certainly." replied Bear.

"I can vouch for Jonathan, his Intel has saved my bacon on many an occasion including the last incident I reported to you today.

"I am aware of that Major Black."

Gus reeled back a little unsure of the new title but he continued,

"If he is still in power, it must be because they are still unaware of his involvement with us."

"Thank you, but that is just speculation. Red Skull march to Dopolis as we speak with the intention of regaining control of Fort Lamont, they perceive one final strike at what they have learnt to be the head of the dragon may end this war. We concur; this battle will decide the fate of Gaelia. We are assembling a force which will meet them in the foothills of Ravenhead and then the die will be cast, but we have one move they may not expect."

Bear paused.

"The knife! We wish you to assemble a small squad with the intent of covertly infiltrating the ranks of Red Skull higher echelons' using the gift the Almighty has given you to rid us of the scourges of both Cutler and Morg. Leaderless the Red Skull will retreat and we will claim back the Burgh, Askdean and our constitutional liberties. Do you accept this mission?"

Gus had no hesitation.

"Yes, sir!"

General Pawlii asked, "Will your conscience be a problem, Marine?"

"No Sir, not this time Sir."

Bear spoke again, "You have two days to assemble your squad and one week to complete your mission before the battle at Ravenhead is unavoidable, report back here tomorrow early evening with your squad."

Gus stood to attention.

"Yes Sir."

Gus motioned to leave but Christiana spoke.

"We're not completely done yet, son, that was just the military business, I'm here for a different reason, sit back down."

General Pawlii spoke.

"Continue to use my office, neither Colonel Bear or I need be here for this."

He indicated to Bear to leave the room which she did.

"Can I just say it has been an honour to meet you, Major Black, your reputation precedes you and I am proud to have trained, commanded and served with a true Marine such as you, may the Almighty bless you, especially today?"

Pawlii saluted and left. Gus again stood to attention and saluted, he was very confused with that last statement. He sat back down.

***

"I have one last piece of news for you, of a personal nature, of a family nature."

Immediately Gus thought of his brother and sister,

"What has happened to Billy and Sissy?"

"It's not them." confirmed Christiana.

"Jimmi, come forward."

The old man he had only known as Black Hawk, stood up and walked slowly out of the shadows.

It was good advice Christiana had given him to sit down or else he would have collapsed.

"Hello, son."

How can this be, his father was dead what cruel trick were they playing on him.

First he felt anger and rage.

"No," he said, "it can't be, you died at Jobo Creek. Why didn't you come home if you were still alive, where have you been all these years when we needed you!"

His voice was at fever pitch and rising in volume till it almost became a scream.

"Why did you abandon us? Why!"

Tears were rolling down both their faces. Jimmi feeling guilt and regret, Gus just couldn't place his emotion, it slid constantly on a scale between anger and ecstasy. He was ecstatic to see his father alive but confused at the same time.

Christiana quickly realised that emotion would not allow Jimmi to speak so began.

"Let me explain. Jimmi come and sit down, I'll help the boy understand."

Jimmi came over and sat down trying to make eye contact with Gus but Gus resisted.

"Your father was wounded at Jobo Creek but in all the chaos listed as MIA / presumed dead."

Jimmi interrupted.

"The carnage at Jobo would have made it impossible to identify everyone who had been killed."

Christiana continued, "It was Morg himself who wounded him but not before he had spoken words of inspiration, and we have just found out today, the same, the exact same words you spoke to him."

Jimmi again interrupted.

"I shivered when you were recounting your story; we seem to have a divine connection."

"Why don't you continue Jimmi, if your able." encouraged Christiana.

He did, "After being wounded, I collapsed and woke up in a Red Skull hospital; I was given special care on instruction from Morg. But once recovered, that stopped. I was sent to Rock Island, as a prisoner of war and spent five year in the most horrendous conditions. Whilst there, I got friendly with some Red Skull guards, not all were convinced of the Red Skull way. They helped me escape and become the Black Hawk helping others to escape from Rock Island and recruiting citizens of Yar to the cause.

Many had heard of the Gaelian resistance and were given hope."

Whilst listening, Gus began to calm down but his stomach was sick, his throat throbbed and ached with the crying. Through the tears he asked, "Why did you still stay away, why did you not come home?"

Jimmi broke down again, "I didn't know!"

Christiana touched his hand and finished the story.

"Gus, your father was told that his family had been killed in the air raids of Caledon, he did not know you were alive. He has lived all these years believing you were dead. We only worked it all out a few days ago, this is as much a shock to him as too you. He came to see you in hospital but you were always sleeping."

Gus's face completely changed as he looked at his father's face, it so resembled Grandfather's.

He looked at the wrinkles and the worry lines; he considered the sacrifice his father had made and the will of the Almighty in how their lives had been intertwined.

He stood up, he felt like running.

Jimmi sensed his panic and stood up as well, he grabbed his hand.

"Son, I am so proud of you and if I could change what happened, I would in the blink of an eye."

Gus took a deep breath, "What about Billy and Sissy, do they know?"

"Yes, I met them yesterday, it was a good day, I'm so proud of you all."

Gus welled up again. Knowing his family was safe was comforting, he turned to his father.

"It's just hard to accept."

"I know."

He grabbed his son and held him tight, they both, once again burst into tears.

Chapter 14 - Impulses

Gus and his father left the office after an hour. Speaking, telling stories, it was Gus who mostly spoke, his father held him by the elbows.

"I'll be in Lamont WHEN you return; I have given information," he looked at Smithy, "to this young man. Information that will allow you access to higher places within the Red Skull than you can imagine. There are many who are unhappy with Cutler, Morg and the Red Skull way. They have saw the resolve of the Gaelian's standing against evil and will help you get close enough to use the Almighty's gift, ridding us all of this evil."

Jimmi bowed his head and placed his hand on his son's shoulder.

"Guide and protect my son, you have redeemed what the locust has eaten, redeem him again, use him as you have promised."

He hugged him for one last time and walked away, as he did so Gus was filled with so many mixed emotions. He was glad his father was alive so why did he feel such ambivalence, he felt thankful but also angry and hostile. He bonded with his father and accepted what happened was outside his control. Part of a divine plan but there were so many cruel words he could have said during the conversation. He wisely chose to keep them to himself. Even though it was honestly how he felt at that moment, he recognised how destructive in the long-term it would be. Some truths are better left unspoken. Tolerating the hatred toward the man he loved would be no easy task, the ambivalence would be tolerated or hatred will win out. Through time, he hoped, the ambivalence would fade, he must preserve the love and re-direct his hostility toward Red Skull. This mission was perhaps a blessing in disguise, having an outlet for his hostility would come as a relief and wouldn't tax him as much as coping with real mixed feelings towards his father. He would face the reality of his hostile feelings on another day. This space actually came as a relief.

Both Smithy and Rex were standing to attention,

"What are your orders, Sir?"

Gus was feeling tired, emotionally drained.

"Do we have a squad for the mission?"

"Yes, Sir." replied Smithy.

"Chosen, recruited and briefing scheduled for eight hundred hours tomorrow, Sir!"

"Good!" exclaimed Gus.

"Drop the Sir nonsense and let's hit a bar, I need a drink."

"You sure that's a good idea, Gus?" asked Rex.

"We brief tomorrow and are on mission tomorrow night, we need to prepare."

Gus looked despairingly but admiringly at Rex because of his commitment and earnestness.

"You guys have been out that hellhole for a week while I've been in a hospital bed, 'resting', you prepare all you like Rex, and I need a drink!"

"I'm with you, Gus." exclaimed Smithy.

"We have lived close to death long enough let's do some living, tonight may be all we have."

The three comrades walked away together, Smithy knew exactly where to go.

***

Even when a student in the Burgh, it was rare for Gus to frequent a bar, he sat with his friends, inspecting behind the bar, stained-glass shelve with many coloured bottles.

The bartender poured liquid into his glass.

"Everything alright, buddy." he listened with a sympathetic smile.

"Yes, thanks, just day dreaming."

At end of the bar sat a pair of unattractive ladies with too much makeup and disgustingly drunk. Their continual screams and whoops were beginning to grate on Gus. He swung on his stool, in a booth opposite sat a couple, and they were getting friendly. Gus wondered if they would leave here and spend the night together, he watched for a moment as they spoke in whispers. She stroked his hair while he gently touched her knee as he took a sip of his whisky and she nibbled on the bread sticks. He realised he was intruding in a private moment. In the booth next to them sat a lonely man in a suit drinking beer, the ladies at the bar were trying to flirt with him, having failed to attract the attention of the Marines.

"How much longer do we have to stay here?" asked Rex.

"Where did you find this place Smithy? It's a dive."

"Sorry!" said Smithy.

"I was daydreaming, this isn't the end of the night, and it's just the start, besides there aren't many places like this open in the middle of the day."

Gus mused.

"It's been so long since I've done anything like this, these people, do they even know or understand what we've sacrificed? They go on living, making wrong decisions, is this why so many died to allow people to make wrong decisions? I wish I had more time."

He turned to Rex.

"Do I even have a billet for tonight?"

"You do Sir." replied Rex.

"I'll take you there right now."

"Rex you go back to barracks, you too Smithy, I'll join you both in a while."

"Good idea, Rex, you go get Gus's bunk ready but I'm staying with you buddy, at least for a while."

Smithy insisted.

Rex did as he was told as always.

Smithy turned to Gus.

"Explain it all to me? I don't quite get it?"

Smithy sat on the barstool beside Gus.

"What is going on in that head of yours?"

Gus didn't say anything at first, he just sipped his drink.

"Well?", insisted Smithy.

"I don't feel much like talking about it. Right now, all I want to do is drink till my head goes numb."

"No you don't," said Smithy, "c'mon spill it."

"It just seems all we've done, what difference has it all made. I studied philosophy at college and theology in the temple, I've led group discussions and even lectured on the meaning of life but right now it's all just words and ideas with no substance. Let me pose some questions, I would like to hear your thoughts, brother, only you can possibly understand."

"Well, Gus, this is slightly random, but I'll answer." confirmed Smithy.

"No, I apologise, I'm just moody."

He took another sip from his glass and grimaced.

"I'm here till the death mate, so hit me!"

Gus gulped.

"I know, as Marines, 'Ours is not to reason why,' but what is it within us that make us feel obligated to help others? I mean, how essential is it having a meaningful life? Look around you; these guys don't seem to feel obligated. We, you and I Smithy, have lived a moral life. We needed to, to be a part of the Marines but can you have a meaningful life whilst being immoral? Can we create our own meaning and morality or does it have to come from the Almighty? Is it just our parents, our teachers, our siblings, that teach us our moralities, our obligations? Look at these guys, they don't care about obligations or even morals, tonight they'll make choices, probably bad ones, but does that mean they won't help their neighbour tomorrow and they won't feel good about it, gain meaning? Surely, helping others, no matter what obligates you, is all that matters."

"Wow!" exclaimed Smithy.

"Where did that all come from? You do know, man that it was always you we thought had it all together. You were easy to follow because you were so certain about everything; meaning is so much more than doing stuff. It springs from community, family, being together, the difference between you and these guys, you have someone. Do you know why I joined the Marines?"

Gus sat up and paid attention.

"No, I do not, you've never said."

Smithy laughed.

"Yeah, it's all about you man, well, I had no one. Yes, I had a mum and dad but I was an only child and they were professionals, they concentrated on their career. I was sent to private school at eight, I saw my parents twice a year, boy, what I would give to swap with you. You don't help because you're obligated, you help because you care. You actually want to lighten burdens. You don't do it because you're told to, although that may be so. You do it because it helps, it make a difference. Gus, we have made a difference and tomorrow we will make history!"

He turned to face the bar and finished his beer.

"Does that answer your question?"

Gus stood up and gave Smithy a man hug.

Smithy finished, "You are not like these guys, Gus, and you are made for greatness."

"Still," replied Gus, "I need to do something spontaneous!"

Then it hit him, he indicated to the barman to bring him the phone. He reached into his pocket and pulled out the piece of paper Melody had placed in his hand and started to dial the number. It made him happy; he wanted to be impulsive and knew right now he would do anything for Melody, anything. He remembered her features, they were flawless, he felt sheer happiness of being able to know her, he felt warm inside. Now, as the number rang he felt nervous, butterflies. He may be the potential proclaimed saviour of Gaelia but he felt like a giddy teenager. Standing toe to toe with Morg, not a twitch, but phone Melody, he felt faint, seriously faint. It's not that he hadn't been in love or had a crush before, in fact it was because of this he knew this was different, it was like being slapped in the face, and this was not a crush. His whole face was one big smile, it seemed an age as the phone kept ringing and then, she picked it up.

She spoke, "Hello."

He felt a glow like someone had turned on a gas burner inside, realising there had been a big pause.

"Hi," he replied, "you said to call; I hope you've been thinking about me."

"Wow...that's weird. I was just thinking about, I'm just finished shift, how did you know? Are you stalking me?"

He found it hard to concentrate; it's difficult to be nonchalant when it feels like a truck load of little insects are fluttering around inside your stomach, causing massive waves of happiness, excitement and hope.

He continued, "I'm drinking at *'iKandy'* bar, you want to come over?"

He realised how bad an idea that was, it's a very seedy bar, did he really want to spend an evening with Melody in this place, and he regretted the invitation.

"I don't think so; it's not really my scene."

His heart dropped, he knew it was a mistake once he had said it but it picked up again when she replied.

"There's a lovely cafe just beside me called Jeffrey's, I'll meet you there?"

That moment took his breath away, it was like she had placed her warm hands around his heart, and his skin was tingling,

"That'd be great. Just try not to dress too beautiful, you may cause an accident on the road."

He stopped and cringed at the stupidity of his last statement, she giggled though.

"Stop it you big cheese ball, see you in an hour?"

He stuttered, "Looking forward to seeing you."

He hung up,

"Well!" said Smithy.

"That's me dumped."

"Yea," replied Gus, "I think I may be in love?"

Smithy whistled.

"You're sure on an emotional roller coaster today."

"Sorry mate, see you at eight hundred hours."

Gus finished his drink and left the bar.

***

Melody had put on her favourite red, flowery dress, it was still warm outside but with a little breeze, she wished she had at least brought a cardigan, the rain from earlier had stopped but it could start again at any time. She was tapping her right foot and chewing at her nails as she sat at the table, waiting on this stranger. She realised what a risk she was taking but there was something different. She felt it, she couldn't explain it, it wasn't logical, and it just felt right. Her eyes darted to the clock, he wasn't late, she said an hour and she was there twenty minutes early.

With an angry expression she sighed.

"Why can't it tick any faster?" she thought to herself.

Each moment seemed to get longer; she stood up and sorted the skirt of her dress, pulling at her sleeves as well. She sat back down and started running her hands through her hair, stealing another peek at the clock.

Only two minutes had passed.

"It must be running slow." she thought but she could hear its ticking, it was working.

She changed her train of thought; she looked out the window and watched the people go passing by. Girls wearing the latest fashion, two girls standing in a doorway probably telling tales or talking about boys, a young, good looking man passed directly in front of the window, he waved, she waved back. Across from her sat an older man, he smiled at her, a kindly smile that eased the pain in her aching heart.

"Are you alright, dear?" he asked.

She smiled back, "Yes, I'm just waiting on a friend."

"Lucky friend!" he returned to his coffee.

Gus had got a taxi from '*iKandy*' but it took him to the wrong cafe. When he asked they directed him, it was just round the corner, he walked quickly and had lost all track of time, he had no idea he was early, and he thought he might be late.

He thought, "I'll tell her I'm sorry."

He turned the corner and the first thing he saw was Melody in the cafe window.

He thought, "You don't know how lovely you are, I'm so glad I've found you but how can I tell you I need you that you set me apart."

He stepped in through the door, Melody stood up, blushing.

Gus found it endearing.

"Glad you came."

She stood up and standing on her tiptoes with her left foot slightly elevated, as some girls do, she kissed him on the cheek.

"Please sit down, do you want a drink?"

He nodded and gestured to the waitress.

"A large black coffee, please."

He sat down, popping a mint into his mouth, worried the smell of alcohol may put her off.

"I know you said it was cheesy, but in all earnestness you make me feel good every time I see you. You look very pretty. If I knew we were to dress up I'd have changed, mind you what I'm wearing is all I have at the moment."

They spoke for over an hour, falling in love is like a friendship on fire, at first you're all excited to get to know them, their life, their secrets, their dreams. You gain their trust and you want to spend every second with them, when you start to touch hands and forearms and elbows. The hour flew past, the hour seemed like minutes. Melody loved being in his presence. Gus forgot about his fugue earlier in the day and what he was faced with tomorrow, today was another existence a brief interlude from the drudgery of duty. She was his, a safe and warm and comfortable security blanket.

The afternoon was drawing to a close.

"Let's go get something to eat." suggested Gus.

"Yes, let's but if I'm honest, I can't be bothered with a fancy restaurant. I live around the corner; let's just get a carry out and a few bottles of cheap wine. I have shift tomorrow at eight so I can't be late out." suggested Melody.

Gus smiled, "Well, actually I'm the exact same, so yea, let's do that."

He looked out the window, now able to concentrate beyond Melody.

"Actually, this is close to where I used to live, it's changed a lot because they've rebuilt but my house was close, it'll be gone, though, it got bombed."

"Oh, what a shame, if you want, when we get our meal, we can trade bomb stories."

They left the cafe, Gus noticed that there were now different people sat around them, and they both had been oblivious to any changes until now. After they got their meal and wine they casually walked along the street, Melody slipped her hand into his.

"Do you mind?" she asked.

"Not in the slightest."

They walked casually along the street, with no rush.

"Just around this corner and we're here." instructed Melody.

As they turned the corner Gus dropped Melody's hand, he could not believe his eyes but standing before him was his old house, refurbished, rebuilt and now divided into professional apartments, but it was his house. Melody saw the look on his face.

"Are you alright?"

His face had drained of blood.

"This is, sorry, was my house!"

"What?" replied Melody.

"You're having me on, stop being such a torment."

"No!" insisted Gus.

"This is where I used to live, oh it's been modernised and refurbished but I lived here as a child, up till the bombing and we were all evacuated."

"That is too weird for words, are you still wanting to come in."

"Try to stop me!"

He grabbed Melody's hand and stepped at such a pace he was almost dragging her along.

Melody fumbled in her bag for the keys, Gus stood on the doorstep with excited anticipation, he remembered the time he ran in and out of these steps with his playmates, and companions.

Joyful school-days, old familiar faces flooded into his mind. Memories of laughing, jostling, and staying out till the street lights came on, all gone now but in his memory, it was on these very steps he had his first kiss, how ironic he stood here again with possibly the love of his life. The house felt like a friend and kinder friend he never had, he felt like an ingrate who had left his friend abruptly.

It stood before him ghost like, haunting his childhood memories, like a friend who he thought had died, who had left him but is now restored, like his father. Melody opened the door and suddenly, his eagerness left him, he felt a cold shiver run down his back. It suddenly felt like he was entering a catacomb, the happy memories were replaced with those standing in the rubble and knowing his brothers had lain dead underneath with his mother dying. He stepped over the threshold, the dread disappeared like a mist when he realised the interior looked nothing like he had remembered. It had been fully refurbished and converted, he allowed Melody past, she walked up the stairs to her front door, she opened it and they walked in to a small hallway and then a big open apartment.

It consisted of two rooms, a bedroom and an open area which was set up in different areas, a dining area, a living area and a kitchen. The bathroom, more like a cupboard, came off from the bedroom.

This is where it became spooky again.

The large area had been where he and his brothers slept, a wall had been knocked down to make the space bigger and the bedroom was where Cissy and mother slept.

"This was my mother's room."

"Can I go in?"

Melody replied, "It's a little messy but yes."

He slowly opened the door, you could hear the slow creak, he looked in but apart from the dimensions, nothing was familiar until he looked beyond, he gasped.

"Are you alright?" asked Melody concerned.

"The balcony is still there; can you still go out on it?"

"Of course, feel free, take your time, I'll prepare the food whilst you do, before it gets too cold."

Gus walked across the room avoiding some clothes left on the floor, opened the balcony doors and walked onto the balcony.

The nights he had spent with his grandfather and brothers sitting here watching the blitz of Caledon, the sounds and smells came flooding back, as did some of the anger at how that event had ripped the security from his life and ultimately led him here to this point. Again in this place he had known as home, a place where he felt comfortable, felt love, the memory tarnished, snatched out of his hand by the actions of the Red Skull. Melody called him, the anger eased, he was not going to let these thoughts ruin this gift he had been given. To spend an evening with a beautiful woman who obviously cared for him, in his childhood home. The Almighty does have high demands but in His unusual way he gives ointment that soothes the wound. He entered the building and back into the open area, the dusk was settling and darkness was overcoming the light. Melody had set her dining table with the food, now on plates and a couple of candles. Romantic as it was, Gus got the feeling this wasn't a special effort, and she normally ate in this way.

"Hurry and sit down, it's getting cold."

Gus sat down as Melody poured a glass of wine, there was no conversation whilst they ate, they were too hungry and the food was too good. Once finished they both topped up their glasses and sat on the sofa, Gus sat fully back with his arm across the back, Melody on its edge. It was like a dream, after spending four year in Askdean, living in a hovel, always hiding, running, fighting, eating scraps and rations. He felt like shaking himself, it did not feel real.

"So tell me all about this house then, I can't believe you lived here!"

Melody broke into his thoughts.

"We didn't own it, it was my grandfather who did, he had worked for years in the steel mill and bought it for his retirement but when my father went to fight the Red Skull at Jobo Creek and didn't return, he took us in, we were here only a few years."

Gus paused and took a sip of his wine.

"Then the blitz came."

His eyes began to well up, Melody held his knee.

"You don't have to go on if you don't want to." she reassured him.

"It was towards the end of the blitz, we thought we had survived, it was the last day of bombing in fact, and we were hit direct, my two brothers and my mother all died, in this house."

The tears were flowing now; Melody moved across and snuggled into his chest.

"It's ok, don't say any more, I understand. I've lost my father and older brother to the war as well, not both in Caledon. We two, my younger brother and I were evacuated with my Aunt to Lamont."

"Really?" asked Gus.

"You forget it's happening to hundreds of others as well, you assume it's just you that's hurting but really there must be hundreds, thousands who have been affected by this madness."

Melody pulled in closer.

"My brother and I both went to the Burgh University, I did my nursing before being transferred back to Caledon Loyal, and my brother went into the Marines, like you."

She popped her head up.

"Maybe you knew him, I haven't heard from him for over four years, I don't know where he is or even if he's alive, his name was Msipha, Captain Msipha."

"Yes.", said Gus.

"I served with him in the Seige of Askdean, I think he's still alive but he was in a different unit, he may have been extracted with us."

Melody sat bolt upright.

"Never, he won't have contacted me because I was in the Burgh the last we spoke; he won't know I'm in Caledon."

"I will find out where he is when I return to base tomorrow."

"Oh, thank you so much, I knew you would be my hero."

She grabbed his face and gave him the biggest kiss possible. The kiss quickly turned from a kiss of thanks into a kiss of passion, the explosion of emotion was inevitable with two people, each with their own emotional baggage and the elision of their life, now merging their separate paths into one. They had both reached a point where it was taken for granted that they were destined, meant to be, and designed for each other by the Almighty Himself. Before she could fathom the strangely uncomfortable feelings and position they found themselves in, Melody lost all train of thought. Previous conversations melted away, her now chaotic thoughts were overcome with desire but something warned her inside. How was she not prepared for this? Gus left her feeling utterly boneless every time he touched her. Their lips had met and locked, sweeping reality away like a tidal wave of emotion. She had promised herself she would be mild. She'd met and dated a lot of other men and had always been in control with them but Gus brought out this reckless spirit, a feeling of abandonment normally associated with youth.

He was sexy, dark, and dangerous. Raw emotion bubbled just barely suppressed below the surface, his face was impossibly handsome, and his eyes seemed to hold all worries of the world making her wanting to care for him. He was an enigma that needed solving. She had no doubt she loved him like she had never loved anyone before. At that moment she would have given him everything of herself with no guilt or self-conscience. She tried to swallow but it became difficult to breath, she did not want the kiss to end but it had too. He reached for and stroked her thigh with his left hand and then went straight for the buttons on her dress. He was like a teenager, fumbling at the tiny buttons. She could feel his hot hands through the fabric against her skin, she so wanted this to go to the full conclusion but she grabbed his wrist.

"No, Gus! It's too early, I so want this to happen but no Gus!"

Tears filled her eyes, Gus naturally, thought he had overstepped and offended her but it was frustration that brought the tears. Her body so wanted him to continue in this unexpected worship of her but her heart told her that it was wrong. It was tenderness that was required tonight, not crude, needy, greedy, passion.

Gus stood up as she moved away.

"I'm sorry, I didn't mean too..." stammered Gus.

She also stood and met his eyes, she held his hands.

"I so want this Gus, but search your own heart, we just met and I hope you feel as I do, I never want to be anywhere but with you. Let's not rush, let's not cheapen what we could have."

She could do no wrong in his eyes, he leant over she curled into his arms, she again found it difficult to breathe, speak, swallow or hear anything outside of her own heartbeat, she felt like a rabbit caught in headlights.

"I'm sorry, yes, you are right, it's too fast. Let's do something else."

She managed to swallow past the lump in her throat, she choked out.

"I'm sorry if I've led you on."

"No, you haven't, I've rushed things, misread things, and you did tell me not to get the wrong idea, remember."

He held her shoulders.

"We'll do anything else, bake cakes, read a book, watch old movies, you name it."

Her heart leapt in her chest, she was afraid she would do something stupid like say, "I love you!!!" and she did. His hand slid down her face and then his fingers tangled with a strand of her hair.

They both sat down on the sofa, his hands holding her tightly as she curled into his muscly torso, she could hear the constant beat of his heart, the rhythm acted as a lullaby and they both slept comfortable in each other's arms.

Chapter 15 - Plans Unfold

Gus woke up at 5am.

Melody had rolled over and curled up on the other side of the sofa, enough for him to extract himself, he found a notepad and pen, he wrote a note;

Dear Melody,

I can't wait to see your smile again, that one that makes my troubles disappears. It's like hearing you favourite song in an unexpected place, which cheers my heart. I couldn't stay to say goodbye and I'm sorry you have to wait but I know the day is coming when I won't have to leave. That day I'll hear you laugh again, the way that you laugh when you get silly. I can't wait to see you in my arms until the wounds so deep inside my heart are healed for good, I know that day is coming. I can't wait to dance with you again, knowing that this time it will never have to end. I can't wait to see your brother's face when he realises who's dating his sister. I have loved my evening with you, pray for me, and think of me, you don't have to ask me to do the same as you are indelibly marked in my soul.

I love you, I will be back.

Gus

He placed the note on the table in front. She stirred a little; Gus hesitated, not wanting to wake her. She settled again, he kissed her on the head and carefully left, closing the door slowly. The door went click, her subconscious registered the door closing but didn't immediately respond. Then she realised what just happened. She woke with a start, she saw the note on the table, it registered he wasn't there. She rushed to the door but he was gone, she rushed through her bedroom and onto the balcony she looked left, nothing, then right, there he was.

"Gus!" she shouted.

"Wait!"

He turned and his heart was filled with excitement. She again ran to the door and downstairs, rushing to him and throwing her arms and legs around him. They kissed again, it was the most amazing moment in his life, and no one had ever shown such unreserved, unconditional love to him before. He felt the softness of her lips which contradicted the vice grip of her arms and legs around him. It felt as if she would never let go, it was loving, romantic, passionate.

She stopped and said, "I am missing you already, do you have to go, can't you stay a little longer?" She still clung to him; he was amazed at her strength.

"I should have gone back last night, I need to get back before they send out the MP's. I left a note.

If all goes well, I'll be back in just over a week. You don't have to look out for me, I will be straight here when I am done, I love you, Melody, now I've found you I'm never giving you up."

He realised how cheesy that sounded but he didn't care, he kissed her tender lips again, holding her head with his right hand and supporting her with his left hand under her buttocks. Feeling her silky hair, catching her smell, remembering her touch and hoping it wouldn't be their final kiss.

Right now it was as if they were the only two people on the planet.

"You're going to have to let me go, if you don't you'll have to come with me."

"Can I?"

Gus laughed.

"The guys might wonder what the new growth attached to me was, might be a bit awkward."

She let go and they kissed once more, she turned away still holding his hand until the reach was too long to keep holding. He stayed watching her, admiring her, taking in every detail till she disappeared through the door of his childhood home. The home that gave him comfort, it felt like she was being looked after by an old friend.

He turned and walked away saying under his breath, "Goodbye, my love."

She ran upstairs and again to the balcony just in time to see him turn the corner. Her emotions were uncertain, she felt glad she had caught him but disappointed he had tried to leave without saying goodbye. She felt elated about him but wondered what she had done, so freely falling in love with a soldier, like her father, like her brother. The same dread she felt when they left swallowed her, the reality that she actually might never see him again hit her. She knew little of warfare but knew they were at war. He said just over a week, that's a mission, he would be fighting. Could she stand to lose another loved one to the Red Skull? Regret would be too strong a word but she began to think she had been too foolish to rush into his arms. She saw the note, opened it, read it and those doubts left her like a footprint being washed away in the sand by the constant tide. She readied herself for work, she also had a duty.

***

Gus marched into HQ, looking dishevelled but he was early enough to brush up in the officer's latrines. He found his locker which was stocked with his new uniform, Major insignia attached.

"Good old Rex knew I could count on you."

As he dressed, Smithy entered the room.

"Do I need to file a report, bud?"

"Nothing happened, we talked, we ate, and we slept."

Smithy's eyes popped wide open.

"You slept? Is that some kind of euphemism for you know what?"

Gus dropped his hands and stared at Smithy.

"No, it means we slept. We could have had sex, if that's what you mean, but we didn't. We slept."

Gus continued dressing.

"Do you remember Captain Msipha? He was part of the initial push on Askdean. Think he was in Vulcan under Major James, and then got allocated to a unit north of us.

If so do you know what happened to him and where he is now?"

Smithy chuckled, "Yea, he got extracted, you taught him at your sniper school."

"That's where I know him from!" interrupted Gus.

"As to his location, how about in the briefing room waiting for you, he's in the squad."

Gus stopped what he was doing again.

"Oh, right!"

Smithy continued, "I was told to recruit the best and he is, he's second in close combat only to Rex. His legendary status is comparable with yours."

Gus was stuck for words then glibly stated.

"Wouldn't be a good time to say I slept with his sister last night then."

Smithy's face lit up and the smile covered it from ear to ear.

"No, not a good time."

Gus continued, "Don't want to get off on a bad footing with my future brother in law."

Now Smithy was speechless.

"Yes!", said Gus emphatically.

"When we get back from this, I am going to ask Melody to marry me."

Gus smiled and finished dressing snapping his tunic downwards to smarten it.

"Close your mouth Smithy, it really isn't attractive, quite nauseating in fact."

They walked into the briefing room; he acknowledged Rex and Lulla clocking Captain Des Msipha and two others grunts he didn't know. Everyone stood to attention as Major Black walked to the front of the room and turned to face them.

"Please sit down men, Captain Smith will brief you on our mission?"

Gus sat on the front desk as Smithy started to speak.

"You have all been chosen for this mission because you have shown excellent covert skills whilst in operations at Askdean and you have served with honour. It has been explained to you that this mission had been voluntary but from here on in, your choice is nil. If you are sitting in this room you are now under orders and obligated. It goes without saying, this is confidential, only those in the highest ranks know what I'm about to share, is that clear!"

"Yes, Sir!" came the reply.

Smithy continued, "Major Black is well known to us all, the Almighty has blessed him in his actions and gifted him with a weapon which will win this war."

Rex stood producing the Promethean knife and bringing it to Gus, Smithy had heard of this knife and had often saw it as Gus carried it but he had never saw it up close and had certainly never handled it. It was silver in colour, within the blade was a very intricate pattern and had, what appeared to be, an ivory handle. The cracks and colours in the ivory complimented the swirls in the Maskeg design on the blade. Looking at it, it just looked an old knife in a brown leather sheath, the cracks and the colours in the handle contributed to the character and confirmed it was old, he could believe it was indeed a millennia in age.

"This dagger is the only weapon which can rid us of the Immortal threat; one cut from this knife will render the Immortal non-existent. We have drawn up plans to rid us of Morg and Cutler rendering the Red Skull in Gaelia leaderless. We have Red Skull leaders who will take command once they are disposed and withdraw Red Skull from Gaelia. They are not allies, they are belligerents of convenience."

Smithy held up a report and indicated to the copies in front of them.

"The documents you are about to look at will detail the proposed assassination plan that forms Operation Dead Fox. This report details the objectives, lists the locations and identifies the habits of the targets, please study carefully. Included is a map of the area of the Ravenhead and the schematics of Red Skull HQ in Dopolis, study and memorise these maps carefully. Throughout their long existence, Cutler and Morg have had various assassination attempts but they survived them all. Bombs, shootings and even poisoning, all failed. They were doomed to fail; Immortals are invulnerable to any mortal weapon. Any attempts on their lives by members of their own staff or enemies were brutally dealt with. Even if we succeed we still face capture, interrogation and execution, even by those who seek to assist us. Be aware they will not risk their position to help you, Red Skull is merciless, and it is their tradition as ours is grace. Morg and Cutler are not beyond reprisals within the civilian population as we have witnessed in Askdean and the Burgh, their weakness is their arrogance. We have been created to undertake all and any action, by way of subversion and sabotage, to provide access for Major Black to both Immortals to use this immortal weapon against them. Whether we succeed or fail, our actions over the next seven days will change the course of the war and history."

Gus stood up.

"Thank you, Captain Smith. If you have any questions refer them to the Captain. After you have read the brief, we will return here fully briefed and ready for task allocation at 1800 hours. We will be ready for operations by 2100 hours and dispatched by 2200 hours, as you will read we will be dropped five mile outside Dopolis. We have two days to infiltrate and five to complete our mission, make sure you are aware of every detail."

Gus picked up his brief and left the room with Smithy following.

"Show me my office and then bring Captain Msipha, I have news for him."

"Still don't think it's time to tell him you slept with his sister." quipped Smithy.

Gus stopped in the corridor; his face clearly showed he wasn't happy with the quip.

"No, but it might be nice to let him know she's alive and living in Caledon."

Smithy stood to attention and saluted.

"Of course, sorry Sir, right away Sir."

He escorted Gus to his office and then returned to get Captain Msipha.

***

Gus entered his office; it had a red oak door with his name and rank printed on it. He still had not fully come to terms with his promotion, it was still sinking in. He saw a cherry desk that seemed almost unnecessary, since there was no paperwork to be seen. A black leather desk chair that reclined to an obscene angle, two small angle poise table lamps, in the corner sat a coffee table and two blue soft chairs that clashed with the rest of the room. The sunlight streamed in through the window and blinds casting shadows into the corners, spilling under the desk. The deep red curtains were drawn to one side painting the far wall in sunlight, there were no pictures making the room seem blank and lacking character. He turned to hang his jacket on a hook and spotted his one and only filing cabinet, suspiciously locked and coated in dust. He then realised he had no computer console or even a telephone, only a requisition form, presumably to request such items.

There was a knock at the door.

"Enter."

The door opened and Captain Msipha entered, "You asked for me Sir?"

"Yes, please sit down."

Des sat down obviously anxious, he knew Major Black, but who didn't.

"I have some news for you Captain."

"Oh!" he replied.

"I hope not bad news."

"No.", replied Gus.

"I understand you have a sister whom you have not seen for over four years because of your service in Askdean."

Des's face changed at the mention of his sister, unsure of how to respond.

"Yes Sir, she's in the Burgh, I believe, so I have been unable to contact her."

Gus broke into a smile, he couldn't help himself.

"You are mistaken, she is in Caledon currently on shift in Caledon Loyal Hospital, and you have two hours leave from now if you wish to meet with her before we go on this mission. Ensure you are fully briefed and ready for operations by eighteen hundred hours."

Des was shocked.

"Do you understand what I have just informed you?"

"Yes Sir!" he replied.

"Well what are you waiting for; time is not on your side."

Des stood to attention and saluted.

"Thank you, Sir" and left.

Gus could not restrain his joy, leant back and laughed out loud.

He picked up the briefing he had received and read it, he quickly flicked past the first pages which had the usual blurb about 'For Your Eyes Only', confidentiality and all the regulations you'll be breaking if you share this information with unauthorised persons.

Page 3 listed the objectives;

'Objective 1: The elimination of Morg, Cutler and any high-ranking Red Skull who may be present at the attempt.

Objective 2: Derailment and destruction of Cutlers personal train by explosives; clandestine means.

Scene of operations: The most recent information available on Cutler's movements narrows down to two locations:
1. HQ in Dopolis 2. Cutlers personal train.
The Ravenhead area includes the town of Dopolis but is surrounded by mountainous valleys, there is only one way in and out, the Hofberg road.

Locations for mission: 1. Kalesh sidings 2. Red Skull HQ Dopolis.'

Gus quickly flicked to the maps at the back; he studied the town of Dopolis. He had visited it on a few occasions in his younger days to see some of the theatre it was famous for. Figure three was a more extensive map of the Ravenhead valley and surrounding mountains, memories came flooding back of the many occasions he had travelled on the train through that valley, travelling back to the Burgh after holidays in Lamont during his time at university. Suddenly like a revelation from above, he realised where he had saw Des Msipha for the first time, it had not been on South Pier or during the sniper training but it was he and that girl on the train, who had imprinted on his memory like a tattoo on his soul. It was Melody, even way back then. He twirled on his chair like a giddy teenager, his heart soared and his thoughts wandered to the last few days and the time spent with Melody. That confirmed it to him that they were destined. No matter the outcome of this mission, he was coming back for her. He noticed some fruit juice had been left on the coffee table. He moved across to the lounge chair and poured some juice. It was apple, his favourite. It was sweet, but not too sweet and not artificial sweet like some can be. Refreshing! He realised this was the first time he had drank apple juice in four years. He drank the whole glass in one go before filling the glass up again. He returned to the map, he considered Cutler's wisdom in choosing Dopolis, it was a natural fortress, and no large army could be marched down the valley quickly so afforded protection to those already bastioned there. His eyes then glanced to the opening valley of Ravenhead which merged into the Vale of Lamont. Now, that was perfect for a battle with the mountains behind preventing any rear guard action, this was no whim this had been carefully planned, he flicked back to the report.

'You will be dropped five mile outside Dopolis; you have two days to infiltrate and five to complete the mission.

Fig. 1 shows a detailed map of Dopolis.

Fig. 2 shows Dopolis station.

Fig. 3, show the Kalesh sidings, Cutler's train is currently being, serviced at the Kalesh sidings occupying the position shown in Fig. 3. Neither Cutler nor Morg will be on the train at this time but its destruction will cause sufficient distraction and delay in Dopolis to achieve our primary objective. The coaches are cleaned by Dopolis workers dressed in black overalls without distinguishing marks. We must infiltrate these workers to set explosives. As this will not be considered a high risk target, the guards will be local security whose attention could be diverted for the necessary time by our operatives.

The lighting at Kalesh sidings is described as extremely poor.

Fig.4 is a schematic, floor by floor of the HQ building.'

Possible Method of assassination:

Poison (a consideration for dispatch); the medium (now known as old lace) is tasteless and odourless, neither hard nor soft water is visibly affected by the addition of one lethal dose (2 grams to 2 pints).

Black coffee treated with old lace in the same ratio indicates no perceptible change in appearance. Nor would the addition of milk make any immediate difference in the appearance of the beverage.

Tea, with milk, treated as above shows no detectable change, but without milk it immediately becomes opalescent and in the course of an hour or so becomes quite turbid and deposits brown sediment.

Fruit such as apples and prunes, and vegetables, stewed or boiled in water containing one lethal dose of old lace, (2 grams to 2 pints of water), shows no abnormality compared with the same materials boiled in ordinary tap water. Though only insignificant quantities of old lace would be absorbed by the fruit or vegetable, the juice would be lethal.

The addition of old lace at the rate of one lethal dose to 1/2 pint of beer causes no alteration whatever in appearance.

Wines and spirits treated with old lace become turbid or cloudy at once and gradually deposit dark brown sediment.

Gus immediately dismissed the idea of poison on the Immortals as it would not kill them, which was the objective, but he did wonder if it would have any effect, if not lethal, it may slow them down. Cutler was well known as a tea addict, always with milk, meticulously, on pain of death, the milk had to be poured first into the cup. Some had in fact died by his hand because they had not poured the milk first. The report said that tea became opalescent, different colours, but that would not be noticed as it came from the teapot being poured into milk. It could be an advantage but at the very least it should be used to dispatch some of the guards or other officers who joined them for tea, bettering the odds. He paused and considered the plan whilst sipping more apple juice. He continued on in the report, skipping past the sketchy details about the Promethean knife.

The first indication of Cutler's presence in the Dopolis HQ is the Red Skull flag which is flown on such occasions from the flagpole at the car park. Amongst other view-points this flag is visible from the Bergun Road, the Cafe roof and the doctor's surgery, both in Dopolis town Centre (Fig. 1).

The second indication is the presence of the Red Skull elite Sonder Guard for Cutler's protection. They are marked with black raven on their armour.

The third indication to Cutler's presence is provided by the clientele of the Warthog tavern much frequented in the evening by members of the

Red Skull Kommando Guard, your equivalent in training and skill, they frequent here when off duty.

If all indicators are present, the plan will unfold thus; date still to be determined;

1. **Distraction 1**: Resistance disguised as cleaners, with one of our operatives in assistance, will sabotage Cutler's train in Kalesh sidings at 0945 hours distracting a large part of the Kommando Guard reducing possibility of detection in Dopolis.

2. **Distraction 2:** Cutler has developed a habit of a daily walk to the teahouse in Fig.2. Cutler is reported to set out for the tea house between 0900 and 0915 hours following the route marked in Fig.2. He walks alone. Cutler is under observation throughout his walk by the Sonder Guard which follows him at a discreet distance. He returns at between 0945 and 1000. The approach will be as in Fig.2 through the woods to the wire fence near the point at which the concrete bypass cuts the route followed by Cutler in his walk. The operatives should be in position, between this point and the teahouse, not earlier than 0940 hours, to give the dog patrol time to have passed. The position taken up should be within 100-200 yards of the route, as he returns one operative will attempt to shoot Cutler. They will fail, and then they will assist the second operative in the next distraction.

3. **Distraction 3:** Morg is expected by car from his billet when he returns to meet Cutler at 1015 hours, we will attack his car. This attack will be made from the previous two operatives firing a Bazooka from the woods. These operatives will not take up position until after the explosion at Kalesh; this would avoid the risk of detection by any patrols in the neighbourhood whose attention will be drawn in the opposite direction. This attempt will also fail.

4. **Assassinations:** A second car will appear taking Morg away safely to his meeting with Cutler, this car will be driven by one of our operatives, with two guards on motorcycles, also our operatives, and they will accompany Morg to the briefing room, as is custom and make opportunity to dispatch Morg, Cutler and any other officers.

5. **NB**: The explosion and the sniper's attempts are a diversion, we know Cutler and Morg can't be killed by explosives and bolts, this will only make them over confident as having two supposed attempts on their lives fail they will not assume a third. The Sonder Guard will be sent for post haste following the sniper's attempt and a fourth distraction by the external operatives should be considered to allow the internal operatives as much time as required.

6. **Escape:** operative from Kalesh distraction will obtain a vehicle for extraction for those who remain alive and be available in Dopolis town square by no later than 1100 hours.

Notes:

- **Weapon and equipment:** bolt pistols or guns (depending on rank), sniper's rifle with telescopic sight (sniper only), explosive bolts in magazine, wire-cutters, grenades carried for close protection and assistance in making getaway.
- **Disguise:** Kommando Guard uniform, Dopolis workers overalls (obtained at mission site).
- **Vehicles:** Staff car with Sonder Guard insignia, two motor cycles, troop carrier (preferably armoured) for extraction purposes, (all to be obtained at mission site).

The report continued for a further twenty pages listing the careers of the seven men chosen for this mission, including the grunts he didn't know, Sergeant Ethan Girvan and Corporal Campbell 'CJ' Jay. These were followed by portfolios of Cutler, Morg and two other chiefs of staff. The day had worn on it was now three in the afternoon, he looked out of his window. He realised he actually had a decent office. The HQ sat on a hill so gave him a good view. The first thing he noticed was a busy road with a large park opposite, and the fire station just behind the park. The sky was grey and promised rain. To the right he saw the main courtyard which lead to the entrance it had a big Neem tree, working with Billy in the garden centre had left him knowledgable in plant life. His mind wandered to them, his father, Billy and Cissy. He regretted his feelings from yesterday and wished he had more time to see them, spend one more evening with his family but it was an impossible hope, the feelings of anger which almost became hate were now washing away with wave after wave of emotion, sympathy, empathy, regret but most of all love.

Tears began again to fall. "Get a grip man!" he said to himself.

"You've cried enough for just now, leave the tears for when they will matter."

He distracted himself by looking to his left, the airbase, where they would be in less than seven hours, was barely visible, around three miles away. He heard a dog barking and turned to see it digging in the ground next to the Neem tree, the owner, embarrassed, grabbed the dog and dragged it away, still barking.

Someone drove past with a brand new all- terrain vehicle, "I got to get one of those, if my life ever turns normal."

He now dreamed of his possible life with Melody, big house, big car, two point four children, Major and Mrs.Black.

"O Lord, I have given myself to you willingly and all those years ago in the temple, I gladly vowed, anything for your glory. That has not changed but surely you are not cruel to bring someone so beautiful into my life to harshly wrench her away. I serve you and I continue to serve you, but I can't help but feel that I deserve this. Forgive me if I am being sinful to desire such things but let me return safe to my beloved so as I can live in peace. Make my hands swift, my heart true and my mind sound, may your arms protect me once more, may they protect us all."

He looked again at the square the rose bushes, intricate paving and walls but what caught his heart and pulled at it were the new recruits. All smartly dressed, all eager to march to victory and rid this world of the evil Red Skull, in the middle he saw the big tree, he concluded his prayer.

"Let me request success for our mission that we may avoid the nightmare of battle for these young men and women, let my success mean they need never face what so many have faced before.

Let our sacrifice mean they need never have too again. As the Neem tree stands tall with its boughs shading those who shelter under it from sun and rain, let our deeds stand tall to protect future generations from what we have had to endure. Bless you, Holy and Almighty one."

He took his cup and realised he had drunk all his apple juice.

"I think it's time to go to the mess hall."

Chapter 16 - Dark Deeds

The next day, Cutler was sitting in the Klause Cafe in the town of Dopolis, sipping tea and admiring the view, as was his habit. The mountains were spectacular, the air was crisp, he enjoyed this quiet time he had reserved for himself, and he sipped his tea again. He enjoyed many types of teas; he was particularly fond of stronger tea, where the milk tempers the strong flavour. He had found that the lighter the tea the less likely it was that it needed milk and he liked it with milk. He avoided green, white and yellow teas as well as aromatic and floral teas; it wasn't tea if you have to drink it without milk. He did not care for the so called delicate flavour, these light teas are so easily overwhelmed by the milk, and he wanted to taste its strength. Cutler was surprising in appearance, tall as Immortals are, but his facial features resembled a teenage boy's. His eyes were piercing blue and would seem to be innocent if you were unaware of his history. They were eyes you could trust but it was his heart that was rotten, compassion was nothing more than a word and a weakness. Where Morg was a genius strategist in battle Cutler was incomparable in political tactics, he had not been fooled by Pawlii's misdirection, he had engineered it to the climax it was now. He knew about the build-up of arms, he had sent Morg to Askdean to distract him, like sending a dog after a ball. He would have insisted in declaring all-out war too early, this approaching battle would finally rid him of the Gaelian resistance, fighting in open combat gave him the irrepressible advantage, instead of street fighting which Morg had been lured into in both Askdean and Caledon. He had drawn the weasel from their holes. He had been sent by Nefarious to penetrate and destroy the resistance in Gaelia and carried out his task with unmatched brutality; he knew this strategy was a long term one. The mark of his success was in the fact that Pawlii believed he had made these events occur, that he had hidden his actions, when all along, Cutler had simply allowed them. The cafe owner's cat entered the room and sat on his lap, he caressed the cat, anyone looking at him right now, could not imagine that he could be evil. They could not imagine that he was a master of torture, sadistic in every way. Stories from survivors told of people being dragged by the hair out of houses, beatings and punchings, these were the milder stories. One survivor spoke of nearly being drowned in a bathtub, she was hung up by hand cuffs with spikes inside them and beaten with a rubber bar, then put into a tub filled with freezing water, her legs were tied to a bar across the tub and Cutler yanked a chain attached to the bar to pull and hold her underwater until he released it. Others spoke of being laid flat on a chair and struck on the back with a spiked ball attached to a chain, breaking vertebrae. He sat drinking milky tea, caressing a cat, with the face of innocence but he was a monster. He was savage, it was unimaginable, a dedicated sadist, responsible for many individual atrocities, including the capture and deportation to Rock Island of thousands of prisoners of war and resistance fighters, many never seen again. If Nefarious had such a thing, Cutler was his favourite; he was awarded, by Nefarious, many citations and medals for his methods and results. He was nicknamed the '*Butcher*', responsible for the torture and death of thousands of people. He finished his tea, placed the cat on the floor and walked back slowly to his HQ to start his day's work. This included the continued interrogation of the mayor of Dopolis, John Marley. The cafe had a path which led to his HQ, formerly the town hall; it also led to a concrete bypass and then into a dense, heavily wooded area. He enjoyed his walk; it was peaceful in that part of the woodland. The outskirt of the wood was surrounded by shrubs and many different plants and greenery. As he walked further into the wood, he felt alone and surrounded by nature, he never ever felt alone except for here and he enjoyed it. It was green, deep, dark but with light filtering through the top branches, smelling the composting leaves, crackling branches as he walked through. Branches touching above as he walked below them, hidden wonders, green meadows hidden in the folds of the forest, the earthy smell of life and death brought pleasure to his senses. Every time it felt like a brand new start, giving him a feeling of lightness before he began his dark deeds. He stopped at the edge of the woods before he walked the final two hundred yards into the HQ. He closed his eyes, listened to the bird song, the rustle of the leaves, and the wind on his face, it reminded of, in a small way of the gardens of grace which he enjoyed millennia ago. He stood, gleaning as much from the moment as he could. Morg was still detained with the main force of the 4th Army at Ravenhead, he was not due to return until the day after next, and he had no need to rush so he walked slowly. He entered the front door and heading straight to the detention centre in the basement, the guard saluted and opened the first security gate by placing his palm on the sensor panel, it swung open and Cutler walked in. On his left were two detainees hung upside-down. In their interrogation they had been deprived of air, kicked, whipped, beaten, given electric shocks, all in the name of gaining intel. There were forty two people detained in cage type cells receiving routine and systematic torture at the hands of their interrogator Cutler. All were accused of aiding and abetting terrorism, many were forced to sign false confessions, allowing and justifying Cutler's actions. He passed another cell which had one detainee being mocked and then kicked. He stood to watch as the interrogator placed a plastic bag over the detainees head, he struggled as his air supply was stopped; he held it for over two minutes and took it off just before he passed out. The tormentor zapped him with a taser prod to bring him back to his senses and continued his questions. Many methods of coercion were used including whipping detainees with heavy cables, pulling out fingernails and toenails, burning with acid and cigarettes, and smashing teeth. There was, of course mental torture, with threats against wives, mothers, sisters, or daughters, the interrogation sessions usually lasted three or four hours and occurred every other day, not to relieve the interrogated but the interrogators. Torture was tiring, emotionally and physically, it did allow the interrogated time to heal, think, regret, and fear what may be next. Detainees had no access to their families or legal counsel; they were not issued any official documents, only dragged from houses, usually at night. A judge heard cases in the council chambers, one floor above the torture chambers, to pretend due process had been carried out but all were convicted with no evidence or jury, only corrupted witnesses. Cutler continued to walk down the hall. He opened a secure cell door with another palm scanner. The smell of sweat, blood and decay wafted into his nostrils, the room had been in darkness but lights came on as the thick security door swung open. Inside lay John Marley, lying on what looked like a mortuary table. He was not dead but had been mercilessly tortured by Cutler and his men. Cutler had used all his favourites, hot needles, fingers between the hinges of a door and repeatedly slammed until the knuckles broke. Screw levered handcuffs which tightened until they bit through his flesh and broke through the bones of the wrists. He would not talk. He was whipped, he was beaten until his face was an unrecognisable pulp and only a mute rattle came out of his swollen lips. He lay on the table unconscious, his eyes dug in as though they had been punched through his head. An ugly blue wound scarred his temple. John Marley had been unconscious for days. He was now used as an example to new interns who were shown what could happen to them if they did not cooperate. He walked up to John's unconscious form sprawled on the table. His face was yellow; his breathing heavy, he was now beyond gaining Intel by physical torment but Marley had been a close companion of Pawlii, collaborating, providing passage for supplies and troops through his narrow valley. He knew facts, strengths and perhaps strategies. Physical torture had harvested nothing useable, he would search his mind and rip it apart, if necessary, to gain the info he needed. Cutler pulled a stool next to his head and began. He closed his eyes and stepped into his mind, it was like a large room with many sections partitioned by heavy green felt curtain. He walked and swept the first curtain aside. It was a memory of his first day in the detention centre. The interrogators had tied his arms behind his back and blindfolded him before they hung him upside down and beat him. They suffocated him with a bag until he passed out and woke him with an electric shock. He swept aside the next curtain, it was ten days later and he was enduring a horrific beating. He had severe leg injuries and had lost several front teeth. The guard circled him like a vulture shouting threats against his family if he did not cooperate. He swept back the third curtain, finally, he was getting deeper, and it was a childhood memory. He was in a small suburb. All the houses were on stilts, made from wood and outside toilets. Children were playing, Cutler took a moment to enjoy the children's joy, he felt the breeze, and it was a sea breeze. The house was located a few hundred meters away from the seaside. He moved aside a fourth curtain, this memory was of a family outing, they were crammed into a car and all piled out of the car, there were trees, the smell of something was strong in the air, he could not decide what. They played football as a lady set out the food and they all descended on the food like locusts. The smell was clear now; it was bar-b-q. Cutler sat, observing the actions for a while until he grew tired of observing, so moved on through the fifth curtain. This pleased him; it was Marley and Pawlii drinking coffee in, of all places, the Klause Cafe. They finished and walked up the path towards the woods and the town hall, they stopped at the concrete bypass, leaning on a metal rail. Cutler only heard some of the conversation, he heard the words, *'Black Hawk'* and listened intently but no identification was given. He heard *'assassination'* and *'Captain Black'*, Morg had spoken of this man who caused them so much grief. He heard *'Promethean dagger'*, these words made him catch his breath. Morg had spoken of this but did not take any credence to his story, Morg was prone to exaggerations. Now dread filled his heart, he heard, *'Welcome Cutler, make him comfortable so as he drops his guard.'* Cutler guessed Marley regretted this advice now, he grew tired, and this prancing through people's memories tired him. He had enough information to comfortably assume the fool Pawlii meant to try an assassination of himself here in Dopolis. But who would be foolish enough to face an Immortal with nothing more than a dagger. Well, if Morg's story is true, this Captain Black perhaps but that was ludicrous, still he will make precautions. If it was to be made it must surely be in the next few days before battle at Ravenhead. He closed his eyes in the memory and opened them again in the real world. He stood up, left the room, closing the strong door and plunging it into darkness again.

"It must be time for tea."

He walked through the hellish halls, ignoring the rancid smells and screams. He went upstairs towards his office. He reached the ground floor passing through the entrance hall as before but this time he climbed the oval staircase. At the top of the stair, he faced the round drawing room which he had commandeered as his office. The views were clear. He could see the whole town from these windows which opened up onto a classical balcony.

He picked up the phone and called the kitchen.

"Tea and lunch, Tagliatelle al Salmone Affumicato with a pot of Yunnan tea."

He hung up and stepped through to the balcony, the sun was at its fullest, he heard children playing in the distance, birds singing and again stopped to appreciate the breeze in his face. He turned and walked back into the office at a knock on the door. His secretary entered, she had white skin, snow white, petite, only five foot two, thin, weighing ninety nine pounds, naturally pale blonde hair which was long and straight, big green eyes with a gold ring, not unattractive but not desirable in what would be considered the norm.

"I have letters you need to read and sign, you have a war council at 1pm and your lunch has arrived, oh, we need a new maid, shall I interview or shall you be doing it."

Cutler was slightly annoyed by trivial matters.

"I have no time for such matters."

He signed the letters, a maid entered with a trolley and his lunch; it was set out on the table.

He sat and waited on the maid pouring his tea. Her hand shook as she poured the milk first and then the tea, not that Cutler noticed her nerves. He had '*dispensed*' the last maid because she hadn't.

She backed off leaving Cutler to his lunch, he took his first bite, he enjoyed its full bodied and slightly peppery taste, and he sipped his tea, enjoying its light maple sweetness.

All was right again. He had his milky, strong tea.

***

Morg had been recalled from Askdean with his army, now waiting to head off to Dopolis to discuss with Cutler the battle plans for the massive army at the head of the Ravenhead valley. He had inspected his troops and now sat at a campfire with four Red Skull commanders. His thoughts turned to that day in Askdean when his bane, Gus Black, had shown him mercy. A concept he knew but had never practised or experienced, Arix, sitting beside him saw the expression on his face.

"Are you alright, lord?"

Morg spoke with no emotion.

"You realise, as an Immortal you will not receive redemption from the Almighty no matter how much you sacrifice because your responsibility was great and that makes your fall even greater. You are then left with only one option, you give yourself over to the dark side and vainly hope the Almighty has lied, that his truth can be changed, otherwise all your actions become vanity, hedonistic and ultimately meaningless."

Arix responded, "Our cause is glorious, our redemption is built on the blood of those we send to glory."

Morg smirked.

"Faithful Arix, you have no doubt, but let me ask you a question? Consider it a test. What if Nefarious is wrong? No doubt you ask, is that a question to which human beings can even give an answer with any certainty."

"But surely even to contemplate this is blasphemy, lord?" exclaimed Arix.

The other commanders slept unaware of the conversation except Sandl who now sat bolt up surprised at the way the conversation was heading, he was a thin faced and contrived man.

"But as my Lord has said, as a test, surely a reasonable and traditional guess, based on your own experiences of going wrong, can be offered."

He was not interested in an answer. He only sought opportunity to make Arix look foolish.

Morg recognised this and stopped the conversation.

"Let me answer for you, Arix, to save tarnishing your reputation, and Sandl, there are no enemies here in your brethren except for your own self-loathing within, not every conversation is an opportunity to advance yourself."

Morg rose to his full height, he turned and took a step towards the cliff top, taking in the full splendour of the valley before him.

"From the moment you realise you have a self, there is a possibility of putting yourself first, we Immortals, even Nefarious can be selfish, wanting to be the centre, wanting to be the Almighty, in fact. If we are wrong what we call glory is in fact sin. Is this our sin, to be dissatisfied with the course the Almighty set before us, if so, then that is the sin we taught the human race? Some people think the weakness of mankind has something to do with sex, but that is a mistake. What we put into the heads of your forefathers was the idea that they could be like gods. They could set up on their own as if they had created themselves, be their own masters and invent some sort of happiness for themselves outside of the Almighty's plans. We never even suggested it may be a hopeless attempt and maybe we were just part of His ultimate course of action to bring all who faithfully, with free will, follow Him to redemption. Nearly all that we call human history, love of money, circles of poverty, blind ambition, merciless war, demeaning prostitution, divisive class systems, empires made of dust, the ugliness of slavery. This is the long terrible story of mankind trying to fulfil the lie we fed your forefathers. That something other than the Almighty will make him happy."

Sandl now stood up, a much less impressive man, only five feet, skin and bone, the uniform hung on him like a damp cloth.

"Your words are disturbing, Morg, I take hope in the fact you did state that this was a test so I stand firm and confess my continued faith in the cause of Nefarious."

These words would have sounded brave and honourable if said by anyone else, someone like Arix but from Sandl it just sounded contrived, seedy and insipid.

Morg turned and looked him straight in his eyes.

"It is good to look for help in that which is stronger than yourself. You can't change your regrets they will always be there but if we learn from them and use them to improve our next actions, our next decisions. On a battlefield, there are two types of men, dead ones and those about to die and when a man is about to die he either calls out to the Almighty or his mother. Which will you cry for Sandl?"

Sandl became very uneasy. Arix was just confused, was Morg becoming insane.

Morg continued, "Most people who are called heroes don't think they are, they are just people who do what they have to do, doing the best that they can do it, whereas we have made choices, wrong choices. You think you are the righteous ones but two wrongs don't make a right but sometimes it feels right. We have sent many innocent and guilty to Glory, the innocent, peace of mind is there reward for the treacherous their reward is set."

Morg's tone changed from an emotionless droll to an impassioned plea aimed at Arix,

"Have you never wondered, if the Almighty is almighty why does He not land in this enemy occupied world, oh,

His faithful say his Servant will one day. But I wonder whether people who ask the Almighty to interfere openly realise what it will be like. When He does, it will be the end of the world. When the author and finisher of this creation steps into our existence, choice will be removed, what good is there of choosing your side then, when all that is temporary melts away like a dream and something else that even the faithful have never conceived, comes crashing in; something so marvellous and beautiful but at the same time so terrible that joy or terror will be your only choice and that already predetermined by your actions in this world. But why does He delay? Is it that He is not strong enough? What foolishness if you think that, mark my words, He is going to land in force; even Nefarious does not know when. But why is He delaying? He wants to give you the chance of joining His side freely. We would not think much of anyone who waited till the war was won before they pledged their allegiance, have no doubt my faithful Arix, the Almighty will invade. It will be something so overwhelming that it will strike either love or horror into everything in creation. It will be too late then to choose your side. That will not be the time for choosing: it will be the time when we discover which side we really have chosen, then we will discover whether we are wrong."

Morg's face turned into stone, he stood with his feet apart, flicking his coat over to reveal his photon pistol. He let his tin cup fall over the fire. It clattered and the two sleeping commanders woke, startled. They were confused as they saw Morg standing over them with pistol ready.

Morg spoke, "Whether you realise it or not. Now, today, this moment, is our chance to choose the right side. Some of you sleep when the truth is revealed because you are oblivious to it, even when it is shown clearly."

Morg looked straight at Sandl, "Some have no concern for the truth, only for their own needs, whilst others, Arix, remain faithful to the end. The Almighty is holding back but it will not last for ever. Today, you choose, take it or leave it."

Sandl, ever the opportunist, drew his pistol in vain hope. Morg already had his drawn before it fully left the holster; Sandl caught the full blast, followed by the commander on the left. The last ran for his life only to get shot in the back, Arix lay with wounds to his right arm and stomach from the side impact of the shot on Sandl.

Arix spoke, "I do not understand, do I pass the test?"

Morg took him in his arms and gave him a sip from his flask.

Arix spluttered, "What has this achieved?"

Morg replied, "A mighty storm is first announced by a mild breeze and a little spark is enough to light the fires of rebellion. You have been a good friend and that has helped me see what the Almighty sees in mankind. Beauty in spirit, integrity, sincerity, a childlike trust I can only envy. I remember once, standing in the devastation of the city of Caledon, a female, her house was gone, her family scattered or dead, she stood there and said, *'I only washed my windows yesterday!'*

To live such a life where her faith in the Almighty nullifies the evil around her so as the insignificant becomes significant, I long for that."

Morg stared blankly into space and then continued.

"I will not lie to you now, this is not a test. All that the followers of the Almighty say is true. You are too good a man to continue in the deception, repent your actions, seek His face and today you will be in glory!"

Arix could feel the life drain from him.

"Almighty, here my cry, I am repentant of my misinformed deeds!"

His vision dimmed, but he began to see in focus, a man appearing.

"Look!" said Morg, "Can you see my old comrade, Andreas. From the shadows he appears and makes the Almighty's presence real."

Andreas, an Ancient, stepped out of the shadows of the other world; Morg lifted Arix and placed him in Andeas' arms.

"Why did you assist this mortal soul when you have misled so many, you know being an Immortal who has looked upon the face of the Almighty there is no redemption for you."

Morg stood back.

"My actions are not meant to earn me redemption; they are simply because I have done so much wrong, I now simply choose to do what's right. I do not desire or expect to see glory. My fate is set; I shall spend eternity with the cries of those I misled eternally in my ears and in the dark. I can only make sure I do not add to the voices of my damnation. Arix is one less voice, today I vow there will be no more voices added."

Andreas closed the eyes of Arix.

"Your repentance is true and you will see glory today."

Andreas disappeared again into the shadows leaving Morg alone with the dead and deceived.

He turned again to look over the valley, so many mislead, souls he had mislead, he spoke, not to himself because he knew the Almighty always heard.

"I have burned my tomorrows and as I stand at the edge of the future, I can see all my dreams fading away. I promise you today, I will face my destroyer who ambushed me with a lie. You judge me for falling but this wounded heart will rise as I again see the light of true purpose. Today, I begin to burn my shadow so as its casting will no longer bring fear. Today I begin my dispersal into the nothing."

He walked away to join Cutler in Dopolis.

"We end this now."

Chapter 17 - Let's End This

Gus walked into the briefing room, eighteen hundred hours. He was uncomfortable in his Red Skull Kommando uniform, not just because it was a bit tight, being made for someone else. Looking around the room at his men dressed in Red Skull uniforms made him uneasy, the familiar faces made it bearable but the subconscious wanted to act out the fight or flight response. After four years of either killing or running from anyone in these uniforms made you edgy, they all stood to attention as he walked in the room, everyone was here. He saw Des Msipha; his face was thoughtful but hard to read. He would have paid a fortune for his thoughts right now, did Melody say anything about them. How would he be feeling about it, about them, how would his feelings affect this mission?

"At ease, men, you may be seated."

They sat down. Captain Smith now spoke.

"OK, you rabbits, I assume you are all fully briefed. We shall discuss the logistics shortly but Major Black wishes to say something first."

Gus sat on the edge of the table.

"First, let me say, you are all looking extremely lovely tonight. I have never seen a more handsome bunch of nit heads; you make these uniforms look good. That may be a problem because we all know how pot ugly the Red Skull gooks are. You're extremely handsome features may give us away."

The squad laughed but more out of politeness.

"I take it that you're familiar with the part I was given in the Almighty's plan, just in case, here's the inside story, not just what you read in the brief. It describes the knife, it gives you the scriptures that refer to it and what it can do but that is just the semantics. You need to understand the sacrifice our comrades made to get us here. It is a mystery that none of our predecessors were privileged to fathom, only in our time has it been made clear how we will rid ourselves of the Immortal curse. This knife places us, mortal and Immortal, on the same ground before the Almighty. It came as a sheer gift to me but at a real cost, the day I received this knife from the hand of an Ancient, I received a commission and lost two close friends. So understand that any choice I make or have made is not trivial, it is considered. I was the least qualified of any but the Almighty saw to it that I was equipped. It has nothing to do with my natural abilities. There are two in this room who are more able assassins than I. You may ask, why didn't I kill Morg when I had the chance, was I way over my head, did sentimentality cause me to be overly gracious? Neither. I truly wanted to thrust this knife in his back but the words spoken by the Ancient checked me. I truly believe that I was to spare Morg that day. I cannot say why but my decisions were genuine. I am fully aware we lost another four good men that day because of my decision, I shall live with that daily but the Almighty's reasons will be brought out in the open and it will be made plain what the Almighty, who created all, has been doing. Through our actions, this extraordinary plan of the Almighty is becoming known and shall be talked about in generations to come, even among the Ancients! We shall proceed along lines planned, by the Almighty's Grace and executed by us. When we trust in him, we're free to say whatever needs to be said, frankness in this room will be accepted as we discuss the process, rank will have no bearing. Be bold to speak about whatever we need to. Don't let past troubles and issues bog us down but be unafraid to express your concerns. Be proud, you have been predestined for this day! Let us bring the events to the Almighty."

Gus bowed his head, as did the rest.

"Father, magnificent Father, who watches over all heaven and earth. I ask to strengthen us, not merely a brute strength but a glorious inner strength. I ask that with both feet planted firmly in your grace, we'll be able to take in the extravagant dimensions of your mercy. Reach out and experience the breadth, test its length, plumb the depths, rise to the heights, live full lives, in your fullness. Through you, we can do anything, far more than we could ever imagine or guess or request in our wildest dreams! You do it not by pushing us around but by working within us, deeply and gently within us. Glory to Marines! Glory to Gaelia! Glory to you!"

Gus opened his eyes, paused and asked.

"So, let's be frank, before we allocate tasks in 'Operation Dead Fox' have you any questions?"

Gus knew what he was doing from the very onset but decided to offer it out to suggestions, seven minds are better than one and they may have an angle he hadn't seen. Letting the squad shape the plan would give them investment, if they didn't have already. His concern, they were veterans already with no real R & R since extraction. He had already spotted signs of PTSD in Rex. He had caught him a few times just sitting on his bunk staring at a blank wall with blank eyes. This concerned him. They were weary of war, unlike Red Skull. They gained no pleasure and saw no glory in death and dying. He looked at the faces of each man as they sat in silence and wondered how their lives would have been shaped if this hellish war had not shaped it. But he was glad about the Almighty's decision to make these guys part of his life. Greater, more honourable guys he could not have chosen, they were all called by name to fulfil the Almighty's plan. The other day, he was filled with doubt, today; his faith in the Almighty soared as he saw He was in control. He had set them on a solid base and would stay with them to the end, gloriously completing what He had begun.

The silence was growing uncomfortable, "Nothing guys, and shall we move on? OK, With the Almighty on our side, how can we lose? We shouldn't hesitate to put everything on the line because we know there isn't anything He wouldn't gladly and freely do for us. I know you are weary but this one action will change the course of the war, whatever is behind you, leave it there. It may return to us but not today, today is a day of new beginnings; we are the storm winds that will rid us off the old."

Deborah stuck up her hand.

"Can I speak, Sir?"

Gus responded, "No need for permission, whilst in this room you speak your mind."

Deborah stood up, "There's a story my mother has told me hundreds of times that's always fascinated me. The beginnings of my determination to be a part of this war may well stem from this. It's the story of one of my family heroes, my handsome eighteen year old uncle, who was accepted to study philosophy at University and who, when the call for Caledon volunteers came out, set out for the front to fight. Of course his father, my grandfather, tried to stop him. But he was determined. My mother remembers him dressed in the impeccable uniform of the Volunteers, strolling down the town, all the girls crazy about him. For her, and for the whole family, that boy was a hero, because he'd gone off to fight in defence of family, Gaelia and the Almighty. He was killed during the first barrage of the battle of Jobo Creek, without ever firing a shot or facing an enemy. Was his actions, in vain, no, he died bravely and I'll fight anyone who says different. He died the only decent way to die, fighting for what your conscience dictates. My mother has recounted many times the moment when the coffin arrived at the house and how my grandmother, received it with her arm raised, shouting,

'Arise Gaelia, avenge my son!' My mother has also told me that one morning, a few years later, she got out of bed when it was still dark, went out into the yard, and found her mother burning my uncle's letters. She got angry, watching her burn the hero's letters; she failed to understand that for her, it was too painful. She'd rather forget all about it, burn it from history, after all history is only what is recorded, what is forgotten, remains forgotten and the healing of the pain can begin. If you say this blade will burn these vile creatures from history, to become nothing more than mere myths then let us get down to the task, let us burn them and let the healing of much pain begin."

Deborah sat back down, everyone responded positively in grunts or nods of the head.

CJ punched the air saying, "Yeah!"

"Thank you, Corporal, I've known you for all these years and that's the first you've told me that story. We fight and die together, guys but we forget to live together."

Rex began to speak. He never spoke at briefings. He took his orders and never questioned, perhaps Deborah's story brought home issues he had hid for years, now amongst friends with no threat of danger, he could finally let go.

"I have a theory; I've never studied in university, like you la-DI-da officers."

Coming from anyone else that would have sounded insubordinate or resentful.

"We find ourselves living in a bubble, all is light and fine then pop it isn't. Your goals change and you begin to justify killing in war, you justify things that would have been abhorrent to you before. You justify the fighting by saying it's just. This changes when an unjust aggressor and just defender fight, it reduces the killing in war to nothing more than gang warfare, as what happened in Askdean. No one is wrong because all are wrong, this grates and troubles the soul of the educated, informed, morally guided soldiers of today but we cannot abdicate our responsibility to respect others' human rights. We took an oath; we have a huge responsibility to protect the innocent. I do think we are morally obligated to fight; I am convinced that this war is just. We cannot be selective, we defend freedom. We will not abandon our comrades."

Everyone sat silent in contemplation,

Ethan then spoke.

"The last guy I killed was in an assault vehicle during a resource raid, the patrol came from nowhere. He tried to evade as I lowered my bolt gun, I opened up and a couple resistance fighters with me began to shoot at the AV as well. I zeroed twenty eight bolts of a thirty bolt magazine into the passenger and driver. The driver was hit but not killed immediately, and he managed to back the AV up another three hundred meters and smashed into a wall before he died. What I'll never forget about that engagement is, as I looked at him inside of the AV, did he have family, were they expecting him to return after his tour of duty? DUTY, was he just doing his duty? Did he believe in his cause as deeply as mine? It makes you wonder. Hey, I've experienced the Red Skull and they are evil SOB's but are they all like that? You got to wonder."

The floodgates were now open, Des contributed.

"I just got back from seeing my sister, my only family and I haven't seen her in four years.

She feared I was dead. I heard of how happy she was, how she has found a new love."

Des glanced at Gus but Gus still couldn't judge how Des felt.

"I wrestled with this deployment. I was taught morality and values that focused on everyone's right to life. I really grapple with the fact that I take human life. In my mind I try to explain it, excuse it, or justify it. I want to feel okay with what I have done, I spoke with my sister, Melody, I told her I didn't think I could ever forgive myself, she said there is nothing to forgive. She was supportive and very proud of me she tried to impress upon me that killing in war is justified and not the same as murder and that I did what I was trained to do, and did it well. It was then I realised why we fight, why we kill, because it's personal. They attack our family and our values. We fight because to do anything less means we are defeated. Let's end this; if this ends it, I'm in."

This time CJ stood up, punched the air and said, "Yeah!"

No one else contributed so Captain Smith focused their attention as they began to plan the details.

***

Twenty two hundred hours came quicker than they expected they were waiting to board the Scorpion class copter, a smaller class than the Roach, but sufficient to get them past the Red Skull lines. They all climbed on board the Scorpion and fixed themselves into their seats; it would be a two hour flight with estimated landing dispatch at zero hundred hours. It was an indirect flight path, a straight route would be suspicious to Red Skull radar flying from Caledon, so they would fly south before heading east and then north, appearing to be a scout ship returning from the south.

As the copter took off they were all strapped in except for Captain Smith who held on by a strap from the ceiling.

"OK, dog faces, you all understand your roles. Girvan and CJ, you're sniping from the hill, so, you will go immediately to ground once we reach checkpoint two. I'm on train sabotage, Major Black, Captain Msipha and Sergeant Yu on assassination along with Corporal Dance, Dance our contact has secured you a job as a maid in HQ giving us opportunity to drug the guards."

Deborah moaned, "Yeah, find that slightly sexist, Sir."

Smithy chortled, "Sorry Deborah, Rex tried on the maid uniform but it looked nasty, least you'll look good in it, so suck it up princess."

Deborah screwed up her face and mumbled.

"Didn't join the Marines to look like a dolly bird!"

"Didn't quite hear that Dance?" asked Smithy.

"Nothing Sir, didn't say nothing." she replied.

"Finally, Major Black is CO, I'm ExO and Sergeant Yu is senior NCO, you may be the same rank in normal life but not on this mission, CJ is the Band Aid, do you understood, boonie rats."

They responded with a grunt.

Smithy turned to CJ and said, "You're in my chair, soldier, move your butt."

CJ unstrapped and moved, before he sat down beside Ethan.

He checked his backpack; he scratched his head, searched and called out.

"Oh man!"

"What is it buddy?" asked Ethan.

"I forgot my toothbrush."

Ethan guffawed.

"You can place a requisition order for one when we get back, I'll even help you fill it out."

CJ sat down heavily in his chair and strapped in.

"You don't understand, it's specially designed to break up plaque and massage the gums."

Ethan continued chuckling, "Yeah. Okay. Whatever."

CJ continued, "What do you think about Deborah?"

Ethan looked puzzled, "In what way?"

"Well, you know, she's got a nice body, don't you think?"

Ethan smiled and placed his arm on his shoulder.

"They say she has a thing for guys with scars."

CJ's face lit up, "I've heard. I've got a few myself. Do you think that'll secure the deal?"

Ethan continued, "I've seen the way you look at her. Surprised your pants haven't caught fire."

CJ pushed his arm away, "Do you have to make it sound so tawdry?"

Ethan shrugged, "If you like her ask her, what are you worried about?"

CJ replied, "A broken jaw and a broken heart."

Ethan nudged him, "She's looking at you. Quick! Look Cuter!"

"Uh, I don't think that's gonna work." CJ responded.

"Seriously, Ethan, do you think I'd have a shot."

Ethan paused, "I don't know, man, it's got to be natural. You need chemistry. She's definitely crazy, like you and kinda hot, unlike you."

CJ dunted him, "Ask if she's got a boyfriend, 'cause I'm in love!"

He kept on knocking his elbow saying, "Ask her! Ask her!" he did it a dozen times.

Ethan, now disgruntled, said, "I'll pay you not to do that."

CJ continued, "Hook me up with Deborah and we have a deal."

Ethan sighed, "You're a pirate, ask her yourself."

CJ screwed up his face, "I hate you."

"Good." replied Ethan.

CJ screwed up some courage.

"Hey, Dance, don't you get a little weirded out by you being here because you're the only woman."

Deborah looked over in disgust.

"I'm a woman? By the Almighty, I'm a woman! Where did these bumps on my chest come from? Hey guys tell the

341

pilot to turn back, I'm unfit for duty, I think I've got chest mumps. I hope I don't get anymore."

CJ embarrassed, fumbled his words.

"S..S..Sorry, I didn't mean it like that."

She continued her verbal attack.

"So what did you mean?" she asked.

"Well!" digging the hole deeper, "Well, us guys, when we've got a problem, a good show of force sorts things out. But the ladies like to, talk about it. Then think about it. Then talk about it some more. No offence."

Deborah shook her head she was getting a bit antsy.

"Believe it or not, we women sometimes have good ideas. You should try listening."

CJ, who clearly didn't know when to shut up.

"Yeah, but you ladies have so many of them. So, sometimes I pretend to listen."

Deborah retorted.

"Anyone teach you to make up nonsense like that, or did you figure it by yourself?"

CJ shrugged and said, "It's a gift."

Ethan decided to throw in his tuppence.

"He's got the hots for you Deborah; he's just upset he won't see you in the maids outfit."

She grunted, "Don't remind me!"

"What are you complaining at; at least you won't have to wear this ugly uniform, the maid uniform will give you more flexibility."

CJ's eyes rolled up, "Yeah, sweet, sweet flexibility."

Deborah protested, "I'm right here, CJ."

CJ replied huskily, "Yes you are. Yes you are."

Deborah shivered. "Just wait till this is over. If I find you have some kind of weird shrine of me, I will be very unhappy."

CJ quipped, "It's just a poster and a few candles. It's very tasteful."

Deborah screwed up her face, "Gads. Can we stop this? You're creeping me out. Ew!"

CJ continued, "So, is that a yes to me and you going dancing when we get back?"

Ethan jumped in, "Everyone knows you can't dance!"

CJ contested, "There are a few people who've seen me in action. They seemed impressed."

Ethan laughed sarcastically.

"Yeah, but I've actually seen you dance and that was pity admiration."

"Touché.", replied CJ.

Smithy decided to join in.

"In the interest of science, CJ. How does your species mate?"

Des, who had remained quiet till now called out, "Very clumsily."

CJ responded, "Good one, Sir, permission to request you go back to sleep, Sir. I had to sign up with a squad who thinks they're funny. All right, my turn. What's the first order we want a Red Skull commander to give at the start of combat?"

Des replied, "Uh, I give up."

Smirking CJ finished, "Correct."

Des sat forward laughing, "All right, big guy. What do you call it when a Red Skull gets killed by a big, fat, hairy rat?"

CJ quickly responded, "Friendly fire. Come on, that one goes way back."

Des retorted, "Gotta respect the classics."

Gus piped up, "My turn, how do you know when a Red Skull is out of ammo?"

He answered before anyone else could.

"He switches to the stick up his backside as a backup weapon."

"Good one, Sir, good one." said CJ.

Just at that, Rex, who was sleeping, gave out a huge snore. Gus kicked him, he startled.

Gus remarked, "Let me know if it's too quiet for you, and I'll find you someplace louder to sleep."

Rex simply said, "Hmm.", and fell straight back to sleep.

CJ asked, "Captain Msipha is it true what I heard? Did you really kill three Red Skull with one bolt?"

Des laughed it off, "No, that was an exaggeration, it was only two. The third guy died of a heart attack."

Again the copter filled with laughter.

"I also heard CJ that you are quite a sharpshooter." continued Gus.

"Yes.", said CJ.

"I always have been I was the junior clay pigeon shooting champion at the age of twelve."

Ethan quipped, "When the clay pigeons rise and attack we'll know who to turn to."

CJ retorted, "I was famous in my day, I'll let you know."

Ethan snorted, keeping the laugh in.

"Last time I was at Caledon, I didn't see a statue in your honour." he chuckled.

"Go and eat flies!" snapped CJ.

"Go and lick your eye ball." replied Ethan.

CJ requested, "Official request, Sir, I insist you allow me to throw him out of the door."

Gus asked, "But I thought you and Ethan were joined at the hip? That'd mean throwing yourself out as well."

"Ahh," said CJ, "I see your point Sir."

Rex rumbled in his sleep and said in a deadpan voice.

"Sometimes I'm not sure whether this Scorpion is carrying a crack Marine squad or a travelling freak show. Where do we find these people?"

Gus encouraged them, "Don't worry, when all off this is over, I will buy us all drinks back in that seedy bar Captain Smith took me to, I promise."

Smithy said defensively, " 'iKandy', It's a great bar! I only go to the best places."

They all settled back for the rest of the journey, all sat quiet for the next while.

Des turned to Gus, "Sir, can I be frank."

Gus replied, "Of course."

Des continued, "I thought you might have asked me about Melody?"

Gus gulped, unsure of how to answer.

"If I'm honest, I didn't know how you would react or even if you knew."

Des also hesitated, "Well how do you think I feel? When I heard about the whole thing, I immediately wanted to hate you. I certainly was very suspicious of your motives but you've won my sister's heart. So far, I can't find anything to level against you, you certainly have a winning personality but maybe you were right to say nothing. For now let's get back to doing what Marines do best, saving everyone else from the Red Skull!"

Gus asked, "Don't you have any questions?"

"Actually, I have a million but we'll wait till this is over, then I'll have time to pace myself. Let's make a pact, let's make sure at least one of us survive, to get back to her. She couldn't cope losing us both."

Gus nodded, "Agreed!"

They all sat in silence for the remainder of the journey; the only sound was the rhythmic snoring of Rex which brought the group a sense of comfort, except for Deborah. Still disgruntled about being the maid, she requested that she either shoot Rex or herself in the head, either way it would give her peace.

***

They reached the dispatch area at zero hundred hours. They unfastened from the seat and hooked up to the overhead rail. They weren't landing, it wasn't wise for the copter to hang around, so they were performing Red Skull style airdrop.

CJ nudged Ethan, "So apart from the fact we're wearing Red Skull disguise, why are we performing an airdrop, is there a reason?"

Ethan shrugged, "Maybe we were refused landing permission because the Red Skull won't validate our parking?"

CJ smirked and shook his head.

"OK, weasels." shouted Captain Smith at the top of his voice.

"It's time to pull the cord and jump, just make sure it's not the fire alarm, that's not due tested till next week."

Deborah was right next to him and it resonated in her ear.

"Ah! Sir, your voice, Sir! Not so loud, please, thank you."

Smithy gave her a disparaging look as one by one they jumped.

First Ethan then CJ, Deborah, Smithy and followed by Rex, Des and lastly Gus. As Ethan was first to land, he disengaged his rope which twisted back into the copter he crouched placing his night vision visor over his eyes, nothing to be seen when suddenly he was hit from behind. He tumbled, finding himself on his back, it was CJ who had misjudged his landing, and there he lay with CJ on top in a compromising position.

CJ blurted, "Sorry man, it's too dark. You're not going to tell anyone about this? Like Deborah, she definitely doesn't need to know."

Ethan gladly replied, "I guarantee that Deborah will not learn about it from me but I'm not the issue."

CJ realised that Deborah jumped after him, "She's standing right there, isn't she?"

Deborah shook her head, "I wish I wasn't, if you like, I can give you two some privacy."

She walked on only to be followed by Smithy and the rest. Smithy quipped, "Mating between different species is a pointless exercise and against regulations." Rex asked, "You want me to arrest them on charges? I could put a bolt in their heads but we can't spare the ammo."

Des just chuckled and Gus stopped, "Shall I get a room so we can work it out."

Ethan replied, "I bet you say that to every guy."

Gus responded, "Only the cute ones."

Ethan pushed CJ off, "C'mon, man, get off."

CJ fell backwards and put his hand on a cow pat, he lifted his hand up.

"No way."

Ethan piped up.

"Hey, Deborah, he bought you chocolate?"

CJ jumped to his feet, "Yeah, I saw this chocolate and thought of you, Ethan, get my drift?"

A mild breeze blew down wind carrying the smell.

"Oh man, I'm catching your drift right now, Major Black, may I request CJ goes on point as that's upwind."

Rex snapped, "OK, jokers, that's enough, back to the task."

They all filed in line for their hour long march to the next checkpoint just outside Dopolis.

"CJ, I think Girvan is right, you're on point."

As he walked past, everyone waved away the smell or held their nose as it became apparent he had fell on more than one pat and it was on more than just his hand, and they were fresh.

Chapter 18 - Pour the Milk First

After landing, they marched off in military single file. They had an hour quick march till they reached their next checkpoint. Des marched behind Gus.

He pulled up beside him, "Sir, do you still want to talk?"

Gus responded, "What did you have in mind?"

Des replied sardonically"Something that doesn't involve us fighting Red Skull would be nice."

"That's hard to do these days. I guess we could catch a poetry reading."

Des chuckled.

"No offence, Sir, but if the end of the Gaelia is coming, I'm not going out on flowery prose."

He hesitated, "Not looking forward to what we're about to do, beginning to have doubts about whether I'm up to it, if I'm honest."

Gus refrained from the surprise he felt, Des paused before his next statement.

"It's just, I've been thinking, the future of so many are in our hands, I wonder if we're putting all our eggs into one basket. Hey, I'll roll up my sleeves, put my mind in gear, be totally ready to perform my duty using this fatal gift the Almighty has given us but I wonder even if we are successful will our comrades still have to face the Red Skull hordes. We are relying on the words of evil men who cannot be trusted. They promise to withdraw but what if they lazily slip back into those old grooves of evil, doing just what they feel like doing."

Gus grunted in agreement, "Trust is a difficult thing. You can trust that good people will sometimes do the wrong thing but what if you have to trust bad people to do the right thing. In the end you can only trust your heart, what does your heart say? I consider maybe they don't know any better; we do. As obedient children, we let ourselves be pulled into a way of life shaped by the Almighty, a life energetic and blazing with grace. We call out to Him for help and He helps, he's a good Father that way. It is only lately, at the end of the age perhaps that the Almighty's will has become public knowledge. The Almighty always knew what He was going to do. It's because we trust the Almighty that we know we have a future. Before we left Caledon, I got to meet my father.

I hadn't seen him in fifteen years; he spent five years in Rock Island."

Des whistled, "Sorry man, I didn't know, I loathe the Red Skull, I mean, what kind of soldier looks at a place that pretends to be a refuge for war survivors, which is really a death camp to conduct experiments, and think, '*Hey, that's something I'd really like to be a part off!*' Sorry, I interrupted."

Gus continued, "When he finally escaped he was told all his family was dead. He didn't give up, he hoped and he helped those who still had family, return home. Glad he could give them what he longed for. Whatever destiny lies before us over the next few days, it is ours, and whatever lies before our comrades is theirs. My father discovered less than a week ago he still had a family. That was his reward for his faithfulness. Our reward, their reward is still to be revealed, we will fulfil our destiny, and they will fulfil theirs."

Des was comforted by these words, he could see why so many trusted him, why he had the reputation he had, and he trusted him.

"Thank you, Sir. That has helped."

They continued their march in silence.

***

As they approached checkpoint two, they came across an unexpected obstacle, a generator fence blocked their way.

They hadn't brought a tech.

Gus gathered them around, "Anyone any ideas or are we stuck before we start? Blast intel, we should have been told about this."

CJ put up his hand, "Uh, tech's not my specialty, but I'll pull a few wires, see what comes out."

"No!" said Gus, "You'll set it off like a firework display."

Ethan then spoke, "My brother, Digger, he's a tech, he used to babble on all the time. Mostly I ignored him but sometimes things went in. If I'm right, this is a type X-3, he said it had a glitch every odd pole, if you knocked it at the bottom it would switch off for a limited time but not every time."

Gus shook his head, "You won't set it off will you? We are meant to be covert."

Ethan continued, "No, as long as we get through before it resets but we need to be quick, it's not exact, it could switch back on anytime."

"By the Almighty!"

He looked skyward. "You do like to test our faith. OK, do it."

Ethan stood up, he braced himself, "Yes, Sir!"

"OK, you boots!" called out Rex.

"Let's get jiggy, Intel have let us down. Major Black, Sir, you take Slack-man, everyone else in behind, CJ you're on rear. Understood!"

They all acknowledged. Ethan walked over to the post, scratched his head in bewilderment, and then kicked it. Repeatedly. Third time the fence went off, he took a second, and he looked back.

Gus called out, "GO!!"

He jumped as did the rest, with CJ last, as he landed in a heap, the fence came back on.

"Did you touch that beam, CJ?"

"No Sarge, don't think so Sarge."

"You better had not!"

"But Sir, I think I tore something, jumping through, I think I'm starting to black out from the pain!"

"Ethan. Are you familiar with band aid skills?"

"I have sufficient knowledge, Sir."

"Tend to CJ, then both of you go to ground as planned, if he is unable to assist, I expect you to complete your mission solo."

"Yes, Sir."

The five man bird-dog team set off to the town leaving eagle team, apparently with one broken wing. Ethan examined CJ, he had what initially appeared to be a dislocated knee but on further examination it was a subluxation, similar but not as severe as a knee dislocation. It's only a partial dislocation giving the sensation that occurs when the knee gives way due to a damaged ligament.

A knee dislocation must be reset into proper position, compared to a subluxation that will slip back in to position fairly easily.

Ethan went into CJ's medic kit and pulled out what looked like an epi-pen but it was pain relief.

"Brace yourself bud."

He jabbed the pen into his knee releasing the pain relief, CJ squealed.

"Not so rough, pinhead."

"It's going to get worse, it's partially dislocated, I'll have to slip it back in"

CJ knew what that meant.

"No, Ethan, it's not that bad, I'll be fine."

Ethan smiled in reassurance.

"I know you will."

He quickly slipped his knee back in to place.

CJ's eyes began to roll up into his head, "Yeah! It's happening, okay, I'm really blacking out."

And he did. Ten minutes CJ was out, by that time Ethan had applied a support bandage and found him a big stick to aid his walking.

"You done sleeping, I know we got a day and only over a mile to go but I don't want caught here in the daylight, let's move it Nancy. We got to find a fox hole to hide in till tomorrow."

CJ got up slowly, the pain had eased and he could walk fairly well but not quickly.

"Lead the way McDuffer!"

Ethan lead and marched off at double speed, he turned round and saw CJ hobbling behind.

"How's the leg? Are you getting tired already? You're still slow!"

CJ snapped back, "I'm only slow because I'm not running! Slow down!"

Ethan slowed down, they reached just outside checkpoint three, and it would be dawn in an hour.

He settled CJ down and went to find their foxhole, he returned in ten minutes.

"Your room awaits, Sir, couldn't get the honeymoon suite but I think it'll do."

He helped CJ to the den, CJ climbed in. It was small, damp, dark and filled with cobwebs.

CJ hated spiders.

"Spiders. Seriously. Spiders. You know I hate them."

Ethan also climbed in, "I super care about you, CJ. And the good kind of caring! Not the creepy kind but shut up, go to sleep and rest that leg, I'm going to need you tomorrow."

CJ for once, didn't reply and did what he was told.

***

Warthog Tavern was on the outskirts of the town, that's why the Kommando unit liked it, away from the prying eye of the Sonder. Even Kommando thought those guys were fanatics and sticklers for discipline. The tavern was right next to the river you could see HQ in the distance, to the extent it was on high ground but a good mile away at least. The river had several bridges over it to cross into the town, all had manned ID points. They had been issued with fake ID but it wouldn't take much scrutiny to see they weren't real. So, Gus thought bluffing there way past the ID point would work best. They approached the ID point, several guards were in a wooden cabin, even at this hour, and security was tight. Gus pretended to be drunk and the rest were carrying him as if he couldn't walk. There hope, they would be waved through regardless, the night was reaching its darkest and coldest, the guard was hopefully lagging and not wishing any hassle.

As they approached, Gus was being held up by Rex and Des whilst Smithy stepped forward to use his charm.

"Hi, it's been such a long night, I was in my bed when I realised this guy, my buddy. His names Chuck by the way, I'm Andy and you are?"

He reached out his hand, the guard was young, couldn't have been much older than 18 maybe 20. He did not take Smithy's hand.

"Anyway, I see him missing and I hear from Pete, that's Pete."

Des waves.

"That he's got drunk and decided to go take on the Gaelian army by himself, all for glory, you know how it is. Anyway we finally catch up with him, spent all morning getting him this sober, we just want to get him back to barracks without any fuss, our NCO will lynch him if he catches him in this state."

The young guard looked at them, he fell for the story.

"Yeah, OK, I can see that. My NCO's a SOB a well."

He was just about to let them through when the aforementioned NCO came from the cabin.

"What's going on here? What kind of disgraceful state is this trooper in?"

The guard stood to attention.

"Just returning to barracks, Sir."

The Sergeant looked all of them up and down pacing either side slowly.

He stood in front of Gus and lifted his head; it flopped as he lets it go.

"Do you have papers?"

"Yes, Sir, we do but as I was trying to explain to our friend here..."

The NCO interrupted, "He is not your friend and neither am I. I need to see your papers ASAP."

They all started to fumble about their pockets but before any papers were found, Gus let off one of his famous farts. It truly smelt like something had crawled up his anus a fortnight ago and died there. The whole company started to gag, the young guard could not hold it any longer, he ran to the bridge and vomited into the river, it was that heinous. Quickly the NCO waved them on.

"By all that is unholy, get that man out of here, this won't be the last, I will be filing a report and I'll locate you."

Gus let off another; the NCO began to dry baulk and ran into the cabin.

They all walked quickly away, especially to get away from the smell.

Smithy through the gagging said, "Sometimes I worry about you, man. Seriously, when we get back, go see a doctor. That's not natural!"

Des chipped in, "It's quite ironic though. His ass just saved our ass."

They turned a corner into an alleyway and regrouped. Dopolis was over eight hundred year old, making it one of the oldest known towns in Gaelia. It became a theatre town and important trading route junction and even had ship traffic a long time ago. Dopolis still had a temple with a ninety nine metre high spire. The third highest in Gaelia at one time but probably now the highest as many temples has been ransacked or burnt down, it would appear to be being used as a local command centre for Kommando unit. He had met its elder on a couple of occasions; his name was Stephen, at temple events in the Burgh. That was an eternity ago in what seemed like another life. As they walked they saw the remains of a bombed house, a museum and parts of the former town walls could still be seen as with many of these older towns. They walked past a small theatre which was housed in the refurbished public baths. They walked past a memorial stone commemorating the brave dead of Jobo Creek; it was made of granite and said, '*For peace, freedom and democracy.*'

It had been vandalised by Red Skull and the five men's anger rose, it was most evident in Rex's face.

"Keep it together Yu."

On the hill was Dopolis' only industry, an aluminium plant. They reached the Warthog tavern. Drunken, off duty Red Skull soldiers and locals were pouring out, as the tavern was closing, last orders had been an hour ago. It was just around the corner from the main concert and opera house where Gus had gained his theatrical education. The town was different in the dark of the early morning but it was the dark cloud of Red Skull that changed the atmosphere.

They walked into the tavern, the barman, who was trying to lock up, called out.

"We're closed; it's almost three in the morning, no more beer."

Smithy replied, "I hear you serve pork medallions, I prefer chicken."

The man's eyes popped open; it was the code he had been waiting on all night.

"We have sesame encrusted salmon?" was the coded reply.

To which Smithy replied, "Just cheese and beer."

The man waved them over to the bar, "I was expecting you at midnight."

Smithy responded, "No, that's when we landed, were here now, show us our billet."

He opened the bar flap and then a trap door.

"This way, quickly, you can rest here before you reconnoitre tomorrow."

They all filed down into the cellar, underneath the floors was a large cellar it was easily as big as the two rooms combined above it, and it was accessed by two more trap-doors including an external one, probably where the deliveries were made. They were encompassed by darkness, with the only light coming from tiny holes in the floor and from the house stairway at the very back of the cellar.

The barman followed.

"I am Gustavo, I own this tavern."

He went round the cellar putting on switches, lighting up the room, the full scope of its size became apparent as well as the large quantities of beer barrels, cheeses, wines and sausage, plenty of sausage.

"I shall bring you food; tomorrow you can do your spying. Also you will meet your contacts."

He looked and then pointed at Deborah.

"Is this the maid?"

Deborah snorted, "I am Corporal Deborah Dance of the Loyal Naval Marines, and I am not '*the maid*."

Smithy concurred, "Corporal, pipe down, yes, this is the Marine who will take the role of the maid."

"Good.", he said.

"Cutler likes them pretty, she will do well. Your contacts will be here tomorrow, noon; they will take you to the next stages, now food and then rest."

He returned with the food quickly, it was fresh as well; it was, yes, pork medallions which were very good, beer and apple strudel, the crust was soggy but the flavour was good.

They settled and slept.

***

First light, Smithy and Rex were out reconnoitring making plans, ensuring there was nothing to hinder their plans. They marked out where they would place the vehicles till the attack. They saw the hill overlooking the cafe and the road Morg would drive up, it was all as planned, Intel had actually been accurate for once. When they returned, the first of the contacts had arrived.

He was a young man in his mid- twenties, 5'6" browny blond hair, very sharp features.

"Hello, my name is Ian; I will be taking you to the sidings, which one shall be with me."

Smithy stepped forward, "That'll be me, Captain Smith, Francis Smith."

Gus spoke, "... and who will be our HQ contact?"

"She is here?" answered Gustavo.

A slight, thin pair of ankles walked down the stairs, the black suit made her white skin and face more prominent, it was Cutler's secretary.

Gustavo spoke, "This is Pieta, she is part of Cutler's staff, and it is because of her we are here. She has relayed the desires of the Red Skull command to rid us of Cutler and Morg."

Pieta completed the rest of the steps and shook Captain Black's hand.

She looked like a child next to the Marines.

"It is a pleasure to meet you Sir, your reputation precedes you, and those in the Red Skull command admire your gall. Very few have stood before Morg as an equal."

They spoke of the arrangements.

She had arranged the vehicles and would ensure they were parked in the allocated street.

After thirty minutes they concluded.

Deborah had changed into civilian clothes and left with Pieta.

Smithy with Ian.

"Keep it sharp, keep to the plan." called out Gus.

"I have a bad feeling about this, Sir; it feels like we just handed over two good Marines to the enemy, I especially don't trust that Pieta." said Rex.

"Mmmmm.", agreed Gus.

"It does seem strange that someone so close to Cutler is our contact, don't know, is it justified or are we just too suspicious. There ways are different; betrayal is a way of life to them which in itself breeds suspicion. I agree that Pieta was unusual, creepy, but it is hard to say if it was her manner or just how she appeared. We are too far down the line to change now, they were picked because they can handle themselves and they volunteered. We must move on, after all, it is all going to plan."

Rex's face was perplexed, "Still, got a feeling!"

Gus acknowledged, "I trust your gut Rex, better than any Intel report, let's keep sharp."

Deborah followed Pieta; she walked just behind her as they climbed the hill. She was at least a foot taller and although fairly well built, was slender but Pieta was stick thin. The town hall, currently Cutler's HQ, was formerly the old palace, in the times of kings. Dopolis was the summer retreat.

It was a crenellated fortress and among the most impressive town halls of Gaelia. It overlooked the town centre, looking down was a statue of Prince Michael 1, the first prince to unite Gaelia over one thousand year ago. Above the front entrance door, there is a notable ornamental marble frontispiece, in the middle, flanked by two gilded lions, is a monogram of the Almighty, surrounded by glory. This was covered by Red Skull banners. She entered the first courtyard, in the lunettes, high around the courtyard, were crests of the temple and City Guilds. In the centre, was a porphyry fountain with water flowing through the nose of a dolphin. In the niches, in front of the fountain stood various statues, the frescoes on the walls, represented scenes of famous Gaelian battles, the harmoniously proportioned columns, were smooth. She had to resist touching them as they were richly decorated with gilt stuccoes. She climbed the marble staircase onto the first floor, still following Pieta. This was being used mainly for offices, Pieta walked past all these and then down again, down a narrow stone staircase, it led outside through a stone corridor. On these walls were frescoes painted with a perspectival illusion of the temple. In the lunettes above were mythical heroes of Gaelia with kings fighting alongside.

This lead to a door in the wall which lead to another building.

"These are the servant's quarters."

It was still grand flanked by two dark marble pillars, Pieta lead her to her room opened the door.

"You'll find your uniforms in the wardrobe, be in the kitchen by four, you do not want to be late for Cutler, it will upset him and that is why we have a vacancy."

Pieta left, she sat on the bed and wondered.

"What have I volunteered for?"

She fell backwards on the bed; the carved ceiling was full of the Lilies, golden lilies decorated on blue background.

"Been in worse billets though."

She relaxed, after awhile, she opened the wardrobe door.

It was filled with maid uniforms, some too large, some too small but she found one that fitted perfect. She opened her bag and brought out two vials containing old lace, placing them at the rear of the wardrobe for later. She looked at the time it was twenty minutes till four, she realised she didn't know where the kitchen was, a knock came to the door.

There stood an older, well dressed, very stern faced man.

"Follow me."

She followed him out of the building and down the same stone corridor she had walked down an hour or so earlier and into the main building. The kitchen was large and busy; she was led to a trolley which had a teapot, china cup and a plate with Haute Cuisine. The older gent, who Deborah now realised was the butler, said, "Take this trolley, I will show you where as it is your first day.

It contains tea and a meal for Lord Cutler, if he asks it is cauliflower and squid with roast squid juice, also a soothing bowl of black sauce and tender white pieces of vegetable and seafood. When you pour his tea, pour his milk first, by all that you hold dear pour the milk first."

She followed him to an upstairs room, using a service elevator, as instructed.

***

The day wore on and rather than hide in the cellar they mingled with the clientele of the tavern.

The ambiance was good, the beer tasty but mild, Gustavo brought food, sesame encrusted salmon. Gus began to think their passwords weren't that great, it was breaded and fried with cheese sauce on the side, and he had never been on a covert mission with full board service before. It was perfectly cooked but by no means haute cuisine. If it hadn't been for the mission, he would be enjoying himself, it was surreal. The tavern had a nice, warm, cosy atmosphere and he imagined it would get better at night. As the afternoon wore into evening, the Red Skull troopers started to fill the tavern. It was now getting crowded and Gus began to think they should maybe return to their hole. Just at that, a small detachment of Sonder Guard entered. Rex kicked Gus, "My gut feelings just soared."

The guards blocked the entrances and the NCO called for silence.

"We are just doing a spot check of papers; it would seem we have an incursion. This won't take long; your full cooperation will be appreciated!"

The dissatisfaction of the Kommando troopers rippled through the place, it was clear Kommando had no love for the Sonder. The commanding officer, a Major, scanned the room. He walked from table to table as if he knew what he was looking for. He stood at Rex's right shoulder, walked on a step; Des gave out an audible sigh. He turned back, looked at Gus, pulled out a chair and sat down, Rex reached for a knife in his boot. Gus stopped him.

"I think your CO is giving you good advice, Sergeant Yu?"

He raised his arm and summoned Gustavo.

"Good evening, Gustavo, can we have some of your good non Gaelian wines, I find it bitter and I only want the best for our heroes, especially Major Black."

Gustavo brought him the wine, his hand shook as he poured, he realised they had been betrayed and his days were now numbered. As he finished pouring, the Red Skull Major grabbed his wrist.

"Don't leave, let you staff deal with the customers."

He kicked a chair.

"Please join us."

The Major took the bottle and poured Gustavo a glass.

"Allow me to serve you."

Gustavo took the wine and gulped it down spilling some down his chin; he wiped it with the back of his hand. None of the Marines drank.

"I am disappointed you won't partake in my hospitality, never mind we will have plenty of time to converse over the next few days, I am aware there are more members too your group, although I have been unable to locate them."

This gave Gus hope, but which ones, had Smithy and Deborah been marched straight into custody or had they escaped. That witch Pieta must be at the end of this betrayal, perhaps it had been a trap all along, and he wished he had listened to Rex's gut all along.

The Major continued, "We can do this messily. I know all your reputations, I am aware that each of you could kill me where I sit and many around us but it would be futile and pointless. I can see in your comrades' eyes that is their desire, Major Black. I hope you can see the futility and choose the rational course, leaving without a fuss."

Major Black looked around the room, there were a lot of Red Skull troopers but there were also women, children, families, he had no choice.

"We will come with you quietly."

Rex's face distorted but Gus again grabbed his arm.

"Look around you Rex, there are civilians and children, let's get some space."

Rex settled and they all left quietly, as they left the building they all felt a sharp blow to the back of the head. Rex was first followed by Des, as Gus saw what happened he began to struggle but was restrained by three guards, he was hit, and he fell. As he fell he looked across at Gustavo who was pushed to his knees and a Red Skull trooper put his bolt pistol to his head, executing him on the street. One more blow to his head and unconsciousness overwhelmed Gus.

Chapter 19 - Out of the Fire

Deborah followed the butler into what was a most imposing chamber it was nearly two hundred foot long and seventy foot wide. Cutler sat at a desk on the end, she felt awkward and hypocritical. Her instinct was to shoot him not serve him tea. The trolley squealed as it rolled along the oak floor which was amplified by the immenseness of the room. It was as if the trolley was expressing her feelings off revulsion which had to remain hidden. She glanced at the walls with their large and expansive frescoes depicting more battles and military victories, the ceiling was panelled and painted in the same way. On the north side of the room, illuminated by enormous windows, was a raised stage built to receive visitors and guests, on it sat a dining table. At the end of the room Deborah noticed a small side room without windows, she approached the desk, the butler stood in silence, so did she. In a few moments Cutler waved his hand indicating he wished served. The butler took the meal and placed it on the dining table, setting out the cutlery as you would at any silver service. Cutler moved from his desk to the table sitting down as the butler laid a napkin on his knee. The butler indicated to Deborah to serve the tea, she walked around the table and approached from his left, as etiquette demanded. She poured the milk first and then the tea.

As she poured she thought, "If you were a mortal man, how easy would it be to simply snap your neck."

He was Immortal and possibly reading her thoughts right now, she was tempted to test the theory that Immortals can't die but her mission was to infiltrate and lace the tea tomorrow before Major Black arrived with bird dog team. She would be patient.

"Is this the new maid?"

"Yes, my lord."

"She's very pretty," commented Cutler, not once raising his head to acknowledge her,

"Pieta always had good taste, it's a pity she let us all down."

The mention of Pieta's name and the phrase, 'let us all down' gripped Deborah's attention.

What did he mean?

At that moment the door was knocked and a Major entered. The Major who lead the squad that detained Gus and his team, but he stayed at the bottom end of the room till he was summoned.

Cutler spoke to the butler.

"Tell the chef the squid was excellent, you may leave but the maid can stay, I will wish more tea."

He now raised his head and spoke directly to Deborah, her skin crawled.

"Go and wait in the ante room, this is private business, wait there till I call."

She obeyed, the room had a barrel vault wall with paintings but she remained focused and undistracted. She left the door ajar and listened intently. The clump of the Major's feet could be heard clearly on the oak floor as he walked towards Cutler and the clack of his heels as he stood to attention, Cutler moved back to his desk and motioned the Major to speak.

"The insurgents have been detained, mostly, and are ready for interrogation"

The Major hesitated at the word mostly.

"Explain, mostly!" asked Cutler in a dry voice.

"We have Major Black and his two assassins detained, we dispatched Gustavo, and here is the knife."

The Major handed Cutler the Promethean knife. He was surprised to see fear in Cutler's face.

Cutler opened a drawer and retrieved a velvet bag.

"Place it in here, carefully! What of the others?"

The Major continued.

"We know there are others, how many we do not know and their location is also unknown, Pieta broke easily under torture alerting us to Major Black's location but we will gain no further information from her."

Cutler stood, pushing his chair backwards, he moved around the desk so as he stood beside the Major, uncomfortably close breaching his personal space.

He raised his hand and forced the Major to his knees.

"Pieta was my friend; I hope you are not telling me she is dead by your clumsy hand."

The pressure on the top of his head was clear in his face.

"She was so delicate, my lord, we were more gentle than most. She simply expired."

Cutler replied, "Then so shall you."

With a twist of Cutlers hand, his neck was broken and he fell limp on the floor.

Deborah realised that the mission was now a failure with Major Black and his team captured there was no way to kill the Immortals, escape was the only option. Cutler appeared at the door, it startled her and she jumped backward in fright knocking the picture in the alcove slanted.

"I'm sorry, my dear." announced Cutler.

"I did not mean to startle you, I have business elsewhere, and your service is no longer required. Please clear away my dinner dishes and I will arrange for the other garbage to be removed."

He turned and left, Deborah was stunned. Speechless and numb, it was clear this whole mission had been an elaborate trap. She felt her legs weaken and fell against the wall, the painting she knocked now fell to the floor her hand pushed the wall to steady herself from falling completely and a secret door opened. This brought her back to her senses, she stepped inside, and it was covered in cobwebs and had obviously remained secret for many years. It lead to a staircase and a corridor, firstly, she walked along the corridor to its end, a dead end. She searched the walls and found the seams of another door. She pushed; it opened into what were obviously private chambers. The chamber door opened, she quickly closed the door again to hide. It was Cutler; these were the private quarters of Cutler himself. He opened a drawer and placed the Promethean knife, Gus's knife, with the velvet bag into the drawer. Suddenly he looked across; it was like a bloodhound catching a whiff of scent, she was certain he saw her. Her Marine training meant that although the blood was pulsing through her veins and she felt like she couldn't catch breath, she controlled her panic and her breathing. He turned and left the room, reality hit home. Gus was indeed captured but the mission may yet be a success, surely the Almighty had lead her here to redeem the knife Cutler had taken from Gus.

She double checked she was alone in the room, entered and took the knife and placed it in her bosom, in her bra strap. There was nowhere else to place it in this blasted maid uniform.

She quickly left securing the door, she decided to explore further and walked down the carved stone steps, they were simple but elegant and, being on the first floor, it led down past the ground floor with no opening and directly to the cellars. Again she faced what seemed like a dead end but placed her hand on the wall feeling for cracks, she found the door and pushed. Slowly, aware that she was unaware of what might be behind it. She looked out into a whitewashed room. Stepping gingerly, she stepped out completely closing the entrance again leaving it a little ajar, in case she needed an escape. She could see she was in a room that was being used for storage, the wooden door of the room had a small window but she could see the cells and could see, to her joy, Gus. She almost let out a squeal but contained it, she hated being a girl sometimes.

Gus was sat at a table, his hands bound at the back with plastic straps a blindfold on his face and he looked unconscious. She was deciding how to rescue him when she heard footsteps. She peered out of the small pane of glass, it was Cutler again and two troopers. She cursed, if only she had climbed the stairs first, she may have been able to help him before he arrived, this was obviously his other business, again she opened the door a little to hear.

***

Cutler walked up to Gus, his head slouched, and he held his head up. He was unconscious.

He let it go, it fell, "Wake him up!" ordered Cutler.

The guard grabbed a taser rod and put it to Gus's chest, the pain shot all through his body, every nerve tingled, and he felt sick. He was awake but did not know where he was. In a few seconds he realised what had happened and the sick feeling increased his head felt all screwy.

Cutler pulled out a chair and sat on it with his legs crossed.

"Shock him again; he's not yet fully awake?"

The shock made his body jolt, twitch hard and jump involuntarily, his muscles contracted. He felt his heart rhythm becoming irregular, the pain in his chest screeched it felt like his chest was being stomped on by someone wearing work boots, his insides felt jumbled and again he felt like puking.

"Do I have your attention Major Black? I need to know how many others are in your group, what are their plans and locations. Please hurry, I am impatient. Today I have lost a good friend and I have no time for games."

Gus replied, "I have nothing to say.'

Cutler cried, "Bag, use the bag!"

The guard pushed a plastic bag into Gus's mouth and another over his head, he struggled to breath thrashing trying to get air, he felt the plastic sticking to his face and unconsciousness taking over as his lungs emptied of air. Before he blanked out the guard removed both bags and shocked him again. It was a most peculiar pain like he'd just been kicked really hard, there's the first pain of the actual impact, then a dull continuing residual pain. He gulped in the air as panic overwhelmed him.

A third trooper appeared.

"My lord, I have report that lord Morg has returned and is wishing to see you."

Cutler stood, "He is not due till tomorrow, blast his impulsiveness, is he here?"

"No!" came the reply, "but he is imminent and he speaks of vengeance."

"You!"

Cutler spoke to the trooper who had been shocking Gus.

"Stay here with him, you two follow."

They followed and as they walked he said, "Explain to Morg he must wait till he is summoned. Cutler left, his anger had not reached such heights in an age. Although she had betrayed him, he was fond of Pieta and genuinely felt grief but no more than an owner would feel for his faithful dog.

He left.

Deborah looked around and could see no other guards other than the one Cutler left. She crept out the store room and stood flat against the opposite wall, adjacent to the door of the cell. This gave her a better view of the holding cells, there were about forty other people she estimated, including Des and Rex who were chained and hanging from the ceiling, also unconscious. She grabbed a small metal object from the table beside her; she threw it across the hall. This distracted the guard, he walked into the hall, and she grabbed him from behind with a blood choke cutting off the blood supply by squeezing the carotid. Her left arm encircled his neck, with the crook of her elbow against his trachea, grabbing her upper right bicep with her left hand and her right hand on the back of his head bringing her elbows together applying pressure to his neck till he passed out. He collapsed after a few seconds and she slid the limp body down her length to hide the thump.

She ransacked the trooper taking his bolt gun, bolt pistol, dagger and two grenades. She entered the room taking the troopers dagger and cutting Gus's bond. He was surprised and loosed his blindfold. If it hadn't been for the serious nature of their situation he would have burst into laughter as he looked at Deborah standing before him in her maid outfit holding the dagger with the bolt gun draped over her shoulder.

"You are a sight for sore eyes, unless I'm dreaming. Am I dreaming?"

Deborah did not appreciate the comment.

"No Sir, you are not dreaming and I would appreciate it if you could disregard my appearance.

I do not wish to be in anyone's dreams dressed like this."

Gus still felt groggy, his vision still blurred.

"I assume you figured out we have been betrayed, must have been Pieta."

Deborah shook her head.

"Only indirectly, I believe she was detained and tortured and is dead as a result."

This news brought Gus back into a sharp reality; Deborah took out the dagger in the bag.

"I believe this is yours."

He opened the bag and again surprise gripped him.

"Are you sure I'm not hallucinating? You are surely sent by the Almighty. How did you get into the cells, it has guards and security doors?"

She impatiently suggested, "Can we release Des and Rex and get out of here, with respect Sir."

"Of course."

She handed him the bolt pistol and he followed her out the door into the cell area, the trooper still lay unconscious. Deborah searched his pockets again and found the key card that released the cells. Gus went to Des, Deborah to Rex and let them down. They were also groggy as they walked into the open area Deborah went into the next room to get water to refresh them. She found a bath filled with water and in it was Pieta dead, or so she thought. As she walked over she felt pity and regret that they had assumed she had purposely betrayed them but she had suffered at the rough hand of the Red Skull like so many. Her eyes were open, she reached over to close them, as she touched her eyelids, and her wrist was grabbed. It was Pieta, she was still alive. She released her chains, helped her out and wrapped her in a blanket she found on a chair. She sat her down on the chair, "I am sorry, are you ok."

"Who are you?" asked Pieta.

"I'm from the Gaelian squad."

She jerked; it was unclear if it was fear of repercussion of her behaviour or just plain shock.

"I'm sorry!"

"I was too weak, they forced me under water! I thought I was going to die! I thought I was dead! I could feel the life drain from me."

She continued to shiver, "As darkness became my sanctuary suddenly there was light, a man held my head. He called himself Andreas; he spoke, *'Rest child, the Almighty has plans for you. When you were still in your mother's womb He chose and called you! Now He will intervene, today will be your rebirth, it will be painful but once life is returned it brings joy.'* He held my head above water for what seemed like an age, then darkness returned and next I saw you."

Deborah helped her into the open area. Rex had already found an arms locker and handed out arms to Gus and Des, he had found his favourite, a katana. When he saw Pieta, rage filled him; he drew his katana and advanced on her.

Deborah stood in front.

"What are you doing?"

"She betrayed us!"

"And that's the reason why I've found her tortured and close to death. Yes, she talked under torture but we can't condemn her for that. Sit down Rex and think about what you're planning to do."

He backed off a little, Gus, now fully aware, stood up,

"That's an order Sergeant Yu, BACK DOWN! Even if she did betray us, we practice mercy, have you forgotten your Marine code."

He backed way down and re-sheathed his katana.

"We release the prisoners, Des, Rex get to it, Deborah you still haven't told me how you got here."

She explained it all to Gus and then helped release the prisoners, Gus realised that to leave via the vault door would be suicide, he left Des with the six prisoners they had released, the rest were dead,

"We will scout out these stairs and see what we can do from there."

Deborah lead, followed by Gus and Rex.

***

The troopers who followed Cutler walked to the front entrance door as Cutler climbed the stair towards his private quarters. He did not plan to meet Morg without an advantage.

His new prize, the dagger, would give him this. He entered his room and opened the drawer, he searched frantically, and it was gone. He tore the room apart, he left and entered the grand hall, he searched his desk, and he turned it over. He screamed like a banshee, who had the audacity. The troopers stood at the entrance, they were gripped with fear as they saw Morg approach.

Their lives hung by his mood and how he would receive their demand to wait until summoned.

He approached and they gave him Cutler's instruction, Morg was filled with rage at being told he could not see Cutler, who did he think he was? They were equals in every way. He lifted his left hand and kinetically snapped the troopers on the left's neck. The guard on the right responded by reaching for his bolt gun, Morg simply waved his right hand and threw him against the wall with force, he crumpled unconscious. Morg entered into the courtyard, the commotion caused troopers to emerge from the room to the left. Seven troopers all with bolt guns emerged. At first they did not know how to react, after all it was Morg before them but when he drew his broadsword they realised that fighting was the only option. They shot bolts at him; he waved them away and threw back in a balletic motion killing two. One attacked bravely with his own sword, Morg leapt upwards and bringing his blade down in full force, cleaving him in two. He thrust his sword killing a second trooper; he rolled and brought his sword breadth wise across the third trooper, bringing him in between the remaining two. He parried, kicked and punched as they attacked at once; he then punched the floor causing a sonic wave which blasted both men away leaving Morg to move on. He climbed the stair, a trooper from below shot a bolt; he deflected it as it ricocheted off the marble pillar. Two Red Skull Captains met him at the top of the stairs both with melee weapons; he parried the first and pushed the second. He knelt and thrust his sword upwards into the chest cavity of the first, stood up and round house kicked the second who fell backwards over the stair balcony onto the marble ground floor. He walked down the corridor past the offices with office clerks and servants scattering before him, as he approached Cutler's room he pushed the door open and entered.

***

Gus and his team had now reached the ante room, he could see Cutler standing.

He whispered, "Is this the only way, Deborah?"

"There is a corridor which leads to a private chamber and out into the hall."

"There is a back stair that leads through the kitchen and outside."

Gus instructed, "Captain Msipha and you will lead the prisoners to safety whilst Sergeant Yu and I attempt to complete the mission."

She protested, "But, Sir..."

"Those are my orders, Corporal!"

***

Cutler stood with his back to Morg as he advanced; he swung round, drawing his own sword as the steel clashed with Morg bringing his in a downward stroke. Cutler followed with strokes to the left, right and left again, finally a downward stroke pushing Morg to his knees,

Morg kinetically pushed Cutler away. Cutler regained his footing he advanced again but Morg kinetically pulled an ebony cabinet from the wall, smashing it against his back, knocking him from his feet and losing grip of his sword as it slid across the oak floor.

Cutler spoke, "Why are you blowing the horn of battle against your brother? You attack as a demon attacks a warrior."

Morg stood slowly up, he made eye contact.

"We are not and never have been brothers but we are both demons, we end this now."

He kicked Cutler's sword towards him.

"We must withdraw, we must reverse this lie we have propagated, we have been misled, we have misunderstood these humans, I now understand why the Almighty has blessed them with grace and I will no longer have any part in this."

Cutler responded, "No matter how much you protest, we were both born of the same Immortal blood, we are brothers. What divisive argument, comrade, has convinced you that Nefarious's plan is flawed?"

Morg replied, "I have seen and experienced the great power, the very mighty force these humans hold. We belittle grace and mercy but added to their great sense of purpose, it becomes very great."

Cutler spoke again, "Rejoin our cause and I will overlook this temporary lapse in judgement."

Morg replied, "You do not hear my words, so how can you understand my heart or my intent.

These men have minds like rock, they are unmoved, standing defiantly, and unshaken; they practise grace which no delights or provocations can rouse them to wrath or inflame corrupt passions which will betray their purpose. Men such as these, when trouble comes to them, it strengthens not weakens there resolve. They have been trained in noble arts that neither you nor I can comprehend. The lie of Nefarious was that they are lesser beings when in fact they are greater, far greater."

Cutler concluded, "You are deluded, brother."

"Your years in Askdean have bewildered you, leaving you unable to reason, having lost your mental faculties. Your words lack order and clear distinction, shall we fight for eternity. We can cause each other no harm with these mortal weapons."

Morg pursed his lips in a self-satisfied smirk.

"If that is my purpose, to distract you till the Almighty returns, then so be it."

He raised his sword.

***

Meanwhile, as Gus watched these giants battle, Des came up the stair with the six prisoners and Deborah, Gus could tell he was unhappy with the order.

"I signed up to assist in the assassination, not babysit prisoners."

"You signed up to follow orders!"

Gus grabbed his forearm and shoulder.

"We made a pact, I must complete my calling, and you must complete our pact. Get back to Melody; tell her I love her, if I don't return. That's an order, Marine!"

Des hugged Gus and followed Deborah down the hall; he wanted to protest more but could see in his eyes that his mind was made. He watched them disappear through the secret door and felt his stomach drop as he realised his future was leaving with him. He turned to Rex, you keep behind me. If I fail, take the knife and attempt to strike. This is too the death, ours or theirs."

Rex's eyes were dark and blank.

"Sir, I have followed you for many years and never disobeyed your orders, today is the first. I will attack. Take your opportunity as you see it."

He drew his katana and slung his bolt gun over his shoulder to support him holding it in one hand,

"It's been a pleasure serving with you."

He stepped out and charged at Cutler, shooting bolts at Morg, shouting, "For the Almighty!"

The speed and ferocity of his attack caught them both off guard, Morg felt the bolts pierce his skin like steel shards of lightning, Rex's katana sliced Cutler across the midriff both felt the pain, searing but both stood defiant as their Immortal biology healed over the wounds. Cutler reached out and grabbed Rex by the throat, throwing him a good hundred feet across the room. Gus took his opportunity and jumped at Cutler with a lunge of the dagger. Cutler felt his presence, swung round, catching him with his forearm across the chest and knocking him on his back to the floor. The knife fell out of his hand and slid across the floor stopping at Morg's feet. Cutler now faced the entrance to the ante room, standing in the doorway was Pieta, and he stood motionless with a disturbing surprise.

"You are dead, my love."

He felt emotions that were alien to him colliding violently inside.

"I was but the grace of the Almighty saved me, grace I fear you will never know."

At that moment, Morg, who had lifted the knife, plunged it into Cutler's back.

"Correct me if I'm wrong or do I smell the scent of retribution."

He collapsed to his knees, Pieta ran to him as he collapsed into her arms.

"You crush your opponent so completely that he realises he was wrong to stand against you in the beginning. I was wrong to stand against you Morg but why did they not crumple, what strength do they have that has defeated me."

Pieta simply said, "I loved you but I could no longer live under this evil."

"I know." he replied and he slowly disintegrated.

All that was left in Pieta's arms was dust, he no longer existed.

***

Gus stood up and took in the fullness of the vista before him as his vision narrowed and all he could focus on was

Morg standing with the Promethean knife soaked in immortal blood.

Morg spoke, "A good man will look for ways to save lives and to gain the victory but a great man will find a way to stop the actions of men they know are wrong no matter who that man is."

Morg looked at Pieta and then at the crumpled body of Rex across the room, he saw the desperation in their eyes.

"The bond between brothers is the sword that defends your faith, your lifestyle, and your hopes. That is what has defeated Cutler and will ultimately bring the demise of Nefarious. My task is incomplete. I shall vanish and wait till my destiny is revealed."

He waved his hand pushing the balcony doors wide, ran and leapt. He landed on the lawn and ran disappearing into the distance. Gus turned and saw Rex, he rushed to him.

His trachea was crushed; the force of the throw had broken his lower back and neck.

"It'll be fine Rex! We'll get you out of here."

Rex struggled to speak.

"No, Sir, you won't. I will miss pulling you out of the fire, I enjoyed those old times."

Gus smiled, "What do you mean, as I recall it was always me pulling your backside out of the fire. As I remember, I was the one getting shot at."

Rex replied, "And I gave you the moral support to dodge those bullets! Can you see that light, I'm leaving Gus! I'm pressing on to claim the mark of high calling from the

Almighty. Thank you for being my friend, don't be sad, I can now join my family, with pride."

His eyes closed and Gus held his friends body close to him and wept severely. In his grief, he suddenly felt peace.

He realised that Andreas knelt beside him, his hand on his shoulder.

"Troopers are coming; I will guide your friend. Go now there are others in danger. Go now or you will lose more than you need."

He heard footsteps coming along the corridor, many footsteps. He lay Rex down grabbed Pieta's hand and left through the secret door following the route described by Deborah.

He closed the door to hide their escape.

Chapter 20 – The Almighty is with us

As he left the rear door and entered the stone outdoor corridor, he saw Des and the prisoners.

They were pinned down by bolt fire, behind upturned stone benches he instinctively placed Pieta behind him and crouched; the three troopers pinning them down were unaware of Gus. He took his time, his aim and one by one, BANG, it pierced the first troopers' helmet, the remaining two looked around surprised by the attack, BANG, the second fell as the bolt pierced his neck and arterial blood spurted out. The third now saw Gus and rotated to fire back. Gus dove on top of Pieta to protect her, as the bolt whizzed above his head and then, BANG, a bolt entered the side of the third troopers head, this time from Des.

Gus grabbed Pieta by the hand again and ran the twenty yards to where Des was pinned down.

As he ran a bolt ricocheted at his feet, he dove into the cover with them.

"Sorry, Sir, we got held up with Red Skull security."

Another shot ricocheted beside him. Gus let off a blast of his bolt gun.

"Where are the rest?"

"Deborah is over there, I think she's been hit, don't know how badly."

Gus looked over and saw Deborah lying still with a wound to her shoulder,

"It was the sniper; he caught her as she led us out of the door. We've been pinned down since. Then the troopers arrived."

"It won't be long before there's more from the main building, we can't stay here.", said Gus franticly.

It was almost prophetic as troopers arrived at the door he had just come through.

He sprayed the entrance, killing the first and making the rest jump back.

"It's not looking good Sir."

Des let off a round at the entrance and ducked as they responded in kind.

"At least our deaths will not be in vain." confirmed Gus.

"Rex is dead but so is Cutler, Morg ran."

Des looked surprised, "An Immortal showing cowardice."

Another spray of bolts splattered against the stone bench.

"No, it was something else. The Almighty is with us."

At that moment there was an explosion behind them, they were covered with rubble and dust as the rear garden wall exploded.

"There firing bazookas at us now." shouted Des.

Gus looked through the dust and the biggest smile filled his face, it was Smithy with Ethan and CJ. They followed the bazooka explosion with a volley of bolts.

"If you're enjoying this party you can stay but your taxi is here." CJ piped up.

"Does Red Skull hospitality always come with sharpshooters?"

Des replied, "Stop with the cheesy narrating and get back to shooting."

Des let off a round of bolts and then picked up Deborah and carried her to the stolen Red Skull AV; despite bolts flying some prisoner escapees helped him.

Ethan quipped, referring to Des.

"The way he's speaking, it sounds like he's jealous of your wit and charm."

The sniper shot again catching CJ on the shoulder, he fell to one knee.

"They got me. They got me bad." called CJ.

"No!" exclaimed Ethan.

"You are too aesthetically displeasing to die."

CJ held his shoulder, "Promise me you'll get them, and avenge me."

Ethan kept shooting the heavy bolt gun he had.

"They have already perished, some are currently unaware of it but they soon will be."

CJ stood back up, "I thought you were shot?"

"Nope, my mistake." said CJ.

"It was just an itch, scratched it, all better now!"

Captain Smith jumped into the driving seat.

"OK guys, we're all in, Red Skull getting closer! Time to move."

Ethan called back, "Tell me something I don't know!"

CJ picked up the bazooka and fired again.

"Take that, excellent iron supplement for the Red Skull."

Ethan returned the comment, "They did look a bit pasty."

"Hurry up!" shouted Smithy.

They jumped in, "You always spoil our fun, Sir!"

CJ saw Deborah, she was bad, and he started first aid on her,

"This doesn't look good."

The AV jerked as it pulled away.

"Can you watch Sir? I need it steady to treat this."

"Sorry but this vehicle handles like a drunk rhino!"

Besides the obvious signs and symptoms, pain and bleeding, there was signs of shock and respiratory impairment. Her skin was cool and clammy, she was limp, her skin was pale, and she was sweating profusely. Her pulse was weak and thready with rapid breathing and she was unconscious.

He saw bubbles in the blood.

"I think her lung has collapsed and the bolt has splintered against her clavicle."

He applied pressure to control bleeding, conscious of not pressing too hard in case he constricted the rib cage more, air was traveling in and out of the wound with each breath. He sealed the wound with a field dressing, pulling out a spray can of plastic dressing. He sprayed it creating an airtight bandage on three sides of the field dressing allowing air to escape through this temporary valve during inhalation.

"Come on, Deborah, I'm not losing you, you are not dying, I know you can hear me. Think of my reputation! If you don't survive I'll have to go back and find the SOB who put this hole in you and get him to apologies for his impoliteness."

He placed a blanket on her.

Pieta said, "I'll look after her, I owe her my life, I will not let her go."

He could see the sincerity in her eyes as she laid Deborah's head on her lap.

"You had better; she owes me a dance." responded CJ.

***

Gus sat in the passenger seat as Smithy drove.

"So where are we going Smithy, I am so glad to see your beautiful face."

"Please, Sir." replied Smithy.

"We haven't even dated yet, I was alerted to your plight by the resistance, and they told me of Pieta's arrest, the rest was logic. I found the boys and set up on top of the cafe roof just off Burgen Road, We worked out the weakest point to attack from the maps on the brief. We saw Morg leap from the balcony and thought '*it's happening*,' we attacked the weakest spot and were just as surprised as you to find you there, the Almighty is with us."

Gus laughed, "I just said that!"

Smithy continued, "I contacted the Scorpion pilot, he's extracting us from the aluminium plant.

It's the highest point in the town, and ... here we are!"

He screeched to a halt, everyone emptied the AV; a resistance fighter waved them into a building.

Ian, the resistance leader, spoke with Smithy.

"We have contacted the Scorpion pilot, but he's twenty minutes away, I'm afraid your attack will bring a Red Skull hell upon us."

He was right, within ten minutes they were trapped in the building by intense hostile fire and Gus doubted they would be able to evacuate their wounded and liberated prisoners. CJ had set up the heavy bolt gun on the first floor. This helped to drive back the advancing troopers. The troopers were surprised at the fierce resistance this last stand produced, they suffered heavy casualties.

The first gun to shoot didn't sound like a gun at all. The noise was high and buzzing, like a chain saw. It would stop, and then starts up again; Ethan was firing a modified mini gun the resistance had given him. It was smaller than a heavy bolt but just as powerful. The Red Skull fired back, every second, bolts poured out of the spinning heavy bolt barrels that CJ fired. The pressure from each bolt felt like a punch in the gut. Des was on the roof with glasses as a spotter, he pushed up his helmet, trying to spot targets for CJ and Ethan, sniping individual targets himself. The volume of fire built as two other Sonder squads joined in, these were heavily armed.

Des' spirit dropped as he informed the rest of the advancing troops.

"Expect extreme violence of action."

"Let's make anyone who decides to shoot at us immediately regret that decision."

"Once we start shooting back, we don't stop until every last man is dead." ordered Gus.

"They may have an overwhelming amount of firepower but the Almighty is with us!"

Des on the roof, called down on radio, "Scorpion spotted, ETA five minutes."

It was beginning to get dark which could only aid their escape as dusk claimed the sky.

The details of the flight plan had not indicated heavy fire; the pilot had seen the white flashes from the explosions from miles out. The advantage was the Red Skull assumed it was their air support, until the very manoeuvrable and heavily armed Scorpion retaliated. He flew the copter very low to ground level, to lessen him as a target and fired a laser guided photon missile, the time from pulling the trigger to impact was about twelve seconds. He fired two more into the base of the tower beside where the main Sonder troops where positioned, which buckled the tower, and then two more into the buildings either side. A Red Skull fired a bazooka at the Scorpion but, the skilful pilot manoeuvred out of its way narrowly missing its tail rotor, the Scorpion landed. Gus and Smithy laid down suppressing fire allowing the escapees carrying Deborah to board, over the radio he ordered.

"Des give us cover; shoot every last Charlie that shows an inch."

"Ethan and CJ, get down here, leave that heavy bolt gun, it's time to leave!"

The pilot interrupted.

"That'll be now Sir, I thought this was a secure position, we cannot stay here any longer."

Ethan and CJ ran out and jumped on board.

"Two more minutes, pilot! Des, get your butt moving, transport is leaving."

Des clattered down the stairwell, as he reached the front door, two Red Skull appeared behind him. They smashed him over the head; Gus saw this and watched him being dragged off.

"This is not happening. Captain Smith, get them safe. Pilot, take off!"

Gus jumped off the Scorpion as it took off.

"What are you doing, you madman." called Smithy.

"Get them safe, he's alive and I'm not leaving a Marine who's alive."

Bolts flew around them as Gus chased after Des. The Scorpion was riddled with bolt gun fire as it began to hover. It was by His grace that no major damage or injuries were incurred, Ethan and CJ threw a handful of grenades at the advancing Red Skull squad, a bolt got Ethan in the arm.

"Are you OK." asked CJ.

"Just a flesh wound." he replied.

"I'll decide that, time for me to inflict pain on you, what goes around and all that."

CJ said patting his knee.

The Scorpion turned round towards the firing positions, still being fired on by bolt guns and some small arms fire from troopers aiming at the copter. Its front heavy armour held. Suddenly, a large AV appeared, specially adapted with a photon cannon on the back and it was rotating towards the copter. The Scorpion opened fire with the thirty millimetre bolt cannon, firing about sixty rounds in bursts totalling about six seconds, annihilating the ground troops. The vehicle had lots of ammo in it and this triggered a series of explosions, going off in all directions, sending shock waves. The pilot struggled to control the copter and narrowly missed hitting the building but did and flew off to more random firing, leaving Gus and Des behind. Gus could still see Des with the troopers, a large number of the enemy was advancing on them, and Gus knelt and shot, killing one trooper outright. Des who had initially been knocked senseless by the blow, now regained his senses, pulled the knife from his boot and thrust it into the trooper who held his arm, which he then twisted. Twisting the trooper round and finally after extracting the knife thrust into his neck. He also saw the advancing troopers, grabbed a bolt gun and fired causing them to dive for cover. Des reached Gus and they were receiving bolt gun fire, they were trapped and pinned down.

"So much for keeping our pact." accused Des.

"What can I say; I'm going to need a best man."

The volume of bolts grew as grenades were now launched and exploded around them; it grew louder as bigger explosions blew.

"Well," said Gus, "let's do this!"

"After three."

"3-2-1."

They stood ready to fire and advance combat style, to find, to their surprise all the Red Skull dead. Ian advanced through the smoke with two dozen resistance.

"We've contacted the pilot and rearranged another pick up but it's an hour from here so let's go. There is more Red Skull on their way!"

Ian who was disgruntled at having to rescue the Marines again, they moved double time and unhindered to the extraction point. The Scorpion established radio contact and the patrol indicated they were ready for pickup; this location afforded maximum safety to those being extracted and the aircraft. The aircraft did not land but dropped a rope Des hooked up his harness and secondary safety line. Des gave the winch operator the prearranged signal of lights in the pitch blackness of the night.

As Des was lifted, Gus thanked Ian.

"Are you and your team not being extracted with us?"

"No.", said Ian.

"Our work is in Dopolis."

Gus shook his hand.

"You and your men are true heroes, I thank you."

The winch operator indicated he was ready for next extraction. Gus hooked on, signalled and was winched away. The resistance squad backed off as the copter flew off at seventy knots towards Caledon for the second time.

Gus walked up to the cockpit.

"Did they all get home safely?" asked Gus.

"Yes, Sir." the pilot replied.

"And Deborah, the injured Marine?"

"Don't know, Sir, she was critical."

"Thank you, you deserve a drink. I promised my squad one when we returned. You're welcome to join us."

The pilot smiled.

"Thanks but, with respect, no thanks. I've just attended one of your parties, a bit too wild for me."

Gus laughed loudly, slapped him on the back.

"Understood, airman, understood."

He returned back to the rear and sat with Des; they sat silently, looked at each other and exhaled in relief.

***

A few hours later, Gus and Des stood around Deborah's bed, she was now stable, her wound healing and her lung being re-inflated. The ventilator breathed for her until she could resume breathing naturally. They had also performed a tracheostomy, Lieutenant Patrick entered the room.

"She has come through the worse we will continue to give her intravenous fluids and nutrition through a feeding tube. We continue to give her antibiotics and the anaesthetic should wear off anytime. She is still extremely vulnerable to infection and blood clots, she needs rest so please don't stay long."

The doctor left, just at that, Deborah stirred.

"Is that you, Sir?"

"It's Des."

He held her hand.

"Gus is here as well."

"Where's Rex?"

"He didn't make it.", confirmed Gus as he took her other hand.

"We got Cutler!"

A single tear ran down her face.

"I'll miss his moaning face."

"As will we all." agreed Gus.

She fell asleep again.

***

Melody sat in the hospital canteen, playing with a sandwich and sipping her tea, she felt sad, depressed, she didn't know what she felt. She knew why she felt that way, any moment someone could be telling her she had lost everything she had ever loved. Her thoughts went towards when she first saw Gus and the growing feeling of infatuation, was that all it was, extreme feelings brought about in extreme times.

Lieutenant Patrick walked up to her.

"I take it you're not aware of Gus's return since you sitting here."

"What!"

"Yes.", he replied.

"He's attending to one of his injured in the ward."

She felt angry, at first, because he hadn't come straight to her. She felt furious but as reason took over she realised it wouldn't be deliberate. On his return, she didn't want to start it with her spoiling for a fight. Is having to wait a little longer really worth a confrontation?

Suddenly, fear gripped her, someone injured, was it Des.

"Thank you."

She bolted and walked quickly to the ward.

Was her worst fears realised? Was Des badly hurt, she tried staying calm and seeing the larger picture. As she turned the corner of the corridor, she looked through the glass. She saw Gus, her heart jumped with excitement. Desire and eagerness to run to him but who was with him, would her eagerness interrupt an important or sensitive moment. He moved his head and she saw Des clearly. Her reasons to be alive were confirmed. She didn't care if she appeared foolish; she burst into the room but then hesitated. She caught sight of the wounded Marine, how seriously wounded she was. She felt shame and a little guilty at feeling angry earlier. The expression on Gus's face changed, he beamed. She hesitated at the door. She didn't realise she was capable of such strong emotions, although it was for good reasons. She walked coyly to Gus without saying a word.

Gus grabbed her lifting her from the floor and passionately kissing her, she became more aware of everything, every noise, every smell, every detail, she had never felt this happy. It was like having her own kind of happiness that no one else would ever have, she didn't want this feeling to stop.

"Oi!" called Des.

"Please put my sister down, it's my turn to hug her."

He duly did and Melody hugged him as well, a long brotherly hug.

"I'm as happy as a pig in mud." squealed Melody.

***

As promised, the squad was treated by Gus to a drink at *'that seedy bar' iKandy*; it was dark in the bar with UV lighting and smoke, disco lights with lasers flashed.

A drink was bought for everyone including Deborah and Rex, they raised their glasses.

Gus spoke, "Here's to all our comrades, alive and fallen. Here's to Rex."

As they stood, they saluted and said together.

"We are strong; we are justified, all for the Almighty."

They all turned round.

Melody said, "Do we have to stay here?"

"I agree, sis."

"It is very seedy."

"What you talking about?" asked CJ.

"It's great, Captain Smith, I love this place? Not too many people but crowded, a dance floor."

Patting Ethan on the back.

"A decent wing man, some good looking females."

He walked over to the juke box put on a song.

"Lots of different ranges of music, it's got pop, rock, dance, R&B, hip hop, Latino."

"You can order food, what more do you need, this is a good shout."

He finished his drink.

"Ethan look some nice girls over there let's invite them to the party or am I the only hot blooded male here who wants to flirt."

Ethan shrugged his shoulder and joined CJ.

"We're leaving.", said Gus.

"I'll stay and babysit the children." stated Smithy.

Gus, Melody and Des left.

***

After the assassination of Cutler, Morg returned to Ravenhead, he withdrew the army back to Dopolis. Then the Burgh and within three months all Red Skull had been removed from Gaelia after negotiation with Pawlii. Terms of withdrawal were agreed with lord Necro, immortal ruler of the Kingdom and Jonathan Oliver newly elected into the newly formed post of National Procurator, along with Pieta, whom he appointed as State Ambassador who negotiated the peace with the Kingdom. This hailed one of the longest periods of peace and prosperity in Gaelian history, Jonathan Oliver was compared in terms of Prince Michael 1 in greatness and prowess. Nefarious was informed of the immortal weapon possessed by the Gaelians. Morg with the knife in his possession, disappeared, some say he headed east.

***

The next time they met casually were at the marriage of Gus and Melody and then again at the dedication of their first child, a boy, named Joshua both at ceremonies in Lamont, conducted by Christiana. Christiana felt hugely honoured to be asked.

He stepped down the stairs of the parish house he had been allocated lodgings in, the resident elder accompanying him. He went to turn left towards the town temple but the elder corrected him.

"Beg your pardon elder, it is this way."

He guided him with his elbow turning him to the right.

"Forgive me, Cracken. Old age does not come by itself."

Two women brushed past, apologising. They were hastening to the Fort temple to get best seats. It was five minutes to eleven, service started at eleven thirty.

"That's OK, ladies. It's good to see young women who are keen to get to temple."

They both stopped and gazed back for a moment; then they glanced at each other with a giggle.

"I suspect elder, there may be a little hero worship today. Gus has become a national talking point and broke many hearts when he married Melody."

Christiana just nodded.

Another young lady walked past with a man in tow, it was Deborah and Des.

"Morning elders!"

"Morning?"

Des was in his best dress uniform but Deborah, having resigned from the marines wore a black straw hat, and a rusty coloured dress hanging at a decent, just below the knee skirt length. They walked slower as Deborah still had to take deliberate strides to compensate for her breathlessness caused by her lung injury.

Christiana stopped at the baker's. The combination of scents was not unpleasing and distracted him. "We must visit here when we come back."

Elder Cracken's face was showing impatience.

"You are correct, my friend. We must not dally." confirmed Christiana.

"Yes, we must continue!" he stated, not apologising for his curtness.

"We will get some assorted cakes and pastries on the way back"

"Oh, and some macaroons, please?"

Cracken beckoned him onward.

"I like those macaroons, you know, and it's not often I treat myself. One gets so tired of not spoiling oneself, don't you think?"

He laughed a quick little nervous laugh showing he was not earnest in what he said.

They caught up with Deborah and Des.

Christiana asked Des, "How's that sister of yours getting on?"

"Oh, she's very well, thank you!"

The Fort temple was within walking distance but they had the whole length of the main street to traverse, a half mile of slow stepping due to Deborah's breathlessness and Christiana's age.

As they came to the end of the Main Street, turning right towards the gate, the wide valley opened out, with the far woods withdrawing into the distance.

A full sun beat down on them drying the remnants of the dew.

***

Gus and Melody were already in the temple, sat at the side and front for ease of access to the altar but also to the changing area, just in case.

"Good gracious!" exclaimed Melody.

"You would think we starved the child. He wants fed every two hours. I think I'll try to feed him again."

She left for the changing area, "Let me know when Deborah and Des get here, there late!"

She stood and looked at Joshua. She could not help herself. She smiled and caressed his cheek with her finger, and nodded to him, making little noises.

"I should think they'll be on their way."

Gus looked uneasily at the clock.

Jimmi, who sat beside him said, "The clock's fast! Don't fidget!"

She went into the next room.

As soon as she was gone, Jimmi said, "I would have thought they'd have been here by now."

Gus did not answer.

Smithy marched up from the front door.

"They're here; you can stop your panicking."

A few minutes later Deborah hurried into the temple, taking off her coat.

"Where have you been? Can't do this without Godparents." said Jimmi sharply.

Christiana entered, he seemed nervous. He went straight to Gus.

"Ah, how are you?" he asked musically, peering sides ways at Jimmi nodding in greeting.

His voice was full of gentleness.

"Hope I haven't held things up?" he said comfortingly.

He took out a white handkerchief and rubbed his nose.

"Not at all." reassured Gus.

He glanced at Jimmi and then nodded towards the room behind indicating Melody.

"Some were getting worried that you weren't coming."

Jimmi's face clearly showed he did not appreciate the reproach, scowling with an unconscious retaliation to Gus's remark. The elder smiled, wistfully but indulgently.

Melody appeared from the room.

"He won't take; I hope he's settled for the blessing."

Christiana turned to the young mother, who was now flushed because she did not realise Christiana was there and wouldn't dream of talking about breast feeding in front of him normally.

"How are you?" he asked, very softly, intending to deflect her embarrassment.

"I'm all right," she replied, awkwardly shaking his hand as she sat.

"Good!" he peered down at the baby.

"Is he not taking to breast feeding?" he asked in an attempt to make the subject of the conversation normal.

"Yes, yes." she replied. Her face reddened again.

"Just not at the moment."

He went towards the altar, "Good!"

The temple elder attempted to help Christiana up the steps to his chair.

"I can go by myself, thank you; I'm not ready for that kind of assistance yet."

Soon all were seated, waiting for the service too start.

"Are we all here?" asked the elder.

The temple doors opened again and everyone looked round, it was Lillibet and Annie.

"Sorry we're late, went to wrong temple."

They slunk into their chairs, Christiana smiled.

"It's ok, we hadn't yet begun."

Annie was stunning in a dress of green voile, whereas Lilibet wore a red lady's suit made from leather and hide. They returned the welcome from the elder with hand signals and eye contact trying to show reverence whilst keeping some assumption of dignity.

"Shall we begin!" announced Christiana glancing at Melody nursing the restless baby.

Once the resident elder had conducted the main service, he handed over to Christiana.

"Well, we've come here to dedicate this child. I'm sure we're very thankful."

He paused and motioned to the family to approach the altar.

Christiana spoke in his soft, lingering voice.

"It is hard for you today, for like so many, you have lost dearly in the years past. So many not here who should be but yet some who are who may not have been."

He glanced in the direction of Jimmi and Deborah.

"The Almighty gives comfort in His time. A child is born to us, therefore let us rejoice and be glad."

He went on with his discourse for a few more minutes. He then motioned to Melody who lifted the whimpering infant; her fingers clasped the body of the child beautifully. He placed his right hand on the baby and his left on Melody's head.

"We ask Almighty, to look after this child. As you have marked his father, grandfather and great grandfather before him for greatness, let it be so for Joshua. Do not let any shade discourage him but let him grow like a tree in the sunshine bringing life and hope to those around him. As for Melody let her be like a stream of clear water flowing beside him, making him strong, bless this family beyond their expectation, almighty you know they deserve it."

The service ended after a Sissy sang accompanied by Nathan.

They all retired into the community hall where a fine buffet waited for them.

Not surprisingly, the crowd levitated towards Melody and the baby.

Smithy, Ethan and CJ walked towards them to congratulate.

Gus spoke, "Glad you could make it boys. Heard you got promotions?"

"Yes we did." replied Ethan.

CJ was making noises at the baby.

"Believe it or not in linguistics and communication."

Ethan thumped CJs shoulder.

"You do know gibberish isn't a linguistic requirement, though you would get straight A's."

Smithy intervened, "Let me introduce you to the buffet table, boys. These kind people have plenty more 'normal' people to speak to."

He almost huckled them towards the food.

Taking their opportunity Des and Deborah snuck in.

"That worked out well." said Des slapping Gus on the back.

Melody spoke to Deborah.

"Not long till the big day now?"

Deborah sighed, "Can't wait! It's dragging in. Pity he'll be too small to be a Paige boy."

Jimmi approached them; he motioned to hold the baby. Melody gladly handed him over.

Holding the baby in one hand he used a spoon against a glass to get everyone's attention.

"I would like to say some words."

Everyone stopped and turned.

"This is a day I thought I would never see, a gladness I would never bear. Billy, my eldest surviving son has never married, unless you count to his business."

Everyone laughed.

"Sissy and Nathan are still a little too young, but maybe one day. So it has fallen to Gus to carry on the Black name and he has done so to my pride. When Joshua was born I told everyone I knew about my new grandson. This is an incredibly special moment for us all; I have gone from being all alone in the world to being a custodian of a great generation. I look forward to my retirement and the many long hours with Joshua. Look out for me; I will be walking about the town of Lamont displaying my sheer delight to all I come across. I am overjoyed at the arrival of my first grandchild. It is an incredibly special moment for us all and we are so thrilled on the birth of this baby boy. Grandparenthood is a unique moment in anyone's life, as countless kind people have told me in recent months. So I am enormously proud and happy to be a grandfather for the first time and I am eagerly looking forward to helping with the baby."

***

He did indeed get involved in the child's upbringing, making up for all the years he missed with his own children happily changing his nappies and buying toys. Jimmi kept a diary of stories of all his grandchildren.

He loved them all, but Joshua was his favourite, he was smart and funny from a young age.

Stories such as when he was in temple bible class, the teacher was asked by his younger sister about the Almighty's edicts, after falling out with Joshua.

"I understand what you say about honouring your father and mother but is there a commandment that teaches us how to treat our brothers and sisters?"

Without missing a beat, Joshua interrupted, "You shall not kill."

When he was five years old he asked Jimmi,

"How old are you, I bet you're forty. No, fifty! Sixty!! You can't be seventy, that's when you die."

Or the day he came running home and Jimmi said, "Wow, you sound out of breath."

He replied, "No, I have more."

Every night Jimmi told stories, like his father before him. Grandfather was talking about sacrifice one day, when he asked what sacrifice was, Jimmi explained it was giving things up, he asked what would Joshua give up.

"I'd give up homework."

Jimmi laughed, "No, Joshua, the idea was to give up something you liked."

He said, "But I like homework!"

"OK, is there anything else?"

Joshua replied, "How about fighting with my sister. I like that as well but I can give it up."

The one he liked most was when Jimmi asked him what he wanted to be when he grew up.

"Well, Grandfather, that's an easy question, when I grow up I want to be a brave, honest and a great man just like you."

This would always make Jimmi beam with pride.

"I believe you will be braver, more honest and greater than us both, do you know why you're called Joshua?"

Joshua would reply.

"Yes, I do. I am a gift from the Almighty, the proof that the Almighty is with us!"

Lightning Source UK Ltd.
Milton Keynes UK
UKOW06f1152091116

287237UK00011B/191/P